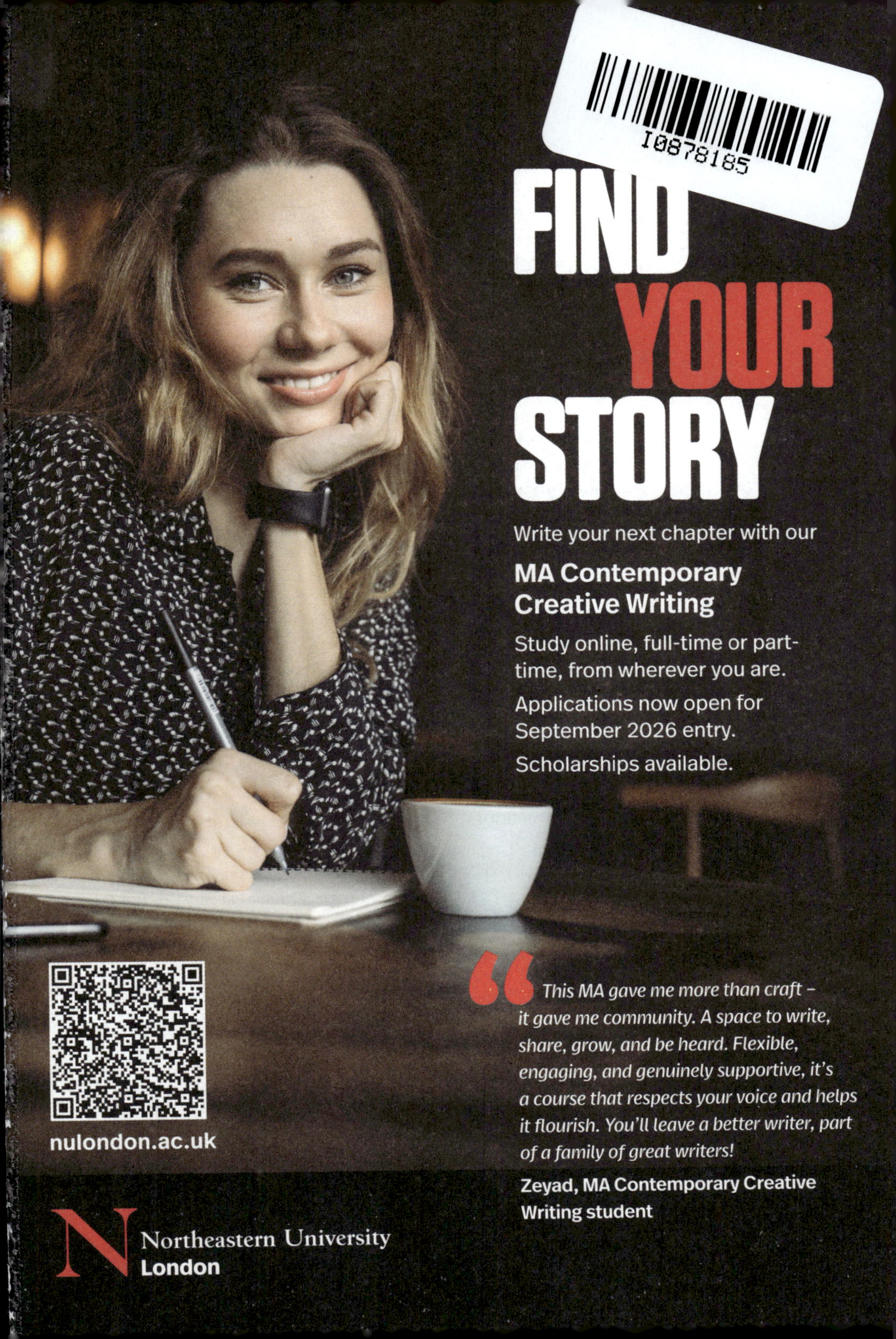
FIND YOUR STORY
Write your next chapter with our
MA Contemporary Creative Writing
Study online, full-time or part-time, from wherever you are.
Applications now open for September 2026 entry.
Scholarships available.
"This MA gave me more than craft – it gave me community. A space to write, share, grow, and be heard. Flexible, engaging, and genuinely supportive, it's a course that respects your voice and helps it flourish. You'll leave a better writer, part of a family of great writers!
Zeyad, MA Contemporary Creative Writing student
nulondon.ac.uk
Northeastern University London

GRANTA

12 Addison Avenue, London W11 4QR | email: editorial@granta.com
To subscribe visit subscribe.granta.com, or call +44 (0)1371 851873

ISSUE 176: SUMMER 2026

Granta (ISSN 173231 USPS 508) is published four times a year by Granta Trust, 12 Addison Avenue, London, W11 4QR, UK.

Airfreight and mailing in the USA by agent named World Container Inc., 150–15, 183rd Street, Jamaica, NY 11413, USA.

Periodicals postage paid at Brooklyn, NY 11256.

Postmaster: Send address changes to *Granta*, ESco, Trinity House, Sculpins Lane, Wethersfield, Braintree, CM7 4AY, UK.

Subscription records are maintained at *Granta*, c/o ESco Business Services Ltd, Wethersfield, Essex, CM7 4AY, UK.

Air Business Ltd is acting as our mailing agent.

The manufacturer's authorised representative in the EU for product safety is Authorised Rep Compliance Ltd, 71 Lower Baggot Street, Dublin D02 P593, Ireland (arccompliance.com)

Granta is printed and bound in Italy by Legoprint. This magazine is printed on paper that fulfils the criteria for 'Paper for permanent document' according to ISO 9706 and the American Library Standard ANSI/NIZO Z39.48-1992 and has been certified by the Forest Stewardship Council® (FSC®). *Granta* is indexed in the American Humanities Index.

ISBN 978-1-909-889-82-8

MIX
Paper | Supporting responsible forestry
FSC® C023419

CONTENTS

7 **The American Berserk**
Thomas Meaney

15 **Intercession**
Mary Gaitskill

29 **Arc de Trump**
Antonia Hitchens

40 **Study for American Interior (Monday)**
Kathryn Scanlan

45 **Dathun**
Amie Barrodale

61 **Blood Boy**
Hansen Shi

80 **People Keep Finding Bodies in Joshua Tree**
Michael Robbins

93 **Nothing Personal**
Nikita Teryoshin, with an introduction by Seth Harp

115 **The Acute Wing**
John Jeremiah Sullivan

157 **Mussolini in Milan, The Death of My Dog & Hinky Dinky Parlez-Vous**
Frederick Seidel

165 **Gold Can Stay**
Rebecca Curtis

191 **Hawaiian Fauna**
Tao Lin

200 **First Year Sober & Sentimentality**
Maggie Millner

206 **He Trains My Hands for War**
Zora J Murff, with an introduction by Ciarán Finlayson

227 **The Year of the Rat**
Halle Hill

242 **What Was Your Hair Color as a Child?, What Sports Team Do You Love to See Lose? & On Which Wrist Do You Wear Your Watch?**
Osdany Morales, tr. Harry Bauld

247 **Making Cuba Great Again**
William T. Vollmann

276 **r/Nostalgia, Goodnight Moon & The Subject Had Become Poetic Logic**
Patricia Lockwood

286 **Notes on contributors**

If our Lord is sovereign even over the sparrow's fallings, you can be assured that he is sovereign over everything else that falls in this world, including Tomahawk and Minuteman missiles . . .

– Brooks Potteiger, Christian, husband, father, pastor, woodworker, spiritual advisor to the Secretary of War

The American Berserk

It's a strange fate being an American. One of its small burdens is a national reality that notoriously outruns its fictional portrayals. Away from the country, I sometimes turn to that outmoded source of information, the nightly news on television. It begins with the latest natural disaster: wildfires, floods, tornadoes pulling roofs off houses, plywood and corrugated metal flying, and an interview with an ashen-faced pioneer: 'We lost everything.' Then, there is a story about local carnage. A man in the back of a police cruiser wriggles free of his handcuffs; the cop rushes around the car to detain him, only for the man to leap to the front seat, take the wheel and shift into high gear down the highway, until the cop, now in the backseat, tasers him and sends the car careening into a retaining wall. Next comes the White House Correspondent, reporting on foreign affairs: Clinton bombing a pharmaceutical factory in Sudan; Bush Jr revving up the Global War on Terror; Obama droning a Pakistani wedding party; Biden striking Syria; Trump obliterating a girls' school in Iran. It ends with an upbeat segment. A beloved postman is fêted on the eve of his retirement. A baby deer is rescued from a drain.

What is the American Berserk? It's there on the vomit-splattered decks of the *Mayflower*, and in John Winthrop's terror that there might not even be enough wilderness in the New World. It's the angel Moroni guiding Joseph Smith to unearth the golden plates that contain the ancient history of the continent. It's John Brown loading his .52-caliber Beecher's Bible. It's 1st Platoon, C Company opening fire at Mỹ Lai. It's Newt Gingrich demanding that giant mirrors direct the rays of the sun into American ghettos at night to prevent crime. It's US forces invading Afghanistan, and setting up model Afghan villages in Louisiana where, in war games, Afghan refugees play themselves. Ancient Judea had the Virgin Birth, but

California has the Octomom. The Berserk reaches us through the police body cam: dizzying, grainy, point-blank. It's in the military hardware named after decimated Native American tribes: Apache, Black Hawk, Chinook. It's Donald Trump presiding over an AI-generated advertisement for the 'Gaza Riviera'. The American Berserk is characterized by world-historical excess. It is the mood of a country convinced of its chosenness but drenched in self-pity about that chosenness not working out.

We owe the phrase 'the American Berserk' to Philip Roth. It first appears in the opening section of *American Pastoral*. Set in the Vietnam years, the novel is about a thoroughly assimilated Jewish family in Newark, New Jersey. Swede Levov is an all-star athlete who inherits his father's glove-making business and solidifies his standing in the upper middle class. But his daughter Merry rejects the life he provides. As a member of an antiwar terror cell, she blows up a local bank, killing four people. What drives her is unclear – her father may have overstepped in his affection for her when she was young; she may be a dupe of left-wing propaganda – but she becomes the enemy of everything that is wholesome in go-along-to-get-along America: its 'angry, rebarbative spitting-out daughter' who transports her father 'out of the longed-for American pastoral and into everything that is its antithesis and its enemy, into the fury, the violence, and the desperation of the counterpastoral – into the indigenous American berserk'.

The American Berserk is what Saul Bellow, in a letter to Roth, described as 'the purgation one can obtain only through rage'. It is a stringent will to clear away the flotsam of the country – to bulldoze accumulated corruptions – and pave the way for an idealized freedom. The 'American Berserk' is not a condition imported from elsewhere – Old Europe, Asiatic Bolshevism – in which the true country remains innocent. It comes from within the American experience; it is a force without direction, a desire without a clear objective. This is why it could change political coordinates even in

Roth's lifetime. First hurled against the extra-parliamentary Left, it now more firmly attaches to the rabble-rousers of the Right. Since 2016, headline after headline has warned of the resurrection of the berserk: DONALD TRUMP IS THE AUTHENTIC AMERICAN BERSERK; HOW SOCIAL MEDIA, THE GREAT RECESSION AND DONALD TRUMP COMBINED TO BRING OUT THE INDIGENOUS AMERICAN BERSERK. 'If you're not writing about the berserk, you're not writing about America,' chided the historian Rick Perlstein in 2020. 'Is there a way for us to make the "American berserk" a little less . . . berserk?' wondered the *New York Times* four years later.

Though it seethes with contempt for 'political correctness', Roth's late work was hardly proto-MAGA. But it was an extended paean to When America Was Great – when she was good. A firm nod in this direction comes early in *American Pastoral* when Roth, in the guise of his alter ego Nathan Zuckerman, lashes out against Leo Tolstoy's *The Death of Ivan Ilyich*. The novella tells of a well-to-do judge living in comfort in St Petersburg, who begins to die a nasty death and realizes, at the last moment, that he lived his life in the wrong way. 'Maybe in Russia in 1886,' Zuckerman counters. 'But in Old Rimrock, New Jersey, in 1995, when the Ivan Ilyiches come trooping back to lunch at the clubhouse after their morning round of golf and start to crow, "It doesn't get any better than this," they may be a lot closer to the truth than Leo Tolstoy ever was.'

In 1962, Edmund Wilson adopted the same view. 'I don't believe that a man like Ivan Ilyich could ever look back on his life and find it so empty and futile', Wilson wrote in his diary. America's greatest literary critic and one of its finest novelists together form part of a literary tradition that cannot admit the bitter wisdom of the Russian: that worldliness is doomed. The false idols of America – security, comfort, supremacy – have only been smashed by an alternative breed of writers who refuse to insist on the country's inveterate decency.

America's conflicted view of its mission has long been a source of unhappiness about its actions in the world. At the zenith of American power, in the 1940s and 1950s, there was little need for Washington to distinguish between husbanding global capitalism and America's domestic well-being – they were very nearly the same thing. In the 1970s and 1980s, these two commitments diverged. It was no longer self-evident that the American working classes benefited from the world that the US's political classes were shaping. Various insurgent candidates – Jesse Jackson, Ross Perot, Ralph Nader, Pat Buchanan, Bernie Sanders – challenged the status quo, but each was put in their place. The mission of the country – to maintain primacy in world affairs – remained consistent. But the cost of the empire, especially when it included building up rivals like Japan and West Germany, was retrospectively viewed as too high. When China entered the World Trade Organization in 2001, American elites could still convince themselves it was an ideological victory. It would not be considered one for long. Could the US continue to keep its primacy through trusted methods, or would it need a decisively new posture?

Donald Trump takes the second view, or at least pretends to. If his trolling about annexing Greenland or the Panama Canal shocked some, it effectively publicized that nothing was off the table for the new administration. Trump's great attraction for Americans is not that he flatters them or harnesses their rage or reverses the tide of elite condescension. The reason Trump appeals is that, in a country where there exists no plausible opposition to the present political-economic order, and in a world where the US's room for maneuver has been drastically curtailed, the figure who can best simulate agency is king.

For all his bombast, and for all his periodic baiting of American elites by flirting with tariffs, threatening to defund NATO, and mocking of the Supreme Court, Trump's policies are for the most part conventional. Even his blundering into war against Iran was par for the course. Trump's sheer unscriptedness, his sore winning, his stand-up antics, his ability to turn the electorate into rubberneckers watching him lick his own wounds: all of this keeps him at the center in a country where attention is the coin of the realm. When asked in 2017 if Trump, as the new emblem of the 'American Berserk', outstripped his imagination, Roth responded, 'It isn't Trump as a character, a human type – the real-estate type, the callow and callous killer capitalist – that outstrips the imagination. It is Trump as President of the United States.'

The writers for *Granta*'s American Berserk edition did not need instruction on what the berserk was. They nodded and got to work. Mary Gaitskill is the country's greatest anatomist of the subterranean connections between pain and pleasure, and the national capacity for personal degradation. In her comic story 'Intercession', two new friends speak on the phone about the forms of punishing desire that crowd their aging lives, and the slinking sense that sanity is a chimera in today's America.

It is hard to find a young American writer of reportage who does not look up to John Jeremiah Sullivan, one of its most abundantly talented practitioners. From the memoir of his sportswriter father, *Blood Horses*, to the essays on American music and television and literature, Sullivan writes with open wonder about his country. He belongs to the American line of writers that runs from the great old Southern masters through David Foster Wallace and Donald Antrim and, in his story for this issue, Ken Kesey. In 'The Acute Wing', which is set in a low-end psychiatric institution, a man confesses a terrible truth, and finds that, contrary to the cathartic promises of therapeutic culture, confession only amplifies the damage.

Christian Lorentzen once argued that the American literature of the Obama years could be categorized into four modes: autofiction; fables of meritocracy; stories of trauma, 'in which suffering confers meaning in an otherwise comfortable world'; and historical novels that take place in the near past, 'locating in recent decades the romantic grit and violence their nostalgic authors find lacking in the present'. What about the literature of the Trump era? The earliest fiction of the MAGA years was often marred by the sense that writers were trying to remain unsullied by a vulgar blip in history. Recent offerings are more farcically dystopian. Amie Barrodale recently satirized America's diseased judicial branch; here, in 'Dathun', she turns to the executive, in a story where a Trump-like figure serves as the vestigial mascot of a regime that has perfected its sadism. In Rebecca Curtis's 'Gold Can Stay', a wife frets over her security fence in post-apocalyptic America, while her husband, 'H-Bomb', plots with a 'world-famous sextillionaire neodymium magnate' to end global poverty and restock the oceans by culling 'the globe's sapien-load by ninety-five percent'. Hansen Shi's 'Blood Boy' transports us to San Francisco, where conniving young technologists trade dumplings and kinky sex to profit off the hottest AI deals. In Halle Hill's 'The Year of the Rat', a Tennessee motel clerk seeks deliverance in conspiracy theories, hare-brained schemes and self-help videos. Kathryn Scanlan's 'Study for American Interior (Monday)' is a feat of acoustic attention that transforms the sounds outside a house – cars, squirrels, construction – into strange poetry.

In 'Hawaiian Fauna', Tao Lin picks up a hitchhiking astrologist who is as conversant with extraterrestrials and planetary realignment as the author. Antonia Hitchens's 'Arc de Trump' plunges into the underbelly of Washington, D.C.'s officials, lobbyists and influencers, and offers up a portrait of a court culture where Christian-maxxing and toadying are full-time jobs. For this issue, William T. Vollmann took to the streets of Havana, where the US energy blockade has further ravaged the people. With Ernest Hemingway, José Martí, and Tomás Gutiérrez Alea as his guides, Vollmann and his companions speak to Cubans from across the political spectrum about Trump and Marco Rubio's lust for regime change.

In our poetry we feature Frederick Seidel, the great bard of the berserk, whose poems of sex and death create a rapturous, bouncing music. Patricia Lockwood uses the Reddit forum r/Nostalgia to write an oblique elegy for John Ashbery. In his deadpan poem 'People Keep Finding Bodies in Joshua Tree', Michael Robbins drives through the desert, listening for the voices of departed singers and friends. Maggie Millner finds the crushing beauty in unloved things: 'A broadside printed COFFEE MAKES YOU QUEER, / McGovern button, shoebox of Hitachi Magic Wands'. In three poems from his series 'Security Questions', the Cuban poet Osdany Morales moves from questions asked of him by US Immigration and Customs to fragments of his own history.

In our photography, Ciarán Finlayson writes about the work of Zora J Murff, who reckons with the compromises and commitments of a black artist ascendant in the academy, while Seth Harp, lately subpoenaed by Congress for his exposé *The Fort Bragg Cartel*, writes about the weapons industry, captured in all its shiny banality by the Russian-born photographer Nikita Teryoshin.

Next up for *Granta* is an issue devoted to the literature of Nigeria, to be followed by issues on the Koreas and Mexico. There will also be a special issue called 'Humiliation', which could just as easily have been the title for this one. ■

TM

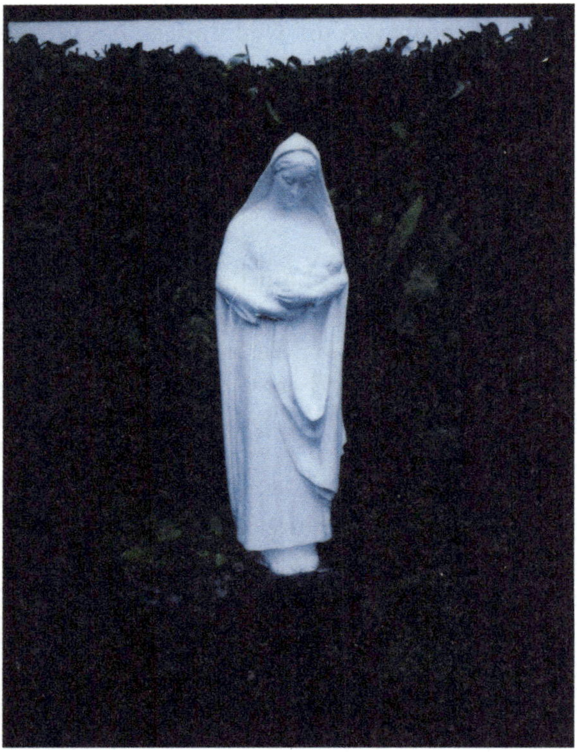

SUZIE HOWELL
From, *A Bowl of Tears to Drink*

INTERCESSION

Mary Gaitskill

That day another one of Laurie's friends had gone crazy. This made three in the last two years which to Laurie seemed like a lot. She had been taking a walk around the convent near her home, drawing stunted comfort from its roughhewn statuary (St Francis, lambs, white plaster Mary everywhere) and brooding on the 'loneliness epidemic' plus her marriage when Eileen's text pinged in her pocket. *Can you talk now? I need to talk.*

Laurie was not Catholic; she was a retired English professor with chaotic and half-formed spiritual ideas, most of which came to her while she lay awake and terrified at 4 a.m. Still, the convent – spacious, enchantingly wooded, with multiple walking paths – was her place of respite in her new 'forever home', a decaying still-beautiful town that was mysterious and closed to her. She and her husband had moved there right before the pandemic, and they had made few friends. Eileen, a self-described rogue RN/pelvic-floor therapist whom they'd met at a yard party, was one of them. The woman had extra social allure because, in addition to being a nurse/pelvic-floor etc., she was an amateur actress who'd had a brief off-off-Broadway moment in NYC and who still did occasional community theater. And so Laurie pulled herself from her trance before beautiful decay to respond.

'Hi hi hi!' cried her new pal. 'Are you alone? Can you talk for a sec? Something's really going on with me! It's not something I'd share with everybody. But I really need to talk about this and I feel like you'll understand –'

'Thank you,' said Laurie.

'– because of the situation in your marriage. Which is kind of like mine. Anyway, I've been having a thing with this guy. It's, or rather it *was* mostly very heady, like, totally online – but it's the most mind-blowing sex I've ever had. We met at a Zoom theater workshop he ran last year, he's a director and a playwright and we had this *incredible* chemistry. After the workshop was over, he messaged me to say that he felt so struck by my intuitive understanding of character that he wondered if he could discuss and develop *his* work with me. We were texting every week, then every other day, it became very emotional, and we, we –'

The ribbon of her voice poured off its spool with alarming speed as she described vertiginous bonding on increasingly powerful erotic levels: Zoom workshop exercises that spontaneously exploded into chthonic sexual role playing, multi-layered virtual fucking that ended with her sobbing or dancing around her room to Stevie Nicks. Which was great, but then it got weird. He got her involved with an online site dedicated to dominance and submission and supervised her there in increasingly disturbing fantasies involving very young girls, role plays which were meant to be healing but –

'Wait,' said Laurie. 'How did he supervise you?'

'He, you know, texted me suggestions, blah blah. But before I say more, I need to ask, do you know something about this already?' Emphatically, Laurie said she did not know about this! And so Eileen explained that 'this' was the director/playwright's baroque revenge when Eileen started to say no, to assert the reality of her marriage. He had somehow hooked up with a board member and diva of the local community theater ('I'm going to call her "Jen"') who had also participated in his workshop. Eileen had intuited that something was going on because of the way Jen had begun to avoid her eyes in public;

eventually she realized that the director had turned her erstwhile friend so totally against her that she had become a vicious enemy, not only talking shit all over town but also using multiple online personae to spread virtual crap too. In fact she and the director had found the time to create multiple false sites essentially portraying Eileen as a groomer, presenting the transformative role play as real-life sickness for all the world to see.

Laurie listened with oh-no-not-again dismay. A few months back a former colleague from the city (Cara) had shared a story of fantastical persecution in which she was being undermined in the English department by assholes who, newly empowered by the anti-DEI bloodbath, had spread rumors about her incompetence, hinting that she had only been hired to appease the old regime's BS. Which unfortunately did not sound paranoid – until Cara expanded the story to declare that these people had not only blackballed her in the department, they had not only smeared her university-wide; they had done it on a national level where they were trying to make it impossible for her to publish. Hundreds of people were involved she said and it wasn't only coming from anti-DEI pricks; she had no allies among her fellow queers because of some inconsequential thing she'd once put in an email about needing to be 'a warrior' on behalf of young girls who were 'cutting their breasts off' in order to transition – a pure terror response to being female in Cara's opinion. 'I don't even remember that email,' one of her erstwhile allies had said when Cara confronted them. 'I just don't like you.'

'And that was just the start,' said Eileen. 'There was this other woman on the dom/sub site, like, kind of *famous* in the theater world – older but still beautiful and incredibly seductive, I mean emotionally; we started messaging and I kind of fell in love with her. And he knew that, and so he went to use her as a weapon. He basically replaced me with her, except that they're using the work I did with him – she's basically stealing the characters I created with him, this rich, famous woman is stealing from me! After pretending to be my friend and even –'

Laurie turned off the main walkway and took a narrow path down into the landscaped convent grounds, past wood-cut Stations of the Cross nailed to a series of quietly triumphant trees leading to a stony rise; a stone female acolyte stood with face uplifted in joyful prayer before a stone crypt built into the earth, half hidden like a child's secret. She seated herself on a bench, rested her phone on her thigh and gazed beyond the grounds at the gentle swells of wooded earth, subsiding toward a distant flash of river . . .

'It's just insane!' cried Eileen. 'But honestly I don't care about the big star. Because she is evil and I think it's going to all blow up on her. It's just a matter of time. I'm more upset about Jen partly because she can do more immediate damage and also because I don't think she's really responsible for this. She isn't that strong or that malicious and frankly – even though she's the star of Brickbat Theater *and* a member of the board, she's always seemed kind of lacking a center. Some people need to be at the center exactly because they lack a center. And he's a total, I mean *total* dom. But he wouldn't scare her because he comes on like a good Daddy – that's how he gets in. Acting very protective, very moral, always asks permission, blah blah. I could see him totally controlling her mind. I think he is, actually. I can see it on her face. He's making her do this.'

'Wait,' said Laurie. 'How do you think he's doing that?'

'I can't describe it! But I can sense it, you know what I mean? You must've seen relationships like that?'

'No,' said Laurie. 'Not really. Not actual *mind control.*'

'I forgot, you don't really go online,' said Eileen. 'That's a different zone. It's a world of psyche, people are exchanging on an energetic level at high speed – boundary-dissolving happens quickly. That's what makes it so exciting. And also dangerous. Things happen that wouldn't happen in real life. I went places with this guy I'd never go with someone in real life. It alters you. It *infiltrates* you.'

Laurie remembered the time she'd first met Eileen at the yard party, how bright and big-spirited she was – artlessly so in her gauzy flower-print dress. She was youthful and bare-limbed in late middle-age, a natural redhead with an unstable voice and the voluble hands of a silent film star. They'd exchanged numbers and, days later, Laurie and her husband were traveling to the more upscale side of the river to attend a party hosted by Eileen and her husband on the spacious screened porch of their elegant A-frame house. It had been a charming candlelit evening. Eileen proved skilled at drawing people out and then linking them, orchestrating conversations in tandem with the esoteric movements of her long, nimble fingers, half hidden in her lap. The other guests were themselves relatively new to the area yet already involved in food banks and town hall meetings; they told stories of contested real estate, and who was vying for what, of local eccentrics nearly coming to blows over the fate of an old baseball field and, of course, the local theater. In the candlelight, shadows of aged trees stirred and silently signaled on the one bare wall; out the back window, a boat moved heavily down the river, linking this small social intimacy to the vast impersonal world. Laurie and her husband had been heartened to feel that they could find a home in this place.

As if she'd sensed the residual warmth of Laurie's memory, Eileen's tone shifted. 'I realize this must sound crazy,' she said convivially. 'Do you think it sounds crazy?'

'I don't really know,' said Laurie. And she didn't. She thought of her old friend Sugar, a writer who had gotten a menacing dirty voicemail from a complete stranger ('Your pussy stinks! You deserve to be kicked and punched! You're a satan walking this earth and you deserve to die horribly!'), which Sugar thought she had summoned via an inner monologue with a dark 'unintegrated part' that her therapist was helping her work with. When Laurie had asked if she was afraid, Sugar had said no, not really. Because people 'just do this now, they make death threats. It's normal.'

Which was true. Politicians got death threats, lawyers and judges and jurors got death threats, people expressing opinions or making jokes online got death threats – even the president made death threats. And sometimes, it wasn't just threats. People killed senators, judges, podcasters and schoolchildren; they killed their neighbors over lawn disputes and yard signs and unruly pets and facial expressions. Citizens were shot in the streets by masked men paid by the government. That part was new; people had always killed neighbors etc. But who knew, maybe even that would soon be normal.

'So here's an example of what I mean by mind control,' said Eileen. 'You'll totally get this, basically everybody got this.' And she proceeded to raise the topic of a months-old controversy about a revered, recently deceased writer ('M') who had been exposed as enabling the abuse of her young daughter, or ignoring it, or, on the other hand, as being the erotically helpless victim of the man who did it, depending on your point of view. People were flinging previously beloved books into the garbage or even flinging them into the street and then running over them until they were pulped. Other people were enraged at those people for judging, especially for judging the complex and actually sacred intersection of motherhood and erotic love, the place of ultimate instinctual blur. Other people thought only art should matter and that you should just keep reading the books regardless of your feelings which shouldn't count.

'It's obvious that this man was controlling her mind to the point that she could not protect her daughter,' said Eileen. 'She was just so vulnerable to him. Which is why I think people are so furious at her. People are just so uncomfortable with vulnerability!'

'That's ridiculous!' said Laurie. 'She was a powerful woman, she wielded influence globally, she blew people's minds!'

'That's exactly why people could not forgive her for being vulnerable. They hated it that this powerful lady genius cared about sex so much, that she was in thrall, that she actually admitted she needed sex to do her art – like, how dare a *mom* be like that? The abuse happened years before she found out about it, she couldn't do anything at that point and she was old by then, if she had left him where could she get what she needed?'

'Excuse me, that's not vulnerable, that's ruthless. I see no reason to believe he was making her do or not do anything she didn't want. If you want to talk about vulnerable, I'd say the little girl was the one who –'

'Yes. She was even more vulnerable. But he was the one who abused the child, not M. Really, it's so sad, for everybody. And you're right, young girls are always the ones who wind up paying the price.'

'Actually, old women pay at least as much. And they don't even look good doing it either.'

Eileen laughed, a bit hysterically.

'I think people are furious at her because she was the rare old woman who didn't pay a price,' said Laurie. 'She bested a beautiful young rival – that would be her daughter – and she kept hold of the sexy scumbag and got famous while the poor kid got shoved aside by everybody! She won!'

Eileen laughed a lot, hysterically.

Then they went back to the horrible director, the big star and the hapless treachery of 'Jen'.

'I feel sorry for her,' she said. 'But I think it's time for me to defend myself. I've finally told Brickbat's director what's been going on, and I think he's going to intervene.'

I really hope you didn't actually do that, thought Laurie.

As they got off the phone, Eileen said, 'I love you. I'm so glad I have you to talk to.' Laurie said, 'Me too.' Then she put her phone in her pocket and thought *Why are my friends crazy? What does that say about me? Why do my husband and I love each other but we have sex with other people?*

She gazed at the flashing river, at a stand of trees under which sheltered Mary blessed a circle of beseeching children. It was undeniable: the whole world was crazy. But maybe these particular friends were particularly crazy because – like her – they'd never had children. Perhaps this explained why her marriage was weird? What would it have been like if they'd had kids? She didn't want to go there, but it had become hard not to. All at once, hordes of important businesspeople, powerful politicians and inexhaustible influencers were saying that a birthrate collapse had put humanity at risk of extinction, and it was the fault of spoiled, despicable women who were not doing their part. If they were married it was their husbands' fault too. These opinions pounded down near-daily and sometimes Laurie imagined herself trying to push them back with her hands as she paced around her house arguing with invisible hectoring natalists.

'*I know most people want children, need children. Children are great! I love children! But some people are different, some people are just built a little different. The aggregate dominates of course! But life is more interesting when there's room for those on the margins. Think of the wonderful poems and stories written by the childless, I mean childfree! Emily Dickinson, Jane Austen, Flannery O'Connor!*'

'*Those women are to be pitied,*' intoned the invisible opposition. '*They were tragically ill, their contribution came out of lack.*'

'*Everyone contributes what they can! What if you've got bad genes, what if there was no love in your family, what if you were abused as a child and your mother didn't protect you, what if she actually didn't like you and so you don't have normal maternal patterning? Isn't it better for the world if you don't produce more people with that coding? And instead –*'

'*What you describe is, again, tragic. But people with stories of abuse far worse than that have transformed their history with selfless parenting. If you can't do that then – get out of the way! Women past child-bearing years who exist in sterile partnerships are selfishly hoarding a resource: a sixty-year-old man can father children and should not be taken up by an old woman. The only role for an old woman is to care for children – data proves that is the sole reason for superior female longevity.*'

Absolutely: *Old women pay at least as much*. And what do they get for it?

Peripheral motion disturbed, then alerted her; the nuns were coming down the path, conversing. The younger of them – she was about thirty – spoke intently, her face focused as if some wonderful problem had just yielded itself to her. The older woman – at least sixty – listened patiently, mouth gently frowning, eyes scanning a universe invisible to Laurie; a place of refuge or complexity or both.

'*What about nuns?*' she thought at her invisible scolds. '*They don't have children and yet they . . .*'

'. . . *hide from life*,' came the curt reply. '*And they don't even look good doing it.*'

But actually the nuns did look pretty good. They rode bikes all over the neighborhood, they played basketball on the convent court, they gardened and joked around. Laurie and her husband smiled to see bands of them riding down the street with pleasureful energy, their habits tied up around their ankles. How robust they were in this realm of ancient words and fairy-tale statues grounded in the earth, Mother Mary with her open arms; a whole system that held them in place.

In Laurie's mind, the imp of the perverse dancingly appeared, obscuring Mary and her sisters with another remembered story of obscene license and abuse: a young woman who'd worked as a live-in servant for a fanatically beloved but sexually abusive male writer had taken a selfie after he'd (for the umpteenth time) ass-raped her and made her eat her own shit. She'd posted the image on Instagram, pouting at her device, looking baffled, helpless and very adorable. Which prompted Laurie's friend Sugar to post somewhere that she thought the picture undermined the accusation because it made it seem like the girl was in love with herself as an ass victim. 'It's like *feel my ass pain*,' she wrote.

Which maybe explains the death threat? Laurie thought but didn't say.

Also thought and unsaid: she got why the girl posted the picture. It reminded her of herself as a teen, writing funny feisty journal accounts of miserable, actually degrading things that had happened to her; adorable pictures made of words.

No old woman could console herself with such an image, not even one made of words; it could just not be made to look good. And at least old women didn't get abused like that so much – well, but sometimes they did. The perverted writer had b-fucked his sixty-something housekeeper too – who had actually been willing, in spite of being married.

My God, no wonder young people didn't want to have sex anymore! The adults, even moms and old people were running after them with their pants down, sixty-five-year-old women were roaming sex sites and then writing about their experiences for respected news outlets, elderly couples – like her! – had open relationships. On the one hand it was great, an assertion of life force in fierce rebellion against its own limitations. On the other . . .

The nuns smiled and greeted her as they passed, their faces pale and voices foreign in the absence of makeup or contemporary social cadence. She didn't know these particular women, but there was a nun with whom she'd had some powerful conversations. (Sister Ava: humorous mouth, exalted eyes, skewed gray glasses, one scratched lens.) They had met one day on the broad concrete path surrounding the convent itself and had, with remarkable speed, gone from the weather to Jesus – whether or not he was literally the son of God or more like a complex human vector for divine love – and Mary, a spirit of comfort and forgiveness to whom Laurie sometimes appealed in sort-of prayer.

On another pathway meeting, Laurie had broached the subject of adultery. She had admitted to fear of demonic influence entering her in the form of intense love-hunger, a terrible childish voice that woke her late at night and spoke from her mouth while her husband lay asleep; high, frightened and strange, it begged a nameless *someone* for love (*please love me, why don't you love me?*), love that she could not experience with her husband for reasons she did not understand.

'And do you think you can get this love from someone else, from another man?' asked Sr Ava.

Laurie hesitated and answered, 'Yes. Yes, I can.'

The nun stopped and turned to face her. 'Is that the truth?'

'At first,' Laurie replied. 'And then –' Something scalding, a bright blinding force rising inside her, like a ligature cutting off everything but furious, faceless instinct; chaotic sub-emotive need slamming through her body in response to his body, words coming from her that she could not recall. Joy, terror; terror-joy: the forgiving tenderness of his chest, his arms, his hands.

'I would like us to pray together,' said the nun. And she reached for Laurie's hand.

Then one day she came home and found that she could not be with her husband; even though they were in the same room, she could not fully be with him. Nor could she be with the lover, not really; she could only endure the memory of his force and transitory tenderness, moving in and out of her in subsiding waves. She was more alone than she would be if she were actually alone. The pain of it was stunning.

When the incantation was done, the nun gave her the name and number of an exorcist a couple of towns over – 'just to chat' – and invited her to Mass. 'When you feel the presence of evil, I encourage you to sing. Say the name of Jesus and sing – demons hate it when you sing.' 'Actually,' said Laurie, 'they might enjoy my singing, it is pretty awful.' Sr Ava laughed and said, 'Then just say the name of Jesus; declare that he is Lord.' She'd walked away singing confidently.

Laurie had not been able to resist calling the exorcist who said he thought it sounded more like harassment than possession and who in any case couldn't run a ritual on her if she wasn't Catholic. He said it would be like trying to get rid of squirrels in the attic by installing a high-pitched electronic noise device; you'd just irritate them, and even if they left, they'd come back because the 'holes in the house would still be there'. He urged her to beg God for forgiveness, to go to Mass and learn more about the faith.

And she did go, once. There was hardly anyone there and the priest spent half the sermon bitching about wokeness and lack of funding for the local dioceses. Laurie tried to focus on the other people in the pews, their unknown capacity for love, their will for it, their wish to humbly praise the vastness of . . . whatever this was that they were walking around in. But the priest made it hard to remember that.

Laurie got up off the bench and walked to the statue of Mary; she thought about kneeling among the statue children but considered how uncomfortable that would be, not to mention how kooky and theatrical it would seem if someone saw her. She simply clasped her hands before her and lowered her head. 'Help,' she thought. 'Help.'

The thing about Eileen: you could talk about this stuff with her. Laurie had shared with her the conversation with Sr Ava which Eileen found interesting even if it was based on patriarchal shit which she hoped that Laurie did not believe.

'I don't know what I believe,' said Laurie. 'But I think there might be a reason that every culture in the whole fucking world believes in monogamy –'

'Every culture *does not* believe in it. I think it's only something like –'

'– or at least some sanctimonious pretense of it. For women anyway.'

'Exactly,' said Eileen. '*For women.*'

'And that thing that happens at night, maybe it actually is something evil, like a horror-movie monster-thing that's getting in where I'm weak, that's using me as a vehicle to get into the world and just go around eating –'

'Oh stop,' said Eileen. 'You've hardly eaten at all, it's just been this one guy! You're not evil. You're hurt. You're not evil!'

'I know *I'm* not,' said Laurie. 'But what if something bigger than me is –'

'I don't think it can do that unless you invite it in. I think the good in you is too strong for that, Laurie. And you've got such strong boundaries.'

Forgetting any appearance of kookiness or theatricality, Laurie went to the statue of Mary and put her arms around it. It was of course cold but its shape was gentle and curved. She held it and thought 'Help me. Help Eileen. Help us walk through this. We're not evil. We don't deserve to be made crazy.'

And maybe they didn't. But how in hell was Eileen, 'rogue RN/pelvic-floor therapist', in any position to declare who was good and who was not? She thought of the time her friend had drunkenly revealed the reason for her hinted outcast status: They'd been talking about social and professional backstabbing when she abruptly told the story: several elderly clients had come to her longing for sexual connection; when creams and patches plus pelvic-floor exercises had failed to work she'd referred them to a doctor who would inject estrogen pellets under the skin of their asses or abdomens. For a while everything was great, the women had inundated her with raving emojis describing hot sex with their husbands for the first time in decades! Then two of them started bleeding uncontrollably, and yet another developed some horrible thing involving her endometrial lining growing somewhere it shouldn't be, there was possible cancer and a possible lawsuit – and they couldn't take the damn pellets out.

It sounded horrible and frankly irresponsible but Laurie heard only the pain in her friend's voice as she cried, 'I was just trying to help! They wanted it so badly! And I did help some of them, I did!' Eileen had put her face in her hands and begun to cry. 'But nobody knows about them because they're too embarrassed to talk about it!' Laurie had put her arms around Eileen and stroked her hair and said, 'Well *I* know. I know honey.'

But she didn't know. She really did not know what to think about any of this. And still she had to walk through it. A lot of it.

Her phone pinged; it was her husband wanting to know when she was coming back and what she wanted for dinner. She typed *What are the choices?*

Orange and avocado salad plus bread. Pasta with tomatoes and basil.

Maybe something with beans? I don't think we're getting enough fiber. And then *I think Eileen is crazy.*

Why?

She was thinking about answering when she saw that a nun was standing on the path, watching her. On realizing that she had been noticed, the sister resumed walking, but slowly, still keeping her eye on Laurie – the stranger who was standing oddly close to the statue of the Virgin. Raising her hand in a static wave, Laurie moved away from Mary, respectfully skirting the prayerful children. The nun waved back.

She texted her husband *I'll tell you about it when I get home. I still like her. But she is crazy.*

You realize you're both crazy, right?

Ha ha she replied. *See you soon.* And she made her way back up the path. ■

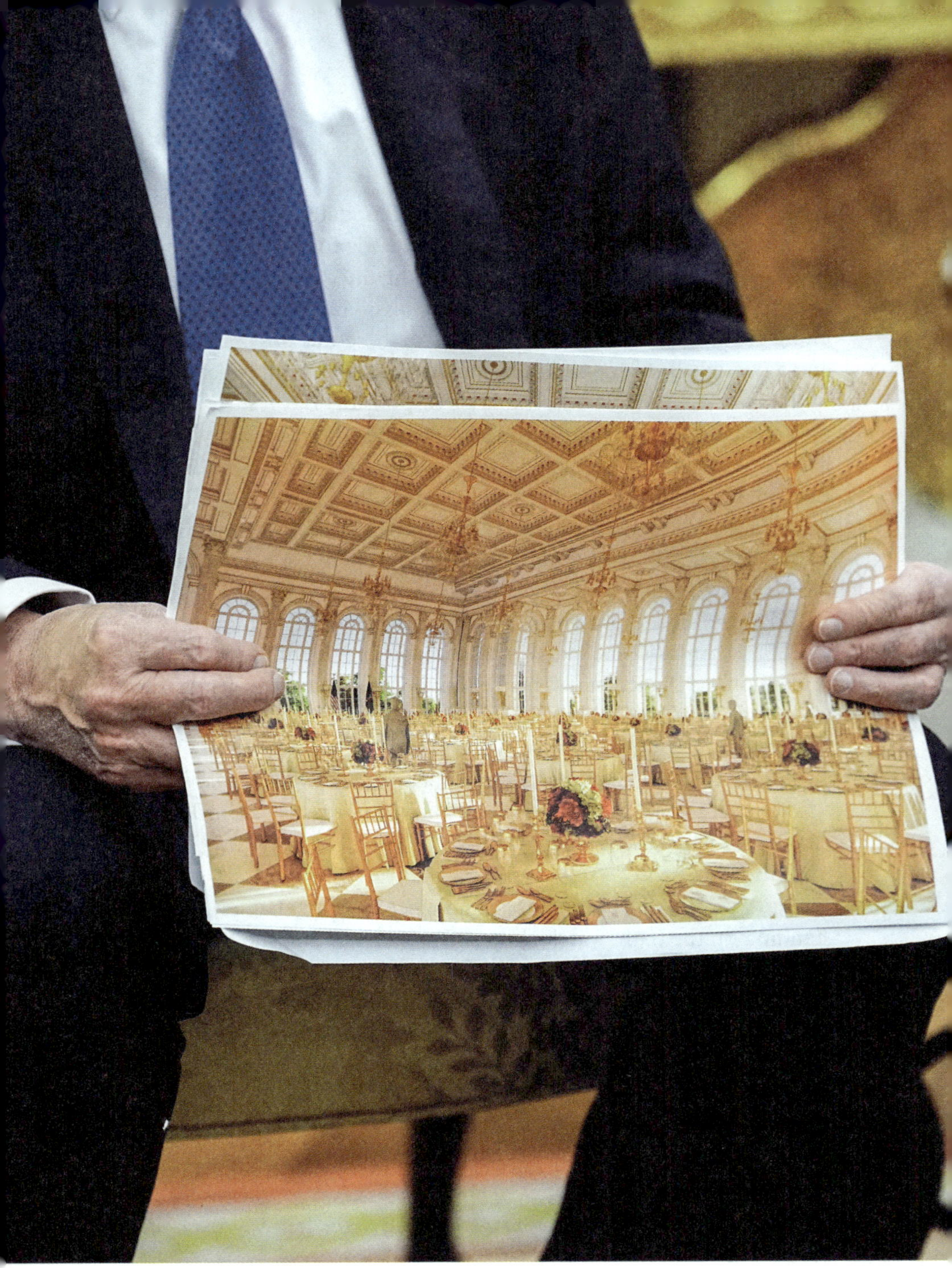

GETTY IMAGES

ARC DE TRUMP

Antonia Hitchens

Donald Trump doesn't use a computer. 'He doesn't even have an *email* address,' Stephanie, a lobbyist, said to me over lunch, lowering her voice as though revealing classified information. She was pushed out of the President's first campaign in 2016, and has spent the past decade finding ways to reach Trump indirectly. Much of her work in Washington now revolves around getting the occasional piece of paper slipped into the stack of social media printouts that she says is piled on the Resolute Desk in the morning. A staffer nicknamed 'the human printer' – she carries a desktop printer in her backpack – gives Trump hardcopies of tweets. 'He usually looks through them before his daily intelligence briefing,' Stephanie told me.

Since being dismissed, she's found 'new angles' to work her way in from the outside. 'I'm here to solve issues,' she said. 'Business is always going to be business. Money is always going to be made. Deals will always be had. Okay?' One of Stephanie's recent ventures is paying people to post about specific subjects on X. 'I write every word of it for them, they just press send,' Stephanie said. 'Then the President might see it.' I used to wonder why the stream of pro-Trump influencers populating my feed would take sudden and fleeting positions on flavored vapes, the Congo, a little-known person Trump should consider for a political appointment, a mineral deal.

Stephanie sends them a monthly fee of ten thousand dollars in exchange for two posts obliquely introducing her clients' needs.

We were at a new members' club downtown, frequented by administration officials, political strategists, and an expanding class of MAGA hangers-on. On the wraparound terrace overlooking the Treasury building, chefs were slicing an enormous tuna into sashimi. The fish, they said, 'woke up in the Pacific Ocean' that morning before being flown to Washington. When I went in to meet Stephanie, she was on the phone. 'I don't think he understands what is at stake or who these players are,' she was saying as she waved me to her small, round table. The club's 'no public phone calls' policy means that there is a certain amount of spectacle in answering, and then ending, calls in the public rooms. Stephanie put down her phone and announced that the person she'd been speaking to was trying to kill her deal. 'This individual is coming back and saying, "Yeah, no, this dog ain't going to hunt."' She went on, 'I'm sad because I love this individual and he's a known brand. I can't say his name, but you know who he is and he's a titan and people love him and the President loves him and he's in the news all the time and he's a brand. So of course I want to make him money. I want the President to give him an "attaboy!" on this one.'

Stephanie speaks in a register of abstraction and generality: D.C. is a 'small town' where, she says, 'perspective matters' and it's 'all about the influence that you have over decision makers, period'. She knew I'd seen leaked documents from Trump's first term in which she laid out her fee structure for trying to secure presidential pardons for clients. She would only occasionally mention a detail about her current work. Over coffee, she told me that, when visiting a foreign country to meet a prospective client, she'd had her own motorcade and an armed guard outside her bedroom door. One way that she liked to be specific was by citing how often someone talked to Trump. When I asked about 'this individual', she said, 'I can't go into detail too much because I'm NDA'd, but let's just put it this way, the person we're dealing with is a one-percenter – a verified one-percenter.

Okay?' She went on, 'He's very close to the President. He speaks to him *weekly.*'

In Washington, I often hear discussions about who is a true believer, and who is cosplaying belief. 'He's not even really racist,' a longtime consultant sighed to me recently when I brought up one of his associates. 'It's honestly cooler to be philosemitic now,' another strategist told me, as the trend of paid-influencer-generated antisemitism reached its peak. 'You'll start to see a pivot,' he said.

The new style of political performance could be demanding. At drinks, an official complained to me about how poorly the administration was handling some of its high-profile legal cases. The problem was that 'it's like everyone has this MAGA id, where you give yourself over to something you know is irrational'.

I was surprised when I saw this official's iPhone background was Trump raising his bloodied fist and mouthing 'fight' after the alleged assassination attempt against him in Butler, Pennsylvania. He explained that he hadn't wanted to buy the branded Trump iPhone, but it had briefly seemed like everyone in Washington was expected to purchase one. At least with this background, he said, if he were out to dinner with other officials and they all put their phones on the table, his wallpaper selection would color him as sufficiently loyal.

He speculated on which brawls had been staged, which assassination attempts were real, which tragedies were faked. When a Christian influencer's wife, who had posted a pregnancy 'reveal' video on Instagram, followed up with a teary announcement about her miscarriage, one source mused that it might be some kind of elaborate engagement-farming. 'What does it even mean to be Christian? They're all pretending to be Christian now,' a former conservative news producer said to me.

Sometimes the influencers' handlers got sloppy with timing and pacing, or a flurry of personae used the exact same language and punctuation. That's when the pay-to-play contrivance becomes obvious. Last summer, Trump knocked down the East Wing of the

White House in order to start developing an enormous ballroom he'd designed; a federal judge had recently ordered him to stop construction. I was at the White House Correspondents' Dinner when an armed man tried to storm the cavernous Hilton ballroom where Trump and his Cabinet were eating dinner with the press corps. Within minutes of the shooting – apparently another assassination attempt, carried out by a man who'd checked into the Hilton and tried to run through its magnetometers with a long gun – dozens of influencers posted that Trump's ballroom was now a national security necessity. 'This is why we need a ballroom,' they implored in unison, while the President was still in a secret evacuation tunnel underneath the old hotel. The two competing narratives of the Correspondents night were that the shooting had been staged and that the ballroom needed to be built.

In Congress, the response to an encroaching sense of cynicism and collective disbelief – the suspicion that unknown forces were pulling all the strings – was to 'restore trust' by releasing as many classified documents as possible: on Epstein, UFOs, MKUltra, and Havana syndrome. I met with an intelligence official who told me that under Trump, his agency was finally 'bringing back normal Americans' faith in the intelligence community after they knew it was weaponized against them'. He had just been at a meeting about declassifying documents that, he said, showed how the Biden-era intelligence officials had apparently targeted stay-at-home moms as the new sleeper agents of transnational white supremacy. Another senior official characterized MAGA as a movement that attracted a lot of converts. 'Your mind becomes too porous when you keep converting as an adult,' she told me. 'It's not good to be so open to things' – becoming a post-liberal, or a Catholic, or deciding to believe in demons. There was a lot of talk in Washington now of visions and demons. I ran into a War Room producer who told me to 'look at the ancient alchemical tarograms. What do you see? Hermaphrodites.' It took me a second to realize he was joking.

Some administration officials came off of the internet and into the office buildings around the capital and quickly became disillusioned. Before one staffer, Liam, joined the administration, he made music and spent a lot of time on X, where he had an anonymous account. 'I'd been extremely online for the past ten years in an explosion of political education,' he told me. 'I was looking for the most interesting dopamine hit.' He thought working for Trump would deliver it. 'The whole end of history thing had been my life. An autopilot default liberal order – why challenge it? Things you thought were never possible, questions that were finite, then you hit the center of the earth. When narrative starts to fail, there starts to be a reformation.' The freshness of this new order curdled within a few months on the job. When I last saw him, he said, 'I get no dopamine from this stuff anymore. It's all folklore.'

Since Trump's second inauguration, young DOGE engineers and administration officials have been gathering at Hugo's house in an ongoing victory-lap against what came before them. They say things like, 'We're gonna ignore the courts.' Hugo went from being nearly cast out of Washington society to a sought-after Trump-world fixer who often works on 'all five sides of a deal'. He used to wear a MAGA hat around the city when it was still sacrilegious to do so. One day, when we met at a coffee shop, he pointed out that we were next to a former soup-kitchen where he'd had to do community service after stealing snacks from a convenience store while on a bender. The police chased him and caught him flushing the cookies he hadn't yet stuffed in his mouth down the toilet.

Sometimes while we were speaking, Hugo would get calls on Signal from a prominent tech mogul. Over lunch, when he was showing me something on his phone, I saw him telling an influencer what to post. ('Quote tweet that,' he'd written alongside a link. 'Retweet it.') One night at a bar, an official drunkenly sniped at someone questioning Hugo's credentials: 'He's who you hire if you want a settlement to go through.' Hugo told me he never went into the Department of Justice 'through the front entrance', because then he'd have to sign in on the logs.

Recently, Hugo found out a newspaper reporter might be writing about him. 'Nobody knows how I make money,' Hugo said. 'I don't *do* anything,' he told me. He said that barely anyone showed up at his next party after the paper started calling around about him.

Hugo was engrossed in a legal action against a MAGA activist named Dave. Some Republicans wanted to help clear his name; Hugo – or his clients – seemed to want Dave to go to prison for reasons of their own. Hugo hired someone to pose as a videographer to follow Dave around. 'He thinks they're making a documentary about him,' Hugo told me. He'd contrived the whole fake project; the concocted film gave Dave's detractors footage of his whereabouts and circumstances so they could strategize about bringing him down. 'He's so fucked,' he told me.

One evening, when I was having a drink at an Italian restaurant across the street from the DOJ, I noticed a huge banner of Donald Trump hanging from the side of the building. 'It's all so cringe,' Hugo said. When he wasn't trying to point me toward stories that would presumably serve his clients, he urged me to write about those in his political universe that he found most disreputable and tacky. 'This administration is so corrupt they'll have to come up with new laws to address the inventiveness,' he said. 'Paolo Zampolli is disgusting,' he told me, referring to one of Trump's special envoys, a former modeling executive who was trying to get the administration to deport his ex after they had a fight. (Zampolli denies the accusation.)

I'd been at an event on the National Mall called Rededicate 250, twelve hours of prayer and political speech to 'rededicate' the nation to Christianity for its semiquincentennial. There was a lot of the usual talk about how God had saved Trump, and T-shirts printed with I'VE READ THE FINAL CHAPTER: GOD WINS. The following day, Doug, a person close to the administration, invited me to a film screening at the recently renamed Trump Kennedy Center. It was a documentary built on a report published by the White House Task Force to Eradicate Anti-Christian Bias. Trump had created the group following claims that Biden's Justice Department had attempted to 'squelch faith'. 'You should come to this if you want to Christian-maxx,' Doug told me, of the premiere.

The evening had an end-of-days feel. There was a late-spring heatwave, and attendees were sweating off their make-up onto their black tie. There was no water. All the concession stands were already shuttered; Trump was about to close the Kennedy Center for two years of renovations. A few 'VIPs' walked down a makeshift red carpet, taking questions from esoteric right-wing streaming networks. In the mostly empty theater before the show started, several enthusiasts were on their feet swaying to acoustic Christian rock. Doug and I joined a group of lawyers he knew. He'd just given a speech to a law firm audience hoping to better understand the administration's policies. 'It wasn't really political. It was sort of in exchange for not getting subpoenaed,' he said. He told the lawyers in the theater about going with their boss to the funeral of one of his former professors. 'Nobody would talk to us,' he said, listing the various people from previous presidential administrations who'd been in attendance. 'Oh, that's really deep state,' one guy responded.

The woman next to me had worked on the film, tracking down documents supposedly showing evidence of anti-Christian bias in the FBI. She was on rotation from a department where she worked to one of the presidential advisory boards. She told me the timing was good; she'd just broken up with another official in her department. I asked why it didn't work out. 'He didn't believe in God,' she said, 'and he didn't love me.'

A Trump official and I were waiting for Diet Cokes at the club. He was checking the prediction markets to see the odds on whether his boss, a Cabinet secretary, would be fired that afternoon. Betting markets were everywhere. Brokers had flooded Washington with lobbying money for the betting industry, and were popularizing placing wagers on any event that the political class tracked. Polymarket opened a 'monitoring the situation' pop-up cocktail bar. A journalist received a request to change his news story ahead of publication to mirror the outcome one user had bet a lot of money on. A military guy was arrested for making hundreds of thousands of dollars betting on his early knowledge of the Venezuela raid. (Some members of Congress claimed it was unfair to punish him; he was basically just engaging in the same behavior as Congressional stock-trading.) The markets 'honestly work better if there's insider trading, because it makes them more accurate', an administration official told me at the club. When asked about the new trend of betting on politics a few days later, Trump said, 'The whole world, unfortunately, has become somewhat of a casino.'

'There are deals to be had right now, because there's a geopolitical shift happening,' Stephanie said to me. 'Does that make sense? It's not that hard.' Stephanie was one of the many people manically pitching herself into the new Trump-led world order. 'It's a gold rush to get in on the permanent infrastructure,' another consultant told me.

I met with a MAGA lobbyist at his office downtown. He had just arrived in the city, but was already in high demand as all sorts of companies were puzzling over how to best engage the administration. He suggested we talk as he drove to his next meeting, and led me to a brand-new Escalade with custom leather bucket seats. 'Take me to the State Department,' he said to his driver, 'then take her anywhere she wants to go.' He told me a long story about talking to the President about poisonous snakes as we rode down the Mall. He discussed the statues Trump planned to put up in his 'National Garden of American Heroes'. All around Trump's construction projects were other gut renovations of the capital, promises to renew fusty establishment avenues like K Street from the inside out.

There were cranes everywhere. Trump would look down on them from the Marine One helicopter as he flew back to Washington after weekends away. He would have the military pilots circle over the areas he wanted to transform. He'd sandblasted the Lincoln Memorial's reflecting pool and had his 'pool guy' advise on repainting it 'American Flag Blue'. (Soon after, algal bloom had turned the pool green.) Now he was planning to build a triumphal memorial arch for himself in the style of the Arc de Triomphe. I sat in on planning commission meetings stocked with Trump appointees who were fighting with local organizers and historians about the implications of putting white paint on historic granite, about whether the arch would impede flight paths. 'Washington is not a static city,' the panel chairman said, before motioning to fast-track construction project approval for Trump.

At Trump's direction, the National Guard had been in Washington since August last year, pacing the sweltering streets in their fatigues, putting up checkpoints near a few epicenters of nightlife. A handmade sign on a lamppost in my neighborhood cautioned people against reporting their neighbors to ICE or the Guard. STITCHES FOR SNITCHES, it read. I was walking at nightfall when a synchronized clamor erupted out of the windows of residential buildings, like a version of the Covid-era pot-and-pan banging for health workers. I asked someone on the street what the cheers were for, and she snapped: they're clapping for our occupied city. A guy who threw a sandwich at federal agents became the new symbol of the resistance.

Mostly I saw the guardsmen as they tried out new restaurants on their dinner breaks, or stood bored outside boutiques like Rag & Bone in Georgetown, or rode the Metro's escalators up and down in packs. Just after Thanksgiving two West Virginia guardsmen were shot downtown by an Afghan national who'd worked with the CIA in Afghanistan during the war. One died. In the January snowstorms, residents wondered whether the guardsmens' mandate included shoveling the black ice that remained after days of unplowed streets. This summer they helped enforce a night-time curfew for teens, who were ordered by the city to be indoors by 11 p.m. The guardsmen's presence, like the construction, was part of Trump's capital 'beautification project'. I did hear residents permitting themselves to praise the working fountains in Malcolm X Park. As long as I could remember they'd been empty, fetid squares where mosquitos bred. Trump had the park service turn on cascades of running water for the first time in years.

'Let him build his shit,' Stephanie told me. 'This is a city of monuments. We put one up for Martin Luther King and World War Two and Roosevelt. There's monuments that have been put up. You want to halt his construction and just have a gaping hole?' Trump was moving fast because he knew he might lose the midterms and get bogged down in investigations and impeachment. 'Everything is in hyper-expedited speed, hyperdrive, now,' Stephanie said. 'Donald Trump is not going to have a five-year study done on it to see if we should do it.'

Her five o'clock meeting arrived, another Trump 2016 veteran who was trying to stay in the mix. He pointed at the view out the window, which framed the Washington Monument. 'Look at that,' he said. 'Do you know what's on top of the Washington Monument? It's a piece of aluminum. When they built that, aluminum was the most expensive metal in the world, and the largest piece of aluminum ever is the very tippy top of that.' He gestured to where the color of the blocks of marble subtly changed color midway through the monument; around the Civil War, when construction was halted, it stood half-finished for several years. The operative and Stephanie, occasional colleagues, were meeting a new client. 'He's from a foreign country,' Stephanie said, 'where shenanigans ensued last year.' She went on, 'We help him with a range of issues. He's a nice guy. I mean he's a lion. He will be president of that country one day.' Her colleague cut in. 'I tell you what, there's more there than meets the eye. That's the problem with him. He doesn't talk much. The things he's done are just . . .' Stephanie stopped him. 'I'm sitting with a reporter,' she said. He looked at her like: why? 'I was just giving her some insights.' ■

Names have been changed to protect the privacy of sources.

KATHRYN SCANLAN

A saw squeals in the half-built house across the street; a man shouts: *Hey hey hey!*; a car speeds by on the road out front; the neighbor thuds across the floor on the other side of the wall; a hammer strikes; men speak; a car door slams; an engine starts; an airplane thunders by; an engine idles at the curb; a saw stutters; boards clatter to the ground; a truck rattles by; the neighbor shoves something hard against the other side of the wall; heavy things are dropped into the bed of a truck; a saw shrieks; metal clangs on concrete; a hammer rings; a hammer patters; a car goes by; a car goes by; a car goes by; a drill spins; a sander groans; metal strikes metal; a car speeds by blasting its radio; the high mechanical choir of a courtyard neighbor's electric car can be heard reversing into the street; *Yes right no definitely*, says a man on the sidewalk; a saw roars; a saw shrieks; a hammer pounds; a car goes by; a car goes by; a car goes by; an empty bucket hits the ground; a man lets out a sharp whistle; a man shouts: *Yo!*; the neighbor speaks on the other side of the wall; a crow caws; a car goes by; crows caw; a car goes by; a car goes by; a heavy truck clanks down the hill; the dog in the yard across the street (blue house) barks; a dog with a higher-pitched voice barks; a third dog barks; three dogs bark at each other; a startled crow caws; a car goes by; the blue-house dog snarls against its fence; frantic dog claws scratch the sidewalk; a woman says: *Leave it!*; my chair creaks; a car goes by; the neighbor coughs on the other side of the wall; a drill squeals; a saw shrieks; a hammer strikes; a sander drones; a hawk cries; a car speeds by; a car honks; a man shouts: *Fuck you, idiot!*; a cat gallops across the roof; a tree jostles; a squirrel lets out a string of sharp rebukes; a sander drones; a grinder groans; a squirrel scolds; a drill stutters; a car goes by; a car goes by; a car goes by; a squirrel mutters; a saw whines; a drill squeals; a car goes by; I sneeze; a cat growls; a clanking truck thunders by; I sneeze; a motorcycle putters past; metal strikes metal;

a board clatters to the ground; a man sings; a police helicopter chops air; a car goes by; a car goes by; a saw shrieks; a police helicopter throbs overhead; the windows in my room rattle in their frames; the neighbor drops something heavy on the other side of the wall; a police helicopter recedes; a car door slams; a car vibrates at the curb out front; a grinder groans; hammers strike; a bird warbles; the neighbor's plumbing rattles in the wall; a car goes by; a car goes by; a car goes by; a gas-powered leaf blower riffs at the white house across the street; a car goes by; a leaf blower's engine catches; a leaf blower roars; a saw spins; a saw sputters; a leaf blower drones; a car goes by; a car goes by; a waste bin is banged along the ground; a leaf blower whines; a car goes by; a car goes by; a saw shrieks; hammers pound; a rake scrapes pavement; a leaf blower gets louder; my elbow squeaks on the desktop; a heavy truck rattles by; a drill squeals; a leaf blower whines; a rake scrapes; a waste bin is banged along the ground; the mail truck roars up the street blasting its radio at top volume; the mail truck grinds to a stop out front; the mail truck's engine quits; *He's got that same feel the gunman had*, says the mail truck's radio; a guttural vehicle motors by; the mail truck's heavy metal door slides open; a car goes by; a car goes by; a leaf blower drones; the mail carrier's package scanner beeps; a package hits the next-door neighbor's stoop; *Exactly, it's hereditary*, says the mail truck's radio; the mail carrier's package scanner beeps; another package hits the next-door neighbor's stoop; a leaf blower whines; a rake scrapes; the metal lid of my mailbox opens; the metal lid of my mailbox slams shut; the metal lid of the next-door neighbor's mailbox opens; the metal lid of the next-door neighbor's mailbox slams shut; a leaf blower roars; *She would just swing like this and she'd hit you*, says the mail truck's radio; the mail truck's heavy metal door slides shut; a car goes by; the mail truck's engine struggles to start; a car goes by; a car goes by; a leaf blower drones; a rake scrapes; a sander groans; the mail truck roars up the street; a drill spins; a saw squeals; boards clatter to the ground; a siren wails; a man says, *Hee hee!*; an emergency vehicle blasts its horn; heavy bass issues from a car idling out front; the windows in my room vibrate; a car honks; a car speeds by; a siren wails; on the other side of the patio wall the next-door neighbor says, *Cancel my reservation*; a hawk screams; a leaf blower drones; a car goes by; a car goes by; a car goes by; from the courtyard apartments a new baby bawls; a saw splutters; a drill stutters; men shout; a bird trills; a heavy delivery truck roars up the street; the new baby mewls; the delivery truck stops out front; a leaf blower screams; a rake scrapes pavement; the delivery truck's hazards tick clocklike; a hammer strikes; a sander groans; the delivery truck's heavy door slides open; a man says, *Hey how are you*; a car goes by; a car goes by; a car goes by; a drill squeals; a man says, *OK I appreciate it*; the delivery truck's heavy door slides shut; a sander groans; *It's just so good*, says a woman on the sidewalk; a car goes by; a car goes by; the delivery truck roars up the street; a leaf blower drones; a crow caws; a crow mutters; a car speeds by; the next-door neighbor's door opens; the blue-house dog barks viciously; the next-door neighbor calls to the dog: *Hi, Izzy!*; the blue-house dog barks savagely; the next-door neighbor calls: *Hi, sweetheart!*; the blue-house dog barks crazily; a jay whistles; a car goes by; a car goes by; a saw shrieks; boards clatter to the ground; crows chatter as they fly over the building; a car goes by; a car goes by; a car goes by; a leaf blower whines; a bird chirps; a sander groans; a drill squeals; a man sneezes; my chair creaks; a heavy truck beeps in reverse; a car speeds by blasting its radio; a motorcycle sputters past; a bird chirps; a truck beeps in reverse; old-fashioned music is switched on in the tap-dance studio up the street; apprentice tap dancers stomp the floor of the tap-dance studio up the street; the tap dancers sound like heavy bags dropped and lifted, dropped and lifted with no particular rhythm or unison; a car goes by; an airplane goes by; a hawk cries; a car pulls up to the curb and idles there; a phone rings at top volume from the car's stereo system; a woman's voice says *Hello?* at top volume from the car's stereo system; a heavy truck comes clanking down the hill; *Where are you?* says a woman's voice at top volume from the car's stereo system; a drill shrieks; hammers pound; a fast-moving military helicopter thunders over the building; a heavy truck shudders up the hill; a car goes by; a car goes by; a hawk squeaks; old-fashioned music tinkles from the tap-dance studio; tap dancers stomp; in the courtyard a woman says: *Go pee-pee, Charlie*; a saw screeches; a car goes by; a car goes by; a car goes by; in the courtyard a woman says: *Go pee-pee in the garden*; a hawk squeaks; a car goes by; in the courtyard a child says: *I don't want to!*; a car goes by; metal strikes metal; a sander groans; a car with a bad muffler goes by; a jogger's feet slap the sidewalk; hammers pound; a drill squeals; men shout; a bird chirps; wind-chimes ring from the blue house across the street; a crow caws; a car passes; crows caw; a car passes; a leaf blower starts up at the gray apartment building across the street; a leaf blower roars; a car passes; a sander groans; a leaf blower gets louder; a car speeds by; a heavy truck rattles down the hill; a leaf blower riffs; a drill stutters; a saw splutters; a leaf blower roars; a car goes by; a car goes by; a car goes by; a car goes by; a low-flying plane sounds like thunder in the distance; a low-flying plane ruptures the air; a low-flying plane shakes the building; *Run!* says a child; *Run!* says another child; children laugh; feet strike the sidewalk. ■

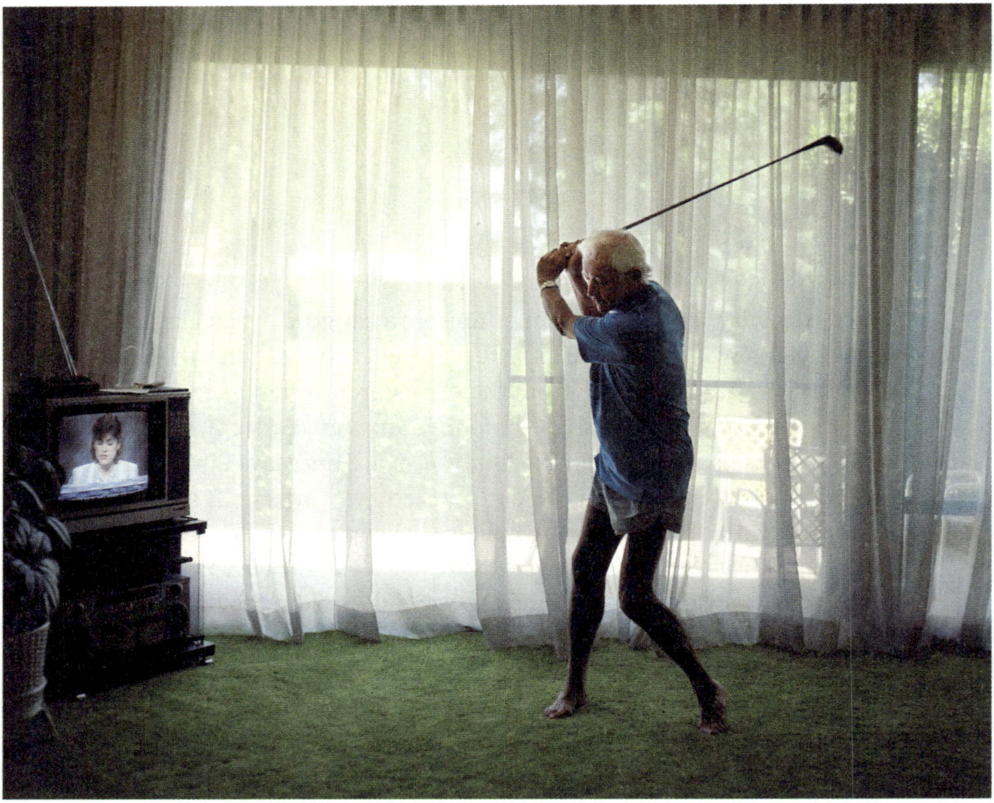

LARRY SULTAN
Practicing Golf Swing, 1986
Courtesy of Casemore Gallery, San Francisco; Yancey Richardson, New York, Galerie Thomas Zander, Cologne; and Estate of Larry Sultan

DATHUN

Amie Barrodale

We would get into a cart and ride out onto the green. Down the fairway, around the slope, past the sand traps and over the rise. Some days I'd take us by the water, which was overpopulated by strange fish. Marty might throw in a piece of bread, bring the surface alive with their bodies. We'd go past that. All the way to the line of trees, and then on foot through the forest about an hour's walk to the trailer. Marty's place before the thing. The AI doomsday or virus or whatever. Before we had to hunker down at my club. Back when he was just the HVAC guy, and an HVAC guy was a guy who didn't matter. Now Marty had a little bit of power, running the AC and the heaters, and over the months, he'd leveraged it. I mean, he treated me like a dog.

He took me to his trailer. It wasn't what I expected. I expected beaten-down carpet, dog food. Cliff Booth-type deal. But he had it set up like a coffee shop. Reclaimed wood, vinyl. Total pussy. I contemplated telling him I liked it, then thought I'd better not.

He gestured for me to sit, opened his little refrigerator, got out two Diet Cokes. 'You like these right?'

He wore dark glasses, club jacket. Had a nasally voice, like reedy.

'Got them for you,' he said.

He opened a can, passed it to me. Opened the other. Took a sip, making a little sound, like *sfffft*. He set the can down, then picked it back up and lifted his dark glasses to read.

'You were in construction?' he said. Set the can down.

I nodded. Took a sip of Diet Coke.

His expression changed. Something shrewd. 'So . . . you want to build me something?'

'Like what?'

'Little road.' He drew a line on the table with a finger.

'A road? Marty, come on.'

'From here, up to, oh . . . there.' He pointed. 'From my trailer to there. Cut through the forest eventually.'

'That's thirty meters. Big job. I'd need a team. Tools, you know. Gravel.'

'There's rocks all over.'

'You're joking. Marty, come on. We don't have the supply chains. Skid loaders. I can't go out and, like, rent a crane.'

He gave me the megawatt smile. Said, 'What about your hands?'

Later that night. I was back in my suite eating steak tacos in bed. I pushed the plate away and called down to the front desk to Reggie, said come and take it. When he got there, I said you know what, Reggie, put on new sheets for me.

I got him to put on my show. Had the covers around my calves. Blue PJs. Called the Department of War. Said, 'Kevin Costner destroyed this show. What he did is such a shame.'

'Try *Lioness*, sir.'

'Backing out before the last season like. And you know, to be honest –'

'Try *Lioness*, sir.'

'I'm putting it on. Reggie?' I snapped, pointed at the *Lioness* DVD.

Reggie put it in. Got it going for me.

I said, 'Is that Nicole Kidman? She looks like shit.'

'Yes, sir.'

'She was a beautiful woman at one time. You see Bradley Cooper?'

'Bleph.'

'I said his hair looks like a doll's.'

'Yes, sir.'

'Fast-forward. Reggie?' The violence went faster, jumpy. 'We need something like this. I don't want any more of that horse mayors shit, gold statues that track the sun shit. I want security. You hear what happened in uh Peapack-Gladstone?'

'A tragedy, sir.'

'I told them to get robots. I said I need robots. Bezos has a million robots, I want two billion. Now we got guys circling the . . . roving bands of thugs, clowns. Do you think our guys can hold?'

'Our guys are solid.'

I hung up the phone. 'Skip me to the second season, Reggie.'

Reggie put me to the second season. Mexican cartels, kicking in doors, dragging people behind automobiles. I let it wind me down. Close to sunrise I dozed. Had a little hypnagogic imagery. Beautiful girl with fluffy blond hair. A little white table. Garbage can on wheels.

I woke with a start. Must have slept two, five minutes.

Marty was waiting for me on the green. Dark shades, suit. Bob Evans look. Sun behind him, broken into light waves, resplendent. I got into the cart, turned it on, felt the hum. Waved at the guards. They fell back, hands folded at their groins.

Marty put the scorecard on the floor. 'Let's check that spot from last time.'

Sent the heat to my pants. I veered left. Back down the fairway, around the slope, to the line of trees. Drove until it got too rough and parked. On foot again, about an hour's walk to the spot.

I figured I'd take the road step by step. See how far I could get. How far did he want me to go? Without him, we'd freeze in winter, roast in summer. He keeps the generators running, nice air flowing.

I marked out the road, stomped the shrubs and grasses. It felt good to kill. I kicked away clumps of dirt and rock, pulled a sapling, tossed it away. Tore the smaller growth. When my hand got sore, I took off my half-zip and used it like a glove. Pulled nettles and scratchy weeds like that.

Marty came out of the trailer and watched. Brought a folding chair. Ate a sandwich. Went back inside. I took the chair. Sat, leaned right, grabbed a fistful of brush, twisted it around my palm. Pulled. Leaned left. Scooted the chair when I had the area around me clear. The sap left the skin on the backs of my hands discolored.

Toward sundown, Marty came out of his trailer. He was holding a cooler, a tube of something. 'Hold out your hands.'

'What's that?'

He squeezed a line of ointment. 'Rub it in.'

I did what he told me. He tilted back, grasped his hips. 'You've earned a reward.' He got out two Diet Cokes from his cooler. I tried to put my half-zip back on, to shield Marty from the disgusting fact of me, but the fabric was grass-stained, stuck with dirt. 'Give me that,' he said. I handed it to him. He went to the trailer, came back with baby wipes, a clean half-zip, same color. 'New uniform,' he said.

'How the hell did you get that?'

I cleaned myself with the wipes. He shook his head. I put on the new half-zip. Said, 'How do I look?'

He shrugged. We drank in silence. Then walked back through the forest, to the cart. I took us to the guard post, where the umbrellas used to line the patio. Marty swung out. Pointed to a guard. 'Stay alert, coyote.'

Alone outside the Gold Room, I looked at the brown-gray streaks of blistered skin on the backs of my hands. Pulled down my shirtsleeves. Lifted my chin and squared my jaw. Made my entrance.

Three dozen tables. Pale-pink tablecloths, lidded boxes of sugar or whatever in the middle. My table by the windows, far end. Platform, velvet rope. Slip knot, bottle service. Delivered to your table. Hooker in a twenty-four-karat gold egg.

Poached whitefish, green beans, grated carrots and raisins. Marty's fucking with the menu. Ordinarily, I wouldn't have touched it, but after all my work I was hungry.

Mid meal I glanced up, made eye contact with a piece of trash. Bimbo. Club member. She smiled, flat line. Loser smile. 'Show some teeth,' I said. 'But you can't, can you? Because they're yellow.'

Couple people laughed. Legacy members, survivors. Hangers-on. People I snap my fingers and they're dead. Out.

'I like to joke,' I said. 'She knows I love her.'

She rolled her eyes.

'Do me a favor and rake the leaves, would you?' I said. 'Improve your mood. You look like junk. Bags under your eyes. You on the rag?' I closed my good eye, obliterating her easily with the circle of damage in my bad eye. From looking at the sun that time. 'I could smell it when I walked by. Burbling in your reusable mug down there.'

Sunset, the light pink. Subdued staff. Faces bent toward trays. Soft eating sounds. I opened my good eye, momentarily troubled by the lingering blur, pushed some whitefish onto the back of my fork, looked at her husband or whatever glaring at me. 'Something on your mind?' I said. 'Something you want to say?'

He took a sip of lemon water. Cleared his throat. 'No. Nothing.'

I swallowed the fish off my fork, washed it down with lemon water. 'No . . .' I said. Mimicking him. 'Nothing.' I said, 'You're so *disrespectful*, you know that?'

He made a face like he was confused, like he understood that I was being aggressive, but my aggression didn't signify. Like he was perplexed by it.

'Try the salad,' I said, gesturing with my butter knife toward my plate. 'It's spicy.'

He said, 'That was about the only thing that you could have said that would make it less appealing.'

I smiled, looked around at the others. Pointed at him with my butter knife. 'He's a loser but he's got backbone.' A couple of them laughed. I said, 'I like that. Don't worry. We're having a good time. Are we having a good time?'

A few people nodded. We *were* having a good time. Then Marty walked in with a plate. Sucked the air out of the room. Crossed toward me, unhooked my velvet rope, dropped it on the carpet. Couple staff members started to come over. I shook my head, waved them off. Marty stepped onto my platform, sat across from me. Sent the heat to my pants. Sat there and ate his food neatly, mechanically, in his way. One of the busboys came over, filled water, picked up the velvet rope, hooked it back in its loop. Marty turned to watch him, then turned back to me. Raised his eyebrows. He pulled the wooden box on the middle of the table toward himself. Lifted the lid and let it fall. Then opened it, pulled out a deck of cards.

'All this time I thought that was sugar,' I said. Looked around at the others. 'You playing solitaire, Marty?'

He looked at me like I'd pay for that later.

'The tarot,' he said.

'Oh, from that fortune-teller lady the other day.' Sometimes people came through. People with talents. 'Forgot about that. Figured that was sugar, or . . . what do they call it?'

Marty spread the cards out face down on the surface of the table and worked them in figure eights with his palms, releasing the smell of frankincense, myrrh.

'Splenda,' he said.

'My guilty pleasure,' I said. The others laughed.

Marty looked up at me, pursed his lips. 'Ask me something.'

I shook my head, set my jaw and looked at him out of the bottom corners of my eyes.

'Okay,' he said, 'we'll do a general reading. A general reading on your life.' He gathered the cards up. Shuffled, blew on the deck, held it out toward me.

I froze, wondering when the cards might last have been cleaned.

The fortune-teller lady had looked a little dirty.

'Go on,' Marty said. 'Take 'em.'

I accepted the deck.

Marty said, 'Sure you don't want to ask me something?'

I shook my head once. Passed the deck back to him. I was afraid he'd be angry with me for telling him no, but he let it go. Fanned the cards. 'Take one.'

I took a card and turned it over. Naked woman by the lake under the stars. That had to be good. I felt a flicker in my pants.

'Set it here.'

I set the card down on the tabletop.

'Inverted.'

'What's that?'

'The Significator. Right-side up, that's inspiration, a solution, but *inverted* . . . as you have it, it's hope dying out.'

He shrugged, laid out more cards, winced. 'The Tower. Spectacular collapse, public and personal. The wheels have spun you to the top, but now they're circling down. You're desperate for vindication, meaning, a little action. Making small wins, sandcastles in clepsydra's funnel. An endless loop of days followed by death.'

'What's that, Marty?'

'I think you heard me fine.'

'Marty. That doesn't make me feel good.'

He wiped his nose with his dinner napkin, shrugged.

I got out my phone. Texted Department of War. 'Got a removal.'

Thumbs up.

'Slut in the faded cardigan. Old.'

Thumbs up. 'Know the one, sir.'

'And the husband if he makes any noise. Tries to impede.'

100. 'Did you try *Lioness*, sir?'

I put my phone away. Glanced out the window. It buzzed in my pocket. Buzzed a few times. I got it out.

'I'm on *Landsman* now.'

'It rocks!'

'*Hell or High Water* slayed me, sir.'

'It fucked up my shit.'

'*sir.'

I put my phone in my pocket. Took a bite of fish.

Later that night, I took a detour. Walked by Marty's room. He had a big one. Not the best one. That one's mine. But the second-best was Marty's.

To be honest, I would often go by his room at night, just to look at his door. Sometimes catch the sound of his voice blurred, the rhythm of it.

I was curious that night. I went out the fire exit, down the emergency stairs. I hid in the shadow of the building, between the brick and the trees. Looked up at Marty's window.

He had his lights on, drapes open.

He was sitting in an armchair, wearing some kind of elaborate device, wearing mesh sunglasses. He sat for a while, not moving. Then he took the glasses off, folded them, set them on his lap. He wore this thing. A sort of crown. It was an elaborate iron bracket assembly bolted at his temples. On the right, a short arm extended out and angled slightly forward. It held a lit candle about a foot from his cheek, just outside his direct line of sight. A second arm on the left held a little mirror. He adjusted the arms, so the mirror was about two feet from his face.

He moved his eyes between the candle and its reflection, shifting his focal range, and images appeared on the wall. Moving pictures. Memories, if I had to guess, judging by the faces, the distinctive chin dimple. Like the flame of the candle was pulling them out through his retinas, projecting them up there and telling him who he was. And that was my question. I wanted to know him, and to know myself.

I'll tell you the truth, I felt left out. I would have given anything to have been in the Oak Room Mansion Suite with Marty.

I stood there for a while watching him. Then I walked back through the darkness, toward my room.

Back in my golf navies that morning, driving up the crest, the wind in our faces.

'You look soft,' Marty said. 'Like a seal.'

I set my jaw.

He instructed me to gather stones from a creek bed, carry them to the site, put them in a neat pile. After a few trips I figured out it was easier to carry them if I bent forward and held them across my back like a donkey.

I developed a large, chafed patch of skin between my shoulder blades. It got pretty inflamed.

A week, maybe ten days in, Marty came out to look at my pile. He picked up a stone, tested its weight. Dropped it. 'That's enough for now.'

He lay a hand on my chafed skin. Maybe this is all I'll get, I thought. Or maybe this is just the start. He lifted his hand, turned and walked toward the trailer. I followed him, half bent, dizzy from hunger. At the door, he paused and looked back at me with a questioning glance.

I realized then, he hadn't asked me in. I said, 'Oh, I'm sorry.'

'That's all right. Let's get you a Coke.'

Inside, the air smelled like leather. He gave me a Diet Coke, sat on the edge of the table, and watched me drink.

'Maybe sometime the two of us could . . .' He paused, held a hand above my forearm for a sec. Lifted it. 'We'll see.'

That night in the early-morning hours, in the blue light of my television screen, I spilled my guts. I wrote a love note for Marty. It started out as a break-up letter, saying this can't go on, you don't appreciate me, you never ask me about myself. You never give anything away. I said the other day when you looked at me, I felt it. Did you feel it? Like you were touching my energetic field with your eyes. Said I'd never felt that before. Said, I didn't know it was possible. To be touched by glances. I said I have no idea who I am.

It was stupid. I tore the note up and flushed it down the toilet. Then I worried someone would find it. Imagined it clogging the pipes, then a plumber comes, unfolds the documents, puts it all together on the floor. So, I stood over the toilet and flushed three times. Then went back to my bedroom, sat on the edge of the bed and thought about texting him something normal, like, 'Nice round today.' Not that we were playing golf. Maybe, 'Incredible round.'

Reggie kept texting me. Club stuff. Food supply. 'What about this? What about that?' I gave him the thumbs-up emoji. 'Thumbs up to what?' he wrote. I put my phone on the blanket, screen down, and went to make sure my love note hadn't circled back up. Flipped on the bathroom lights, looked in the toilet. Flushed again. Waited. Went one more time. 'Looks pretty good,' I said aloud.

I need that machine. That incinerator that burns the papers and compresses the smoke into a powder. Sprinkle it on the green.

Dew on the grass, the wheels left dark trails. We crested, went into the forest. Cut the engine, and Marty told me to hoof it to the site. Said he'd come around later.

I walked down, started laying the stones in place roughly interlocking. The chafed area on my back broke open, soaking my shirt. It hurt, but I was happy. After a few hours, my road stretched seven feet. Like, I was amazed. I was happy with my work.

Then Marty came down. Golf club under his arm like a switch. 'What's this?' he said.

I set down the rock I was holding.

'Hmm,' he said. 'Tear it up.'

'What? Marty why?'

'Put all those stones back in the creek bed where you found them. Then when you've done that, start again. This time do it right.' He sniffed, looked around. 'I don't want to see you looking in the Oak Room again.'

'What's that?'

'You. Standing outside my window, spying on me in the Oak Room. I can't have it. I'm working in there. It's private stuff. Top-level stuff.'

I said, 'Like, Marty, to no uncertain degree, everything that you see in any direction, is mine.'

His face twitched. Then white flash. I felt the impact of his golf club on my forehead. It pounded outward. Concentric circles of pain. I fell onto my knees and caught myself on his trousers. He brushed away my hands, stepped back. Tucked the golf club back under his armpit.

His phone buzzed. He reached into his pocket and checked the screen. 'I have to take this.'

He turned, took a few steps away. 'Yes, thank you. Nishant. Let me just get the . . . So yeah, as I said –'

I fell forward onto my hands and knees. My blood made a patting sound in the dirt. I felt a dropping sensation, like I was falling down through the ground. I imagined my body slipping to the center of the earth, a place full of seaweed, no gravity. I rested my head on the ground. Flashed on French fries. Scalp surgery. Italian loafers.

Marty kicked some dirt in my face. 'Did that,' he said. 'And then next, I get the error message. Yes, I'll hold.'

I lifted my face.

Marty pointed at his own forehead and winked. 'Aloe vera on that scrape,' he said. 'And concealer.'

I got a fever. We had no antibiotics. You believe that?

So it was visions of the reaper in the wood grain and on the ceiling. Reclining in a hammock in shadows cast by a crystal glass. Holding my remotes. Cloak draped open, scythe resting near bent fingers. Swarovski. Bulgari. Herman Melville Crazy. My father gazing out over the world in flames, fastening a scrap of cloth to a stick. Waving it in the air, saying, 'Do I have a son?'

And then it was Marty. Had track from a toy train set up in two straight lines in the middle of the floor of his trailer. Actual train wheels sewn onto a pair of gloves. So he crouched, lined up the glove-wheels to the track, shot forward, and I woke up.

The phone was ringing. Reggie from the desk. Said, 'Marty left you a package.'

'Bring it up. Open it.'

Reggie let himself in, opened a cardboard box, took out a medical halo and a set of perforated sunglasses, an envelope, a candle and a mirror.

'Give me the note,' I said. Tore it open, released the smell of leather. 'Hey kid,' Marty wrote. 'Thought you might like to pop the hood.'

I dropped the note on the floor. 'Set it up,' I said to Reggie. 'Actually, set yourself up. You first.'

Reggie opened the halo, fitted it around his head, tightened the screws, then took it back off. He threaded the two arms into their collar fittings. Clamped the candle onto its mount, then the mirror. Put the halo back on. Angled the arms in place, tilted them slowly until the candle appeared in the mirror, lowered it a bit. Then lit the candle.

'Don't forget the sunglasses,' I said. 'He starts with those.'

Reggie put on the sunglasses and waited.

'Let your mind go blank,' I said. 'Now take them off. Take off the glasses.'

Reggie looked irritated. Waved a hand at me. Took a little time, then folded the mesh sunglasses and set them on his leg. He looked back and forth. Slow at first, then images beginning to appear on the wall. Rush week. Peanut butter out of the jar.

He turned to me. Jacked. Said, 'I feel like you're seeing my entire life.'

'All right, all right. Get up. My turn.'

Reggie took off the halo and stood.

I did the whole thing, put on the halo, sunglasses, then slipped the sunglasses back off and started moving my eyes. Glanced from candle to mirror. I thought I would see my mother and father. Quarter bouncing off a sheet, or that one guy who said I had a lisp.

I barely made a glow. Then some grains of sand, like little pills, and the visual field became white. I was nowhere, then the pixels of light reassembled themselves, and I was alone in a bright, cramped room.

I was sitting in an ordinary chair. It was next to a door, with its back pushed up to the wall, its right arm against a narrow desk. Paper calendar with ballpoint doodles of a naked lady, slim keyboard. Set of keys, nail clippings, lanyard with a hospital ID. On the other side of the desk, diagnostic equipment, long metal arms.

The man on the ID had an oval face with high cheekbones, slightly hooded eyes, a straight thin nose, and a delicate, pointy jaw. His cheeks were full, hair straight, jet black and fine. He wore it combed back, lifted off of his scalp, sort of like a pompadour, but like it just did that. Bar soap and a comb. Dancer from the seventies, philosopher.

The door swung open and the man from the picture introduced himself. Sterilized his hands. Asked what brought me in, and swung a device up against my cheek. Began to examine my eyes.

'Give me the tiniest line you can read.'

I read a string of letters.

He adjusted something. 'Clearer? Or about the same?'

'About the same.'

'Try this.' He clicked something. 'Sharper . . . or softer?'

'Same, I think.'

'Better here . . . or here?'

'It's all about the same. Wobbling.'

'Look at my left ear, now back at the dot.'

The doctor leaned back, looked at me. 'I'm going to refer you to somebody else. Whatever this is, it's not an issue that requires glasses.'

As he was printing out my referral, I cleared my throat.

He rolled his stool backwards and looked at me. 'You're a great sinner,' he said.

I shrugged.

He rolled back to his desk. Brushed his nail clippings into a pile. Put a hand to his mouth and faced me again. 'I can kill you, if you like.'

'I don't think so.'

He frowned. 'Lay on your belly.'

I looked around the room.

He pointed at the ground.

I got down on the ground.

'On your belly,' he said.

I got on my belly.

'Pants down,' he said.

I undid my buckle, pulled down my pants.

'Drawers, too.'

I got them down, and heard him rustling around. Something made like a farting sound. He made a little pinched hand with his thumb and fingers. Pumped me. Or, I thought it was him. When I turned around, I saw it was a lot of people. Like everybody. One of them wiped his hand off on my sleeve.

Then it was the opposite of what came before. The room filled with fog, went white, and when it cleared I was in my suite, wearing the halo device, turning from the wall to Reggie.

'That was fucked up,' Reggie said.

I took off the halo. Said, 'Get out.'

I was gnawing a golf tee, laying the final stretch of the road, when Marty came down in his ATV. Parked by his trailer, went in. I was thinking maybe this is it. Like, I did it. But then I was like, no, it's not going to happen.

The music from Marty's hi-fi occasionally drifted down, otherwise it was nothing, just the sound of my breath, the rocks and the dirt. The sore on my back was itchy, but I barely noticed it. One stone filled my mind. It was perfect. I had found it in a hole, about three feet down, but I couldn't get it out. Dug around its edges and tried to pull it from the earth all day.

In the afternoon, Marty came out of the trailer and stood over me for a while. He said, 'Try a little water,' and passed me a thermos.

I did as he told me. Dug around the rock, lifted it, and the sky fanned open, like whatever you call it.

'It's a choking hazard,' Marty said. He pointed at the golf tee in my mouth. 'Small parts.'

'Not mine,' I said. I lifted the rock. Stepped out of the hole. Balancing. Stood. So we were eye to eye.

He brushed a twig out of my hair. Took the tee out of my mouth. 'You're not empty,' he said. 'Not really.'

'But I'm stupid.'

'I say so.' Marty shrugged. He got into his ATV, gunned it. Pointed at the sky. 'We'll always have this,' he said and shot off down my road, wind in his hair, jacket snapping. I held up my hand. Forefinger pointed, relaxed number one. ■

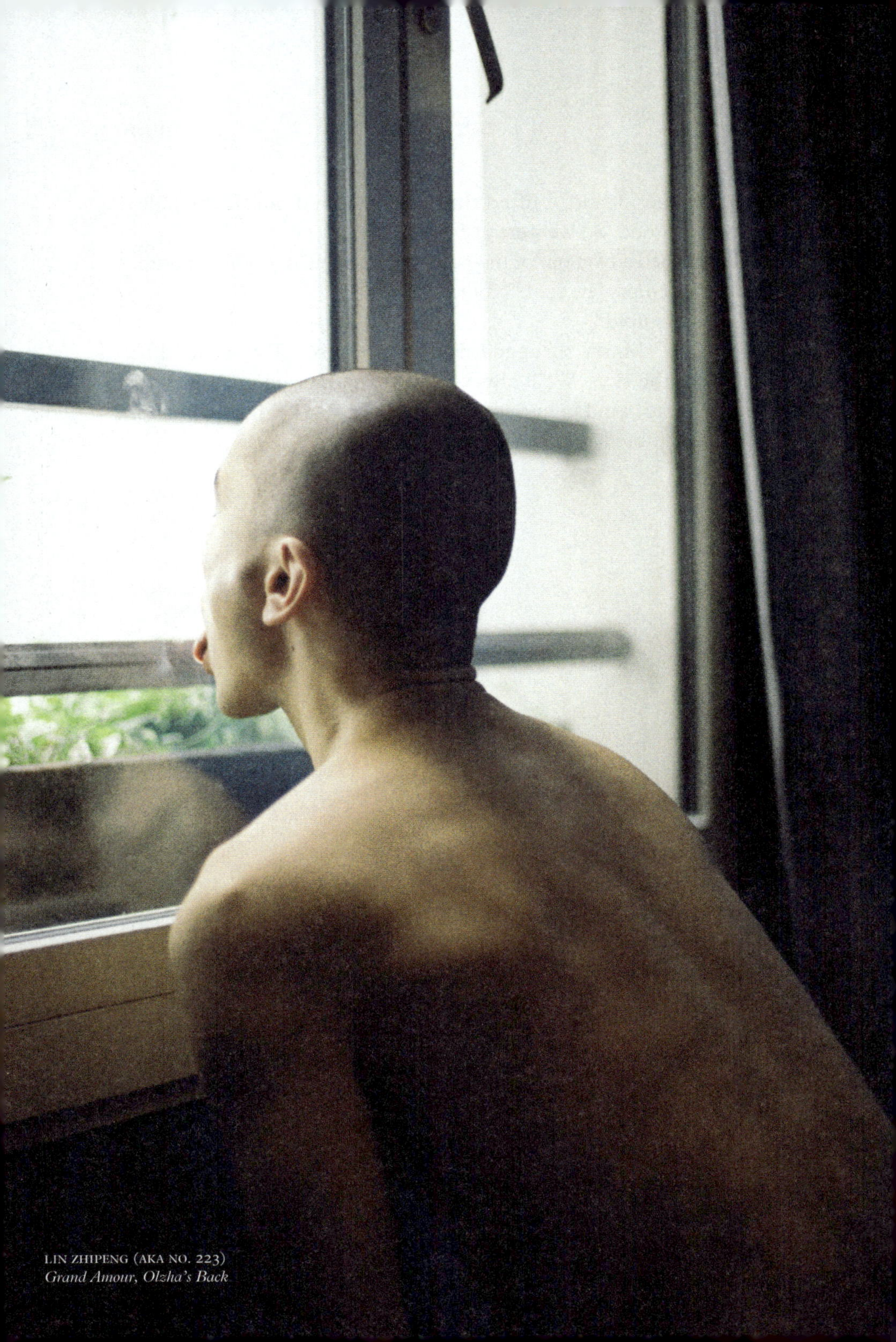

LIN ZHIPENG (AKA NO. 223)
Grand Amour, Olzha's Back

BLOOD BOY

Hansen Shi

The key was to make everyone as indebted to you as possible. That's why I made the dumplings for my Super Smash Sundays from scratch and made sure my guests always saw me folding them by hand. The user journey looked like this: you take off your shoes and put on the pair of animal-themed house slippers I've selected for you, grab a glass of home-brewed *mugicha* from the kitchen, choose your favorite color GameCube controller from the bin, then find your tourney partner in the living room based on whoever had your matching pair of slippers. Between games, you'd mingle with the other guests; even though you've always considered yourself an introvert, the conversation would flow easily because I would have made sure you'd have at least three mutual friends in the room. You'd feel like you already knew everyone, that this is where you belong. If it was your first time, I'd take a flattering Polaroid of you and ask you to sign it, then add it to my community wall. Every thirty minutes or so, the steaming plate of fresh dumplings in the play area would be refilled without you having to move an inch – just like at your mom's house.

My presence would be felt, but not overtly. My regulars always asked me to play in the tourney but I made a show of being too busy clearing plates or refilling drinks. I took on the MC role of deciding the team pairings and matchup sequence, live-updating the tourney bracket and then announcing the winner. This ensured that my guests would subconsciously think of me as both a provider and an authority figure, the benevolent administrator of their social lives.

I knew I had achieved product-market fit for Smash Sundays when white VC bros I barely knew who lived in the Marina started DMing me asking if they could 'roll through'. *Yo – saw [insert founder they were chasing] post about Smash Sundays on Instagram. Looked super lit can I join for the next?? I'll bring Chinese food!* We had a name for these interlopers: Marco Polos, or marcos for short. The marcos sought an audience with the Yuan court of modern San Francisco, the elite inner circle of overwhelmingly male and Asian American AI researchers, engineers, and founders that the entire future of American capitalism seemed to hinge on. The marcos were constantly trying to take advantage of my people and poach them for less than they were worth. That's why every time they hit me up to join, I declined. Their self-centered motives would taint the spirit of Smash Sundays, which was about trust. My people knew that I was the only one who really had their best interests at heart. That's why whenever my AI researchers received job offers, they came to me first to help them parse the fine print behind the often eye-wateringly high headline numbers, to make sure they weren't getting ripped off. That's why whenever my founders needed to hire AI engineers, they entrusted me to make thoughtful and discreet introductions. I was the honest broker, a role I treated with reverence. My people understood that even though I wasn't 'technical', I was one of them. We were bonded by the shared experience of spending every Sunday in Chinese school, playing *MapleStory*, watching the same Asian YouTubers, eating Costco pizza, training for Mathcounts/AMC, résumé-padding at a hyper-competitive 50 percent+ Asian public high school, and watching the CCTV New Year's Gala.

I was proud to see our community take care of each other. Since I started hosting Smash Sundays, my regulars had invited me – unprompted, by the way – to invest in three of the hottest AI deals of the year, which turned me into a rising star at work. That encouraged me to create even more opportunities for the community to come together. I started with Friday poker nights, which were an instant success and got me a foothold into the weekend rotation. After that I secured a recurring pickleball court reservation in the Mission every Saturday morning, followed by afternoon sessions at the indoor climbing gym. This meant I had 2–3× weekly touchpoints with the key SF AI talents, guaranteeing that they saw me more frequently than any other investor in the city. Except for the ten-mile run through the Presidio that I took every Sunday morning to clear my head, I was spending every minute of every weekend tending to my flock.

At 9 a.m. on Monday my boss Danny, one of the younger partners at the VC fund I worked at, asked me why we missed the Zelion deal.

I stiffened, feeling the hyena eyes of Eric and Kenneth, my two rivals in the associate cohort, boring into my neck from across the bullpen. 'Are you sure? They only raised their Series A four months ago. I just saw Kelvin last week and he promised he would save an allocation for us.'

'Pre-empted by Velar Capital. Go figure out what happened and fix it.'

That night I took a Sharpie and scribbled out Kelvin's face from his Polaroid on the community wall. Velar Capital's involvement meant only one thing – Colter, the Tribeca-based Golden Boy of Silicon Alley. My hands quivering with anger, I pulled up Colter's Instagram story and there he was, my so-called friend Kelvin (the CEO of Zelion) playing poker on a Velar yacht in Nassau wearing some ridiculous Kith hoodie custom-embroidered with the Zelion logo that Colter had obviously special-ordered for him. The video ended with Colter turning the camera on selfie mode and doing his lip-bite-fist-pump dance move while EDM blasted in the background. Seething with indignation, I replayed the story, pausing at the frame where a glimpse of Colter's upper abs rippled out from under his nearly unbuttoned shirt.

Colter was only a few years older than me but had already made general partner at Velar, the high-flying New York hedge fund that had carpet-bagged its way into venture capital after the tech bubble burst. He was one of those Park Avenue frat types who never seemed to take anything seriously then mysteriously appeared on the summa cum laude list at graduation. I'd actually known him during college through a 9 a.m. linear algebra class we had together when he was a senior and I was a freshman. I still had his number saved from when I used to send him pictures of my completed homework psets. He usually found me in the library the night before exams to catch him up on all the material from the lectures he'd skipped. After every late-night study sesh he'd insist we needed to hang out outside of class, 'grab lunch or something', but never followed through.

The last time I saw him was at a Penn young alums event in the city two years ago. I'd spent the entire night floating at the edge of the conversational clusters that formed around Colter, but he never seemed to spot me. Finally, as I was standing at the bar waiting to order a drink, Colter walked right over – only to cut in line at the bar as if he couldn't see me. Then, with two lagers in hand, he accidentally bumped into me and splashed my shirtsleeve with beer. We looked straight at each other; I wiped my sleeve and smiled at him warmly. He scanned my face without a trace of recognition, said a quick 'my fault my fault' and went on his way.

Every time I think about that encounter I feel soaked from inside with a tingling, piss-warm indignation. And since then, I've become addicted to watching Colter's Instagram stories, deliberately seeking out that burning tinge of parasocial resentment.

Which is why Colter's re-entry into my life was so insulting. To encroach, as a *marco*, on my turf, and have the nerve to shower Kelvin with his attention when he couldn't even remember my name – I couldn't tolerate it.

I reminded myself that this was a temporary humiliation. In this business, whoever controlled the talent controlled everything. Next time I'd be the one leading the deal, and when Colter came to me to ask for allocation, I'd make him beg. I tried to ice out my anxiety by taking out my phone and opening up the iMessage app. But instead of Kelvin, I swallowed my pride and texted Rex.

In Rex's guest bedroom I changed into the kimono he laid out on the bed and admired his collection of Joseon-era moon jars that seemed to float on the ambiently backlit cypress shelves. On his bedstand were two mini bottles of Fiji water arranged neatly behind the lamp like in a hotel room, a discreet wooden tissue box filled with baby wipes, and a yolk-yellow quart of 'Boy Butter' lube.

'You're early this month. Did you prep?'

Even though I should be used to it by now, I was always struck by how remarkably tense Rex was. His acute autism made it impossible for him to sustain eye contact, so I locked my gaze on the engorged blue vein splitting his forehead. 'Yes,' I lied, in the alluring breathy voice I reserved for such occasions. 'I just couldn't wait to see you.' He had a weird fixation that for the twenty-four hours before every rendezvous I had to cleanse myself by only consuming barley tea and *seolleongtang*. Eyeing me suspiciously, he lifted my kimono to inspect my chastity cage with feigned disgust and nodded curtly. That was my cue to put on the blindfold.

I'd been seeing Rex (if you could call it that) for about six months now. He was in his early fifties but his Mephistophelian devotion to scientific anti-aging practices had embalmed an unnatural tautness in his skin, which seemed to revolt by taking on a cadaverous gray hue. The one time I jokingly asked Rex if he had a blood boy he'd gotten defensive and changed the topic. Rex was one of the leading men in Silicon Valley. Though our relationship was an unrecognized state, he had shown a promising anger the one time I mentioned going on a date. After that I deleted all my dating apps. Any rumors could result in a blackball and my file had to be clean.

Rex did have a type – the last three boys before me had all been Asian, Korean to be precise, and I was the first Chinese one. Everyone knew this. None of them had lasted more than four months, though all three had got something meaningful out of it in the end. The last boy had even gotten his own small VC fund to run.

After he finished, Rex collapsed onto the bed and lay half prone with his head on my chest. Cautiously, I ran my fingers through his hair and, feeling his breathing slow, timed my opening. I only had a few minutes before the post-coital hormones wore off. This was the Sisyphean game I played every month – how to contrive a reason to linger, ferment intimacy, and thereby alchemize our recurring appointment into a committed relationship.

'Should we put on a movie? Maybe you can explain *Metropolis* to me again!' That was Rex's favorite movie. He had a habit of replaying random scenes from it while I was over and doom-staring into the screen.

I felt his neck muscles contract. 'No, it'll impact my sleep score. I have to be awake in six hours,' he said, rolling off me to the other side of the bed. I sighed – it was only 9 p.m. Rex and his ilk lived like inverse vampires, rarely awake after dusk.

'Is something wrong?'

'You didn't cum hands-free,' he said, an accusatory undertone creeping into his voice. He turned back to face me and blinked furiously. Rex blinked a lot when he was upset. 'Have you been cheating on the cage?'

'No, of course not! You're the only one who has the key,' I pleaded.

'That's not what I meant,' he snapped. My heart lit up with a glimmer of hope. Was he jealous?

'I couldn't take more than what you give me, even if it's just once a month,' I said coquettishly. Rex shot me a disdainful look.

'Why do you always make me wear these kimonos anyway?' I said playfully, trying to change the topic.

I could tell that was the wrong thing to say because it set off a thunderstorm of aggressive blinking.

'Um, I don't know what you mean by that. These are hanboks, not kimonos. You thought I was giving you kimonos like some stereotypical *otaku* creep?' He pronounced the word 'otaku' with a Japanese accent.

'Of course not!' I cried. 'I guess they're all kind of similar. In China we call them *qipao*.'

Rex fell silent.

'What's wrong?'

'You're not Korean?'

I laughed nervously. 'Of course not silly!' That was my third time saying it. 'I'm Chinese, we talked about this!' I said, even though we hadn't. In fact, the first time I met Rex, I'd purposely steered us into an hour-long conversation about Korean skincare and the quality of coffee shops in the Seongsu neighborhood of Seoul (I'd never been). That's when he added me on Telegram. The last time I was over, I'd made *samgyetang* for him. The mood in the room was quickly souring.

'Not Korean,' he repeated. 'Okay, I see. Go unlock yourself.' He left the key on the nightstand, retrieved a chilled eucalyptus towel from the towel fridge and placed it next to my naked body. Like the eel at the end of omakase, this was a signal that the experience was coming to an end. But this time, the coldness of Rex's manner suggested I might not be invited back.

In Rex's bathroom, I unlocked myself and then, without thinking, hoisted myself onto the corner of the marble vanity top and pressed all my weight down. I held the position for fifteen seconds until I couldn't bear it any longer.

I returned cupping my crotch with my hands. 'Daddy, something's wrong . . . I think I was too hard for you while I was locked up.'

Rex gestured for me to approach his side of the bed and inspected. A moment of disgust flashed his face before melting into something that resembled sympathy.

'Let's put some ice on that,' he said. 'Here, lie down.'

I nodded cutely, drawing the blanket over myself. Rex returned with an ice pack and a cup of hot cordyceps tea. I sat up just far enough to hold my head level and took small, effortful sips. When I noticed him looking at his phone, I feigned chills and started shivering.

Rex touched the back of his hand against my forehead. 'You're hot,' he murmured. He went to his closet and came back with an oat-colored cashmere hoodie. I put the hoodie on, pulling the sleeves over my hands to make it look oversized. He climbed back into bed with me and wrapped an arm around me awkwardly; I let my head roll onto his chest.

'What are your plans for the summer?' Rex asked abruptly.

Though my heart was hammering I continued to 'play dead'. This was the first time he'd ever mentioned the future. 'Just a few weddings,' I lied. 'What about you?'

'I'll be at the chateau in Tahoe,' he said, running his fingers through my hair. Though the shimmering possibility now hung in the air, I waited for him to take the lead.

'It's possible we could arrange to have you visit. I'll have to check my schedule to see if there's a weekend that could make sense,' he said hesitantly.

'That sounds lovely,' I said, taking care not to sound too eager. 'Yes, let me know.'

We stayed like that for a little while longer, anticipation and anxiety rippling through our bodies. Not wanting to overstay my welcome, I told Rex that I called an Uber. This time, he walked me to the door.

'I'm hosting my annual Lunar New Year party here in February. Would you like to come?' he said.

'I'd love to!' I said, beaming through the ache in my groin. The invitation to Rex's party arrived via paperless post the next morning, curing me of any lingering gloom from losing the Zelion deal.

I was at Costco scrambling to buy dumpling ingredients when I got a text from Jerry, one of my most prized assets. I'd been cultivating him since he was a broke postdoc at Stanford and my efforts were about to pay off. Jerry was an early employee at OpenBrain who was in the middle of secret talks to start his own AI company. Since the rumors of his departure began circulating last year he'd been hounded by marcos like Colter pressing him with term sheets. As his trusted friend, I'd taken on the role of shepherding him through these preliminary discussions, nudging him toward potential partners that would ally with me.

Yo bro cool if my friend Alex Chen from Lucid rolls through tonight for SS?

Yes for sure! I texted back immediately. Lucid was one of the hottest new research labs in SF, but Jerry's request was more or less a formality since the answer was always yes – trusted referrals were the lifeblood of my business because the most prized tier of AI technical talent traveled in packs, clustering around tight, impenetrable cohort groups from Google or Stanford. The number of introductions made was a KPI I tracked for every contact in my spreadsheet and on this metric Jerry was an MVN – a Most Valuable Node.

Jerry's track record was so flawless that I hadn't even bothered to look up Alex Chen. So imagine my surprise when Jerry sheepishly walked in accompanied by an attractive Asian woman.

'Ooh, I love your apron! So cute!' she said, using the annoying 'sassy' voice heterosexual women reserve for gay men. 'I brought you some pastries!'

'Thanks!' I said, sizing her up between pleasantries. The first thing I honed in on was the incongruity between her natural attractiveness – based on facial symmetry, skin clarity and physique I guessed she'd probably be around a high eight to low nine on a heterosexual scale – and her stereotypically frumpy tech-girl outfit of Lucid Labs hoodie, leggings, and generic white sneakers. It was unusual for a high eight to low nine to dress like this. At the same time, she was wearing perfect makeup, and I could also detect an assuredness and high social horsepower humming just beneath the surface, which made her unassuming conformist outfit seem like a getup.

I showed Alex her position in the Smash bracket and went to the bathroom to freshen up. When I came back, no one was playing Smash. Jerry and four other engineers had left their controllers on the floor and were clustered around Alex. They were taking turns asking her questions and laughing sycophantically, totally oblivious to Alex's hardcore social engineering. She was throwing out the most basic 'Oh my God no way [insert boba chain / video game / anime] is my favorite too!' and tilting her head while listening and all of it was hitting the targets dead-on, obliterating my friends' psychological defenses.

I fixed my face into my best corporate grin and set a plate of fresh dumplings down in the middle of the circle.

'Hi! So what do you work on at Lucid Labs?' I asked.

'I was a product manager! So, you know, basically just supporting the brilliant researchers at Lucid and getting out of their way.' That drew more tickled laughs from her enamored audience.

'Was?' I pressed gently, taking care to inflect my tone with curiosity, rather than suspicion.

'Oh, yes! I left last month actually. I think what I learned at Lucid was my real passion is supporting the people who are building the AI future generally, not just working on one specific project myself, you know?'

'I see. So you're taking some time off, then?'

Alex laughed modestly. 'Oh no! I actually just signed with Sutton Hale, haha – girl's gotta pay rent!'

This was the first time another venture capitalist had infiltrated Smash Sundays. Besides that, Sutton Hale was a sickeningly prestigious venture-capital firm, one of the most storied names on Sand Hill Road. Rex was a partner there. Hundreds of the most pedigreed analysts tripped over themselves to compete for the two junior spots they had each year. Even the technicals, who usually thought of VCs as talentless hacks, were excited to call their parents to tell them their start-up had raised from Sutton Hale. And here was Alex, acting like it was no big deal.

'Yeah I know, never really thought I'd join the dark side, but they were really convincing!' she said with another fake laugh. 'Anyway, I don't start until next week. Guess we'll just see how it goes.'

When Alex revealed that she had just moved from New York City, the energy of the conversation instantly dialed up a notch.

'No way, I have to show you the best climbing gym . . .'

'. . . the best matcha cafe.'

The night dragged on. Just as I started my solo cleanup ritual, Alex popped into the kitchen to help. I bristled when she casually defied my instructions to let it be and started taking Tupperware out of my cabinets and deftly packing the leftovers. The regulars looked on in awe.

'Hey Miles, can you add Alex to the group chat?' Jerry said as he was putting on his shoes in the hallway.

'Yeah man, add her!' Jerry's friend Kevin echoed.

'Of course!' I said, amping my corporate grin up to its maximum brightness. 'I'll add her right away! Goodnight everyone!'

Alex's LinkedIn raised some questions – she'd deliberately removed the months at Lucid, a classic tactic to cover up a short stint. Her longest employment before Lucid was McKinsey and she'd attended Dartmouth for undergrad – red flags. I switched to Instagram for evidence of sorority involvement or dating white guys. She didn't have any pictures before 2023; everything had been posted in the last two years, zero tagged photos. Her entire grid was dominated by pictures of baking, hiking, matcha, and traveling. The only party picture was her at EDC with a group of all-Asian, approachable-looking sixes or sevens. There wasn't a single male in any of her photos. She was available, down to earth; in other words, she was the perfect girlfriend for an AI researcher, but it was a thin wrapper, just enough to trip over the uncanny valley. I'd seen enough to know something was amiss.

Everyone kept texting me to ask if Alex was coming to Sunday Smash. Attendance reached an all-time high, but nobody seemed interested in playing Smash anymore. Worse still, she started showing up at my Friday poker and Saturday climbing kickbacks too. Like a shitty expense management software billboard ad, suddenly she was everywhere.

Then, three weeks after she arrived, the cancellations started coming in. People who never missed a Smash Sunday for six months in a row were suddenly tied up. Finally, an Instagram story confirmed what I already knew: they were all at Alex's place in Haight-Ashbury.

I sent a text to the Sunday Smash group chat: *Hi everyone!! So my upstairs neighbor flooded their place and it's leaking into mine . . . unfortunately need to cancel tonight* ☹️

That got a bunch of heart reactions and replies like *Oh no!! Hope everything's alright.*

Next, I screenshotted the Instagram story and got ChatGPT to give me the coordinates. Since the party was in the backyard, I just snuck in through the garden gate. Everyone was Asian and all my regulars were there: Jerry with his OpenBrain entourage, Brian and Jason with the Substrate/Monad Labs squads. Even that traitor Kelvin, wearing the same streetwear hoodie I saw in Colter's Instagram story. I picked up a hard yuzu seltzer from the cooler and began a slow lap. Inserting myself into a conversation should've been easy, considering I'd hosted everyone more than a dozen times. But everyone kept giving me these darting and unsettled looks, as if they were embarrassed to see me there, and whenever I brushed up against a circle, it seemed to clench up, its members pointing their feet closer to the imaginary center and turning their backs stiffly on me.

Beaming, Alex walked out of the kitchen wearing a pink apron with a huge, steaming plate of dumplings. She set them down on the picnic table while everyone cheered.

Joining the queue, I seethed as I eavesdropped on the compliments.

'*Honestly I come to these just for the dumplings.*'

'SO good. Low-key the best dumplings I've ever had.'

At the front of the line, Alex was holding court and insincerely thanking people for coming. To my amazement, she pretended not to see me. My hand quivering, I picked one of the dumplings up from the plate and plopped it into my mouth. I recognized the taste – they were frozen Wei-Chuan dumplings from 99 Ranch Market. Soaked with indignation, I stood rooted to the spot, chewing slowly, while people behind me in the line shuffled their feet.

'Hey dude, are you okay?' It was Jerry, standing next to me with a concerned look on his face. 'You're sweating.'

'I'm fine. Just need to freshen up,' I snapped, disappearing into the house. I tracked through the hallways silently until I found Alex's bedroom. I ran my fingertips across her desktop, bookshelf, and nightstand. Then I took a seat on her bed, one of those $5,000 water-controlled smart mattresses tech freaks use to optimize their sleep performance, and contemplated the room. The barren walls, the meticulously made bed, the complete absence of dust or debris – it was the type of living space only an unhinged psychopath could construct. After a moment of hesitation, I tapped the touchpad on her MacBook and found it unlocked. I opened her Notes app and started to read.

'Gratitude Journal 7.2.25'

today grateful for:
kind peeps who made me feel welcome in a new city
biweekly facetimes with my ny girlies
living walking distance from H Mart
ceremonial grade matcha
clean air
new beginnings

I frowned, feeling gaslit, as if she had laid out this implausibly vapid note for me to find on purpose. I was about to read further when I heard voices, so I slipped out of Alex's bedroom into her en suite. Then I pulled my cock out and started urinating on the floor. I was enthralled by the force of the hydraulic pressure stored in my bladder, the thrust and flow rate of my piss surging forth in a steaming, vindictive jet. As I rotated midstream to splash Alex's vanity, her electric toothbrush, the mirror, and her towels, a gleeful cackle escaped from somewhere deep inside me. I was still wearing that deranged grin when I opened the door and found Kelvin waiting. I stammered something incomprehensible before speeding past him into the hallway, down the stairs, and out into the street.

Year-end reviews were starting in two weeks, which is when they were going to tell us which of the three associates would be promoted to partner. My former winning streak had put me in the lead, but after the Zelion mishap I couldn't afford any more mistakes.

Something about the snide tone in Kenneth's voice during our pipeline meeting that morning had put me on edge. Then at noon I got the push notification on my phone: Sutton Hale was leading the seed round for Jerry's new company, Mantle Labs. I immediately recognized the picture they used of Jerry and his co-founder, which I had taken for them at my apartment's co-working lounge. The post already had thirty likes on LinkedIn, including Brian, Jason, and Kevin, as well as several reposts, which kept it at the top of my feed every time I refreshed. Jerry had publicly humiliated me with a quote praising Alex as 'an early believer and an amazing mentor'. After Danny finished viciously dressing me down at my cubicle, I slid into a conference room and called Jerry.

'I'm sorry, man. I know how disappointed you must be,' Jerry said, his voice sounding stilted and rehearsed, like one of those pre-recorded phone trees.

'Disappointed?' I said. 'How many times did I make dinner for you and your friends? Drive you to Costco just because you wanted food-court hot dogs? Edit and caption your Coffee Meets Bagel photos? Promote your DJ sets on my story? Teach you how to use the post office?' I was reading off my spreadsheet and suddenly noticed that I was yelling. 'And *this* is how you treat me?'

'Woah, slow down. I thought the reason you did all that stuff was because you were my friend.'

'Of *course* that's why I did them!' I snapped.

'I hope everything is okay,' he continued shakily. 'Honestly, I've been hearing some pretty weird things about you bro. Between us, I did ask Alex if we could leave some allocation for you in the deal. And she said no. I tried, Miles. I'm sorry.'

I was just about to ask Jerry exactly what he'd heard when he hung up.

The doorman checked my name off the list and brought me to the backyard where the party was being held. Rex's backyard extended to the vanishing edge of the steep cliff overlooking China

Beach and you could see the silhouette of the Marin Headlands through the fog. For his event, Rex had turned the space into a fanciful imperial Chinese garden. On the patio, staff in crisp white uniforms carved Peking ducks and served cocktails at a red lacquer bar. Connecting the patio to the lawn was a garden bridge astride a pond where half a dozen jumbo koi cruised lazy figure eights. From there you took a footpath, illuminated by red-paper lanterns, to a huge red-and-gold party tent made to look like a Chinese pavilion.

I spotted Rex at the cocktail table under the pavilion. He was wearing a purple hanbok and stiffly holding court with a few members of his peerage – the senior VC partners that constituted the merchant-nobility of Menlo-Atherton – and together they formed an impenetrable, cashmere-wrapped circle. Fanning out from the center table, the founders of OpenBrain, Substrate, and Monad Labs were munching duck pancakes with some of the world's leading AI researchers. This was the most valuable cluster in the entire network. I took a deep gulp of my yuzu seltzer and approached. I felt the approving gaze of Rex's guests and found myself standing taller. I imagined the thrilling possibility of becoming familiar to these people, someone they thought of affectionately, shared inside jokes with, invited over for dinner. It was possible, as long as I made sure Rex invited me to Lake Tahoe.

My euphoria was interrupted by a nagging awareness of two heads of black hair bobbing in the golden company. They were two slender Korean men approximately my height and weight whom I recognized as Rex's Tuesday and Thursday boys from last year; the latter I had only recently displaced (fake Grindr screenshots) over the summer. We were all wearing very similar outfits and keeping an eye on each other while refusing to make eye contact. They were both loitering just a few paces away from Rex's table, clearly angling for an opportunity to speak to our host first, which I obviously could not allow, and when Rex left his table, I intercepted him.

For a split second it seemed like he was walking faster to make it inside the house without saying hello. But I shouted his name loud enough that he had to turn around. He gave me a once-over and recoiled slightly.

'Happy new year Rex! I brought you some *maehwa* flowers,' I said, using the Korean word for plum blossom and presenting the seasonally appropriate bouquet. It was probably my imagination but I thought I saw a twinge of annoyance when I said the word *maehwa*.

'Hi, yes, glad you could make it,' Rex said, without uncrossing his arms. 'And thank you for the flowers. Why don't you go put those in the kitchen?'

I couldn't let him go that easily. 'The color matches your hanbok,' I continued winsomely, the bouquet still hanging in the air between us. Then I shifted my expression to a more flirtatious register. 'Isn't it funny how this time *I'm* wearing the suit and *you're* wearing the hanbok? Usually it's the other way around!'

Rex's face was overtaken by an uncontrolled bout of blinking. I winced.

'Wait,' I said, lowering the bouquet to my side. 'I'm sorry – you look stressed. Is there anything for the party I can help you with? I mean, if it would help you relax, I did prep for you before this –'

'*Stop* that,' Rex hissed. Now he looked almost startled, as if he was scared of what I was about to say, or scared to overhear himself participating in our usual exchange. He squeezed his eyes shut but when he opened them again, he was beaming.

'Alex!'

My body seized up. Alex had secured an invite when none of Rex's other junior employees were included. She'd shed her frumpy tech-girl disguise and squeezed herself into a silky red *qipao* that exaggerated her hip to waist ratio and flaunted her toned arms. As I watched them warmly greet one another, I felt threatened by their rapport, the way they whispered excitedly to each other about something as if I wasn't still standing right there, holding the *maehwa* bouquet. Then Alex turned toward me and gave me this super-condescending, apologetic smile – *oh I'm sorry for excluding you, just one moment* – and without saying goodbye, they walked side by side down the footpath.

Rex clinked his glass with a spoon and the partygoers gathered on the lawn below turned their attention to him. He started on a stilted speech about the significance of lunar new year and the contribution of Asian Americans to the tech industry. I was barely listening, focusing instead on wearing my warmest, most admiring smile at the front of the crowd where Rex could see me. But then he started thanking Alex for planning this year's party and the crowd cheered as Alex took her place next to Rex and she gave a shy little bow. Lurking below the pavilion deck, I felt the propitious future I'd seen so clearly when I arrived dissipate.

After the applause died down, Alex was still lingering onstage. Rex went on for another minute about Alex's 'preternatural ability to connect with the world's best AI talent' before announcing that starting next week, she would be Sutton Hale's youngest partner.

I choked down a bitter laugh. There was that piss-warm feeling of indignation again.

Rex told everyone to enjoy themselves, and that in a few minutes a well-known dance troupe from Hong Kong was going to perform their lion dance on the pavilion. Then for the finale of the evening, Alex would light the fireworks.

The crowd dispersed across the lawn while I paced back to the patio to compose myself. But as soon as I got there, the sliding door opened and Colter walked out from the house.

He was wearing a dark suit, a couple of the buttons on his white shirt were undone and he was already drunk, clearly having come from another event. After scanning the crowd, Colter rolled up to the red lacquer bar and ordered two negronis. After fixing my hair, I positioned myself two feet away from him and willed him to say hello. But then he leaned his elbow against the counter to check his phone so that his back was facing me. The bartender placed the drinks on the counter. As Colter reached across to grab them, I pressed my body against his so that when he turned we collided with each other. The splash left a satisfying ruby stain on my white shirt.

'Oh shit, I'm so sorry, bro!' Colter cried, his eyes flicking between my face and the red stain on my shirt.

You're so fine! Wait, didn't we take a class together in college? Your name is Colter, right?

All good bro. Colter, right? Nice work on Zelion, by the way – Kelvin is a close friend.

Déjà vu! Haha remember when this exact *sequence happened last time? How crazy is that!*

But before I could get any words out, he'd mouthed a 'my fault bro' and slipped away.

I watched Colter saunter over the garden bridge toward Alex, who was holding court with a circle of admirers. Smirking, he interrupted their conversation, handed Alex the other negroni, and raised his glass to 'the competition getting hotter'. Alex rolled her eyes and they clinked their glasses together. I watched as Colter launched into a whole routine, practically groveling to get a laugh out of Alex, until I couldn't take it anymore.

I whipped my phone out and took a zoomed-in picture of Colter whispering in Alex's ear.

The caption sparked out from my fingertips like electricity. 'Who could've guessed everyone's favorite golden child is just another MARCO worshipper!!' I sent the picture to the group chat confidently, waiting for the heart and haha reacts to roll in. A few seconds later, my phone began to buzz.

<*Chris Chan has left the group*>

<*Jerry Zhou has left the group*>

<*Eric Qiu has left the group*>

<*Peter Song has left the group*>

I stood alone in the gloam, numb to everything except the haptic feedback from my phone pulsing in my palm. At that exact moment, Rex started tapping his glass again to gather the partygoers.

The crowd applauded and took their seats facing the pavilion, Alex next to Rex, his peerage, and Colter in the front row. While the lion dancers performed, I retreated to the patio bar and got another yuzu seltzer. The only people in this part of the backyard were myself and a drunk guest who was tossing leftover dumplings to the jumbo koi. This sent the koi into a feeding frenzy; they leapt and thrashed against each other to snatch the dumplings, splashing big waves onto the patio. I stared at the back of Rex's and Alex's heads and wondered whether I should hurl myself over the cliff behind the pavilion to ruin the party. Instead, while everyone was watching the lion dancers, I made my way over to the firework setup and poured what was left of the yuzu seltzer down the mortar funnel.

After the dancers cleared the stage, the event staff moved the fireworks to a grassy area next to the pavilion and invited Alex to come up while Rex looked over her shoulder like a proud parent. I felt almost giddy with excitement.

'Oh goodness, I'm kinda nervous,' Alex said, which drew a couple laughs. She crouched down by the base of the mortar and squeezed the barbecue lighter next to the fuse. On her third try, the fuse ignited – the crowd cheered as Alex dashed back to safety and the spark ate its way down the fuse and disappeared into the mortar shaft. Alex was performatively covering her ears and ten, then twenty long seconds passed, but nothing happened. The silence became awkward as we all stood there staring at the dead firework.

'Sorry, that's really weird!' Alex stammered. As I watched her flounder, a cold satisfaction seeped through my entire body.

'No worries, let's move the party inside for now,' Rex said in an unrecognizably gentle voice.

'No! Ah, sorry let me just check,' Alex said. Before anyone could stop her, Alex crouched down beside the firework, inspecting it with her face directly next to the mortar. Even as I felt my body instinctively backing up, a queasy but thrilling anticipation locked me in place – I couldn't look away.

'I think it's dead!' Alex said, looking up with an embarrassed smile. Then there was a flash and a terrible wet bang. ■

Michael Robbins

People Keep Finding Bodies in Joshua Tree

It's hard, in the era of pig,
to remember what it felt like.
Topanga Boulevard winds up
Topanga Canyon
from Topanga Beach.
Charles Manson saw a spaceship
land here while Kenneth Anger
was exorcizing the Pentagon.
The only problem with California
is the fire thing.
And the cars, the mouthwash,
the aerospace industry,
the tech sector, the think tanks,
the subdivisions, the landfills.
The real estate, the scene.
I learned punk rock in Colorado,
Straight Outta Compton
on a janky tape deck
down 285 outside Fairplay.
Grassland basin, bison
nosing turf along the highway.
In Joshua Tree I'm trying
to find a desert tortoise
in the road so I can follow
the Fish and Wildlife Service
instructions for helping
a tortoise cross the road

so they don't get creamed.
Quietly approach the tortoise
is step one.
Last step is wash your hands.
I feel that all my life
without knowing it
I've been perfecting
my quiet tortoise approach.
But I'd like to know how
I'm supposed to wash my hands
in the desert.
I like step two, note the direction
the tortoise was heading.
If only things were that simple.
I decide it makes more sense
to note the direction
before I quietly approach.
But I don't see any tortoises.
I see: rocks, dirt, Joshua trees,
various birds, one jackrabbit.
I only see the jackrabbit
for a second.
And the sky. I see the sky.
I don't know where I'm heading,
but I note the direction
in which some clouds
are crossing the road.

I carefully pick up a cloud
holding it upright
in its normal walking position.
I carry it carefully across the road
no more than a few hundred yards
into the desert
and place it in the shade.

On a dark desert highway
heading in the direction
of Twentynine Palms
I play the song.
Anton LaVey was rumored
to be visible in the high window
on the inner gatefold
just as he was rumored
to play the hairy devil
in *Rosemary's Baby.*
Susan Atkins danced topless
in LaVey's Witches' Workshop
before murdering
Polanski's wife, Sharon Tate,
who was photographed
at Joshua Tree in 1968.
Still those voices are calling
from far away. The desert
is full of old metal
shafts jabbing up
from the void.

Mötley Crüe learned punk rock in Hollywood.
Of course they covered 'Helter Skelter'.
This was long after Charles Manson
stole Doris Day's green telescope.
When Nikki Sixx was working on
'Shout with the Devil'
an Elektra A&R man witnessed
a knife and fork rise from the table
and stick in the ceiling.
He recommended Sixx change
the title to 'Shout *at* the Devil'
forthwith. It's a perfect song,
and in eighth grade
when two metalheads came to my house
looking to beat me up
for insulting their musical taste,
as I had in fact done,
I invited them in,
showed them my metal tapes,
and we all grooved for a while
to Def Leppard and the Crüe,
though they advised me to get serious
and check out Slayer and Iron Maiden,
advice which has served me well
down to the present day.
I don't believe in spontaneous
demonic levitation of flatware.
As Slayer's drummer put it,
'I don't care about all these things.

I play drums. That's it.'
Image is everything, as Andre Agassi
and Baudrillard understood.
I just wanna go real hard.

I'm in Joshua Tree reading an article
called 'People Keep Finding
Bodies in Joshua Tree'.
The author claims that 'bodies
don't bury themselves',
but the late '90s taught me
otherwise. I resolve to find
and quietly approach no more
than one body. Let the dead
raise the dead. I'll put my hand
to the plough and look back.
I like John 8, where they bring
the adulteress to Jesus. They're like,
the law says we should stone her,
and he just stoops down
and writes in the dirt with his finger.
I assume he was writing
lyrics from his favorite bands.

Some assholes cut down
a bunch of Joshua trees.
I hate U2, but I saw them
at the Garden for free,
because I'd never been

to the Garden. I posted
about how bored I was,
and to entertain me, Joshua,
no relation to the trees,
posted a long thing
about how he quit *Spin*,
which blew up online,
and now Joshua's gone, too.
The last song he turned me on to
says 'If you're resourceful
anything can be the right weapon,'
which reminds me of Ani's
'Every tool is a weapon
if you hold it right.'

You can see why all the freaks
end up in the desert.
Saint Anthony, Manson,
Brigham Young. Hard-luck
scrabblers out for gore
or God or both. Rock
pictograph, coyote scrub,
brimstone cowboys.
Strike-slip along the Eureka.
Adrianne Lenker's out here
in a trailer. She just wants to go
real soft. Athanasius says the devil
threw a silver plate in Anthony's path
when he lit out for the desert.

But Anthony had his number:
'May your silver plate go to hell with you.'
These rocks were star-born.
Caught in the devil's bargain.
I've got to get back to the Garden
to see the Knicks play basketball
as the Sugarhill Gang put it in '79.
The Garden is the opposite of the desert.
There are no numbers in the rafters
and no rafters. No emo teens
along 8th Ave. Neither snow
nor rain nor gloom of night.
Just the greatest hits
of the Precambrian Supereon
rolling on like REO Speedwagon.
I wrote the previous line for the sound
but as an afterthought
did a search for the band
and guess where the album cover
with the tuna fish was shot.
People keep finding bodies
in Joshua Tree.

Gram Parsons saw spaceships
out here. The internet says
'Joshua Tree park guides
are given the option
to tell the story
of Parsons' cremation
during tours.'

It should be *Parsons's*.
My grandparents had a sign in their barn
that said *The Robbins*,
which drove me crazy as a teen.
It's in my kitchen now.
Beneath the solecism
is a fairly good painting
of my grandfather's horse,
Shane, named for *Shane*.
Frosty, my grandmother's horse,
was kind of a dick
and once bit her 'on the tit'
as she liked to tell visitors.
Those summers outside
Rose Hill, Kansas, dirt roads
for light years – the Delines
have a song that says
'It was the only time
I ever felt right
about anything.'
And now, visions of bodies
being burned. Every star
is a death star in the end.
Who's gonna pay for all this?

We used to break into the high school,
drink in the classrooms, write
stupid shit on the blackboards.
The Jeep got stuck in the bush.

This was before classrooms
were killing fields, before
footage and stills and drills.
Before they made a desert
and called it peace.
Tacitus says 'the earliest humans,
having no perverse desires,
lived without fault and crime,
without punishment and coercion'.
You shouldn't sit in an exit row
if you're unwilling or unable
to help, but actually every row
is an exit row, and no one knows
whether they can help
until they're called on to do so.
So no one should be punished,
ever, for anything. I don't know
much, but I know that.

I hardly ever notice birds,
then one catches my eye –
that ladder-backed woodpecker
on the Joshua tree that looks like
a giant asterisk had babies,
for instance – and birds are all
I think about for the next hour.

In this respect birds are like
other people. And other people
are like the desert tortoise,
floating in the sky, changing
shape, blotting out the sun.

Bury the dead, they say.
Have faith in the war.
A desert is a warm gun,
and any rock is the first tool.
It's not killing that's wrong
but choosing the wrong target.
Lisa told me the bully
I fantasized about taking apart
fell out of a tree, high,
and died, decades ago.
So I found another body,
without knowing it,
and it buried itself.
And when we were kids
we walked all over town
by ourselves. Our parents
never had a clue where we were.
It's not that they trusted the world
but they consented to live in it.

And my brain is still a map
of that town, and I still name
tornadoes after metal girls
I let copy my homework.
And I learned then that loss
is a thread and the soul
is a needle.

The songs know. Yesterday
I got so old. I want to hurt
the hand inside me. I hate
children, but now, past fifty,
I get why people have them.
They're an anti-loneliness drug.
You can take them to the desert
and they'll scare away
the interesting birds
but you'll have a grand old time
and take pictures
they'll look at when they're old
and lonely and wondering
what the point of anything is.
Maybe I should put it plainly
for once. I want the feeling back.
Making out with a witch
in a coffee truck. Four hundred
cigarettes on Mary's floor.

My old Ford, a fire road.
The little things I didn't know
were everything. But it sounds
stupid when I put it like that.
Midlife baby mourns lost youth.
At least I'm not boring
someone in some dark café.
The wise course would be acceptance.
But I hate wisdom.

NOTHING PERSONAL

Nikita Teryoshin

Introduction by Seth Harp

The Shajareh Tayyebeh School in Minab was clearly marked, in English and Farsi, on Google Maps. The Iranian school's website, preserved on the Internet Archive, shows photos of children, mostly girls, in classrooms and at play. No one could have reasonably mistaken the building for a military site.

Nevertheless, on the morning of 28 February 2026, the United States and Israel declared war on Iran with 'Operation Epic Fury', and the school was among the sites struck by the surprise barrage of missiles and bombs. In typical American and Israeli fashion, the aggressors struck again a short time later in a 'double-tap', which killed rescue workers and other people arriving at the scene.

More than a hundred children – as well as scores of adults including parents, teachers, and the school's principal – were blown to pieces, torn to shreds, burned to death, or crushed by falling concrete. Videos of the aftermath showed parents screaming and crying, bloodstained backpacks scattered around, and the arms and hands of dead children sticking out of the rubble.

'The United States would not deliberately target a school,' Secretary of State Marco Rubio said a few days later. 'We,' said Secretary of Defense Pete Hegseth, weighing in, 'never target civilian targets.'

Video evidence established that the volley of projectiles directed at the school and surrounding area included a subsonic Tomahawk cruise missile, manufactured by the Raytheon corporation and sold to the US government for $2.5 million apiece. Israel doesn't have Tomahawks, and Minab was marked as a strike target on a US military map displayed during a Pentagon news conference. United States Central Command, the formation in charge of American warmaking in the Middle East, implicated itself further by releasing a video of the Navy launching Tomahawk missiles on the day the school was hit.

The schoolhouse was adjacent to a dusty, disused compound, mainly consisting of a pharmacy and medical clinic, supposedly run by the Iranian military. The larger attack damaged or destroyed all fourteen buildings in the compound affiliated with the Islamic Revolutionary Guard Corps, suggesting that the Shajareh Tayyebeh School may have been included in the 'target set' by mistake.

The target set in question was reportedly generated by the Maven Smart System, a software program designed to speed up the targeting process. Maven was developed by Palantir, the company founded – in part with seed money from the CIA – by Jeffrey Epstein's 'great friend' Peter Thiel, and now run by an eccentric sociologist and lawyer named Alex Karp.

Maven enabled the US and Israel to strike over a thousand targets in the first twenty-four hours of their war against Iran. In the past, they might only have been able to strike a tenth as many sites with the same air force and naval assets in an equal amount of time.

Hours after the Americans bombed the elementary school in Minab, Palantir's technology helped deliver another strike on a teenage girls' volleyball team in Lamerd, southern Iran, while they were practicing in a dilapidated gymnasium. That attack was carried out using Lockheed Martin's newly developed Precision Strike Missile, which costs up to $3.5 million and is designed to explode in the air and blast its victims with a deadly spray of tungsten pellets.

Other targets swept into the frenetically paced bombing spree included an Iranian wrestling camp, a bodybuilding and fitness federation, a tennis federation, a rowing club, and the Iranian Red

Crescent Society's Peace Building, as well as a sports stadium, public park, and synagogue in Tehran.

When news of war with Iran broke, Palantir's stock price approached its zenith. Maven's targeting errors, which mirrored the glitchy performance of consumer-facing AI bots, were ignored by market speculators. More war meant more profit for Palantir, whose CEO donated $1 million in 2024 to a Trump-aligned political slush fund.

The Soviet-born, German photographer Nikita Teryoshin has sought to capture the 'back office' of this secretive economy. 'We are rarely afforded a glimpse behind the curtains of the global arms business,' he notes.

Intending to 'document arms fairs on every continent', Teryoshin attended twenty different defense exhibitions, ordinarily closed to the public, between 2016 and 2026. Most were in countries within the sphere of US military hegemony, including Poland, South Korea, Germany, France, UAE, Spain, and Greece; but others took place in China, Russia, Vietnam, India, and Brazil. The ongoing project, published in his book *Nothing Personal*, makes plain the multinational character of the global defense industry and security elites of every stripe.

Teryoshin describes the atmosphere at the arms fairs he attended as 'the complete opposite of a battlefield'. A weapons convention is like 'an oversized playground for adults', he writes, 'with wine, fingerfood and shiny weapons'.

He continues: 'Dead bodies here are mannequins or pixels on screens of a huge number of simulators. Bazookas and machine guns are plugged into flatscreens and war action is staged in an artificial environment in front of a tribune full of high-ranked guests, ministers, heads of states, generals and traders.'

Teryoshin's use of flash in well-lit environments recalls the pervy vibe of VICE and American Apparel in the era of the millennial hipster, but here what is exposed in suggestively raw detail are middle-aged men buying and selling weapons systems in banally luxurious settings. The results are photos of an unnervingly sterile clarity.

The F-35 Joint Strike Fighter program will cost American taxpayers more than the whole Iraq War. The F-35, which is plagued by a host of technical problems, repeatedly appears in these sometimes dryly comical scenes. The positioning of dumpsters in the foreground of one photo, which depicts a Lockheed Martin billboard advertising the F-35 as 'essential to allied airpower', makes it look like the defective boondoggle of a stealth warplane is nosediving into a garbage can. In another, men in suits, looking awkward and uncomfortable in the midday sun, wait in line like children at a fairground to sit in the cockpit of a mock F-35.

At a convention for the Association of the United States Army, three officers in green dress uniforms sit on stools with virtual reality goggles strapped to their faces, experiencing 'the future today'. Textron Systems, which makes the VR goggles, also sells geospatial analytics software to aid in targeting air strikes.

None of the people in these photos have eyes. Or rather, they have eyes but their faces are averted, blocked, occluded, or masked, so that you see at most one eye at a time. Teryoshin seems to be suggesting that these clean-shaven salesmen of death are in a sense blind. Blindness and blandness are among the major themes of these bleak corporate tableaux, which highlight the anonymous and impersonal nature of wars waged with advanced technology against weaker, poorer nations.

Other than a strip of parched grass in a parking lot, there is not one child, animal, or plant to be seen in the photographs selected here. In the full collection of photos from *Nothing Personal*, the near-complete absence of nature is striking. Besides a potted plant, some cut flowers, or a fringe of parched trees beyond an airstrip, the only greenery is the camouflage of military uniforms. The artificiality of the backgrounds is a reminder that war, and the preparations for it, are planned in clean and cordial air-conditioned spaces.

By contrast, children, drawings of animals, and plants abounded in the photos on the website of the Shajareh Tayyebeh School, whose name, a borrowing from Arabic and a scriptural reference, roughly means 'the goodly tree'. One depicted a group of small girls with bows on their heads in front of a mural of a cartoon giraffe.

The United States military killed them. The next trading day, the stock price of the Tomahawk's manufacturer, Raytheon, hit its highest level in the company's hundred-year history. ■

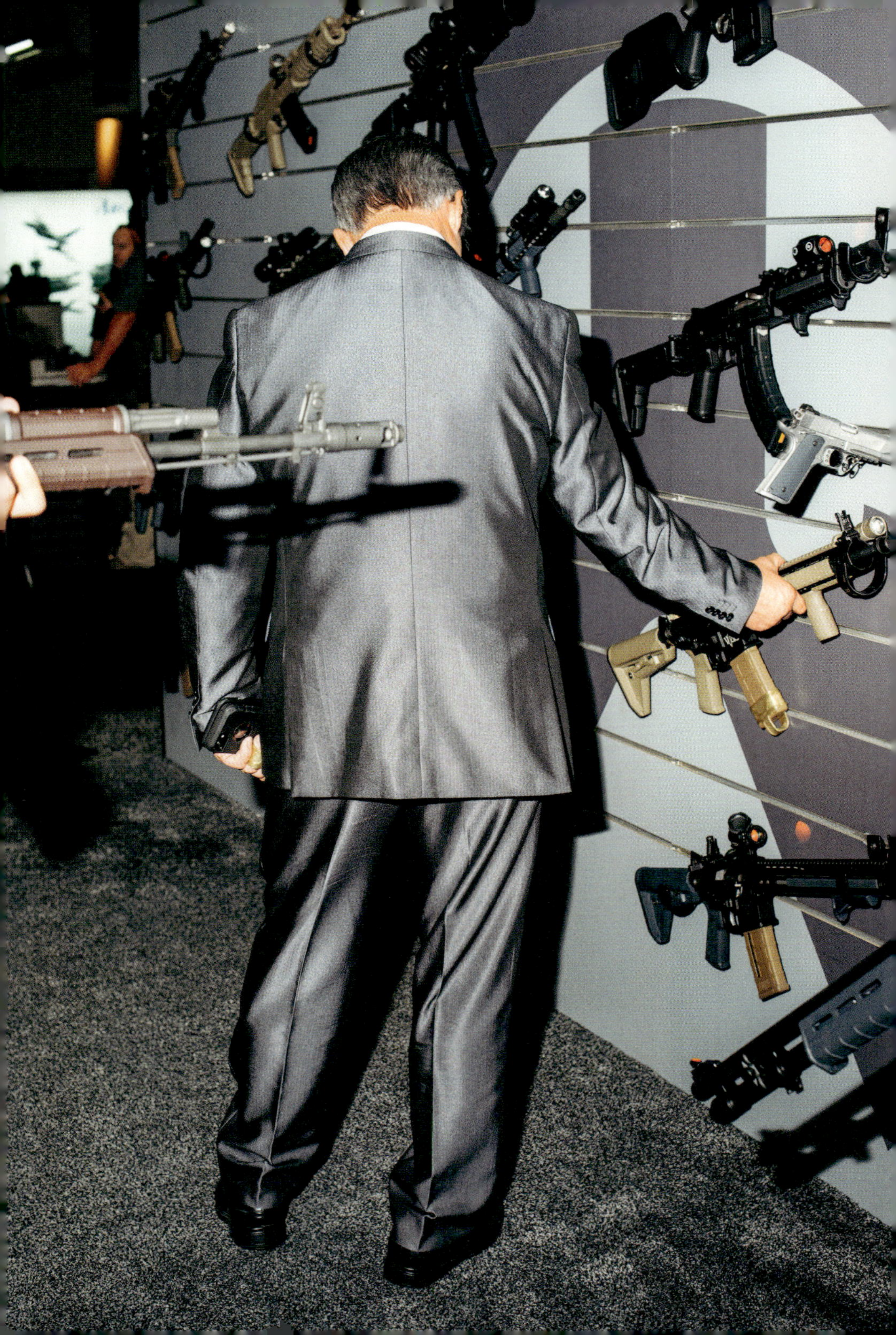

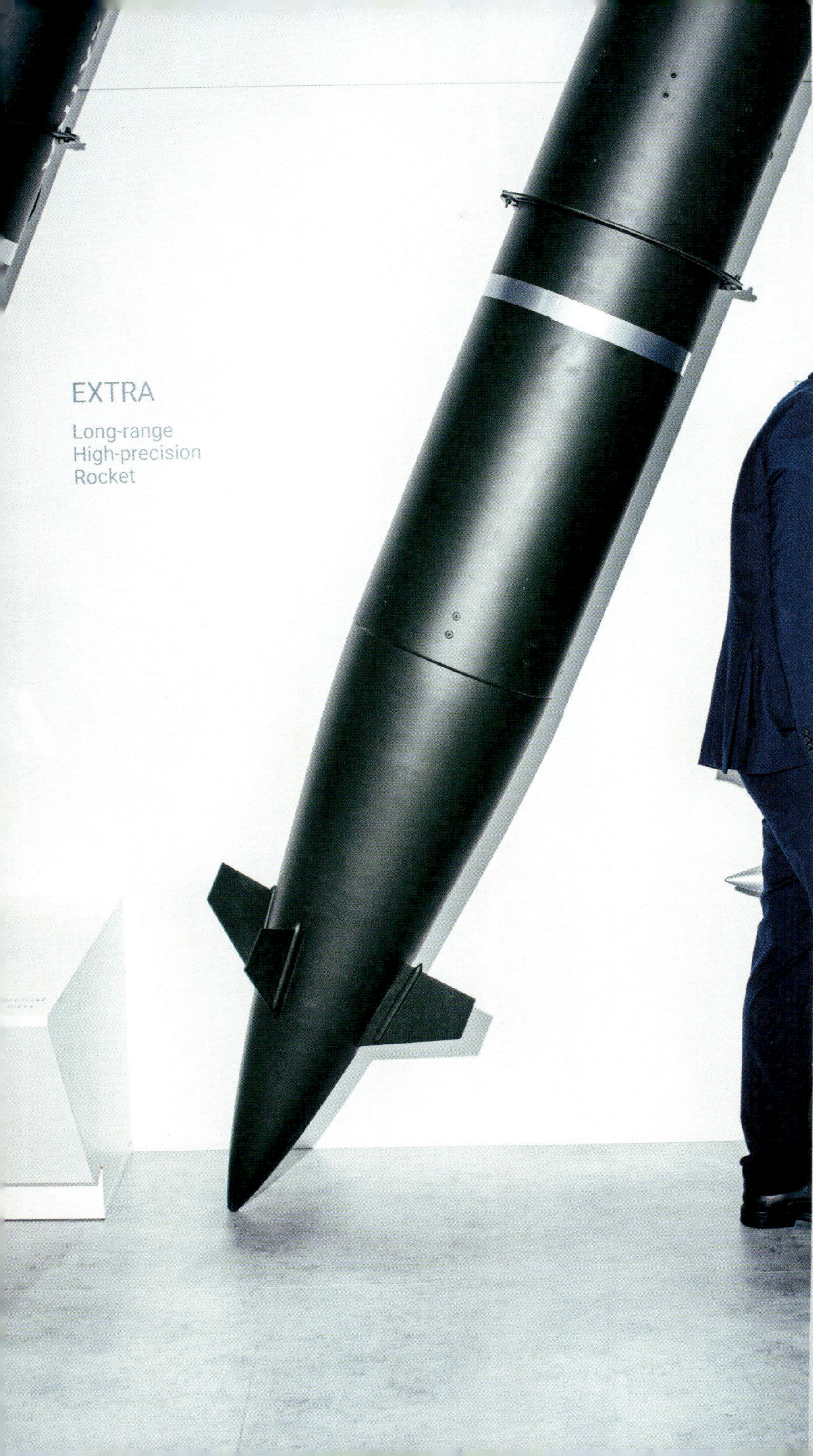
EXTRA
Long-range
High-precision
Rocket

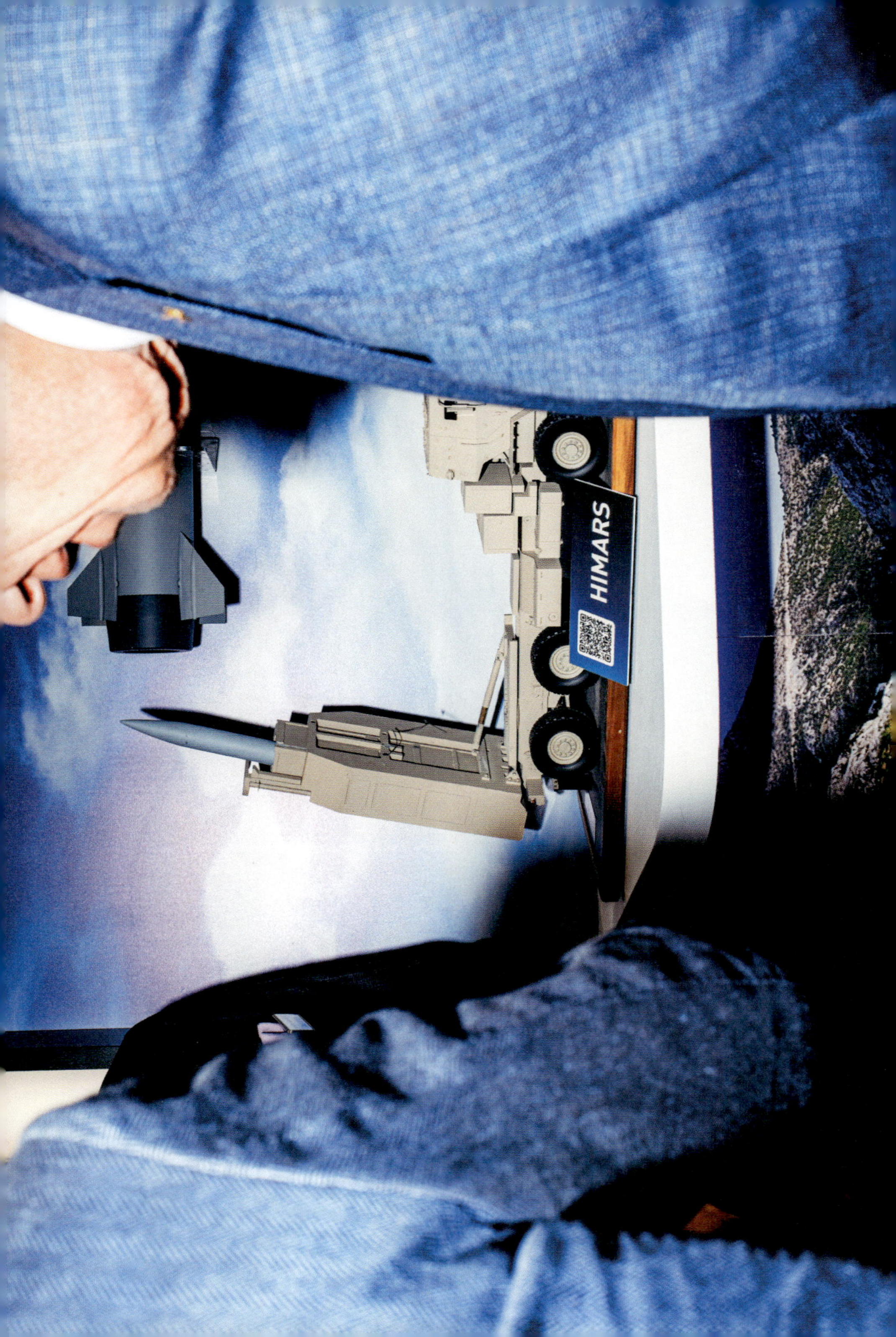
HIMARS

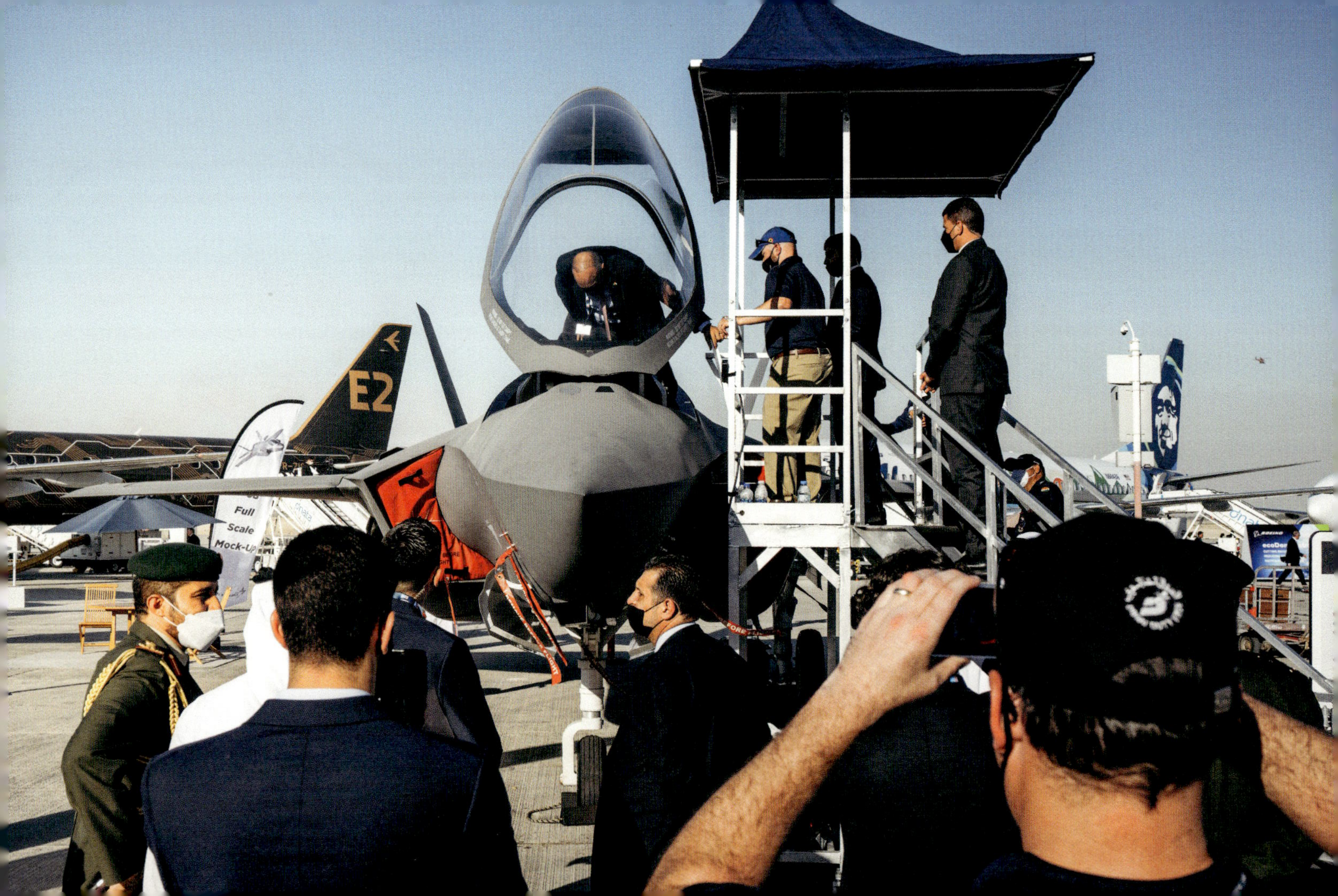
E2
Full
Scale
Mock-Up

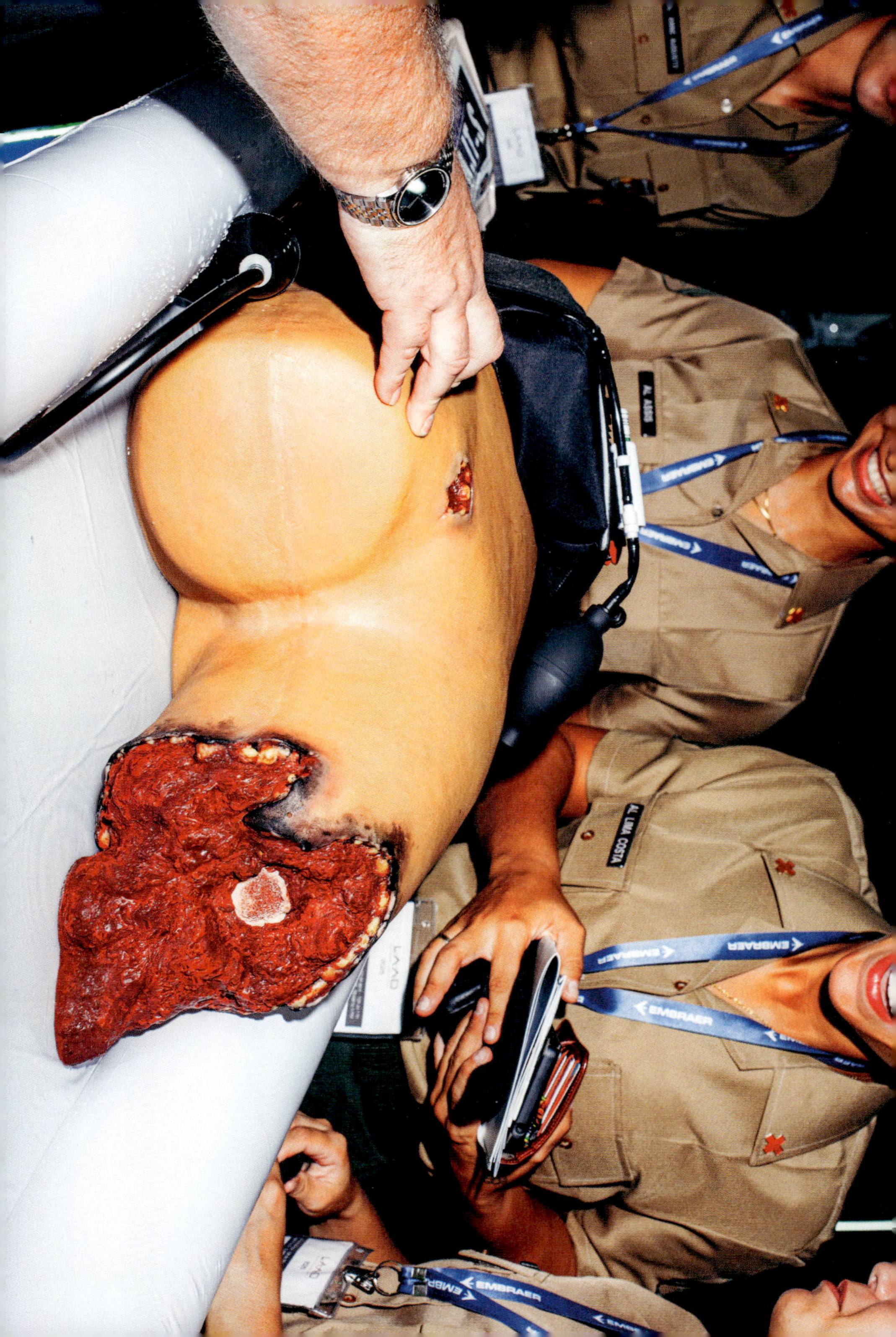
EMBRAER
AL LIMA COSTA

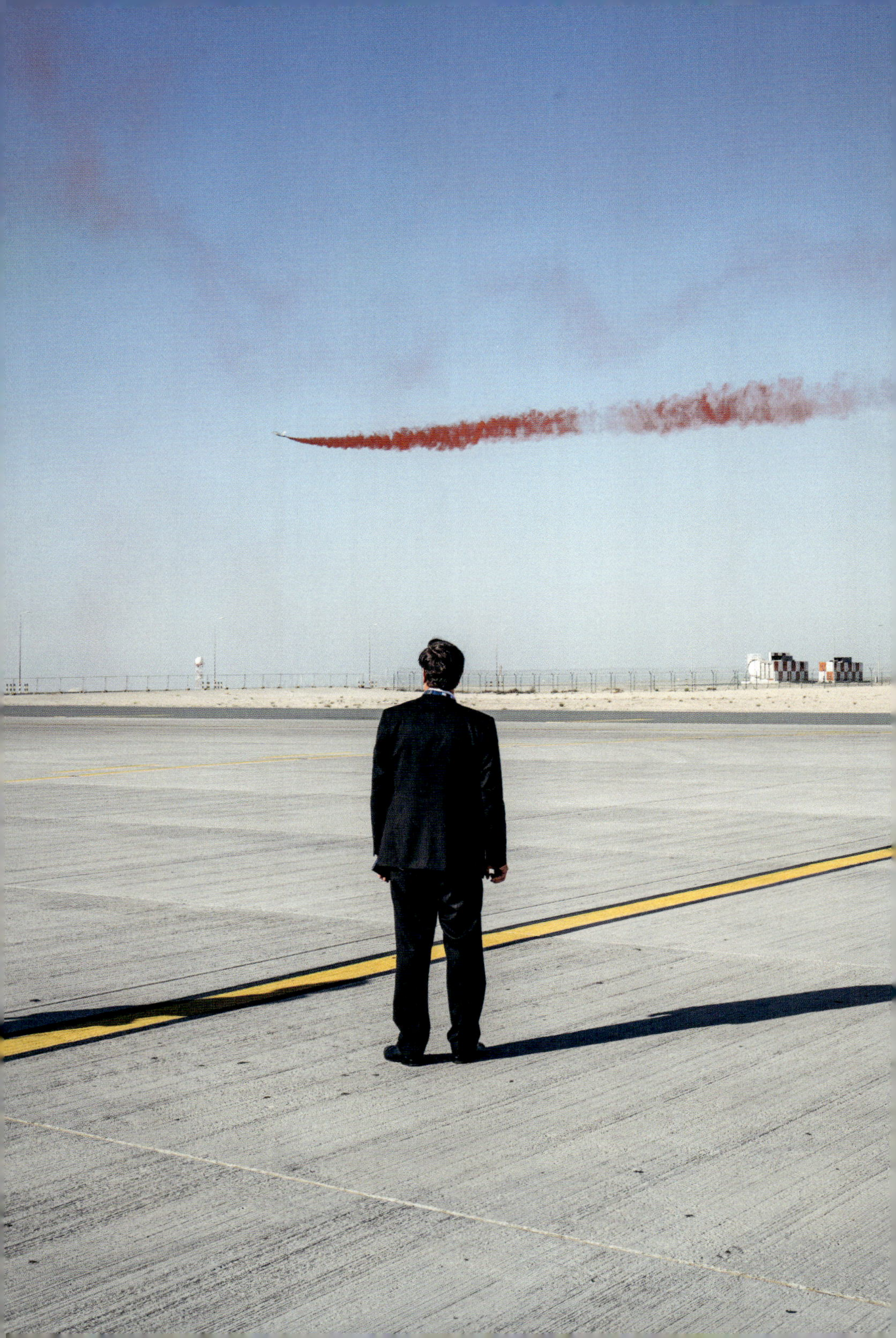

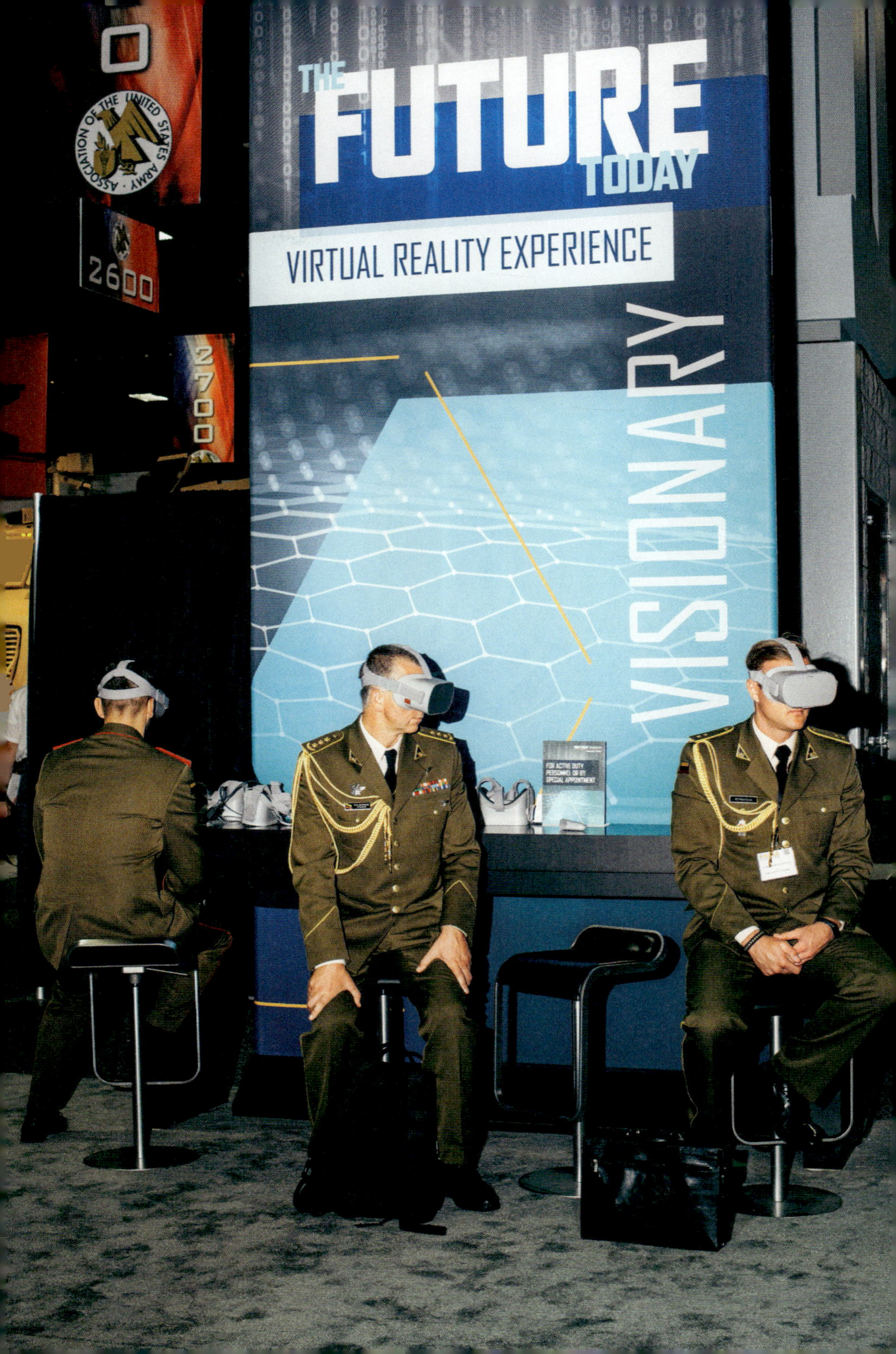

THE FUTURE TODAY
VIRTUAL REALITY EXPERIENCE
VISIONARY
FOR ACTIVE DUTY PERSONNEL OR BY SPECIAL APPOINTMENT
ASSOCIATION OF THE UNITED STATES ARMY
2600
2700

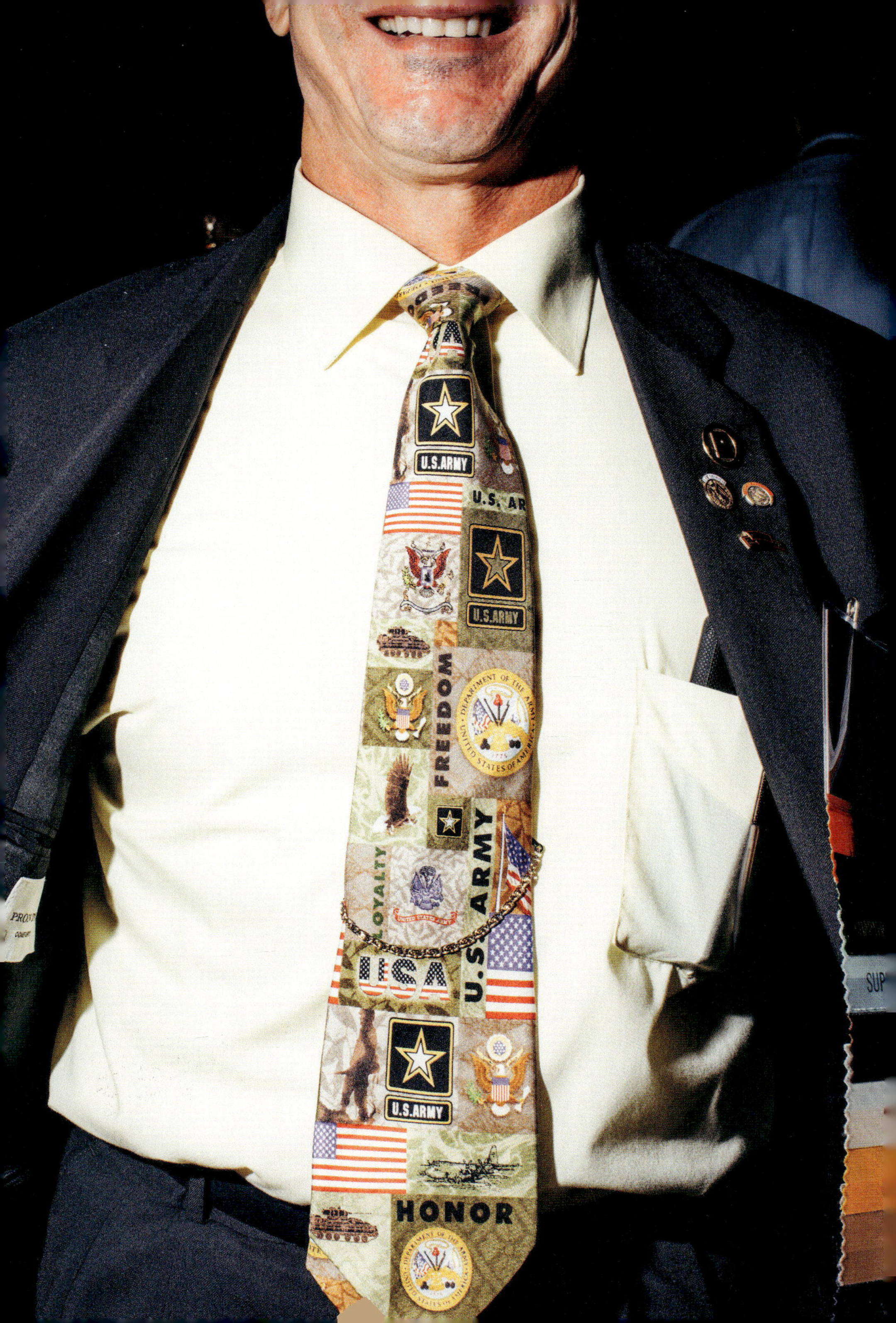
U.S.ARMY
FREEDOM
LOYALTY
ARMY
USA
HONOR

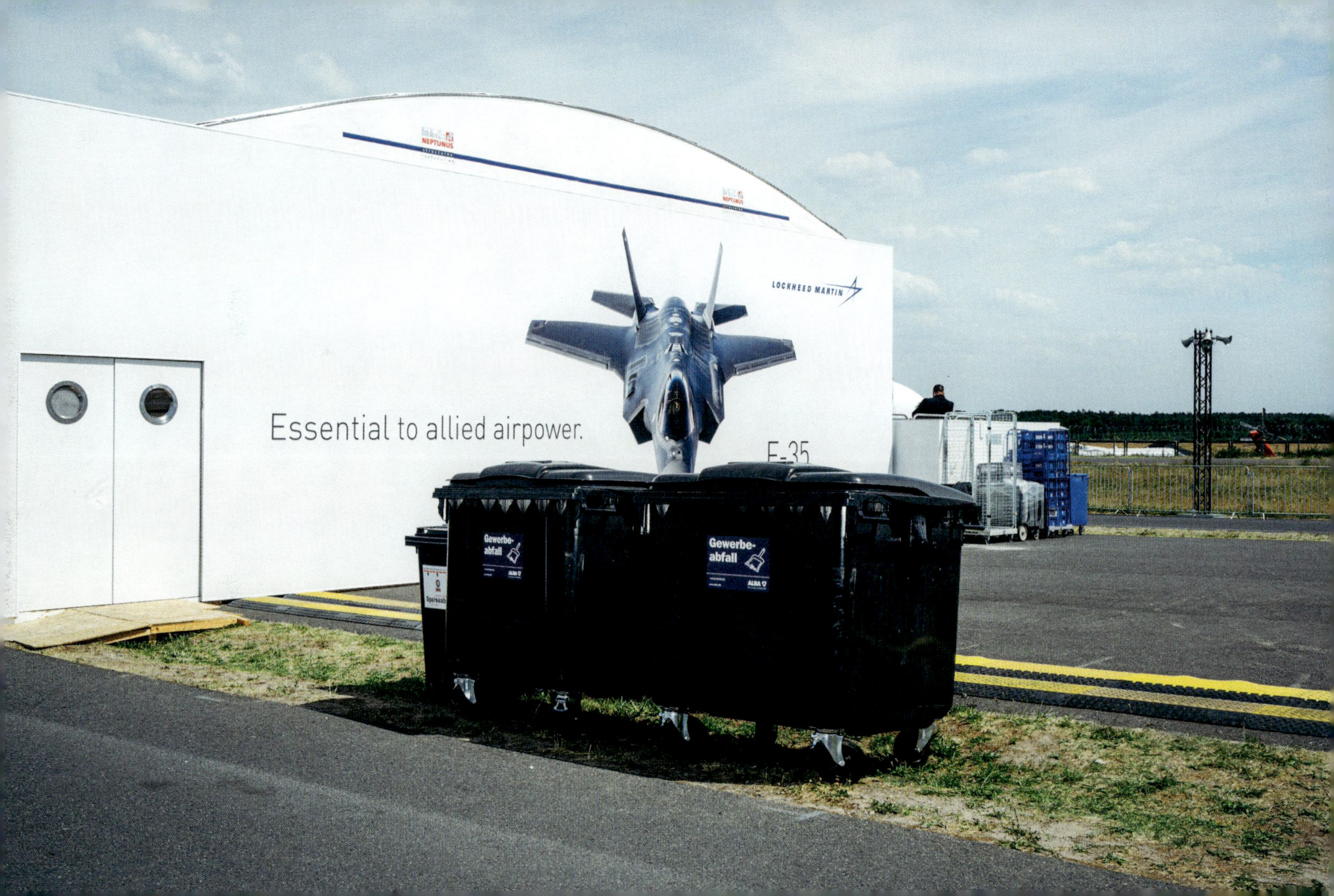
NEPTUNUS
NEPTUNUS
LOCKHEED MARTIN
Essential to allied airpower.
F-35
Gewerbe-
abfall
ALBA
Gewerbe-
abfall
ALBA

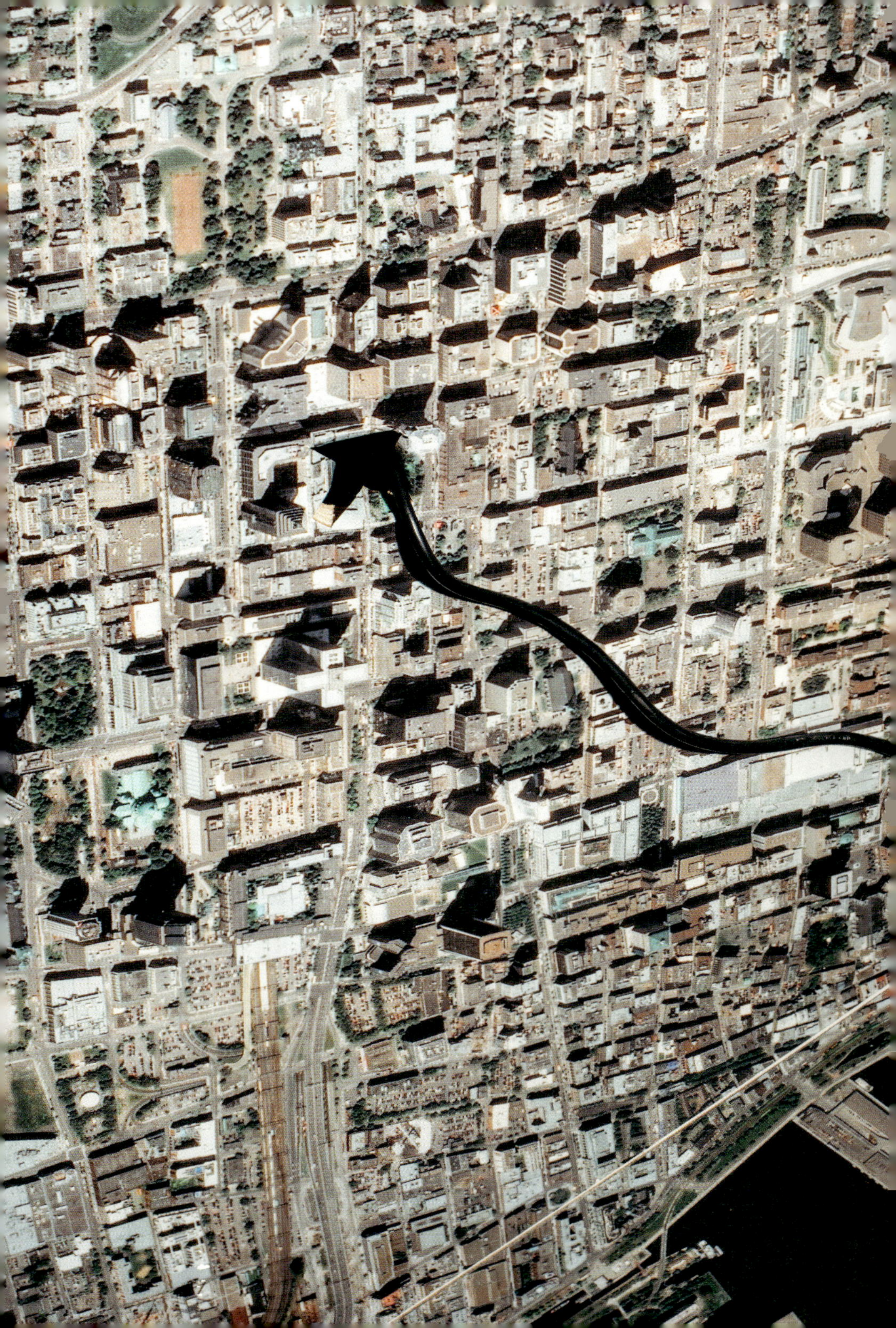

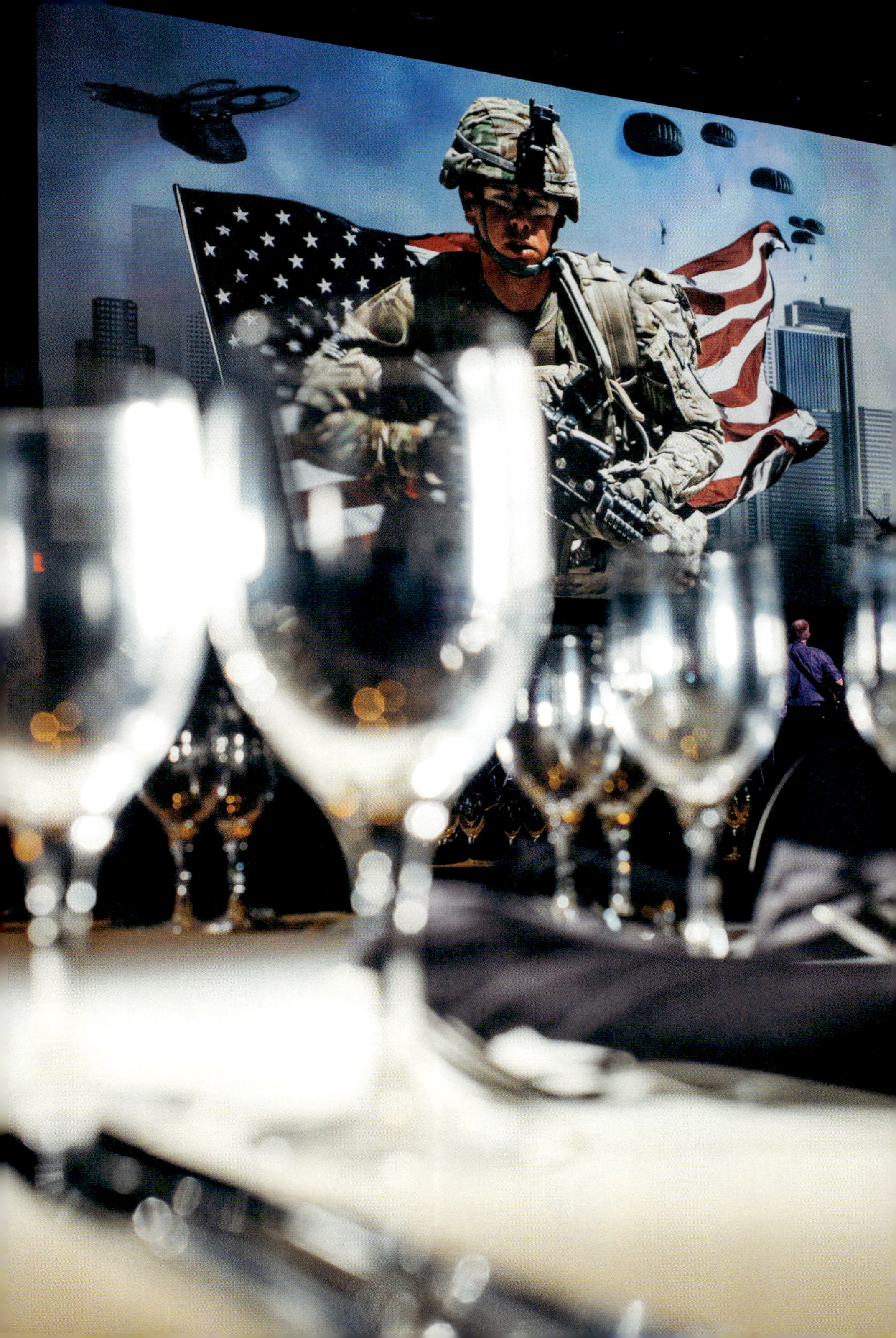

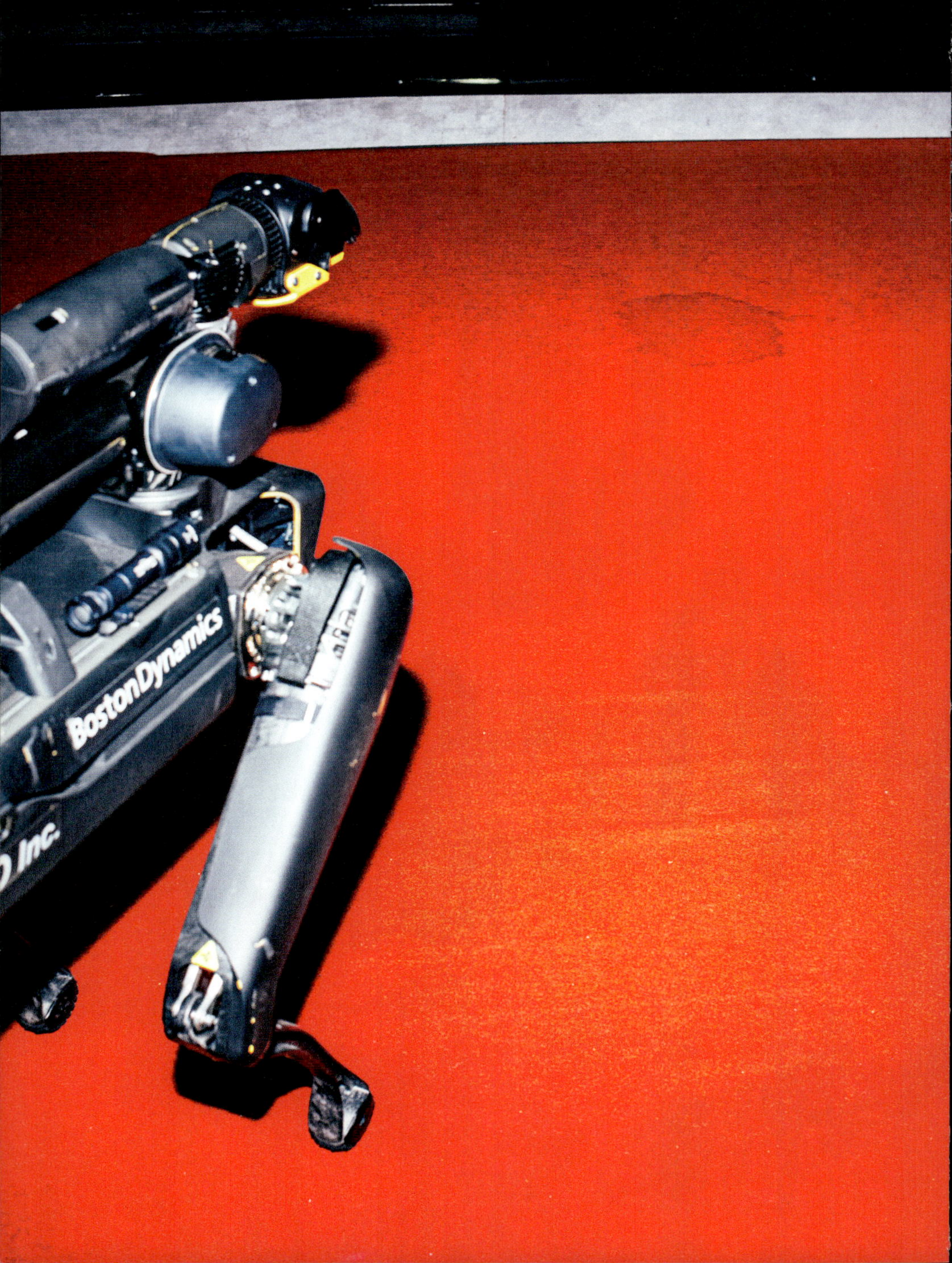
BostonDynamics

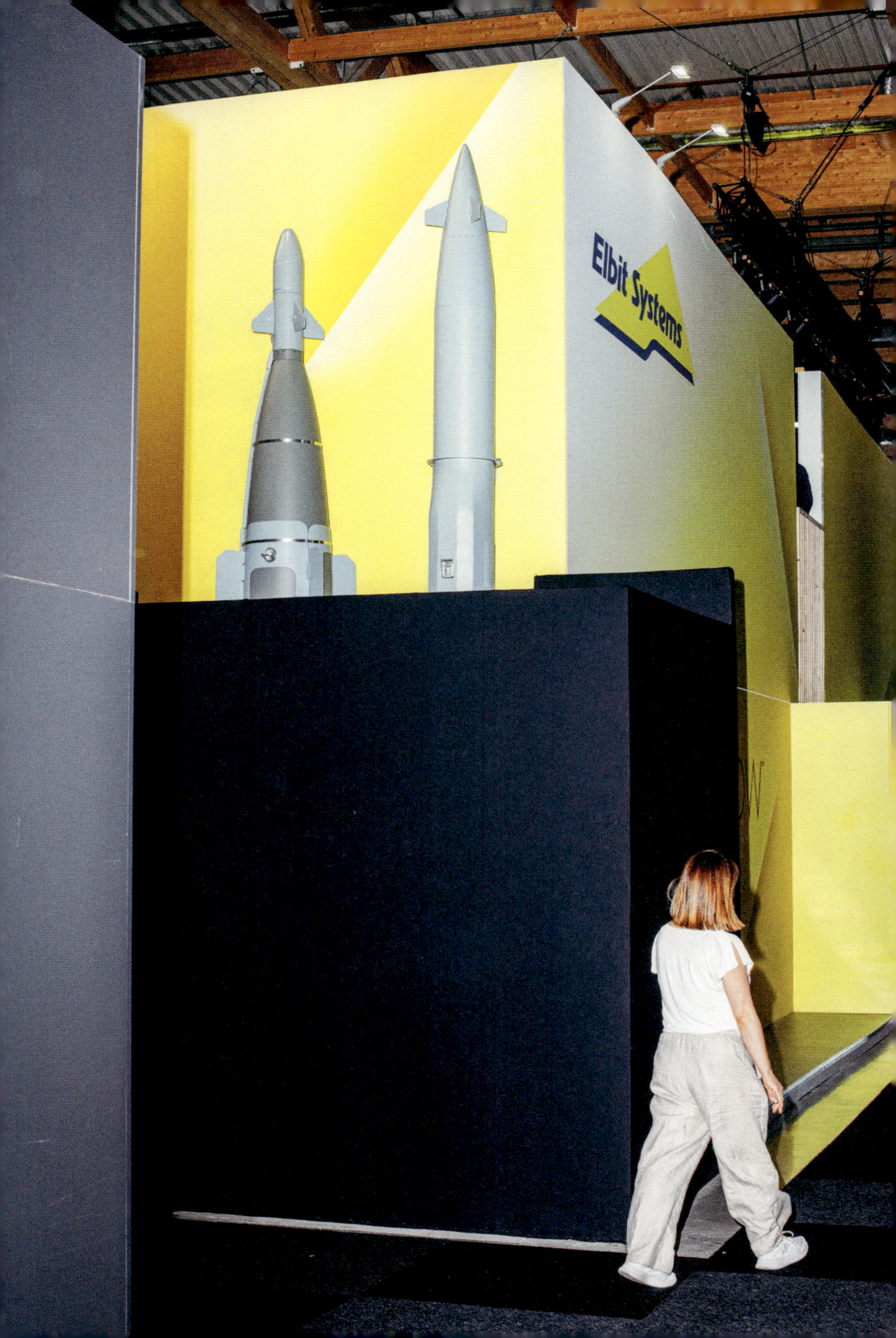
Elbit Systems

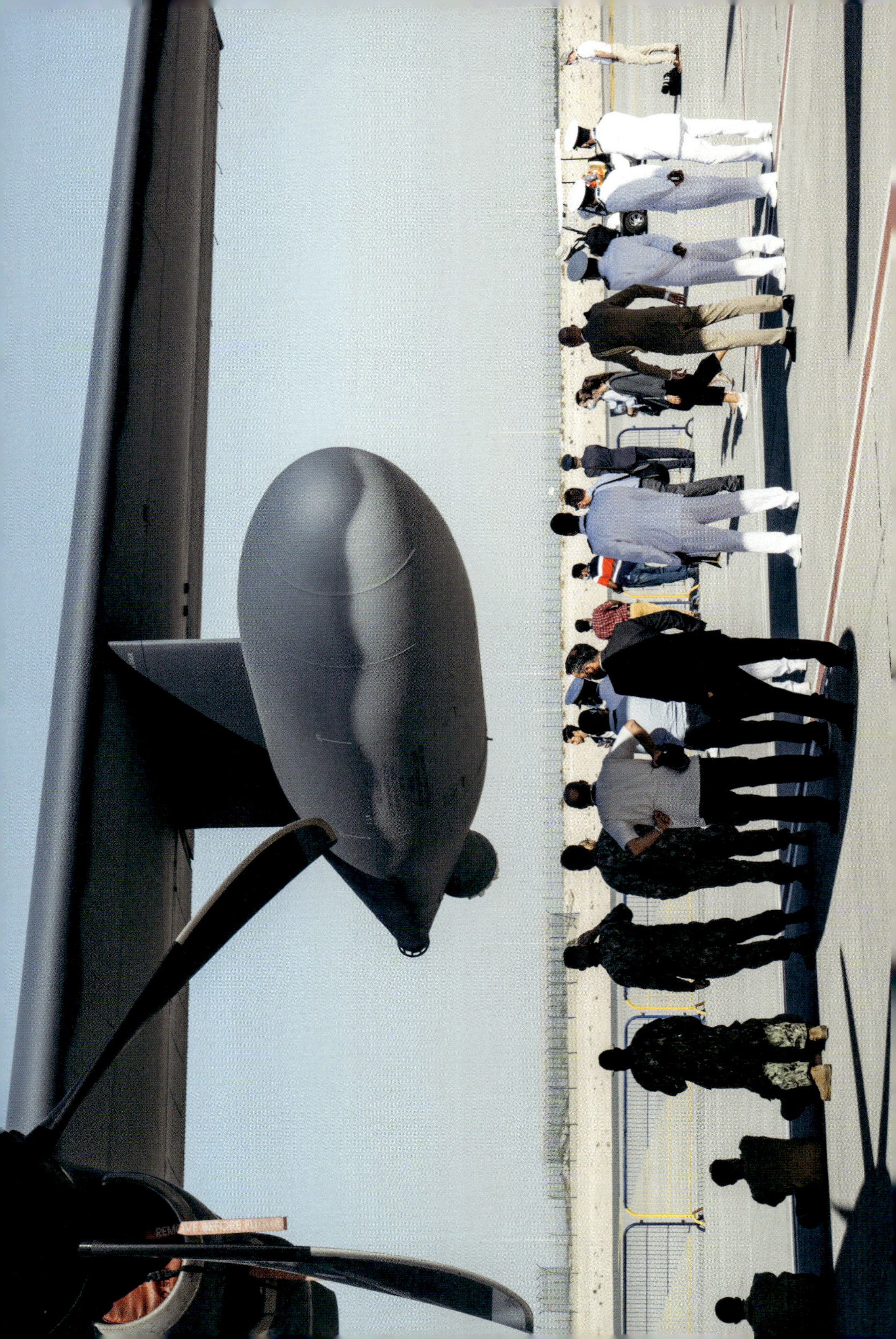
REMOVE BEFORE FL

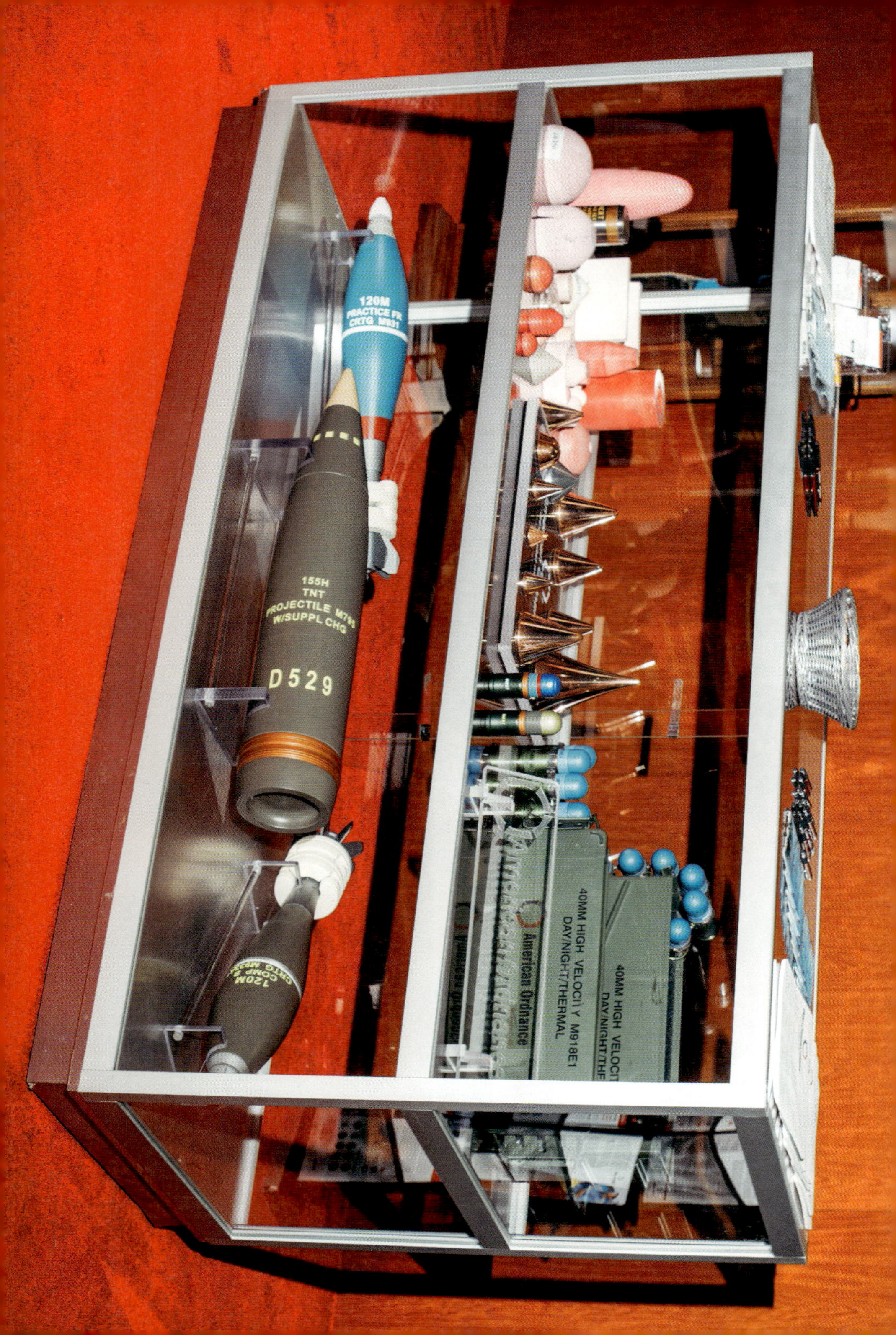
120M
PRACTICE FR
CRTG M931
155H
TNT
PROJECTILE M795
W/SUPPL CHG
D529
40MM HIGH VELOCITY M918E1
DAY/NIGHT/THERMAL
American Ordnance

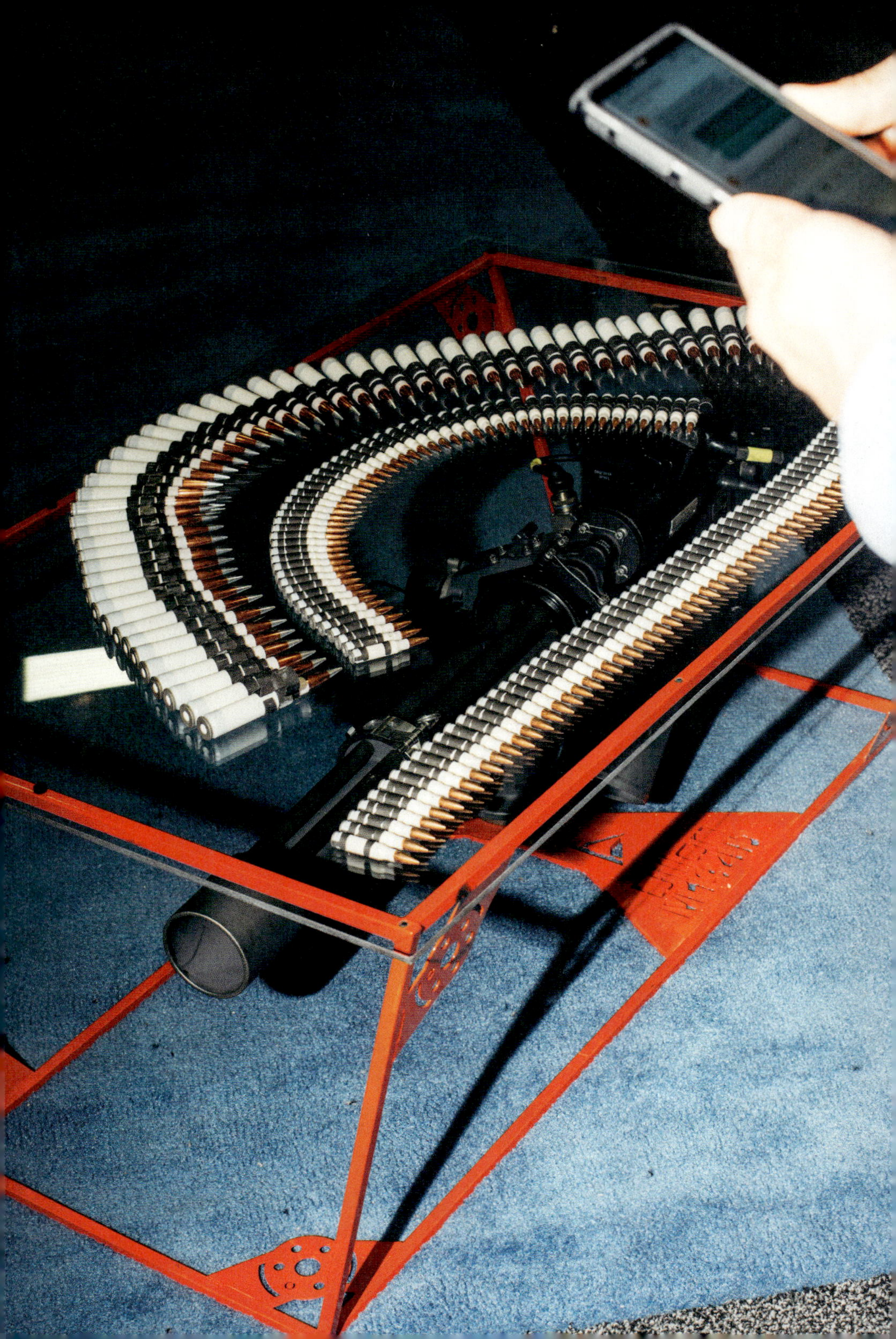

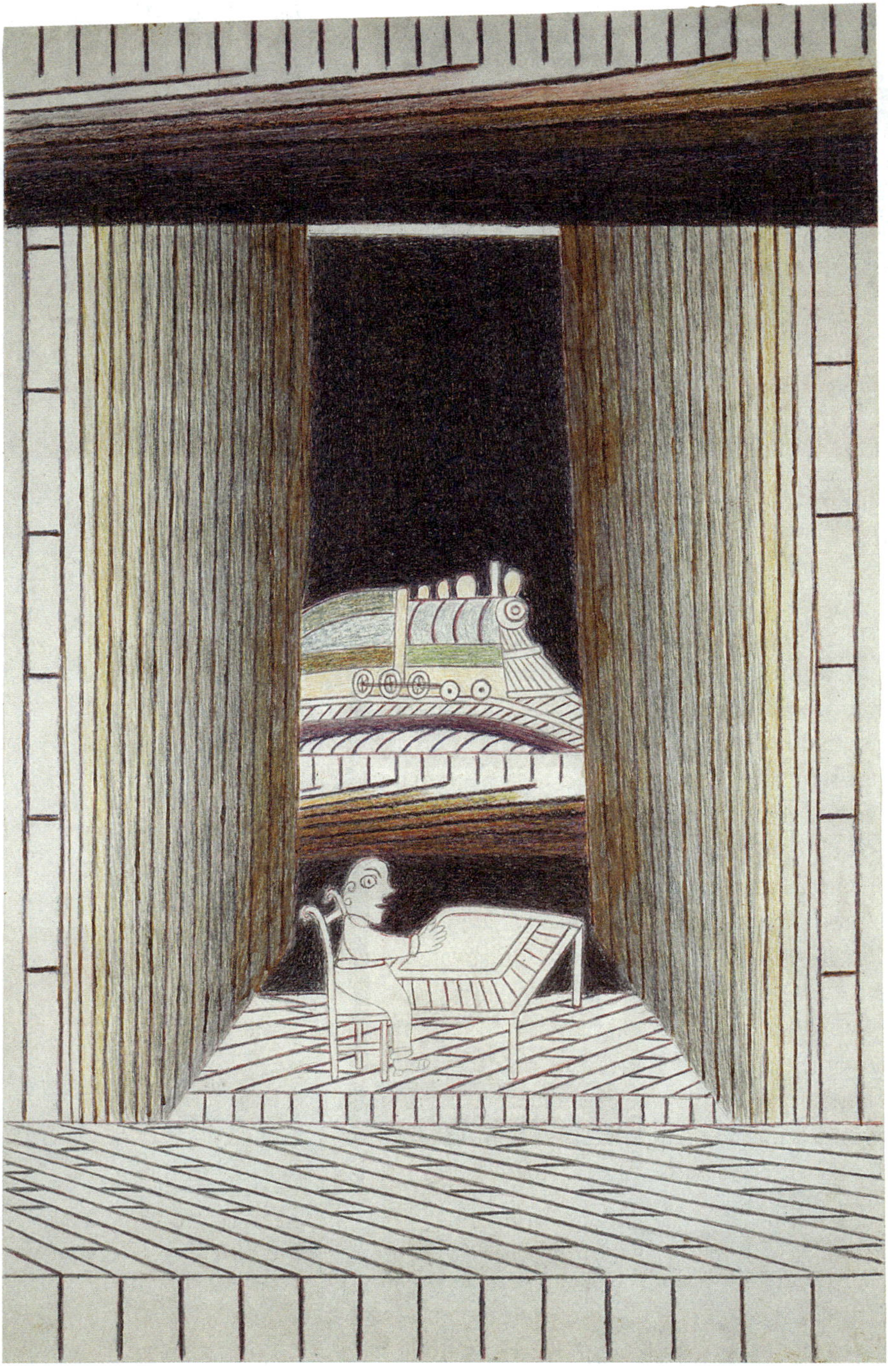

ESTATE OF MARTÍN RAMÍREZ
Martín Ramírez
Untitled (Man at Desk), C. 1950
Courtesy Ricco/Maresca Gallery

THE ACUTE WING

John Jeremiah Sullivan

The man had been on the ward for only a couple of weeks when a nurse was fired, or at least reassigned, for talking to him inappropriately. A woman in her sixties, Julia, who was new. His first day had been one of her first, too. He noticed how she regarded him with a scrutiny that verged on scorn. When he asked her any question, even of the most straightforward kind, she would narrow her eyes and take a few drawn-out seconds to answer. It seemed he could all but hear her thoughts going, 'Hmmmm . . . *you*.' She was often on duty in the middle of the night, when he would stagger out to the desk looking for painkillers, the sadistically weak kind they offer when the system has flagged a history of pill addiction. He kept getting these headaches. Partly it had been the withdrawal, but they persisted beyond the point where that made sense as a cause. They would come on when he was sleeping. He woke to them in the dark, already whimpering. He had been prey to migraines since high school, and like all sufferers had evolved secret, eccentric techniques for surviving them, but these were new. The pain lay somewhere out beyond language, though he made efforts to describe it in the patient journal he'd been encouraged to keep. Like a poison dripped into the ear. Like a virus that had taken root in the muscles where the neck meets the skull and spread from there in a barbed network. The word 'fire' kept trying to insert itself, but fire is cleansing, and although these sensations might at times possess an illusion of burning, or of searing, they were equally a kind of cramp. Acid . . . cancer . . . the words slid down the surface of the thing, like the bloody hands of a stabbing victim down a diner window, and the failure of these attempts was somehow bound up with the pain. A strangeness of migraines, when you're in the middle of one, is that, because they take place in the brain (or cranium), they often seem to be made of thoughts – the pain itself can resemble a form of consciousness, of sick thinking – which a person who doesn't get them might assume would make it easier to articulate, but the opposite is true.

'The etymology of the word "migraine",' he wrote in the journal – feeling, as he spelled the words, that he was appropriating, not quite convincingly, the voice of a man who no longer existed – 'comes from the Greek *hēmikrania*, meaning half a head, which tracks, when you get them, because it seems like that's what you're doing, as you writhe around: searching for the half where it doesn't live.'

One day a couple of neurologists showed up in his room. Two fit brown-haired white guys in white coats, in their thirties, they looked almost as alike as twins. Both seemed tired and leaned against the wall. One was the other's assistant. The assistant glanced around a lot, as if scanning for exits, but the main doctor had a steady, exhausted gaze. Neither seemed pleased to be on the ward. He thought about how it had smelled to him at first, the urine and disinfectant, neglected bodily crevices, burnt-coffee breath, dead nicotine skin, despair pheromones. He couldn't really smell it anymore, except at moments, when the doors of certain rooms and hallways flew open. The main neurologist let fall some vaguely patronizing sentences about how medical science had failed to determine what a migraine really was, and how some researchers suspected there might be a *psychological* dimension.

'But they come on in my sleep,' he said. 'If it's psychological, why would I get them when I'm not even conscious?'

The main neurologist shrugged and repeated his wisdom, that it was mysterious. Both doctors had a strange contempt in their eyes, although the contempt may have seemed strange to him only because he had encountered it so rarely in his life. He was an educated middle-to-upper-middle-class WASP man – conspicuously one, somehow, a sort of throwback, with his old-fashioned politeness – who had washed up at the Pines, the psychiatric wing of the local third-rate county hospital, a facility populated almost entirely by the indigent poor. The doctors and staff were not used to people like him there. People like him could pay to go to nicer, less harrowing places. But he was broke and had shitty insurance, if he still had insurance (they were working to verify that), and the night of his intake had been an emergency. He'd been mumbling to himself incessantly about God and scouring the house for a gun he believed to be there (in the end there was a shotgun in an upstairs closet, kept for snapping at intruders, but no ammunition), and so his wife of many years, who half wanted him dead by that point but was not mean enough to let it happen, loaded him into the back of the station wagon and physically deposited him in the lobby, like a giant foundling. And really he had felt like a baby, going in. A male nurse asked a series of simple questions, and he answered them guilelessly. They took his clothes, shoes, watch, everything, and wrapped him in a gown that felt like wearing paper towel, gave him fuzzy gray socks with grip-pads on the bottom, made him sit in a wheelchair – though he could walk, albeit unsteadily – and off he was rolled.

The first few nights he spent on the Level 1 ward, the acute wing, the lowest circle, a place for psychotics and recently attempted (or plausibly threatened) suicides. His roommate that night had been a pissed-off, grousing fat man with thick bandage-pads on his throat. He had a crusty tan like he'd been sitting by a motel pool his whole life. He kept saying how many times he had read the whole Bible (six), emphasizing that he read it page by page. 'Most people don't do that, see.' It was never clear what these statements were meant to imply. That the man was spiritually superior? Or that he had read it all and found it unavailing? Later, when they had both been moved off the crisis-stabilization wing and wound up 'in group' together, and he heard the man repeat these claims to others, the point remained veiled. Was it a way of saying, 'Alright, God, I read it! Are you gonna *help* me now?' Finally one afternoon he'd asked the man, in front of everyone.

'And what did you *learn*, from all of that?'

'From the Bible?' the man said, as if the question, despite its obviousness, had caught him unawares. 'As far as I can tell, it's totally empty.'

Those words hushed the room. Even the group leader had no response. A handful of the other patients seemed troubled, especially Gloria, a schizophrenic Black woman in her seventies who wore a plain denim dress and prayed under her breath all day. Now she squirmed in her chair and muttered.

'Well, I don't know!' the fat man said, appearing to feel himself cryptically accused.

The incident with the nurse, Julia, happened right after that group meeting. He was sitting at one of the big wooden tables, watching a man named Dusty render precise and elaborate multicolored drawings with dull pencils. That was one of the main activities on the floor. Several of the patients on the ward were meth-heads, and this genre of hyper-fixated activity soothed their nervous systems. They would make pictures as complex and finely executed as Tibetan mandalas then cast them aside like scrap paper. The finished work held no interest, only the doing, although they were always dedicating their pieces to one another: 'For Shasta, the most amazing person I have ever known. Love, Dusty.' The drawings were all the more impressive because the pencils were never sharp. You had to take them up to the nurses' station and ask for a sharpening, and the nurses knew how to grind them down just to the point where they could not be used to stab anything, which was wise, but less than ideal for coloring. The other problem was that the pencils themselves were small and stubby, about four inches long, like the little pencils they keep in baskets of fill-in menus at family restaurants. A person's hand would start to ache almost immediately. Dusty showed him how to make a paper extension-cone and tape it onto the base of the pencil. That helped and was pretty much the only reason the man could maintain the journal.

He studied Dusty, mesmerized by the severity of his focus. A Bruce Willis movie played on the TV, high on the wall. The nurses played a lot of Bruce Willis movies, or movies like that, mainstream action. They were dulling. They kept to the surface. Dusty had his tongue between his teeth. He was small and skinny, with close-cropped hair. He had a beard like a teenager who couldn't grow a real one yet, though he was not much younger than the man, early forties. He had crude, faded tattoos, but only a couple, and no white-supremacist stuff. The man liked Dusty. It seemed to him that Dusty had been kicked around a lot. Maybe Dusty had told him as much, when they'd first met. The man did not remember the first four or five days in the hospital very well. He mentioned it, the localized amnesia, to one of the nurses, who said it was normal.

Dusty finished his drawing – blue and pink, shards of fractals, a bird with an elaborate, fanned tail – and dedicated it to him: 'For L—, great dude and my brother. Stay blessed, Dusty.' The man took it to his room and put it on the little bedside table. He wanted to tack it to the sidewall, so he could look at it when lying on his side at night, but thumbtacks were out of the question. Maybe later he would ask for Scotch tape, or use Band-Aids. He sat down on the bed for a few seconds. He thought about how much the drawing meant to him – a lot, it seemed – and how odd it was that it meant so much. It hadn't even meant much to Dusty, probably. The man retained enough of his mind to realize that. Still, it meant very much to *him*, and he knew that it shouldn't, and this made him cry, but for just a few seconds. The tears dried right up, as if there had been only a few of them in his body. He lifted his eyes, and Dusty was standing just outside the door. 'Smoke break, dawg,' Dusty said.

To smoke cigarettes in those weeks was sensual in its intensity. His blood had not been that clean since his teenage years. There was nothing foreign in it now except two newer psychiatric drugs they were trying, and a modest amount of ADHD medication, to ease the abrupt withdrawal from a hardcore addiction to amphetamines (they didn't tell him it was for the withdrawal; he guessed that they were sheepish about the off-label usage; at the same time he sensed, as was later confirmed, that they were pretty much constantly deploying it like this). The cigarettes made him sweat and calmed him at the same time, as if each were the first he had ever smoked and also one for which he had longed. His reflex was to describe the sensation as euphoric, but that word had intimations of joy in it, and there was no joy in his body. *Feverish* was the word. He sat there with the others on low concrete benches, in the ineffectual shade of some juvenile trees, and smiled at the crazy things everyone said. Shasta sat beside him. She seemed to like him, and he liked her. Their bodies were politely aware of each other. She was pretty, with brown wavy hair and thick eyebrows, but her face had been ravaged by the lifestyle – missing teeth, sun-blasted skin, and at times a sudden glaring look.

Dusty mentioned that, in some wards he'd been on, smoking wasn't allowed, not even outside. They all shook their heads.

'Why would you *do* that to people?' the man said, and the others signaled agreement with wheezy laughter.

On their way back into the facility, Shasta fell into step with him, leaning close. 'Would you do something for me?' she whispered.

'Of course,' the man said.

'When they give you the Adderall this afternoon, try to keep it in your mouth. Don't swallow it. And give it to me?'

'Oh, jeez,' he said. 'I don't know if I can.' He pictured the scenario: the nurse who gave him the pills would stand there until she was confident he had swallowed them. 'Doesn't it dissolve pretty fast?'

'I don't care if it's half-dissolved,' she said. 'We do it all the time.'

The man said he would try but that he wasn't sure. Shasta looked disappointed. But her mind fluttered on to other thoughts, and she scooted away.

Inside they sat down again at the big table, but almost instantly the others stood up. They 'had group', but the man was not in this group. Each person on the ward had a different schedule. The schedules were written fresh each morning on a dry-erase board that hung on the wall directly below the television.

The man rose and went to his room, where he grabbed his journal and cone-extended pencil. He brought them back to the table and started to write. He was alone. He had been writing for maybe five minutes when the nurse, Julia, walked up to the table. Already that was strange. As a rule, the nurses did not venture forth from behind the desk area. They had a protected zone back there. In an emergency they might run out onto the floor, but it was irregular. Her body language seemed off too. She glanced around a couple of times.

The man stopped writing and looked up. 'Hi,' he said. He assumed that she had come to ask him about the migraines. Even though she was never especially warm or solicitous when he stumbled out asking for medicine in the night, he figured she must have some humanity in her, else why become a nurse of this kind?

'I've noticed you're always writing,' she said.

'Yeah,' he said. 'It's part of my therapy. I'm supposed to keep this journal.'

'Hmm,' she said, and slowly nodded. The nod was skeptical. Displeased, even, as if there had been something false in his answer.

'You've been having an affair, right?' she said. 'I read it in your file.'

The shock and mortification hit him at the same time. His face flushed. 'That's true,' he said.

'Well, don't you think you should stop?'

He smiled a smile that was meant to express amazement at her audacity, but he even as it entered his face he could feel it betraying other feelings, ones that he would have preferred to conceal.

'It's complicated,' he said.

'Is it?' She didn't sit, just stood bending over the table, with her palms flat on it. 'See, I've been through that. In my own life.'

A surge of indignation went through him. What *was* this?

'How long have you been married?'

'A very long time,' he said.

'Well, wouldn't you want to just *honor* that?'

He muttered something pitifully vague, and she said, now a little sharply, 'But those are just your *feelings*.'

Then she walked away, and he sat there, slapped. He tried to get back to writing. It was useless. Julia was stewing behind the desk. He could follow her shape in his peripheral vision, as he stared slack-jawed at the TV. A man was running. He wasn't Bruce Willis, but a version of him. Strong, bald, somber, ugly-handsome. After some minutes had passed, Julia re-approached.

'I'm sorry about that,' she said. 'I think maybe I . . .'

'That's okay,' he said, smiling blankly.

He had meant it as a kindness. He felt for her, despite his anger. Or a part of him felt for a part of her, for some quality of woundedness that he noticed in her bearing. But she took the brevity and flatness of his response – along with, it was true, something peremptory in the timing – as a rebuff, and walked away. He felt guilty then, though abstractly aware that he'd been within his rights. This had been a thing with the man for as long as he could remember. He was ashamed of his own self-defense mechanism. He perceived it as a mean, unworthy instinct. At the base of that shame lay a sort of hypertrophied empathy. His conscience was always whispering that other people were every bit as real, registered injuries just as deeply, were twisting no less helplessly in the sea-trash fishing nets of human nature. You experience people as stronger than you, above you (said the voice), in those moments when life's dissolving equations hand them a bit more power, but like you they are losing swiftly and inexorably to death and driven mad by the prospect. How dare you hit them, even under the guise of hitting back? Yet this very habit of forbearance, he more and more strongly suspected, had its roots in brokenness, not authentic mercy. It did no one any good.

He probably would have been content to let the thing with nurse Julia go – or not content, but would have stuck with his habit of quietly stitching the incident into a blanket of troubling memories he pulled over his head at night – but the following morning he made the mistake, if mistake it was, of telling his assigned therapist, Amanda, and Amanda became very angry, as pissed off as he had ever seen a therapist get, and the man had seen many therapists over the span of more than twenty-five years. He was what they called a special case, when it came to therapy, on account of things that had happened to him as a child.

He grew up in rural Oregon, in the northwestern part of the state, in a village called Fern Falls, about twenty miles from the coast. It was a chilly, bosky world of modest frame houses and trailers half-hidden at the ends of gravel roads. The windows were always wet and fogged. Everything had lichens on it. In his freshman year of high school, it had rained more in that town than anywhere else in North America. This was the thing he told people when they asked what it was like there. As factoids of personal trivia go, it was quick and good, both anecdotal and synecdochal. 'What's it like? Well, you know, it's the rainiest place in America . . .' That actually *was* kind of interesting. But he never said anything else about the town. If the conversation moved anywhere from there, it was to rain in the abstract. For all his acquaintances knew, he'd been raised in a palace of rain, living on droplets of mist like those creatures that have evolved in the spray-zones of waterfalls (*hygropetric* was the word – he had looked it up multiple times, could never quite remember it, or else misremembered the first half of it as *hydro*, which means water, of course, whereas *hygro* has to do with moisture). Yet there had once been a solid hometown. The man remembered it better than any place he had lived since. He could summon the texture, humidity-slickened, against his palm, of every erratic boulder of the place; the mottled amber of morning sunlight on damp cedar bark; the greasy pasted-in newspaper liner at the bottoms of kitchen drawers, and the printed words legible there, their meaning truncated by arbitrary folds and corners, yet given some weird incantatory power by how frequently they were seen, unconsciously memorized ('they do it all quietly and with grace / I've never enjoyed any work / in the beautiful milk roaring 20's television'): the human-like gasps that rose in the throats of a few specific pipes just before the notes caught in the organ at the Lutheran church; and the brook that ran behind the house, at the bottom of a hill, with a chain-link fence alongside to keep kids from drowning, and how one night there was a flood, and after the water receded he wandered down in the morning, a toddler, and found that a fish, in the hours when the fence had been submerged, had swum into one of the metal diamonds, got stuck, and now hung in the air, flying dead, and how his parents had not believed him when he tried to describe the sight, or had not understood his language, he was that small, so he led them by their hands down to the fence and pointed.

He kept all of that at the center of a complicated maze.

No. The man scratched out some words with the cone-pencil. From the outside his gestures looked furious, panicked, but inwardly they were driven by sheer meticulousness. Those pencils had no erasers. He wasn't sure why. They'd been chopped flat on the butt ends. He tried to imagine how a person might use an eraser to commit suicide. Ah, right – it was the small metal cylinder that kept it affixed to the wood. You could flatten that out . . .

No, 'all of that', those sensory details, they *were* the maze. It had assembled itself from those fragments. One whole wall of the maze were these flecks of orange thread, seen from extremely close up, in the oatmeal-colored carpet in the basement of that house. One room was a cluster of pop songs that had streamed through the radio vents of his father's beige Volkswagen Beetle in 1981: 'Lady' by Kenny Rogers, 'I Love a Rainy Night' by Eddie Rabbitt, 'Queen of Hearts' by Juice Newton. One sharp left turn in the maze was a sentence, pertaining to him, that he had half heard, when he was twelve, through a closed bathroom door, and spent about a decade deconstructing and reconstructing from the available syllables and silences.

He could make his way to the center, where the what-happened was, when he wanted. And *did* pay regular visits. It was crucial to stay in contact with it. He feared little more than becoming one of those poor souls suspected of having invented their 'recovered' trauma, so he never allowed it to get covered. To others, to the outside world it remained as secret as the coordinates of an undetected star, but for his part he tended it like an old burial plot, from those days when custom frowned on letting grass grow over the grave. The experience was always hovering, even as it occupied a distinct reality. It turned out this was a survivable way to be, or had seemed so for about forty years. Now some bough had snapped and left him here.

He stared at the lined paper of the journal.

Could it be that there was no longer any reason not to speak plainly?

He had been born into one of those families who adopt foster children for a living. He was the only biological child in the household, which meant that for most of his early life people assumed that he too was a foster, to the extent that he stopped correcting them. Very few of the people in Fern Falls could have told you which he was. He grew up with kids of various ages passing through the house. Many of them had behavioral issues, and he had been introduced way too young to a lot of advanced sexual stuff.

Counterintuitively, perhaps, it was not a foster child who had molested him, but a great-uncle – the brother, to be precise, of his maternal grandmother – a man who was a good deal younger than his grandmother, and in fact barely older than his mother, and thus presented to the boy more like a regular uncle, or some other adult relative in his mother's generation. The great-uncle had appeared in Fern Falls one afternoon with a tweed suitcase and talk of a 'rough patch' in his life, and they took him in without hesitation, offering him the newly finished basement bedroom. Unusually, for that household, only one foster was staying there at the time, a girl about four. The man – that is, the boy – had turned six in that year. The great-uncle was fortyish. Slender, trim. Vitalis and engineer's glasses. He dressed in a modest, elegant way. He had a reedy voice and chose his words precisely – two at a time, it often seemed. He had strong forearms covered in wiry black hair.

The 'series of incidents' occurred during a period of about six weeks in the winter of 1980. The younger girl was there each time. A film was made. It continues to circulate in that darkest of undergrounds, where it is known to aficionados as 'Blazer Boy' or 'blazrboy'. He had never watched the film, and learned of its existence only in the mid-nineties when a federal agent, an Interpol liaison at the FBI, had contacted him at his college to inform him that his name and some personal data had been posted in a Central European chatroom. The agency had disappeared ('digitally expunged') the post, but the agent wished him to understand that an indeterminate number of people out there had seen it. The agent suspected that the poster had been the other adult in the film (there is another man, briefly visible, though his face is never seen), but 'the investigation' had 'failed to make headway on that'. The man did not remember a fourth person having been in the room on those mornings, only his great-uncle and the girl. Somehow he had edited out the other adult. He related this to the agent, Russ, a genial, overweight, gray-bearded cyber-security expert, on the night they met, at a chain steakhouse off the highway in East Portland, and for most of the rest of his life – twenty more years and counting – had been replaying the agent's response, 'Well, he was there.'

He did remember the camera. Remembered it well, because it was the first video camera that he had ever seen in person. A tripod, cords. The great-uncle had been 'into electronics'.

A decade after that first meeting, Russ contacted him again, this time via email, which by then had come into popular use. Russ had kept polite tabs on him, knew that he had become a writer, and asked him to produce a victim-impact statement – not on the abuse itself, in any graphic sense, but on the psychic effects of learning about the film and knowing that it was out there, on the Internet.

Russ explained that such a document could help to secure more appropriate sentences in cases similar to his. Naturally the man had agreed, and lost sleep in an effort to craft something 'impactful'. Russ assured him that it was good, and sent him very sporadic notes over the years to let him know that the statement had been introduced at a particular trial or used as a teaching tool at a conference. But those messages stopped after a while.

In truth, the man had felt, from the beginning, a certain remoteness from what he had written. The statement was a lie. Not in the sense that the abuse had never occurred, but because the abuse – what had taken place in the basement – had not been the worst of it, or not the totality of it. He couldn't really tell anyone about the rest, not when his father had still been alive, although he had picked up a faint indication that Russ already possessed some inkling. It had been the tone in the agent's voice when remarking on the fact that the great-uncle had died right around the time the abuse had taken place. 'That's interesting,' Russ had said flatly, and the man had gripped his own knee for a second and released it, and there had been a pause in the flow of their talk, and in that pause the agent had noticed the young man's choosing to let it go, or his not rising to address the observation. The agent had nodded and moved on. The whole non-exchange took maybe two seconds but turned, even as it was happening, into a micro-chapter of the man's life, a hallway of the maze.

What had happened was this. One afternoon, a few days after the last of those three mornings in the basement, the boy had committed a petty naughtiness. Something banal. He had hurt the foster girl. They'd been playing, he'd pushed her, and she had hit her head on the edge of the stone fireplace. She wasn't hurt badly, but it bled, and she cried. His mother stood above him, scolding him, next to the algae-filmed glass of the fish tank in the den. She held his wrist and demanded to know why he had done it. He had no explanation.

In place of one, he tattled and told her about what had been going on in the basement. He could not, as an adult, remember exactly what he, the boy, had said, what words he had used, except for one sentence, 'He made us!'

There had been no calculation in his confession. It was pure deflection. He had hurt the girl, and his mother was displeased with him, so he would tell his mother about something worse that had been done to him – to him *and* to the girl – and that would make it all cease to matter. They would forget like they always did. Still, the boy must have understood that what had happened in the basement was bad. But he had no way of knowing *how* bad. The experience itself had been more confusing than painful. At moments there had been pleasure.

It must have been a weekend day, because the boy's father was home. The father was in the kitchen at that moment, probably stirring instant coffee (the only thing the boy had ever seen him do in the kitchen), and he overheard the boy.

His mother's features assumed a stricken O, and she looked away. He would never know how to describe it, not that he had ever tried to describe it to anyone but himself. The moment of her own death might be the only other time in her life when she would wear that expression, if the death were violent and sudden but left an instant for some reaction.

She put her hands on his ears, but the boy could already hear the muffled pounding of his father's footsteps on the stairs to the basement. He had never heard his father move that fast.

He heard a shrill screaming, like an old woman might have emitted. It happened in two bursts, the second louder than the first. His memory pinched out after that. There was the sound of the ambulance, picked up through the walls of his room; a visit from the police, days later, during which he was told to go outside and play, and did, but hovered at the edge of the neighbor's yard and spied, and watched the two cops, both older men, say goodbye to his father and walk to their car; and finally the sudden deepening of the silence between his parents, and changes in their manner toward him, marked in his mother by a bewildering rage, born of resentment, that she herself was distressed by, and for which she sought to compensate with unfamiliar, desperate displays of affection, and in his father by a kind of chipper formality, accompanied by a new and disconcerting habit of calling him 'buddy'. The atmosphere in the house never re-stabilized. Everything got quieter – in part because his parents stopped taking in fosters. The little girl had been gone within days, back into the system, and then all of that was over. His parents took an endless series of promising jobs. Childhood passed.

One of his many therapists, Dr Pfeiffer – early fifties, second career, twice married with no kids or grown kids, 'burnt out' by the 'corporate world', with soft, curly gray hair, a moustache and sweater, cords and moccasin-like shoes, everything about him furred and fuzz-bearing: you wanted to roll a lint-roller down him – had said to the man, midway through their 'work together', that possibly it had 'stabilized his ego' to know that his father had been willing to commit violence to protect him, that in an admittedly terrible way it may have been the best thing that ever happened to him.

The therapist after that one, Monica, a Jewish woman in her late forties with long black-dyed hair and protruding eyes and New Age tendencies (boots and skirts, bangles along her forearms) had looked at him, after hearing that, and said, with a signature lack of affect, 'You were raped, on at least three occasions, at the age of six. You listened to your father beat your uncle to death, and felt that on some level it was because of something you'd done.'

'My great-uncle,' the man said.

'Right,' she said. 'And since that day, not a single word has been spoken about those events, in your family?'

The man had been silent then.

'I highly, highly doubt that that stabilized anything.'

Then she had asked him to hold two paddles, one in each hand. She delivered an electrical charge into them, using a device that she held in her lap. She made one paddle buzz and then the other, or both at the same time. Oscillating. He gripped them tight, as if in hopes of squeezing out whatever mysterious power they contained. He was hunched over and sweaty. His anxiety had reached a level where it was hard to speak. Was it really possible that this shit helped people? Finally he sputtered, 'This is freaking me out!' and she turned off the machine.

'I'm sorry,' she said, as she gathered the bundle of paddles and wires up out of his lap.

Every therapist had his or her own pet method. Monica had the paddles. The old bespectacled Yankee transplant in Mississippi, the memory of whose name he had left down there, had rubbed his hands together and said, 'Ah, another creative! I love my creatives,' told him to meditate, and prescribed him a generous daily dose of amphetamines. Fuzzy Pfeiffer had been into making his patients do an exercise in which two chairs were placed facing each other. The man was encouraged to move back and forth between the two seats, assuming in each position the role of one side or the other in whatever internal debate underlay the torment. What had been his argument with himself, in those days? It seemed incredible that he could hardly remember . . . some cluster of thought-sensations that he had learned to call depression or anxiety or obsessive-compulsive disorder or most often a hybrid term, whatever the discourse favored in that particular half-decade. Each shrink would prescribe him the antidepressants *du moment*, and he would gamely try them, eventually re-arriving at a plateau of functionality, which he dubbed 'better', while continuing to feel wretched, until after a few years the pain grew intense enough again to trigger a reinitiation of the cycle, and all the while the reasons, the damage, festered down there in the literal and psychic basement. Looked at that way, it made sense that he couldn't remember what the two-chair argument with himself had been, or even what bogus description of the problem he had offered, because he was never telling the truth about his interior world. When you were a person like that, with that kind of backstory, and the double-life it imposes on you right off the gun? The man might as well have been born lying about sex. It was twisted up with his survival instinct. Easier to rip off your own scuba mask a thousand feet down than to tell the truth about that shit. He listened to others, with their endless talk of eschewing secrets and living an honest life, and knew he belonged to a different tribe.

He had made what he told himself at the time was a final effort, with the last of the therapists he saw before the collapse, a man with the unusual name of Stephen Bainbridge de Valdez. This person had not been born with that name. Growing up in Connecticut, he had been called Stevie Bainbridge, which was wieldy enough. He was gay, and in later life had married a much younger Mexican man whose patronymic was de Valdez. On marrying, Bainbridge had taken that name, or taken it on board, and subsequently begun insisting on Stephen, and this was how he came to be called Dr Stephen Bainbridge de Valdez, a name that sounded either fantastically aristocratic or invented. Physically he was startling. About six and a half feet tall, he had a bald head and long rubbery face, one deeply grooved from decades of relentless drinking that by his own account had owed to self-hatred over his sexuality. When patients were talking, he never stopped squirming, and when he talked, his arms and legs flew outward. He kept a tablet device in his lap and was always using it to document or guide or call time on the session. They had started to do this, the therapists, with the devices – it was terribly alienating. You knew that your darkest secrets were continually being uploaded to a not-entirely-sympathetic psychiatric consistory.

The therapeutic system to which Stephen Bainbridge de Valdez subscribed went by an acronym: DCT. The man couldn't remember what it stood for. In this system, much was made of such terms as 'doing a sounding', and 'dropping anchor'. Anxiety and depression, etc., were 'just thoughts', particularly if they did not 'align with one's values'. Stephen Bainbridge de Valdez was always asking the man if he had done his DCT exercises. Fairly soon the man grew irritated by this. He had life-or-death psychological problems and felt that he lacked the time for what seemed like a sales pitch for a pyramid scheme. Finally, during one session, in a reckless spirit, he shared with Stephen Bainbridge de Valdez some details of what had been done to him as a child. He described the initial abuse, in stark this-happened/that-happened terms. Stephen Bainbridge de Valdez had immediately leaned forward to mess with the language, recasting the 'molestation' as 'sexual assault', which sounded wrong to his ears, but whatever. The man pressed on. He explained that it wasn't simply the initial act of abuse; it was the reaction that those events had set off in the boy's body. When kids are fucked with in that fashion, that young, they become sexualized too early. They start rubbing themselves on the world without knowing why (literally – the man could remember rubbing himself on a bedpost). They seek out other children who are also different in this way. Such kids can sense one another in group settings. More problematic experiences occur. The man could remember several of these – naked humping, mutual masturbation that turned to handjobs while the babysitter was on the phone with her boyfriend, stuff that is natural at sixteen, or even at thirteen, but instead is happening at seven. For him, these premature furtive encounters had always involved other boys. He had been gay, in that respect, as a child. Then puberty dawned, and the lodestone of his urges had pivoted toward girls. Transferred overnight, in fact. It was not a case of repression – he wanted those earlier desires back, but his flesh, his very animal, had rejected them. His dick stopped responding to thoughts of naked males. Whereas girls began to affect him in ways that made the original urges seem wan and sickly, like poorly remembered dreams. He spilled all of this, and when he was done Stephen Bainbridge de Valdez lost it. He burst into tears. He began to talk about how his own father had behaved when Stephen Bainbridge de Valdez had decided to come out of the closet. How the father had said to him (in a parked car? . . . in the rain?), at that potentially scarring moment, something warm and reassuring, yet honorably gruff along suitably masculine lines: 'What do I care where you dip your stick? You're my son.' And when he had finished recounting this, Stephen Bainbridge de Valdez had gripped his long face in a large bony hand and sobbed. The man was moved, and had to check an instinct to cross the room and embrace him. He felt that Stephen Bainbridge de Valdez had intended to honor his divulging of past sexual trauma by sharing some of his own. Or something like that, anyway. An uplifting story, in the therapist's case, but what it had lacked in direct relevance it had made up for in spontaneous sincerity. The man's sense of appreciation faded, however, as months passed and the behavior was repeated on three separate occasions, complete with hard crying, and each time Stephen Bainbridge de Valdez had re-imparted, in identical language, the anecdote of his coming out to the father. This exposed a more general problem with Stephen Bainbridge de Valdez, which was that he had a terrible memory. He seemed to rely on the tablet device to do his remembering. For instance, the man had told him several times that he strongly disliked a habit Stephen Bainbridge de Valdez had, bordering on a tic, of visually 'reading' the man's appearance and body language. 'You look *tired*,' Stephen Bainbridge de Valdez would open a session by saying, scrutinizing the man with a grimace. 'Yeah . . . your body language is depressed. Last week you were more *addled*.' The man would then calmly explain, once again, that he hated how these statements made him feel, namely, self-conscious and judged. They shut him down and made him withdraw and rendered the therapy less effective. 'Oh, that's *right*!' Stephen Bainbridge de Valdez would groan, slapping his forehead. 'And I made a *note* of that, too!' He would stab at keys on the device as though to silently reprove it for having neglected to remind him of this. 'Thank you for the criticism,' he made a point to add. 'It makes me a better therapist.'

At last there came a day when the man went in for a session, and Stephen Bainbridge de Valdez failed to appear. The man sat waiting. Five minutes, ten. 'Hey Dr Bainbridge de Valdez!' he texted. 'Just making sure everything's okay. I'm here for my appointment.' About five minutes later the response pinged. 'You forgot about my trip to Mexico!' But the man had never received any such information. In fact, the previous week's session had been cancelled, due to a minor holiday, and there had been no communication at all. 'I'm down here w hubby,' Stephen Bainbridge de Valdez texted, 'celebrating ex-boyfriend's 40th.' 'Oh, okay!' the man replied. 'I didn't realize.'

Several more texts from Stephen Bainbridge de Valdez then flowed rapidly into the man's phone. They sounded manic and contained multiple misspellings or oddities of punctuation. 'am sorry if poor communication has causes inconvenience for us,' the last one read. The man realized that Stephen Bainbridge de Valdez had fallen off the wagon. The man even said, or typed, 'I hope you have fun, but please take care and remember how proud you are of how long you've been sober.' Stephen Bainbridge de Valdez did not answer that text. Nor did he call the next week, when the man was a no-show for his session. They never spoke to or saw each other again. The man came away feeling bruised. Yet another shrink was walking around town and knew all about him, the worst and most shameful parts. The man also felt guilty, in his characteristic mode. If he had been a better person, maybe their work would have gone somewhere. It was that defect in him, weakness of spine masquerading as largeness of soul. Stephen Bainbridge de Valdez had essentially mind-fucked him, and at a moment when he'd been at his most vulnerable, yet the man's inclination was to figure out a way to feel bad for them both. Nor was he merely performing goodness. The incoherence was more profound than that. He wanted Stephen Bainbridge de Valdez to succeed. Had recommended him to more than one friend.

Amanda, his current therapist, the one assigned at the Pines, had actually heard of Dr Stephen Bainbridge de Valdez. This struck the man, in his fragile state, as semi-miraculous, but probably wasn't all that great a coincidence. The man noticed that she was careful not to let her face do much when he mentioned Stephen Bainbridge de Valdez's name. The smile she had worn when the man had embarked on the sentence stayed fixed, as if she were in a momentary trance. 'Yes,' she said, 'I've heard he's a character!'

Amanda was petite and warm, with brown eyes and a brown bob. She wore long patterned sundresses. Greek by extraction, she had grown up in some North Carolina town he'd never heard of, one of the countless North Carolina towns that end in -boro. She listened intently and asked precise questions. Actual questions, not insinuations with question marks at the end of them. She was young, still in her early thirties, and the man knew enough about the mental-health scene in the city to understand that this was a competitive position, to be a lead therapist at the Pines. She must have been very sharp to land it. The job wasn't glamorous, of course, not 'prestigious' in the ordinary sense, but it was maybe something like being a Chief Public Defender in a city with a worse-than-average crime problem. Most of the patients here came in off the street and needed psychiatric triage more than psychotherapy. Amanda's somewhat idealistic attitude was that they should have both. In service of this she worked hours that a battlefield nurse would have respected.

It took only minutes, the first time they met, in her tiny office – a beige-and-white space so bare it seemed to belong to a building that had not yet been formally occupied – for the man to understand that he was in the presence of a deeply gifted psychotherapist, the first he had ever seen, or been seen by. He had heard of these people, these healers, always with a kind of rueful envy. They lived up north, or in London. Now somehow from the wreck of his life he had sloshed up at the feet of one. He told her everything – not just what had been done to him but things he had done. Unlike every time before, he refrained from curating the details. With Amanda he didn't *want* to color the narrative. She made him feel safe enough to submit the unedited transcript. He handed her everything, not just the drugs and the sexual acting out and the self-mutilation and the suicidal thoughts, but the lying too. The gaslighting and double lives. That was the hardest part to confess, because it was so . . . weak? He couldn't say why. It just seemed like you could come back from all the rest of it, be re-admitted into the human family, whereas liars, they are alone. Even if they can trick the others into keeping them around, as he had always been able to do, they are alone. They are out on the plain in a little rock hut, howling. This was what his great-uncle had done to him. Cast him out. That was the real injury.

It was conspicuous, in the context of all this truth-telling, that when it came to the other woman he failed to maintain it. Amanda wanted to know about her. The way she had inquired, the lightness in her voice when she said, 'Will you tell me about her?', made clear she was prepared to think well of this person. She seemed unwilling to frame the situation as one that required a villain. Amanda had met his wife by then. They had taken a walk together in the parking lot, at the end of his second week. He had tried the next day to coax out details of their conversation, but Amanda had been completely discreet, which only increased his trust. And yet when she had asked about the other woman – 'You said she's a filmmaker?' – he idealized her. She was brilliant and beautiful, etc. Talented, magnetic, led a complicated life. None of which was false, exactly. There was a version of her, an avatar, which more or less matched that description. But she and the man had grown too close too quickly, and neither was wise, and there was something ruinous between them, shadowed by cruelty – it was hard, from the outside, to say whether they were trying to save or destroy each other – and the man had been dishonest with her, and with himself, about his feelings for his wife, which were bottomless and not going anywhere, and which he chafed at for precisely that reason, and finally he and the woman had found the worst in each other, the naked selves that show up only in lamplight in the corner of the cell, with the frightened eyes and the mouse tails hanging from their lips. She knew that he couldn't be trusted. He knew she was someone God had given charisma where others have kindness. They were both holding onto a metal sphere that was taking them to the bottom, yet they refused to let go. He had written this to her once, then apologized, and she had texted back, 'No . . . it's the perfect metaphor.'

She was English, and herself still legally married, although she had been separated for a couple of years from her husband, an older, well-to-do gallerist, when she and the man became involved. The live-together part of that marriage had been brief, three or four years. Her reasons for leaving it were vague and shifting. The most frequently voiced was that the husband had been 'an emotional bully', words that, even as they left her mouth, gave off the pleading urgency of the projected confession, although the man had been deaf to it at the time. Or not 'deaf' – he felt something was off, but refused to let it in. He had met the husband on a few occasions, on the street. The husband looked a little like him, which unnerved him, but had seemed friendly enough. Intelligent. A bit blank, maybe, but the man had put that down to strained politeness. The husband had no desire to be meeting the man, after all.

The divorce had been dragging on because the woman was insisting on more money in the settlement, and the husband kept resisting. But the strangest part of the scenario was that, unknown to the husband and his expensive attorneys, yet all too well known to the man (who heard about it whenever she felt like stoking his jealousy), the woman had been sleeping with another man when she and the husband had broken things off, an Austrian academic whom she invariably referred to as 'the Austrian'. This person, who had professed his desire to have a child with the woman, remained very much in her life. They would travel together sometimes, ostensibly to work on a series of short 'essay films' about traveling together, quaintly pointless projects that bore the whiff of excuses to meet in foreign hotels. Her other code name for the Austrian was 'Crowbar'. This she would use laughingly among her friends, the implication being that the Austrian had been a useful tool for prying herself loose from the marriage. It was hard to see how a crowbar could be required, after so few years. 'Spatula' might have been the better term. The man had never met the Austrian. He wanted to – he hated him, just on a primate level, but felt a kinship with him. He knew too much about him. The woman was phenomenally indiscreet, to the extent that it got in the way of the man's feeling properly bad about lying to her, since, in those instances when he did tell the truth about some difficult, painfully intimate thing, it was usually known within hours to countless people whose faces he had never seen, or else had seen and wanted to forget. He wished for her now that she might find a better therapist, an Amanda. He knew how she suffered. At some point she had been diagnosed with bipolar disorder. Granted, it was a moment when all sorts of psychologically mainstream people claimed to have bipolar disorder, but the woman's case manifested as shockingly real-deal. The things she would say in the heat of her volcanoes, as she called them, were nothing short of harrowing. She tended to wait until the very instant when you had laid aside your armor to draw the blade. The man was so full of her insults that he went about in a kind of daze.

There were moments when the woman could be almost self-aware. One night, not long before he had gone into the Pines, she had said to him over the phone, through tears, 'You're the only person who has been able to love me through this.' The man had cried then, too, but whether because it was true or because it was increasingly no longer so, he could not tell.

He told Amanda none of this. It amounted to a huge evasion, one that counterbalanced the disclosures.

Time had run out. He stood up to leave. Amanda looked him meaningly in the eye. 'L—,' she said, 'you are incredible.'

When he got back to the ward, Dusty looked up at him from the coloring table. 'Somebody's on the phone for you,' he said. Shasta was standing at the wall with the phone in her hand. She held it out toward him. 'Is it my wife?' the man asked. Shasta shrugged. 'It's a woman.' It was the woman. He had put her on the list of people who could call. She asked him how he was. 'Ah, you know,' he said. 'Fucked up.' She told him that the night before she had hosted a small party at her apartment in Boston. 'We were talking,' she said, 'and at one point I brought up the fact that every man I've ever been with was molested as a kid. I was like, "Why do you think that is?"' Was she laughing? She had laughed.

He was silent for a few seconds.

'You didn't tell them that about *me*, did you?'

Her voice did this thing it did when she lied, of suddenly dropping into a baritone. 'Noooo,' she said, though of course the little story would have made no sense if she hadn't been talking about him.

'Because I've told, like, three people that in my life.'

Now she was the silent one. Dusty and Shasta were listening. There were two phones on the wall, and the other was occupied by a young Black guy, about twenty, who was always on the phone, never speaking, only listening, now and then muttering, 'Yeah.' Hours and hours of that. Everyone wondered who he was talking to and what the person was saying. The man had never heard him say a word except these Yeahs on the phone.

The man attempted to make small talk, to move on, but he was too stunned, and it faltered. They mumbled goodbyes and hung up.

She had compromised him in the most grotesque way, and managed to be both dishonest and cavalier about it. But had it been fair of him to tell her in the first place? Had he expected her to keep a secret for the first time in her life? Why had he burdened her with it? He had told her very early on in their knowing each other, too. Once she had even questioned him about it. 'Why did you tell me that?' she asked. 'I wanted you to have the full data,' he had answered, 'to know what you were getting into.' But now he wondered. It seemed possible that he had simply wanted people to know. Lacking the courage to tell the world, he had found someone who would do it for him.

'You okay?' Shasta said.

He smiled at her. Nodded. She bent down and hugged him.

'You want to eat?' she said. 'It's dinner.'

Half an hour later, at the table in the small and too brightly lit cafeteria, they finished their coffee and gratuitous dessert. Gratuitous in the sense that nobody was ever really hungry here. It was a place where people unaccustomed to regular life habits, apart from compulsive drug consumption, were suddenly eating three meals a day plus snacks and consequently felt half-stuffed all the time; but when you are bored and depressed and there is cake and everyone else is having the cake, and having the cake means an excuse to stay at the table ten minutes longer and not be alone with your thoughts, you eat the cake, even when the cake is a stale dry pseudo-brownie. Dusty leaned toward him and said softly, 'Look around at all these people.'

The man did so. Saw Shasta, who smiled at him through her dark sun-fried thicket of hair. Saw Shasta's short blonde friend, with the teardrop tattoo on her face, who was always telling intricate lies about her fiancé in Tennessee and how they had been targeted by the cartels, resulting in her forced rendition to the Pines, for her own safety, lies so long and inwardly consistent, and fired at you with such hypnotic rapidity, that it seemed only an alien psychology could invest that much energy in crafting them. He saw the fat man with the bandaged neck. Saw another, older man, skinny, an expressionless shell, with identical bandages. Saw the three Black patients who always sat together in silence: the old woman who was always praying, the kid who never got off the phone, and the young attractive woman who seemed completely normal but had recently, Shasta said, stabbed her boyfriend to death, for reasons that had evidently been deemed justifiable, seeing as how she was here, freely circulating. The man looked back at Dusty.

'Half of them will be dead in a year,' Dusty said.

'Jesus,' said the man, 'why would you say that?'

'Look it up.'

They dumped their trays, and the man went back to his room, a two-bed unit that opened directly onto the main floor. These psych-ward rooms looked like smallish crappy hotel rooms, apart from the odd placement of the bathrooms, which were deliberately located in exposed positions. The staff conducted suicide checks at night, too, all night, which was terrible, because every time they opened the window, it emitted a squeak, and a shaft of light burst into the room. If you were having a hard time sleeping, the sound and light would wake you up, over and over and over. You knew it was coming, you would wait for it, and slept even worse for the anxious waiting. This was horrendous for the man, with his cluster migraines. He tried to talk to the head nurse about maybe giving him a break on the checks. Could it be done once an hour, instead of every fifteen minutes? He swore he didn't want to be dead anymore. She had sort of laughed, like, 'Yeah . . . no.' Anyway, wasn't he roommates with *Jerry*? Did he think they were gonna skip suicide checks on *Jerry*?

Jerry had been living in the room already when the man had been moved off trauma and onto the ward. He had been living alone in the room, and clearly preferred it that way, which meant that relations between the two were never warm. Jerry avoided eye contact and was silent, except for soft weeping into his hands. He had the scarred, calloused palms of a construction worker and an incongruously handsome face, one younger than his years, like the mugshot of a child actor. He rode or rather sat in a wheelchair all day, although he was always moving his legs, shifting about. He seemed to be confined to the chair by sheer psychic devastation. The man would try sometimes to imagine the biographical catastrophe that had produced this human ruin, but there was nothing to work from. He answered the nurses' questions with two-word responses that, despite their brevity, left him breathless with effort. He never went to group. Nor was he ever pressured to go. At mealtimes he made sure to be among the first in line, bolted down a few bites, then wheeled himself back to the room, to sit beside the bed and cry.

The man opened the door with a spasm of dread, ready for the awkwardness of greeting Jerry again, but Jerry was gone, and in his place, was a very different creature, evidently his new roommate, a tall and all-around enormous man who had been lying there in the dark with his hands folded together on his chest, who now slowly stood up and introduced himself in a deep but youthful drawl as Dwayne Chavis. He gave off gentle-giant energy. Big belly, scraggly beard, huge hands with tattooed fingers. He looked mixed-race, with maybe some Native American blood. This was later confirmed: Choctaw father, but from a band of Choctaws who were not formally recognized by the federal government, which classified them as merely an isolated 'mulatto' population and thereby denied them all sorts of benefits, a slight that the people themselves were touchy about, Dwayne said, and one that the man must refrain from mentioning, should he ever visit that corner of Alabama, in the southwesternmost pocket of the state, where the man would otherwise be shielded from all manner of harm by virtue of his friendship with Dwayne Chavis. When Dwayne

Chavis sat back down, the man got a better look at his face, and noticed something striking: tattooed between his eyebrows, just above the line of his eyes, was an eye. A third eye. Not quite photorealistic but close. It gave Dwayne Chavis a truly freaky appearance. As they made small talk, the man kept staring at the central eye. He realized that he was waiting for it to blink.

They wound up rooming together for almost two weeks. At night, in the half hour after lights-out, Dwayne Chavis would lie on his back and tell stories about his life, which in barely thirty years had contained an almost unbelievable amount and level of violence, 'almost' because Dwayne Chavis's stories were instantly, unimpeachably believable, betraying as they did no hint of pride or shame. The man said very little about his own life. All Dwayne Chavis knew was that he had been having 'emotional problems', and Chavis often said generic comforting things, such as, 'You're a good man. I know you'll find you a good woman.' Dwayne Chavis had been in prison twice, once for rape and once for murder. He denied the rape – 'Well, seems like, when we was first in the truck, she wanted it, but later on she got to talking with some of her friends and decided she didn't want it or something like that . . .' The murder, which he had committed in league with a friend, he made no effort to deny, other than to say that the man had deserved it. Dwayne Chavis also confessed to the man something that the authorities had never known about, or at least never charged him with, namely, that he had participated in a second murder. It had involved a man Dwayne Chavis had met in prison. The man was a zoophile (Dwayne Chavis did not use that word). This fellow prisoner was in love with a horse. Charlotte, that was the horse's name. He had been having sex with Charlotte for years. He wore a ring on his finger to symbolize their union. He talked all the time about how much he missed Charlotte, and how good the sex had been, and how he longed to be reunited with her. This is what the other men in the wing refused to tolerate, not the perversity but the brazenness. Finally they gathered in a circle around the man and stomped him to death. No one was charged. The guards had known all about Charlotte. 'Jesus Christ,' the man said, when Dwayne Chavis finished the story.

Dwayne Chavis laughed, softly and darkly. 'Some people are fucked up,' he said.

'Charlotte,' the man said.

There was a moment of silence.

'We shouldn't have killed him, though. I do feel bad about that.'

A week earlier, Dwayne Chavis had been at home in his trailer down in that southwestern county where all the unrecognized Choctaw lived, and swallowed an entire bottle of pills, washed down with an entire bottle of cheap bourbon, fully expecting to die, but his body was so huge and powerful that the attempted overdose had failed to kill him, and his mother had found him. Now he was here. His snoring was like a sound made by a power tool. The man felt bad, because every night when he woke to the face-shredding migraines, and got up to ask nurse Julia for more of the bullshit painkillers, the light from the opened door would wake Dwayne Chavis, but he never complained. Not even when it happened two or three times in a night.

One afternoon after group they were all sitting out on the floor. Another off-brand action movie involving airplanes played on the wall-mounted TV. The man was writing in his journal with his cone-pencil. Dusty was using every colored pencil in the box to fill in a scene of sinuous dragons. Shasta was discussing the ancient perfidy of men with her friend the blonde pathological liar. Dwayne Chavis and the attractive young Black woman who had stabbed her boyfriend sat beside each other, watching the movie. Dwayne Chavis was chewing crushed ice from a Styrofoam cup. The two men with neck bandages sat at a table by themselves. The gaunt one read a novel. The fat one gazed around, as though daring someone to ask him a question.

Everyone was in a mood, because the Black kid who always sat on the phone saying 'Yeah' about every five minutes had tried to kill himself that morning. No one knew how, exactly. All anyone knew was that he had somehow been able to barricade himself in his room during breakfast. First the nurses beat on the door, and then security was called in. Then the doctors came. They wheeled the kid out on the stretcher. Everyone was shaken. Everyone liked the kid, who had managed to seem friendly and dreamy and sweet despite his introverted ways. Everybody asked one another and the nurses what had happened, but policy dictated that staff communicate as little information as possible.

At about one o'clock in the afternoon, without any sound or warning, the old schizophrenic woman, Gloria, came to stand under the television. She faced them all, staring them down, wild-eyed, as though they had cornered her, when it was she who had positioned herself before them. She gripped her dress at the hips like a little girl and swished it back and forth, moving her body in semicircles. Then she lifted her hand and pointed a finger directly at Dwayne Chavis. She began to pray and condemn. It was hard to understand many of her words. It sounded as if she were speaking in tongues, but as he listened closer, and as she went on, certain phrases grew intelligible. She was talking about the devil, and about Dwayne Chavis's third eye. She believed that Satan had been using this third eye like a periscope, to look into and through her.

'I know you think I'm crazy! I know you all think I'm crazy!'

It was terrible how she howled! From inside a whirlwind. And the fear in her face.

Everyone froze. The nurses had begun to creep forward from their station.

Dwayne Chavis sat in his chair, eating his ice, unmoved. His posture did not change, and he seemed to accept this spectacle as the sort of thing that happened when you were watching a movie.

'You ain't gonna get me,' the woman said. It was unclear whether she meant Dwayne Chavis or Satan.

The man stood up from his chair. He stepped around the table, so that there was nothing between himself and the woman. He looked toward her but avoided making prolonged eye contact. His body stayed loose. 'We don't think you're crazy,' he said. 'We respect you.'

The woman looked distressed. Her glance flicked in a triangle between him, Dwayne Chavis, and the floor, but none of those three stations seemed to offer any comfort.

'We all know Dwayne's tattoo is bizarre,' the man said. 'It looks like an eye, but it's just a tattoo.'

She muttered something at Dwayne. They all heard the word 'devil'. Dwayne chuckled softly into his cup. The young woman beside him batted him gently on the shoulder.

'Dwayne is not the devil,' the man said. 'He's my roommate. I know him. He's nice.' The man spoke slowly, evenly. But her suffering was affecting him.

He grabbed his own chair from the table and placed it against the wall beside her. She looked at him as if he might be pulling some trick.

'Let me get you a bottle of water,' he said.

One of the nurses wordlessly handed him a bottle. He held it out to Gloria.

'It's been a messed-up day,' he said, 'what with . . .' He pointed to the room from which they had recently rolled the kid away on the stretcher.

'Reggie,' she said.

'You know his name?'

'He go to my church.'

Gloria sat down. The man unscrewed the cap on the bottle and offered it to her again. This time she took it.

Dwayne Chavis got up and went to their room, and closed the door loudly. Everyone went back to what they had been doing, but in a more subdued way.

Gloria sipped the water and hummed.

'I heard about what you did on the floor yesterday,' Amanda said.

'Oh, yeah,' the man chuckled dismissively. 'With Gloria? That was intense.'

'To me it sounded like more than that.'

She reminded him that she had seen him do something similar, in group. There had been a day when one of the bandage-necked men, the gaunt gray one, had confessed to the others the terrible thing he had done, as a young man, that had led him to attempt taking what he called 'the coward's way out'. He described a night more than fifty years ago when he had abandoned his family, just up and done the actual 'I'm going out to get cigarettes' number, leaving behind a wife and two sons. He drove west, to the desert, and made a new life. He described the pain that this rash decision had wrought on his family – wife had remarried a horrible man; son had committed suicide; daughter was miserable – as well as his lifelong confusion about why he'd done it. 'I just couldn't . . . I felt that I would *die* . . .' At one point he had tried to reconnect, but the experience had only compounded his despair. They barely knew who he was. 'I'm angry that this didn't work,' he said, pointing to the bandage on his neck. It needed to be changed. It had begun to yellow at the edges. The others listened with what appeared to be a combination of horror and contempt. Amanda did not interrupt.

Finally the gaunt gray fellow had run out of words, and Amanda had turned to the group. The man sensed that no one else was going to speak, to address the old man's confession, not even his friend and fellow bandaged man. The silence was so unacceptable. In all the gaunt gray man's seventy-five years of pseudo-life, this was doubtless as close as he had come – or, it was clear, would ever come – to baring his soul, and everyone in the room just stared at him.

The man set his coffee down on the floor between his feet. He looked earnestly at the man as he spoke. 'You have to forgive yourself,' he said. And: 'There is not a single person in this room with you right now who hasn't done things they regret every day.' And: 'The fact that you've been torturing yourself about this for so many years – half your *life*! – *proves* you have a conscience.' The old man was listening. The others were *mm-hmming*. Amanda watched with an expression somewhere between pleasure and scrutiny, or one that seemed to contain a measure of both.

'Are you a priest?' the old man said. His tone was not quite placeable. It caught the man off guard and made him go quiet. He had the same reaction now, listening to Amanda. She was working to bolster his self-esteem. He took this as a sign that she had failed to detect the hidden narcissism in him. This belief, that she had ever failed to detect it, was itself the saddest and most unmistakable sign of that narcissism, but he wasn't there yet.

'Didn't that feel good, when Glen said you'd helped him?'

'You mean when he asked me if I was a priest?'

The man asked that with an edge of skepticism but Amanda seemed taken aback. That wasn't how she remembered it, maybe, or how she'd heard it.

'Sorry,' the man said. 'It's just, when he said that, I heard him saying basically, "Where do you get off?" I mean, I'm one of the most fucked up people in that room. Why am I giving advice?'

She held her smile, but her eyes narrowed quizzically, as though the man had given her something to think about. He couldn't read her thoughts.

'I tell you what,' she said. 'It's almost two, so we have to stop, but I want you to write something about this, for tomorrow. In your journal. Will you do that? Help me understand it?'

In the quiet hour after dinner, everyone was on the floor, but no one paid attention to him. He sat down at a table, slid a new pencil into the paper cone, and smoothed down the tape that held it in.

> On the last plane trip I took before I ended up here, I sat next to a young flight attendant. She wasn't working the flight – she was 'deadheading', flying as a regular passenger. She was watching a movie on her laptop, I don't know the title. A man has a son who becomes a heroin addict. They're fighting to save him. Toward the end of the flight and the end of the film, I looked at the side of her face, and she was sobbing so hard that she couldn't breathe right. She had her uniform on and everything. She was about twenty-six, I think? Blonde

with a round pale face. I tapped her on the arm and asked if she was okay. She pulled out her earbuds and said that she was okay but that she shouldn't have watched the movie. It came too close to her own life. She had a lot of addiction close to her, she said. I asked what she meant and she said that both of her parents were heroin addicts. She was flying into Atlanta because her father had just gotten out of detox there. Her parents were both alive, but divorced, and both heavily addicted, and she said that every night she went to sleep wondering if she'd get 'the call' about one of them. She had two brothers, but they were teenagers, too young to get it or be of any help. She worried about them, that they'd start using, or just how they'd been scarred. They lived with her grandparents. She had moved to Salt Lake City, a place she had no connection to, just to have some kind of life, to feel separate enough from her parents' drama that she could breathe. But she thought about them constantly. 'It's been my whole life,' she said. I told her about my father. Said I knew what it was like to watch self-destructive people kill themselves in slow motion, and to love them but not be able to save them. To want greater closeness but need greater distance. I couldn't believe how much pain was in her face. She was too young for that level of pain. I said I'd pray for her parents. I wanted to laugh at myself then, but it had seemed inhuman not to say it. She said, 'I can't believe I'm having this conversation. You're a total stranger.' I said, 'I know, but it's okay, because I get it.' But I don't know if I did get it, or if I do. And it made me think about myself, this strange ability I have, at moments like that, to empty myself. I could talk to anyone, somebody dying in a field, someone running from the law, and really listen. It's easy. It's gallows kindness. I tell myself that people blow through me like fog. But then, do they

> really? I mean, here I am thinking about her story, and writing about it, and I probably *will* pray for her parents. But I can't shake the feeling that a person more real than I am, or more present, would not have been able or wanted to have that conversation in the first place, would instead have respected the distance. When we were walking off the plane I said, 'Take care of yourself,' and she said, 'Thank you,' and her face was so serious when she said it, so far beyond any politeness. Then you walk off the plane, and you're in the airport, with people streaming by . . .

The following morning, the man sat in his chair and watched Amanda reading this passage in his patient journal. He didn't want to stare at her but couldn't stop glancing at her face. It was full of skeptical attention.

She gave the journal back to the man, then settled back into her office chair and regarded him.

'I need to think about that,' she said, with a wary laugh.

'Totally fair,' he said.

'What do *you* think about it?'

'Well, I . . . like, if it were written by someone else? I would probably think, "Get over yourself."'

She cocked her head to the side. 'Say more.'

'Why does he even care about all that shit? The woman was suffering. He made her feel better. That's what matters. The fact that he's so caught up in his role in their interaction, whether it was pure, whether it's . . . I don't know . . .'

'If you look at the literature,' she said, 'the psychiatric literature, when you're talking about chronic self-deprecation, once you unwind it, there's usually shame at the core. Unresolved trauma.'

'"Self-deprecation" sounds so mild,' he said. 'This is more of almost, like, a phantom feeling. Vampiric or something . . .'

It seemed she took that seriously.

He got the feeling that she enjoyed working with him. The other patients' problems . . . it wasn't that they were less serious. The opposite: they were *so* serious that it was more like social work. Whereas he was giving her some of the old-line bourgeois Freudian family sexual psychosis, the kind of thing she had studied in college. He flattered himself there. Probably lots of the other patients had life experiences like his, but their damage manifested differently, having been compounded by subsequent violence. In any case, he was not wholly wrong about Amanda.

'Tell me what else,' she said. 'Where are you with things? Have you been talking with . . .' She named his wife and the other woman.

That's when he made the mistake. He told Amanda what the nurse, Julia, had done, how she had approached him on the floor, and reproached him.

'I won't lie,' he said. 'It kind of fucked me up.'

Had he been in his right mind, or closer to it, he might have thought about the impact these words could have on Julia and her livelihood. As it was, the idea that he had the power to affect the destiny of somebody who worked at the Pines never occurred to him. He had thought that it was like complaining about a cop. Nor was he clear on the fact that Amanda ranked significantly above Julia in the hospital hierarchy. It should have been clear but wasn't. He saw, by the kindling of a black fire in her eyes, that he had triggered consequences. It was the only time in their many sessions, one-on-one and group, that he witnessed her losing composure. She had to hold the arms of her chair to keep from . . . he didn't know what. Storming off down the hall to the desk to cause a scene. But she quickly regained control, sharply crossing her legs and breathing through her nose.

'I am *extremely* upset to hear that,' she said.

He felt the old panic. And knew exactly the moment it went back to. She saw it, too.

He stammered. 'I'm sure she was trying to do the right thing. To help me or whatever. But I guess it kind of freaked me out that she had read my file. Or that she would confront me with it?'

Amanda opened her mouth to speak but thought twice and said nothing. He guessed that she had pulled back from addressing the matter of the file. The nurses were not supposed to have access to the therapy notes, and they sure as hell weren't allowed to discuss them with patients. It raised a host of issues, partly legal. Mainly, though, she seemed concerned about the psychological harm it could have done, or had already done, to the man. She felt he was making progress toward a mode of existence not centered on shame.

'I'll have to say something about this,' she said, in a measured tone.

The man sighed, squirmed in his chair, straightened himself, put his hands between his knees. 'Please don't do that,' he said. 'I really don't want anything to happen to her.'

'I'm afraid I don't have a choice.'

'Really? But if I'm asking you –'

'Listen,' she said, leaning forward. 'You don't have to feel bad. You're not making the decision, okay? We have a weekly meeting, all the nurses and doctors and staff, and the whole point is to bring up stuff like this. I can't just . . .'

They both, at the same moment, became aware of the same awkwardness. It consisted in how she was talking to him: not as a patient. She wasn't exactly talking to him as an equal or a colleague, either, but something too close to that. It was clear she felt beholden to explain and apologize. They both felt her authority dim. It was terrible, actually. They both needed her authority. Their dynamic, so precious and hard-won, had been destabilized.

That night the man suffered what Amanda later described in his file as 'a significant setback'.

It was brought on by his doing something stupid, a thing he knew that Amanda, and any sane person, would have cautioned against. He logged on to the Internet. They had a computer on the ward, tucked into a corner of the floor, at a blond-wood desk with high sides, like an old library carrel. Hardly anybody touched the machine. The hospital had it set up – deliberately, one had to assume – so that it functioned only with agonizing slowness. But you could type in your gmail or hotmail or whatever and then sit there for ten minutes while the homepage loaded, and then enter your username and password and hit enter and sit there for another ten minutes while the next page loaded, then click the individual message you wanted to read – five minutes. It was pointless, but it allowed the Pines to say that the patients had access to email.

The man had woken up that night with a migraine so bad it scared him. He thought it might be something else, like an aneurysm. He flung his body out to the desk, muttering apologies to Dwayne Chavis as he cracked the door. The nurses, so accustomed by then to watching him lurch out of his room in the middle of the night to ask for pain pills that they had mentally folded it into the ritual of their shift, did not overreact. They gave him the usual medicine and let him sit in one of the big chairs.

One of the many reasons it was stupid of him to look at the computer was that it strained his eyes, potentially worsening the migraine. But then, this is another facet of cluster-migraine pain: in the midst of one, *any* sensation is preferable, even other pain. People stab themselves, prick themselves with needles, smash themselves with hammers, literally beat their faces against walls.

So he checked his email. He had his right hand on top of his head, and with his thumb and fingers he aggressively massaged his temples. He glanced over at the nurses. They were watching him. Julia was absent. Normally she would have been there. He didn't know if this had anything to do with his earlier conversation with Amanda. Maybe this was just her night off. But something felt off. Their looks seemed less friendly. This disturbed him. What if Julia had been right? What if she were some kind of angelic being, the only person telling him the truth, and now he had engineered her banishment. Without meaning to, sure. But was that even true? He was so full of shit, after all.

The screen loaded. It showed a long list of his unopened emails, with their truncated subject headings alongside off to the right. He read down through, looking for personal messages embedded amid the crap. Because of the migraine, which had begun to fade but only barely, he had to keep glancing away. To the nurses it must have looked as if the screen were physically burning his eyes, as if he were jerking his gaze away like you'd snatch your hand from a scalding tap. He knew he looked insane, in other words. There were a few messages from friends: 'Just checking in, man. Sounds like things are intense on the home front.' Some of his friends weren't speaking to him, but a few were, and had written, and it was meaningful. At the same time he was pretty sure that if they knew more about him and what he had been up to, they would have cut him off, too, and this sense of a fraudulently earned concern made him shrink from allowing himself the solace.

There were two bad messages. The first was from his mother, with whom he had not spoken in about five years. It concerned his uncle Patrick, his father's younger brother. His father had been dead for more than twenty years. The man had assumed, or would have assumed if he had given it any thought, that the brother was dead, too, but it turned out that he was still alive, albeit barely. He had tried to kill himself again. That was what his mother was writing to tell him, that his uncle had attempted suicide for the third time. She did not specify what method he had used, only that he had come near enough to success to put himself into a coma. They expected that he would be pulled off of life support soon, but that hadn't happened yet. She just wanted the man to know, in case he 'felt like praying for his uncle'. He did. He tried. He did it out loud, which was weird, with the nurses watching. That was probably the beginning of the episode. As he prayed, he thought about his lanky uncle, that ghost-like whiskered Irish face, prematurely white hair that ran in the family. He replayed for the thousandth time the most vividly remembered and disturbing of his childhood visits to see the uncle, who lived in Portland. His father dropped him off at the apartment and drove into the city for some interview. He was probably eleven? Uncle Patrick sat cross-legged on the floor in front of the boy, who was on the couch, and rolled up a joint. They sat there in silence as the uncle inhaled several times. The boy had nothing else to look at. The uncle was a person who made a point of having no TV. He worked as a substitute teacher. He said it suited him. He would let them know when he was available to work, and the rest of the time . . .

'Ask me a question,' the uncle said, when he was nice and baked. 'Any question.'

The boy thought for a few seconds. There wasn't anything he wanted to know from the uncle. 'What happens to you after you die?' he said.

'What happens to you?'

'Yeah, do you go on being your same self? Is there, like, a heaven, or . . .'

'In Buddhism,' the uncle said, 'there's a term, *Mu*. Have you heard of that?'

'Like *moot*? I've heard of moot.'

'No, this is *Mu*. Basically it means that the seriousness of the question is not equal to the seriousness of the answer.'

'Oh,' the boy said.

'Your question is *Mu*.'

The boy's face reddened.

'Your question is also *moot*,' the uncle said, and laughed so hard he fell sideways.

Now the uncle was almost gone. They let him finish dying four days later.

What most troubled the man about the suicide attempt, however, was not the sad childhood memories it conjured but a different story involving his father and uncle, one that his father had told him shortly before he died. It had to do with the uncle's first psychotic break, which had happened when he was about twenty, sometime in the late sixties. The man's father had received a call that his little brother needed to be committed. His father had raced over to find him in the midst of a full-on raving episode. He was ranting about their father, who had died fairly young, in his fifties. Once, when the uncle was a boy, his leg had been badly broken in a football game, and after the bone was set at the hospital, the grandfather, whom they all worshipped, had carried him out in his arms. This was one of the uncle's most powerful childhood memories, waking up and looking into his own father's face as they had moved down the hallway, through the doors and into the light. Now the uncle, in his madness, had become convinced that because his own father was dead, there would be no way for him ever to leave the hospital. This time he would be trapped there forever. The man's father had been forced to knock him unconscious.

This memory sent the man's mind plunging. And it seemed impossible that the timing of it all could be a coincidence: Here he was, in the hospital, in the psych ward, and his uncle, who had killed himself, almost, was also in the hospital? His uncle was trying to send him a message, to warn him that he would never get out.

The other message was from the woman. He had spotted it instantly, when the list was loading, and froze. Told himself not to click on it. Now he clicked, and waited. A picture started to load. He looked back at the nurses. They were busy at tasks, or telling each other about their kids. He closed his eyes and tried to breathe well. Opened them again.

Her new film was having a premiere at a festival in London, and she wanted him to see the posters for it. She had worked with the organizers to create a limited series of hand-painted posters. They hung in the window of a theater, or maybe it was a restaurant.

There were words on the poster.

The words were words he had written to her. A moony sentence about what survives in the dark. She had turned it into some kind of advertisement.

The man remembered little of what followed, except that he was shouting. Or they were telling someone not to shout. The others had come out onto the floor. He had woken them. Dusty, Shasta, Dwayne, and Gloria, all just stood and stared. Shasta had her hand on her mouth. Was she laughing? A male nurse he had never seen before was approaching with one hand forward.

They drugged him, and he slept without a migraine for the first time in many weeks, and dreamed hard, and in his dreams he re-entered the maze.

One section, a corridor that he hadn't gone down in forever, was lit with fluorescent bulbs that sounded like they had flies buzzing in them. It was the name of a third-grade teacher's assistant, Miss Arlington, a tall and graceful young woman, just out of college, with brown hair that she wore in a bun every day. She was 'doing her training' in his class and must have noticed something, because she put in a request with the principal that she be allowed to visit the boy's home. She had shown up at the door one day on a rainy spring afternoon. She and his mother stood talking in the entryway, and the boy was sent to his room, but he had lingered in the hallway, trying to listen. Miss Arlington was not invited any further into the house – very irregular, socially – and his mother never mentioned the visit or what had been discussed. Nor did the boy ever say anything. He could have asked Miss Arlington, when he saw her at school the following day, 'Why did you come to my house?'

He woke in the room where he had spent that first night, with the horrible fat man. They had transferred him back to the acute wing. His wife was there.

He had woken up in hospital rooms to find her with him before, and she had always been holding his hand, or resting hers on his leg. This time, she had placed her chair a few feet away from his bed. He had lost her. ■

Frederick Seidel

Mussolini in Milan

Here comes our Leader.
He flies in from the sun.
He flies in on Air Force One.
The people of the planet Earth look up gobsmacked.
He gets into the bulletproof limousine.
Its nickname is The Beast.
He wants to know who loves him the most.

I loved almost too much
The Grand Hotel et de Milan,
Which everyone called the 'Millin',
As I have written in another poem,
And lived there probably for months.
Verdi died there – one night I slept in his room –
A big honor the management paid me.

I'm a Missouri Harvard hillbilly and right-wing and really
I'm both Giorgia Meloni and Giorgio Morandi!
I'm the crafty first female prime minister of Italy.
I'm the great Italian artist of silence and simplicity.
I'm Mussolini and his mistress, Clara Petacci,
Executed by partisans who hung the bullet-riddled corpses
Upside down from a metal girder above a gas station.

In Paris, London and Milan,
I lived a life then that was different than.
I was a flashbulb. I popped light.
I was young, I was a junior man,
Sometimes sounding off but suave.
And I was doubly debonaire, but I was also red and rare,
When a pretty motorcycle or girl was near my raving stare.

How to balance work and play
Is don't.
Your life is going away
And can't.
History and mystery and St. Louis, Missouri,
Is what you hear while listening to the mirror.
You roll-and-rock and listen to Bach.

Sing, sorrow!
Today is already tomorrow.
When things will be worse.
We're cursed.
Which can't be reversed.
Can't cope. No hope. We can hope.
Nope.

I opened up the girlie magazine
Sealed in cellophane
I'd bought the night before in the Galleria –
After Verdi at La Scala –
Pages of big breasts I brought up to my room
In the Grand Hotel et de Milan
(Called by everyone the 'Millin').

Porn morning,
And it's early, but too late, but
Too late to masturbate, but God is great,
Even in the little wartime town square
Just outside Milan, on the edge of town,
With Il Duce and Claretta hanging
Naked upside down.

Thus Ben and la Clara a Milano.
The Beast lies down
At the feet of Air Force One.
The heavy door is opened.
Blue suit, white shirt, red tie
Stops at the top to board and waves goodbye.
Goodbye.

The Death of My Dog

Mark Peploe and Jill Fox
Are the great deaths of my life.
My dog Jimmy died.
When Jimmy died I cried.
There was a man.
He had a wife.
They had a happy life. I have a happy life.

A man has spent his happy life
Shooting an apple off the top of the head of his lovely wife
But every time missing,
Even using a shotgun,
A beautiful bespoke Purdey Over-and-Under
Whose designer shotgun shells spread their birdshot bullshit.
Maybe the guy isn't aiming, the wife thinks, yeah, maybe not.

That reminds her of the Beach Boys song
He was singing in her dream as they canoed along.
He was in the stern in the dream as they canoed along.
Then he put down his paddle rather noisily and lifted his arms
In imitation of aiming a gun at the back of her head.
Bang Bang. You're dead.
I'm kidding, he said. It's just a poem. You're dreaming.

Nothing is more beautiful than
A woman straddling the corner of her desk,
Her feet on the floor, her skirt above her hips,
Riding the corner for the intense pleasure it brings
While the man is watching.
He shows her the riding crop
And seeing it, she's beside herself, and both burst into song.

There comes over him at these moments
In the Book of Miracles
A vision of the shoreline:
St. Louis, Paris, London, Milan, Brian Wilson –
Singing to him in the mist – and Leonard Bernstein –
Which lifts the shotgun to his shoulder for one last shot.
Despite his arthritis, he'll shoot until he's not.

Nothing is more beautiful except
The Earth seen from outer space perhaps and
The Sahara in Algeria.
The Algerian Sahara
Is the gorgeous Chippendale highboy that holds your clothes
And the dunes of the Sahara
Know which drawers hold what.

Hinky Dinky Parlez-Vous

Every memorial service for someone
Dead you loved is
Déjà vu all over again
In the immortal words of Yogi Berra
Who is of course dead.
We wrote a few movies together, Mark and I,
And one that he also directed, called *Afraid of the Dark*.

'Dark' is capable of any number of meanings
For the ten-year-old son of a London police officer
Whose childhood bedroom looks out on a local graveyard –
Who imagines his mother is going blind
And imagines she is being pursued
Because he has to be fitted with new eyeglasses
Because he is going blind.

But we are talking about the fears
Of a child named Lucas who is losing his eyesight,
And is losing his mind,
And stabs his beloved dog to death in his mind.
The mother is played by the beautiful French actress
Fanny Ardant, Truffaut's longtime girlfriend.
Hinky Dinky Parlez-Vous

The screensaver on my computer
Is a view from above looking down
At a jungle,
Green running thickly to a beach
And blue ocean warm as a bath
Without waves and blue without foam
In Goa or Kerala. *Tra lala lala*

I am holding my mother's hand
Crossing a cobbled downtown street on the way to the levee
And her club where we'll be having lunch
And jeweled ladies will run their fingers through my curls.
I'm dressed in a fancy white little boy's
Eton collar shirt
And dress-up gray flannel shorts.

Thirty years later I am in London – sixty years ago –
Living it up with my friend for life Mark Peploe.
Today in New York is Thursday, January 26, 2026.
In London today is a memorial
Service for Peploe.
Rest in peace. *Marco!*
Live it up. *Polo!*

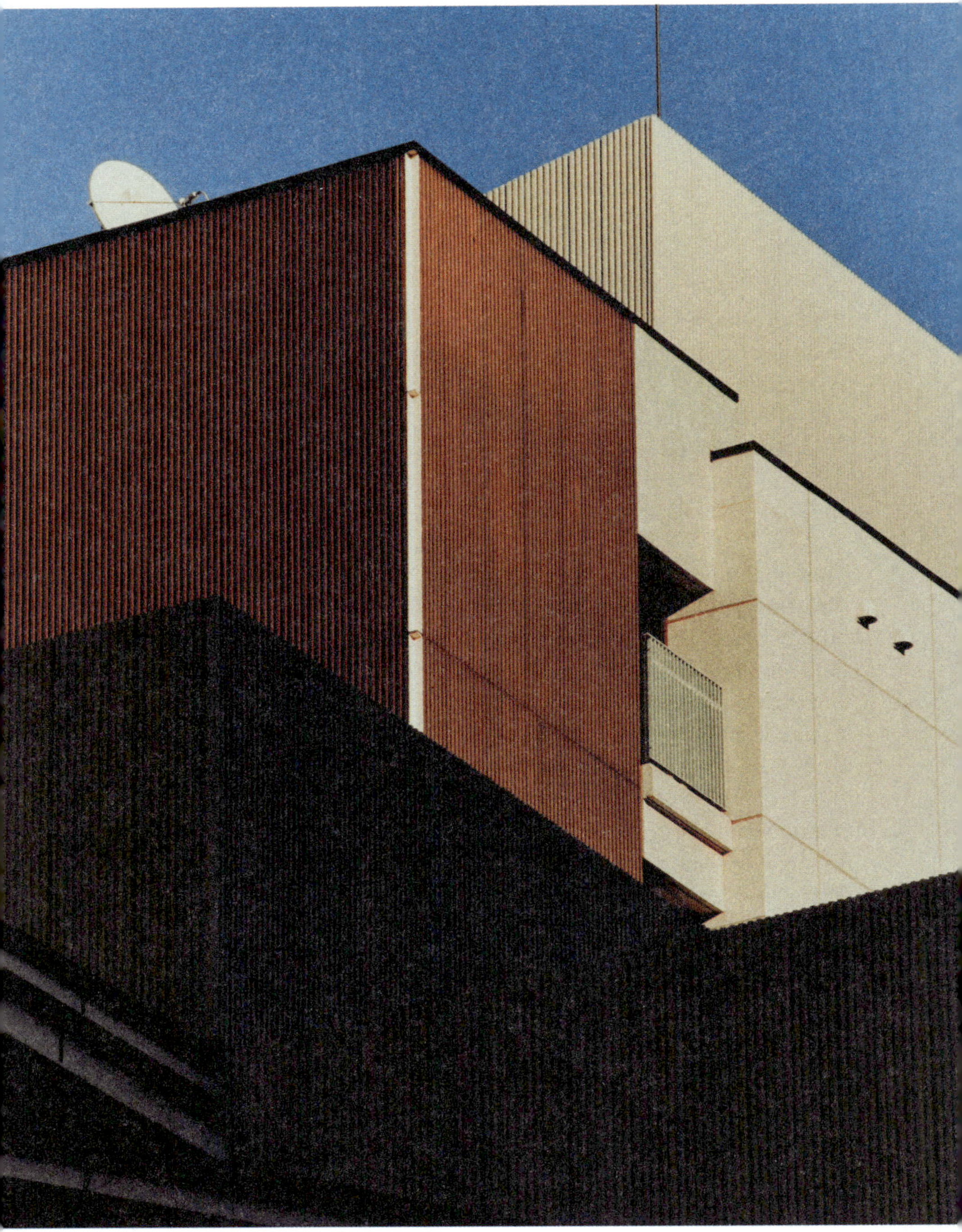

JACK DAVISON
Untitled, 2025

GOLD CAN STAY

Rebecca Curtis

1. Ordinary Day

The air was lemony and dry in Jersey-Ocean Zone 5 that day, and the temperature was eighty-nine degrees. The sky was celadon. A few wisps floated past the sun. August 7, 2066: an ordinary Saturday. *Hawk News* reported that east-coast outzoner activity was mild – a handful of delivery-truck attacks, few successful, and a dozen scrap-rockets, all intercepted, shot into Zones 7 and 13. The *Tick-Tock* did not deliver our paper. Above the green sea and foam-tipped rollers, prop planes flew banners displaying playa bowls, bottled daiquiris, AR15s, and bodyguards. On the bluestone walk beyond our compound, locals strolled through wisteria-scented breezes toward the dunes, Wordle-ing on their minivids, as behind them, refugees pulled loaded carts. Our zone's tower banners were emerald, the perimeter flags were teal, and drone flares were aqua. Everything said: bastion, oasis, calm. By 9 a.m. the beaches were filling with people. One mile north, a pod of finbacks had recently launched themselves onto the shore, they didn't smell bad yet, and when they keened their bodies glinted like sapphires. I had plans: to run along the ocean, seduce my husband, and teach my stepsons – Vladimir, forty-five, and Bone, forty-three – and sons – T-Rex and

Vulcan, both three – to unpack the dishwasher. Also, to write letters to some pals who I hadn't seen in years. The dog days were nearly done. The moon was new. Our zone planned to kill floodlights at ten, so everyone could gather in their yards and watch the Perseids surge. My husband, H-Bomb – a muscular, 62-year-old quantum physicist, who was stressed from his latest hedge-fund-on-hedge-fund-data-theft consulting gig and who doesn't love doing 'family things' – had even agreed to set up his telescope and show our kids Draco the dragon, and the eagle accosting the swan.

That morning, I woke from anxious dreams and decided to investigate my suspicion that our guards were no longer loyal. I headed security at our compound. Over the past week, our guards had seemed oddly smug. I guessed that I was being paranoid. My family lived in a premium green zone. Our north and south flanks were wide, shark-filled rivers. The Atlantic Ocean covered our east side. Our west bank – the only flank against the outside world – was a thirty-three-foot-high wall. Our compound, which was backed against the wall, had two watchtowers and two sentries. I'd been called OCD freak, tight-ass, and necromancer. Because I took herbal supplements and had strange ideas. So I'd investigate sneakily, I decided. Also, I'd be a more supportive spouse. H-Bomb had said recently that I micromanaged him. Actually, he'd been saying that for years, but lately he'd been saying that I micromanaged him and that he'd 'had it'. I'd apologized. I'd promised to improve. But I did feel that my husband was oversensitive to criticism. Also, moody. I'd discover the cause, I'd vowed, and fix the problem by any means necessary, up to and including being the perfect, sexy and obliging wife.

I rose at 6 a.m., just as the mahogany grand-bird clock in our front room struck the common loon. I made coffee, and put on my synthetic foot. I did pull-ups and dead lifts, and checked electric fences along our compound's perimeter. Three were turned off, and one had a bear-sized hole. Made with, it looked like, garden shears. This seemed bad. I wasn't sure whether the guards had made the hole, for some strange – or disturbing – reason, or, just local teenagers, wanting to enjoy midnight frolics in our oversized yard. There were thirteen residential zones on the east coast – some contiguous, some connected by tunnels, some large, others small – but all were crowded, and most yards were one-hundred square feet. Teenagers, I guessed, had to be creative. Every zone was surrounded by stone walls. Supposedly impenetrable. Which was why interior security was lax. I turned on our fences. I told Lou, our maintenance guy, to fix the hole. I checked entrances. Two were unlocked. Someone had been leaving them open. To facilitate grocery-transit, perhaps. Or because someone forgot their keys. But everyone was supposed to have keys with them at all times, and to relock doors upon exit and entry. I felt peeved. I deadbolted the doors. Then I ran three miles along the boardwalk, cased our zone's perimeter, emptied five cases at the shooting range, and arrived home just as H-Bomb was getting T-Rex and Vulcan ready for swim-school. He was shuffling around the kitchen, slowly dropping cookies onto their plates. His long dark hair looked greasy. He hadn't showered much lately. The grand-bird clock struck the House Finch: ten bongs. H-Bomb was running late. On the vidroom couches, T-Rex and Vulcan sucked blue syrup from sippy-swigs and stared at the vidscreen. Their feet waggled. Their hair was snarled, and their cheeks were splotched with fudge. My husband's robe was tied loosely. As he moved, it flapped around his strong calf and his skinny titanium one. He wiped his forehead with his sleeve. He was sad, I knew, because our cat had recently died. Just a long-haired mix I'd found in some outzone woods before I'd met him. She'd seemed happy at first, but then she'd become quiet. For five years, she overgroomed herself, then she grew lumps. For months, H-Bomb made interzone specialists excise masses from her abdomen. But more tumors always grew, and eventually the cat just stumbled around the vidroom, gushing blood. I felt sad about the cat, too. But I wanted our kids to have low A1C levels, I'd disliked watching the beast become demented, and I get nervous when things don't go as planned. So, despite my vow to be a supportive spouse, I critiqued his choice to feed the toddlers fudge cookies for breakfast, and reminded him that processed foods cause diabetes. He promised not to do it again. Then I pointed out that he'd stuffed the toddlers' lunch-bags with high-glycemic syrup-sucks. He shrugged. Then I noted that he'd dressed the kids in stained shorts, and he raged that he couldn't take my constant haggish beatings.

I wasn't perfect, he said. Did I think I was Einstein? What made me think that I knew squat about nutrition? Did I study chemistry in college? Oh wait, he said, I didn't go to college. In fact, he added, I didn't go to middle school! My scientific knowledge, he said, was the level of a five-year-old's. When he met me, he reminded me, I was working at a burlesque bar. I was hairy, dirty, broke, and over the hill, and I'd never entered a zone, used a flush-toilet, or tasted endives. But now, he said, thanks to him, I lived in a palace, and could order any delicacy my heart desired, all because of money he'd provided, by dint of his ceaseless labor, and on top of that, he said, although extremely tired, anxious and depressed, he'd woken at the crack of dawn, today, to take care of our children, so that I could enjoy a jog along the ocean, and furthermore – even though he had a PhD in quantum physics from Aardvark University – he'd prepared their breakfast himself, done the work of a maid, and now, he asked, for dishing up an incorrect meal, he got yelled at? His wine-dark velvet sleeves waved.

Not only was *I* hard on him, he said, but his ex-wife, Ursula, had sicked him with three new court filings at dawn: one to protest Vladimir's choice of graduate schools, one to stop Bone from getting his penis pierced, and another to demand custody of both boys on Halloween. She was determined to eat them, H-Bomb said, and he'd spend his entire life defending them, but constantly speaking with lawyers was aggravating; he could earn hundreds of quadrillions of dollars, he said, manage thousands of underlings at a bank, and dole out trillions in alimony, but he couldn't stop his ex-spouse from harming their sons; she'd hound them across the globe, and no Earthly haven existed. Any more stress, H-Bomb said, and he wasn't sure what he'd do.

I hesitated. I ignored his jabs. Sure, when we met, I'd been dancing and doing security detail at a burlesque bar. But I'd loved my work. And my friends, and the outzone. I'd married H-Bomb because he was hot. I didn't care about flush toilets, or endives. Regarding Ursula, I didn't understand my husband's ex wife, but over time, I'd gathered this: she'd been normal once – or normal enough to appear normal – but now, at sixty-seven, all she wanted to do was punish her enemies. Ursula yearned to torture H-Bomb, and her wrath simply *existed*, like wind. Was it because he'd married her, or because he'd divorced her? Because he'd touched her, or because he hadn't? Because he'd put dishes in the dishwasher badly? No one knew. The court-appointed shrinks had labeled her 'borderline', but I'd decided that she was simply nuts. In the divorce settlement, she'd received a six-bedroom condo in Jersey-Prime Zone 4, two helicopters, and ten quadrillion dollars. Managed carefully, that would have allowed her endless pool-boys, personal trainers, massages and piña coladas; she could have opened a coffee shop, gone back to school, or made art, but all she wanted to do was sue for custody of Vladimir and Bone, send thugs to kidnap them, and harass H-Bomb.

I hugged him. Then I said the phrases that our couples' therapist had taught me: 'That sounds hard', 'I'm sorry you have to deal with that', and 'You are a good father'.

H-Bomb nodded.

He brought the toddlers their backpacks.

I added – on a whim – that he should eliminate Ursula's child support. We had sole custody of my stepsons, basically. The judge *had* ordered them to visit Ursula, but they'd refused. Since they hadn't set a sneaker in her condo for years, H-Bomb was no longer obliged to send Ursula kid-cash. Less cash, I suggested, might mean fewer lawsuits. My husband knelt and put socks on the toddlers. His attorneys advised him to keep paying, he said. Money kept Ursula calm.

I frowned. My brain ached from my last heavy-metal detox-IV. It had been the previous day, but I could still feel my body struggling to expel the lead, cadmium and cesium that the EDTA had released from my kidneys, and deciding to redeposit it all into my head. This felt like a disco party behind my eyebrows. I yelled, Cut her off!

H-Bomb tied the toddlers' shoelaces. Why, he asked, did I believe that I, with no legal training and a third-grade education, knew better than his lawyers?

Lawyers, shmoyers, I said.

If I cut her off, my husband said, searing me with his dark-umber Asiatic eyes, something bad might happen.

When he said that, I felt pain in my missing toes. But I ignored it. I figured: one ex-spouse can't cause *that* much trouble.

Nothing bad will happen! I said.

He said, As you wish.

He took his minivid out. Typed: Hi, J and J. Stop child support, effective immediately. Alert Ursula's counsel. Cheers, Sam.

His face looked tight.

Done, he said. Happy?

I nodded.

He took the toddlers to swim-school.

I walked downtown to the Old Shrew of the Forest Fertility Spa. We'd been trying to have more kids. H-Bomb had sperm, which was great, but the specialists said that my organs contained lead, barium, and radioactive thorium, and that since I was thirty-two, I needed to cleanse every toxin from my body, swallow fifty supplement-pills with each meal, and get five ounces of protein-rich-plasma injected into each ovary. A bummer, but H-Bomb wanted girls.

As I left the spa, PTA Moms were selling cookies in the square, and twenty-somethings were sitting on benches, discussing a pre-cataclysm thing called 'cinema'. I felt worried about the hole that I'd found in our fence. But I vidded our housekeeper, and she said that she'd already walked to the market, selected treats, and marinated short ribs. She said everything was 'fine'. So I headed home. My husband had an important Heartstein Foundation call at

12.30 p.m. with Lucas Balrock, the world's first sextillionaire. Afterwards, H-Bomb's construction partner, Georg, was dropping by to powwow next projects. H-Bomb wanted me to join him and Georg. To be social, he said. My husband was 'retired', but he invested, did charity work and, occasionally, built condos. Every zone needed more housing.

2. The Cataclysm

We had zones, people said, because of August 7, 2037: 'The cataclysm.'

According to liberal newspapers, the cataclysm happened because the US didn't support international efforts to reach an ecologically tenable global accord. They said that America finked on covenants, and colonized poor nations – if not militarily, then through culture and commerce. The *Hampton Sage* said that unchecked Western capitalism had led to hazardous levels of toxic pollution in soil and water, and dangerous levels of CO2 emissions; *that* led to droughts, wildfires, and pestilence, which in turn led to famine and rule by strongmen in many lands. America floated upon a bubble of inequity, the *Malibu Beacon* said, and its technocrats enjoyed wine made from the squashed grapes of global discord. Repelled by squalor, the *Monterey Bell* claimed, America retreated into a protectionist shell. It limited immigration, which had been its lifeline of talent and intellect, slashed scientific research budgets, and let oil barons, tech succubae, and military-industrial-complex crocodiles go undertaxed. It drilled international waters, stole foreign resources, and bombed 'terrorist-affiliated-peoples' at will. Until the day, August 7, 2037, the Leader of Syria came to visit our president, John Dick Lance, to beg him to stop bombing Syria and to lower tariffs. They took tea in the situation room. During the visit, the Syrian Leader petted John Dick Lance's beloved Maine Coon, and the cat bit his hand. It drew blood. John Dick Lance did not apologize. The Syrian Leader said unkind words about the cat. John Dick Lance said unkind words about Syria, such as: stupid shit pond of corrupt lazy low-IQ cretins. The Syrian Leader departed abruptly. That night, BRICKS – Belarus, Russia, Iran, China, North Korea and Syria – hit America with hundreds of nuclear missiles. The next night VAMP – Vietnam, Australia, Myanmar and Pakistan – joined in. The missiles destroyed Washington, D.C., Manhattan, Boston, Chicago, San Francisco, Los Angeles, scores of other cities, many naval yards, and most American military bases. Apparently, artificial intelligence had enabled even broke nations to manufacture weapons that were undetectable by America's missile-deflector systems. Foreign bombers had floated off Nantucket, cloaked in signal-blocking frequencies. The ships had emitted a Chinese-made diffuse diode screen that resembled ocean waves. Thus began the cataclysm.

America nuked Moscow, Damascus, Islamabad and other cities. China blitzed Taiwan. Japan bombed Shanghai, Lebanon blitzed Jerusalem, and, in a paranoia-driven free-for-all, many nations blasted whomever had recently ticked them off. According to conservative news outlets, the catalyst for the spray of 'nocturnal emissions' was not America's isolationism, but its lethargy. Like a feckless giant, *Wolf News* said, America had snoozed for decades. It had assumed that its economic, technological and military dominance would last forever. It had overtaxed its billionaires – whose innovations alone had upheld an otherwise failing economy – until they all moved to New Zealand. To save pennies, it decimated its defense budget. Meanwhile, *Wolf News* said, it spent lavishly on social services, welfare, and hotels for illegal aliens until the interest on its massive national debt toppled it. Like the Eloi, the *Providence Rider* said, fig-brained Americans had frolicked upon hillocks, acting fruity, while in distant lands, dark, squat subterranean Morlocks built weapons.

Some pundits said that President John Dick Lance was a mealy-mouthed psycho. Others, that he should not have had a pussy in the situation room. But *Wolf News* reported that according to knowledgable sources, John Dick Lance's pussy was actually well behaved. They said that, while John Dick Lance was sipping tea, the Syrian Leader had jabbed his puss with a needle to *make* it bite. Foreign missiles had been locked on midnight for months. While John Dick Lance had used the latrine, the Syrian dictator sprinkled cesium-137 all over the situation-room couches, and it was only because John Dick Lance was a nervous pacer that he didn't die. According to *Wolf News*, America's real downfall wasn't Dick Lance's vacillating mores. It was that the United States had believed in the efficacy of world peace groups, American exceptionalism, and the Easter Bunny.

I was only five at the time, but I was taught what happened:

In the chaos that followed the strikes of August 7 and 8, 2037, governments, factories, and power grids shut down. Hospitals closed. Paper money lost value, and hyperinflation tinged the globe. Hordes crossed from one country to the next, seeking safety and food and pillaging, and within six months, two billion migrants crossed into America.

It wasn't the best time to come, but it wasn't the worst. Fallout was deadly within twenty miles of the cities hit by missiles, and poisonous within an elliptical hundred-mile downwind swath. Beyond that, however, land was still good. Travelers arrived from Mexico and Canada, the Pacific and the Atlantic. Ecuadorians, Chinese, Indians, English, Spanish, Afghans, Africans, Indonesians, Brazilians, Poles, Romanians, Turks, Mongolians; Muslims and Hindus, Christians and atheists. They filled cruise ships and sailed over on cargo boats. They landed in passenger jets and in hot-air balloons. Most just wanted to find an empty house and raise families, but many were unscrupulous. The national guard were outnumbered.

John Dick Lance took what he said was the only course available: he fortified protected vales along the seaboards that hadn't been hit by fallout and were still 'mostly American'. He created nineteen zones along the eastern coast and eleven on the west coast, all surrounded by walls, thirty-three feet high and eleven feet thick, modeled after the Aurelian walls of old. Those were meant, Dick Lance explained, to last centuries and to protect Christians from Muslims in the days of the Crusades. The walls had hundred-foot-high guarded towers every thousand feet. He incorporated the government, so that it could more efficiently raise funds, and arranged for the construction of robotic factories, high in the Appalachian Mountains, and in Nevada, Arizona, and Utah. Some grew food or made products, some produced energy, and others mined minerals. All were guarded by drones. Driverless trucks delivered goods from the factories to the enclaves.

President Dick Lance ended term limits, and promised to support all Americans. Fat or thin, tall or short. Most importantly: all blood types. Anyone, he said, who could prove that they'd been an American citizen when the cataclysm occurred, could reside in the zones. Unfortunately, he said, millions of foreigners approached zone entrances with fake birth certificates. Zone officials confiscated these. If they refused to leave, forgers were shot.

Zone laws were strict. But inside them, people had food and medical care. Outside, things were bad. So no one left. That is, not permanently. Day passes cost a few trillion dollars. This was worth it, sometimes, for businessmen who aimed to collect jewelry, antiques or old masters that they knew were stashed in some remote, forgotten warehouse. Others left to slum it, maybe see a show. They brought guards. Most people thought that the land beyond the zones was hell. Perilous. Filthy, toxic, disease-ridden. That was true.

But after a few years, up north at least, things calmed down. Outzone towns had jails and mayors. People 'pitched in' to their mayors, and when needed, they were able to gather a posse. Many people were hungry, and most wild animals were hunted to extinction. Strangers might rob or murder, and some engaged in cannibalism. But towns built fences with barbed wire at their tops. They had watchmen. Farms and farmers' markets. Schools, makeshift theaters. Sometimes electricity. Sometimes travelers brought in newspapers, candy, guns.

The foreigners built their own settlements, or died of exposure or starvation or radiation sickness; or they integrated.

Some villages revived industries they'd had before the cataclysm

– factories, or rare earth mines and processing plants. They didn't have the same safety protections and sanitizing methods in place that they'd once had, and methods were basic. They figured that, due to radiation, they were probably already sick. Boats from Indonesia and China came to collect minerals, and traded rice and pork. Up north, for a while, people felt better off without Washington. Many families had citizenship-documents, but didn't run to the zones. They didn't want to give up their land. They defended it.

That's how things were for thirty years. And people thought, We're fine now, because the worst has already passed.

People from around the world still came to 'America'. But not because America was great. It was just better than everywhere else. My husband remarked that only a few elites knew what had *actually* happened on August 7, 2037 – regulars just knew what they were told. But whatever *had* occurred, he said, was not some episode that entered the atmosphere like a meteor and changed everything – rather, it was a natural series of incidents that sprang from all the ones that had come before them, a predictable result of antecedents. Nothing unexpected had happened, he said.

3. Cat, Mouse

That morning, H-Bomb took calls in his home-office, and watched a ridiculous cartoon about a horny white scientist and his grandson. I know this because at 11 a.m., I entered H-Bomb's office to ask permission to place mousetraps in my stepsons' quarters, and he said, Listen, you overcontrolling, sub-moron, plebeian wench. Don't touch Vladimir or Bone's rooms. You *know* they love mice. Why are you so cruel? Why do you invade my office when I'm paying taxes, earning quadrillions of dollars, and speaking with important people about international problems, and while I'm just *briefly* relaxing by watching *Prometheus and Pando*?

It was because I hate mouse poop. But I didn't answer. Instead, I observed the vidscreen. A pickle with blue eyes lay on a laboratory's floor. From somewhere nearby, machines beeped, and a cat meowed. The pickle accosted a skinny boy. Pando, it said. Check me out. I'm a pickle!

I wondered how a renowned physicist could enjoy a show about a grandpa who leapt through the universe via 'portals'. When I asked, H-Bomb shrugged. The series was relaxing, he said.

At noon, the grand-bird clock bonged upon the red-tailed hawk. H-Bomb had to prep for his call with the neodymium magnate, so I served him lunch: chicken-salad-on-rye, chips and a dill pickle.

4. The Heartstein Falters

Normally, a world-famous sextillionaire neodymium magnate would not bother calling my husband. But H-Bomb was the treasurer of the Heartstein Institute. The Heartstein was a charity created in 1947 by a Jewish Holocaust survivor to fund graduate scholarships for young American® scientists who wanted to devote their careers to national defense. It was the only foundation of its kind. H-Bomb told me that in 1946 Heartstein, scarred and gaunt, had peered far into Earth's future and seen war. Horrible, all-consuming war. Was he just paranoid, I'd asked, from his experience in a concentration camp? No, H-Bomb said. He was smart. A cynic, who yet believed that America® could be a haven for human rights. With his remaining energy he established the Heartstein Institute, and then died. For many decades, the Heartstein had functioned well. Recipients of its scholarships had developed tiny chips that enabled the construction of handheld computers, anti-nuclear missiles, plutonium bombs, patriot missiles, stealth technology, anti-missile missiles, and gallium-alloy weapons. The foundation survived the cataclysm. But recently its board was infiltrated by Belgian sugar-cane heiresses who were awarding all the organization's fellowships to Dutch tweens who aspired to protect Spanish songbirds. Meanwhile, Lucas Balrock said, something foul was rising in the east, and Balrock feared that the foul thing had grown stronger than anyone had guessed. Our government was fiscally irresponsible, Balrock said, and weak. The world needed the Heartstein Institute. Balrock had been calling H-Bomb, sporadically, to pressure him to become chair. H-Bomb was not Jewish. Neither was Balrock. But Heartstein's heirs didn't care. What mattered was national defense. But the position of chair, which was unpaid, required copious time. Balrock was busy, he said, with *his* foundation. He often explained, in op-eds, about the reparations Cheerios boxes he'd sent to families of victims of potassium-cyanide poisoning, and his initiative to send corn-baggies to Eurozoners.

Balrock aspired to end poverty, he'd confessed to H-Bomb. Effective ways to do so existed, he'd said. For example: if you visited England, and gave every skinny wench with starving kids five sacks of kidney beans and squash seeds, and nine goats – the wenches would eat the beans, seeds, and goats, ride their boyfriend's knobs, squeeze out fresh tots, and be hangry again. So that was not the way. This was impolite to say, he said, but true. Teach the French to trawl, he said, and they sauté every fish in the sea. Feed the Slovakians, he said, and their population hops from thirty million to ninety. Earth had a limited capacity to grow food. And – more importantly – limited capacity to process the toxins that billions of people eating food produced. Now, with greater numbers, we needed new energy-creation processes, and more fertilizing and manufacturing machines. One should not speak it, Balrock said, near a gov-cam, but the best way – the *only* way – to end poverty and restock the oceans was to cull the globe's sapien-load by ninety-five percent.

This could be bloodless, he'd pointed out, if all nations would decrease their birth rates. But achieving accord around this solution might be difficult.

He felt lonely, sometimes, he'd said, being one of the few people on Earth who enjoyed calculating the neutron population effects of beryllium compounds, and who understood why fueling solar cells with gallium arsenide was superior to using silicon.

Last month, he told H-Bomb that he'd recently established forty wellness clinics in the Eurozone. He'd staffed each clinic with doctors, nurses, and red-vested guards, and let out that ladies could get free health checks and bread. When patients arrived, their pulses were measured. Then they were handed one Yorkshire pudding, and informed that they could also have five baguettes if they agreed to be injected with a five-year birth-control module. They'd receive thirteen peasant loaves, a block of cheese and a fidget spinner if they got fixed. Pregnant wenches were offered an extra loaf to have an 'accident'. Initially things went well. Most chicks got modules, many got fixed, and loads of pregnant wenches had accidents. But soon delivery boys, mailmen, and meter-maids learned that the clinics were providing child-slaughter and sperm-control.

5. Burn, Baby, Burn

At 12.30 p.m., H-Bomb was on our main porch, reading Toynbee's unabridged *A Study of History*. He had a pile of books on the wicker table. I was also on the porch, being respectful by reading *1984*, a novel that H-Bomb recommended. It was about a mean dictatorship that forbade orgies, and lazewads who complained that the free government candy tasted chalky. The sun was high. The air gold. Beyond our compound, residents strolled toward the beach, talking and looking at their minivids. The fan on the porch ceiling whacked above us.

I didn't want to read. I wanted to quiz our guards, then go into the outzone to scout for anything unusual – though H-Bomb had forbidden me to, and I hadn't gone in months – but I knew that Georg the builder was dropping by.

The vidscreen buzzed.

H-Bomb pressed 'accept', and Balrock's voice boomed, Are you PRIVATE?

H-Bomb looked at me. I was sitting on a wicker chair across from him with a Glock on my lap. I sipped my coffee. H-Bomb placed one finger against his lips.

He said, YES.

I could see Balrock in the mirror behind H-Bomb. He sat behind a huge cherrywood desk. Behind him were gold walls with three tall windows that gazed upon a park filled with thick-trunked elms. Balrock was a pale white guy. Sixty-some. Wrinkly. Small-nosed. His aquamarine eyes glistened. His gray hair swooped boyishly over his forehead. He wore a pink checkered button-down that choked his mauve neck wattle. On the desk sat a young cheetah. Its green eyes stared ahead while it panted. Balrock's right hand scratched the beast's ruff.

Problems, he said.

H-Bomb placed his drink on the white table beside him. Such as?

Balrock sighed.

H-Bomb said, Liberals?

No.

H-Bomb bit his right thumbnail. What then?

Balrock leaned forward. He told H-Bomb to imagine that he was at a party with fantastic food, drinks, music, and hot chicks. However, Balrock said, sometime between midnight and sunrise, gunmen would enter and slay everyone. It was midnight, Balrock said. How long would H-Bomb stay?

H-Bomb said that he'd have a few drinks.

Balrock looked surprised.

H-Bomb said, A little risk is fine. You just can't take *big* risks.

Balrock's right hand flipped, palms upwards.

A solar superflare could devastate our infrastructure, he said. He added, Our yellow dwarf's overdue.

H-Bomb yawned. Is that it?

Balrock's head shook. Gravity on Earth is light, he said, so things seem to move slowly, but time doesn't exist. Also, sometimes it speeds up, but no one notices.

Obviously, H-Bomb said.

He gestured at the porch table. I'm reading a book, he said, about recent developments in time dilation under extreme gravitational fields.

Balrock checked his watch. Mobs destroyed my last clinics today. King's Road and the Strand. He paused. They flayed my guards.

Yikes, H-Bomb said.

They burned my doctors alive.

Urgh, H-Bomb said. He added that the world had plenty of doctors.

I sneezed.

Balrock asked if someone else was on the porch. H-Bomb turned the vidscreen so that Balrock could see me. I waved. Balrock frowned, but H-Bomb explained that I wouldn't be able to repeat their conversation. She's dumb, he whispered. She doesn't know how a transistor works.

Balrock nodded. He said that some of the clinic guards had been his friends.

Lieutenants, H-Bomb agreed.

Balrock's pink nose glistened. His hair drooped with sweat.

He leaned forward, and said that the Heartstein Foundation had to take action. He'd been patient for decades, but – he smiled oddly – nothing lasted forever, he said, and we all knew hearts could change. Eurolazewads, he said, had raved, siesta-d, and begged for American gold for long enough. Now he'd reduce the number of meunière-sauce-licking, half-time-working Euro-peons by adding a tasteless – or perhaps yummy grape-flavored – sterilization compound to their municipal water supplies.

H-Bomb said that Europeans would notice and complain.

Balrock shrugged. We'll say the compound prevents hair loss.

H-Bomb's eyebrows raised. They'll be skeptical. They're not morons.

Balrock lifted his hands, palms up. We'll say that it prevents mange.

H-Bomb's head shook. He said few Europeans *had* mange.

Balrock leaned back, opened a drawer in his desk, took out a half-smoked cigar, and lit it.

We'll say it strengthens teeth!

H-Bomb put his real leg on the ottoman. They'll never believe *that*.

Balrock smoothed the cheetah's ruff. He said that Europeans no longer invented tools or built yurts. They didn't hunt yaks, or bury food in caches for winter. Neither did anyone else. Most people just performed one not-very-hard task over and over, their whole lives, like lab rats, and so their brains went vestigial. Eurozoners, he said, did whatever Euro-yahoos advised. They dumped basil and oregano into their pasta sauce, and mashed fluorosilicic acid into their gums at night. They even drank black and green tea.

Balrock puffed the cigar.

I didn't know you smoked, H-Bomb said.

Balrock exhaled. I don't.

Then what are you doing?

Balrock studied the cigar. This is not a cigar, he said. It's called a Synthgar. It *tastes* like a cigar, and it emits cigar smoke and contains toxic gook that makes your teeth black, but it's not a cigar.

H-Bomb sighed. I did too. H-Bomb's friends were smart, I guessed, but they went on and on. About bond markets, usually.

Anyway, Balrock said. He had news. He'd spoken with Leader Yu of China, and Yu had declared, after breakfast today, that –

6. A Shore Thing

A tall man with broad shoulders and curly red hair strolled up the path, carrying a canvas bag with the words SHORE BUILDERS, A SHORE THING! etched in gold letters on its side. He paused at the electric fence-gate, raised his hand, and saw that H-Bomb was vidding.

Bad time? Shall I come back later?

H-Bomb touched a remote-control, and the gate opened.

On the vidscreen, Balrock frowned. H-Bomb explained that he and Georg, a builder, had constructed an apartment building in Devil's Fork Beach, and that they were meeting to powwow 'next projects'.

Balrock snorted. His news was top-secret, he said.

Hallllloooh! Georg stepped toward the vidscreen. He said that he was incredibly honored to meet Balrock. He was a huge fan of Clean Chip© computers! His company had three! Also, he said, he'd just literally yesterday installed Envirogreen Solar Panels in twelve condominium units! He paused. He'd also recently bought, he said, his nine oldest children their first zero-gravity-super-bounce sneakers, and his kids were – ha ha – over the moon.

Balrock adjusted his pink collar.

H-Bomb made a face that said – Normies, everywhere, nothing you can do, it's fine!

Georg reached into his satchel. He withdrew a red-ribbon-wrapped box, and held it toward H-Bomb. He said, For your family!

H-Bomb thanked him, and pointed toward the table. Georg settled into a wicker chair. H-Bomb asked whether anyone would like a chocolate? as the Polish maid brought more sazeracs.

7. Another Kettle of Fish

As he'd been saying, Balrock said – he looked away from Georg, and coughed. He cleared his throat. He said that Leader Yu of China had confided that his techs had made a virus called 'Forever Yung', which would kill everyone on Earth except Yu's two million closest friends, because he was tired of pollution causing high mercury levels in Dover sole.

I stood and cased the front yard. I was wondering how long they'd yabber. Because I wanted to scout the zone perimeter. I hadn't guessed that world-famous neodymium magnates cared about pollution. I wished my husband and his money-hungry architect friend and his crazy-sextillionaire-tech-titan friend would say cheers and goodbye. Even as I peered into the azalea bushes, checking for spies, grenades, bombs and recorders, I heard Balrock's wheezy voice saying that in 2001 the Environmental Protection Agency had declared that fish should never be eaten by pregnant people, anyone 'sensitive' to methylmercury, or children. Or, he added, in a higher voice, by anyone with neurons in their noggin! He stared at H-Bomb. He put his wrinkled hands on his hips. Fish was too poisonous for humans to eat in 2001, he said. Didn't H-Bomb guess that the release of two thousand TONS of mercury vapor into water, soil and air, *per year*, by the coal- and artisanal gold-mining industries, over the past FIFTY years had increased the mercury levels in the ocean *since* then? Hadn't H-Bomb ever wondered why the 'mercury protection agencies' had not updated their recommendations? Or why, in 2017, the EPA had declared, Hey guys, takes-backsies, everyone should chomp *more* fish? He picked up a purple ink-gel pen from his desk and waved it. Did H-Bomb TRULY believe, that before 2017, the EPA didn't *know* that fish contained iodine?

Georg, who was watching Balrock, appeared confused. Iodine was in salt, he said, right? H-Bomb shushed him.

Had H-Bomb never calculated, Balrock asked, how many thousands of tons of mercury vapor were pumped globally, annually, into the Earth's atmosphere? Did he imagine that the tons of mercury hovered eternally and ineluctably beside a pink cumulus cloud? Where *did* he think all the mercury went? To Candy Mountain? H-Bomb wasn't a child. Did he *really* trust the seafood-association's measurement of the mercury-contents of tuna? Did he BELIEVE a coal-mining magnate's estimate of the mercury content of seafood? Who did he guess ran the EPA, CDC, IDSA, FDA and the ADA? Papa Smurf, Tinkerbell and the tooth fairy?

Dark pink moist patches stained the pits of Balrock's cotton shirt. Cherry-colored spots glowed in his cheeks.

Georg opened the red-ribboned box, removed a milk chocolate, and ate it. While he chewed, he watched H-Bomb's face.

Did H-Bomb not understand, Balrock said, that once swallowed, the methylmercury from fish sallied across the human blood-brain-barrier, solidified inside the pituitary gland, and decimated serotonin and dopamine production, so that most jerks who were regularly exposed, became – in time – listless, nervous, ambitionless, and sad?

Sometimes suicidal? Why did he think that half the world needed to gulp happy-capsules, and the other half needed fake-thyroid-hormone? Didn't he know that mercury slipped inside every cell of the human body and hijacked its mitochondrial energy-production capacities, such that many bimbos felt sluggish now, and most were fat? Why did he think so many dullards were diabetic and hypertensive? For how long, he asked, had H-Bomb eaten fish? Did he ever call his ugly kid by his cute kid's name? Did he ever call his cute kid by his dumb kid's name, or his wife by his girlfriend's? Did he ever misplace his keys? His eyeglasses? His minivid? Did he sometimes forget what he'd gobbled for breakfast? Didn't he feel run-down, tired, anxious, and depressed?

H-Bomb bit his thumbnail. I saw that it was bleeding.

Yes, he said. I'm very anxious. Also I'm very depressed. But that's not because of mercury in fish! That's because – he glanced at me – in my own house, by my own spouse, I get criticized, every day! He added that, moreover, his ex-wife kept hiring thugs to attack his kids.

On the vidscreen, Balrock sighed.

Georg studied a cherry-filled chocolate. He said that he got criticized by his wife, too.

Balrock paced thoughtfully around his circular red office. As he paced, he knocked, sporadically, on a red octagonal cupboard. Each time he knocked, something inside scrambled, and nails clacked wood. After ten laps, Balrock stopped by the large window. He peered at the elms in the green park.

He remarked that he'd vidded H-Bomb because he'd believed that he was sane. More importantly, that he was alive. Was everyone on Earth, he asked, dead? Was every day victory of the pod people? Where was the horn that was blowing? Who was *not* a moron? Who was not *afraid*? Who would join him, now, at the turn of the tide? He felt lonely, he said. Was he, Balrock, an army of one? The only sane man on the sandbar? The only lucid bloke on the ledge?

Georg typed something into his minivid and smiled.

H-Bomb sipped his drink. How did Balrock know that *he* was

sane? he asked. Or that he wasn't just a computer program? By the way, he added, did Balrock have any details about the virus?

Balrock's reptilian eyes peered at me.

His reedy voice said, Do *you* eat fish?

8. The American Clean Slate

Beyond our yard, on the slate walk, I watched tall, pot-bellied men with boogie boards tucked under their arms stride, nearly running, alongside panting children, toward main street. I cocked my gun. I recalled how, that morning, the guards had seemed glib. 'All's normal,' one had said, 'so enjoy your lovely day!' My danger-sensor jolted inside me as I watched tall men pull their meaty kids. I realized that something bad was happening. Why were they leaving the beach? What was happening on the beach? Something more immediate than Balrock's blather.

I said, No, I did not eat seafood. But only because it tasted disgusting.

Balrock sat down at his desk. I too hate fish, he said. But I want them to swim in the ocean.

H-Bomb leaned back and crossed his robed arms over his chest. His handsome face sagged. I winced. Soon he'd be frank and mean.

Time's up, Balrock said. H-Bomb must chair Heartstein NOW, he said. He must expel the debutantes from the board. They never donated to the foundation. They hosted zero galas. Garnered zero endowments. Yet they attended foundation-event dinners, ate the beef cheeks and Bananas Foster, spewed platitudes, and spent Heartstein's cash. H-Bomb could easily slay those dimwits. And as chair, Balrock said, H-Bomb must award scholarships to biochemistry kids who'd swear to create microbe American® Clean Slate.

H-Bomb bit a fingernail. He said the name sounded like detergent. He was busy, he said, with custody battles. Also, his sons, Bone and Vladimir, were each applying to schools, which required him to write many essays – Look, he said, he was swamped now, but in five years

Vladimir would be fifty, legally too old for his mother to interfere with his residency, then –

LATE is the HOUR. Balrock's eyes bulged. All non-morons, he said, were aware that the brightest Shanghainese biochemists had labored – for decades – to craft a fatal bug that would infect only Caucasians, Africans, and Latinos. In bunkered labs, he said, they'd fractured and tweaked the bubonic plague, leprosy, the Coronas, and more. But genomic distinctions between races were subtle, and the best they'd achieved was a virus that killed non-Asians within hours and Asians within weeks. Forever Yung would turn the insides of every sapien who hadn't received the Mandarin vaccine into mustard-colored slime within days of release. Now Leader Yu was a decent guy, Balrock said. A joke-teller. A mensch. He valued harmony, intellectual-property-sharing, profit-sharing, and peace, and he believed that all the world's citizens were equally equal. He even liked kids! However, he'd discovered, years ago, that many sixth-world nations were developing plagues.

Furthermore, Balrock said, Yu had learned that other leaders, and the plague-makers, had all discovered that roguer factions were also developing pathogens. Dominoes have been set in motion, Balrock said, and any rockhead could see the end-tile. Someone would release a virus – soon – and ninety-nine percent of all people alive, he said, would die. This was serious, he said. As a gift, Balrock added, Yu had offered to send Balrock fifty vials of the Forever Yung vaccine. He'd estimated they'd be ready in five months. Balrock guessed that meant three.

H-Bomb must chair Heartstein, Balrock concluded. He sat down. He'd be frank, he said quietly. The Chinese were math demons. They were merciless, soulless, and relentless. They'd calculated exactly what they needed to do to protect themselves, and they were doing it. America needed its own Operation Refresh, for deterrence. And the push had to come from Heartstein. With H-Bomb as chair. Because there were no other effective foundations, and no other candidates with keen vision.

H-Bomb's foot drummed the ottoman. His tear-shaped dark eyes glimmered. He seldom accepted claims at face value. I doubted that he believed Balrock. About most of it. Thallium-loaded kale, mercury-laced sea bass, crazy Asian chemists.

How well did H-Bomb know Balrock? I asked. And did H-Bomb think that he was exaggerating? Not about the toxin stuff, which was clearly woo-woo – about the Chinese virus.

H-Bomb sipped his drink. He knew Balrock only slightly, he said. However, he said, China certainly possessed bioweapons. Most nations did.

I asked whether Balrock's insider-juice about the Forever Yung virus was why H-Bomb cared so much about Balrock.

I was mistaken, he said, if I thought that he cared much about Balrock.

A coolish breeze blew in from the ocean. Salt, smoke. Hot dogs, curry? Saffron?

I felt frustrated. I said, The moral is?

My husband smiled.

I said, Is it, Buy low, sell high? That was usually his moral. But he didn't respond. What then? I asked. Is it, Hope for the best, but expect the worst? Eat the Toad in the morning? I paused. I recalled his fears about global societal decay. I said, Is the moral, The frogs feel pleasantly warm, but the water's getting hot? He sipped his drink and stared past me. I said, A house is not an asset? He stared at the purple leaves of the Japanese maple flipping in the breeze. I said, Is it, Everybody lies? Or, Gold is at an all-time high, AGAIN, so don't buy gold now, as many strumpets are?

H-Bomb took a cigarette. He lit it. He said he could not explain what he didn't yet understand himself. Expect the worst, he said, might apply; but his thoughts ran more toward: prepare for the worst. Always anticipate potential complications, and for each, always devise a plan B.

I said, Okay?

He shrugged. Said that Balrock would call back. When he did, we'd know more. He waved an arm expansively and said that every country in the world was a piece of poop, and that every country was gradually getting worse. One day soon, he said – perhaps very soon – things would fall apart. I watched him smoke. He smoked only when disturbed.

I asked whether he thought that China's leader was about to release a virus that would eliminate mankind.

He shrugged. First of all, he said, Yu's virus would not eliminate mankind; merely unvaccinated humans. Secondly, he said, this sort of thing, he said – the panoramic release of a hemorrhagic fever – sometimes threatened to happen, but never had yet. The sky, he said, was not a neighborhood. Generally, these gestures were sound and fury. Much ado about nothing. Of course, he added, events not yet happening hardly meant that they never would. We will all die, by the way, he added. And, shortly, humans will cease to exist. That might not happen today, but it will happen. Because the only truly certain thing is death.

I said, Good thing I married an optimist.

I excused myself and rounded the compound. The air smelled like beef-on-a-stick in some spots, but in others, like spareribs. That was odd. Usually, the afternoon air smelled like azaleas. But the guards were all in their towers, they all had binoculars nearby and were seated near windows, and when questioned, they said that everything was 'normal'. They said, 'Yup, all's normal,' and, 'Better get that run along the ocean,' and, 'It's a beautiful day to be alive.' ■

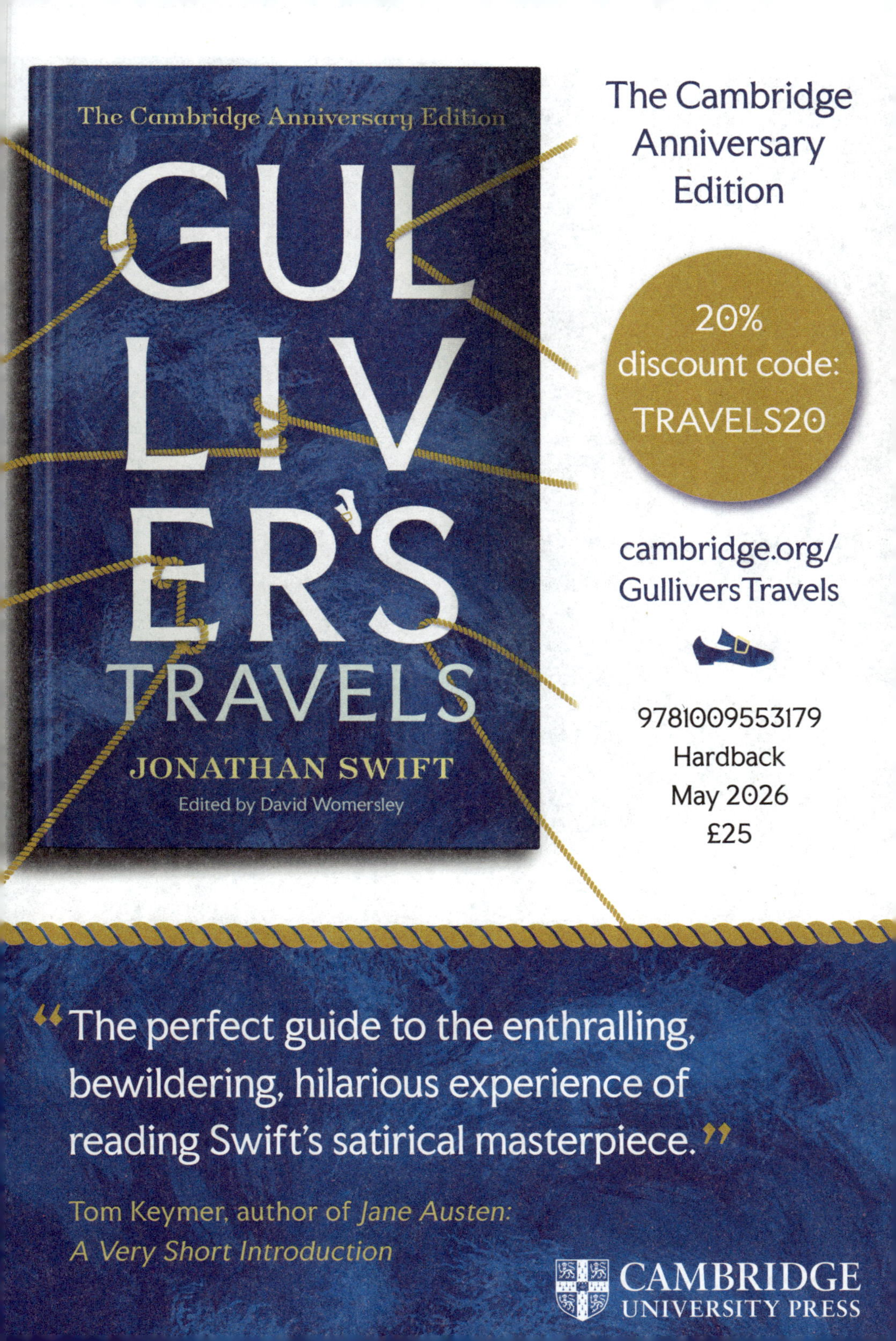
The Cambridge Anniversary Edition
GULLIVER'S TRAVELS
JONATHAN SWIFT
Edited by David Womersley
The Cambridge Anniversary Edition
20% discount code: TRAVELS20
cambridge.org/GulliversTravels
9781009553179
Hardback
May 2026
£25
"The perfect guide to the enthralling, bewildering, hilarious experience of reading Swift's satirical masterpiece."
Tom Keymer, author of Jane Austen: A Very Short Introduction
CAMBRIDGE UNIVERSITY PRESS

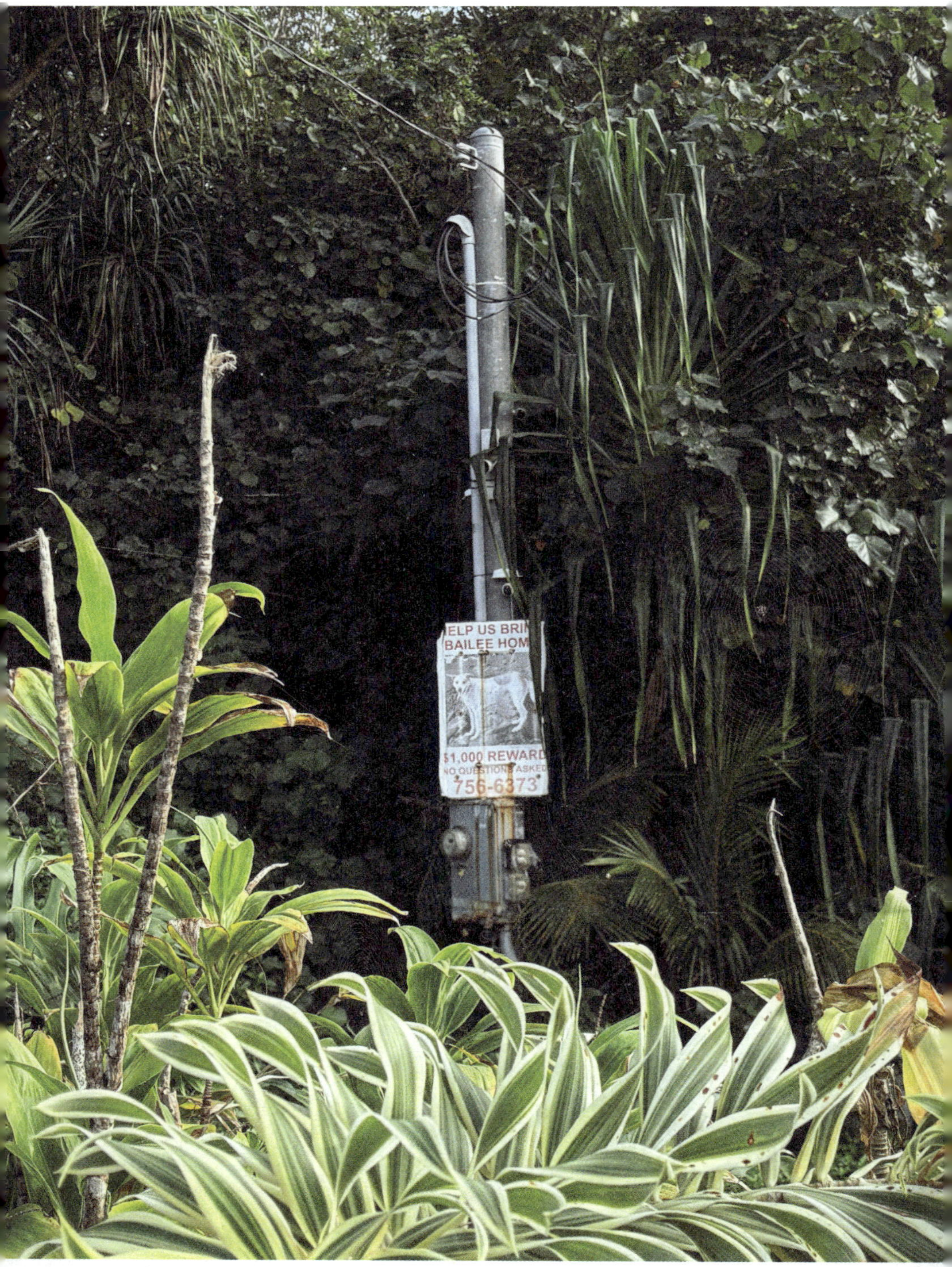

Courtesy of author

HAWAIIAN FAUNA

Tao Lin

TRIGGERFISH

In January 2020, I was house-sitting in Honolulu, on the island of Oahu. My then-girlfriend visited from New York. Walking on a beach, we saw a leathery dead fish.

'It's the state fish,' said a passerby.

'Really?' I said. It looked sewn together from dissimilar parts.

'*Humuhumu*,' he said. '*Humuhumunukunukuāpua'a*.' He continued in the opposite direction.

'I thought he was mocking us,' I said. *Humuhumu* means 'to stitch together', I later learned. The rest of the name means 'snout of a pig'.

ME

After house-sitting for three weeks, I moved to the sparsely populated West Side of the island. I'd decided to stay on Oahu for a while before returning to New York.

On an empty beach, I read an anthology of ancient Chinese poetry and teared at this line: 'The love that is not deep is quickly broken.'

My relationship had lasted more than twice as long as my second-longest relationship. But I had a nagging intuition that I should be alone.

I moved back to Honolulu. Each day, I worked on my fourth novel, tweaking its sentences, then biked to a grocery store or a park.

At night, I researched Earth's shifting magnetic poles. Some people argued that the planet would reorient in the 2040s, placing the ice caps at the equator, resetting civilization.

BAILEE

On the Big Island in 2021, my girlfriend and I saw flyers for a medium-large dog who'd gone missing on Christmas Day, a few days before our arrival. By February, the flyers had grown into signs the size of stick-mounted placards at political rallies. Other 'lost pet' notices – printed on computer paper, stapled to poles – soon vanished. Bailee signs kept appearing.

By the end of 2021, she was probably the most famous life form on this side of the island. Was she an art project or social experiment? No, I decided. She was real. I felt impressed by the power of love, broadcasting a message as ubiquitously, I imagined, as any political or corporate campaign ever done in the area.

In January 2022, our cat Leo went missing. We searched for him twice a day. I went out alone after waking; the second search included my girlfriend, who worked as a book editor from 4 a.m. to past noon. We taped our flyers ($200 reward) to orange cardboard, making them larger than other missing-pet notices except for Bailee's.

We found Leo in May, but he left again in February 2023, by which time I was single. Letting go was easier alone; I had two other cats to care for. Leo would be fine, I thought. Born in the wild, he ate lizards and rodents. Bailee had probably eaten dry dog food her whole life. By then, I'd stopped seeing her signs, though my range of travel had shrunk since the relationship ended.

In 2025, driving by the coast with my parents, I saw one of the signs on an electricity pole, faded but legible. After my parents returned to Taiwan, I searched 'Bailee' in the Facebook group 'Big Island Lost, Missing, And Found Pets'. Her owners, Claudia and

John, had posted twenty-three times. Some excerpts:

> January 15. We get up early in the morning and look for a few hours and then again in the evening. We make and update flyers which we post within and outside our neighborhood because she could be anywhere by now.
>
> January 22. We feel as if suspended in time, our only focus is to find our girl. If someone has her, please call us, no questions asked, we just want her back.
>
> February 5. Bailee is still missing, and it still seems unreal. She is family to us, and we will search for her forever if we have to.
>
> February 18. Our search now includes going door to door in nearby neighborhoods, and hiking the woods.

Some posts included updated flyers or signs. By February 18, the message had been distilled to a near-haiku in red font: HELP US BRING BAILEE HOME / $1,000 REWARD / NO QUESTIONS ASKED.

> March 7. We are not sure what day she was born so we always celebrate the entire month. Before she went missing, we never thought or imagined what not knowing what might have happened to her would feel like.
>
> April 29. Last week I received a call from a very nice officer. He informed me that his department was receiving calls and emails from someone saying that our signs are a hoax and unfortunately he had to follow up.
>
> June 25. Sometimes this sad journey has turned towards crazy, our signs in Hilo and Kurtistown continue to be

> damaged or taken down faster than we can repair and replace.
>
> July 5. Our Bailee remains missing, and the sadness of our journey is unbearable, debilitating, and paralyzing at times.
>
> August 14. Based on some comments we received on a picture we posted recently, we decided to change our signs and expand our search.

There were no posts in September and October. The sole November post included a new sign. HELP US BRING BAILEE HOME was now HELP BRING *BAILEE* HOME . . .

The last post, on Christmas, began:

> Today marks one year since Bailee went missing 💔 To say we are sad, is not enough to describe our feelings. We feel broken, certainly we are not the same people we were last year before this dreadful event. What we want the most is to bring our girl home. Today we went around replacing our signs and posting new ones. We also got a banner and set up almost at the corner of 130 and the Pāhoa school.

The banner, attached to the side of a truck, showed a life-size photo of Bailee in a relaxed Sphinx pose, tongue out. The ellipsis was gone. More words were italicized: *HELP BRING BAILEE HOME*.

I felt sad that they'd stopped posting after one year, even as I wondered if they'd searched too hard, deepening their grief. But what affected me most were the little edits to the signs, honing the simple message.

Bailee had been gone for more than four years. I posted on the Facebook group, asking if anyone knew what happened to her.

Claudia commented the next day:

> Unfortunately we have not found Bailee. It breaks my heart. We still look for her everywhere we go, as long as there's a slim chance of finding her, we will never stop searching. Thank you for thinking about our beautiful gurl.

In another comment, someone had written 'someone is asking about Bailee', tagging Claudia. She'd replied, 'It gives us hope that after all this time people still remember her. It makes my eyes water.'

JOTA

A month later, in May, driving out of the mail store's parking lot in Keaau at 5.50 p.m., I noticed a small old Caucasian man watching me.

'You're going that way?' he said, pointing south.

'Yeah,' I said.

He asked if I could take him home. He'd missed the bus. He had groceries. He lived in Seaview.

'That's far,' I said. My ex and I had hitchhiked a few times during our carless first six months on the island, but I'd never picked up a hitchhiker.

'Where do you live?' he said.

'HPP,' I said.

He asked if I could take him to Pāhoa; if I dropped him off there, someone would take him home. Pāhoa was beyond my neighborhood. He said the next bus wouldn't get him home until eleven.

'Where are your groceries?' I said.

'Over there,' he said, pointing to the bus stop.

'Okay – I'll give you a ride,' I said.

'Thank you!' He got his groceries and put them in the backseat. Momentarily thinking he was going to sit there, I remembered my brother giving teenage-me a ride to the bookstore; I'd sat in back and he'd said, 'I'm not your chauffeur.'

The man sat in front. He had a mild natural scent. Turning right, I said I used to take the bus and knew it was reliable.

He said it was six hours late once. He said he worked on a farm. He said he went to Hilo twice a week for Evolution organic juice. It was cheaper there.

'But time is money,' I said. 'And you're spending so much time.' I regretted saying this. I told myself not to speak mindlessly again.

'Time is money,' he said. He asked if I was Chinese. I said Taiwanese. He'd been in the Taipei airport on the way to Bali and Nepal.

He said society would collapse this year. I asked why this year. He referenced something the president had said. He said three families controlled the president.

Monologuing, he moved past the societal to the cosmic: abnormalities in the sun's electromagnetic activity would cause changes on Earth.

I asked if he was talking about 'the pole shift'. He was. He said extraterrestrials told him the purpose of the Great Pyramid is to 'alleviate axial excursion'. He seemed to be referring to the theorized cyclical shift of Earth's axis.

'Did extraterrestrials personally tell you that the purpose of the Great Pyramid is to alleviate axial excursion?' I said.

'They did,' he said. 'In 1975.'

He showed no surprise or recognition that I seemed to be knowledgeable about the pole shift. I considered mentioning the shafts and chambers that satellite radar had found under the Giza Pyramids, but I decided to just listen and ask questions.

Sometimes I had to interrupt him to ask my questions. It seemed fair for me to direct his monologue, since I was giving him a ride.

'Did the extraterrestrials say the Pyramid had any other purposes besides to alleviate axial excursion?' I said.

I don't remember if he said yes or no. He talked about the number nine, how the Pyramid represented this number. He talked about electrons. He talked about a huge book from 1912 that he'd read in a library.

He said the extraterrestrials who told him about the Pyramid were from Saturn. Not physical Saturn, but a non-physical reality overlapping the planet. He said there were two realities 'below' and 'above' us.

Pāhoa was ahead, a small town of around 1,500 people. A shopping plaza had opened in the past few years. Sprawling and bulky, it reminded me of the ones in Florida, where I grew up. It seemed out of place on the edge of Pāhoa.

'I can drop you off further into town,' I offered.

'Go left,' he said.

'I guess I'll give you a ride home,' I said as I turned onto a road that went south past Pāhoa to Seaview.

'Thank you,' he said. Soon he was talking about diet and herbs. He seemed to have sold herbs in the past. He said he was a 'working astrologer'.

Sometimes interrupting him didn't work – he talked through my interruption. 'Can I interrupt you?' I said.

He looked at me and said, 'Yes.'

I asked if he was in regular contact with the Saturnians. He was. They taught him special things about physics, math, tensors. I asked why they communicated with him, and he said he was 'one of theirs'.

He said he'd also met a non-Saturnian extraterrestrial named Shift, who lived on the Big Island.

We passed where one could hike down to a nude beach. My ex and I had gone once or twice; around 10 percent of the people had been nude.

The man said we were a kilometer from his place. I asked if he had any tips for 'making contact with extraterrestrials'.

He said Shift had told him to think, 'I've had enough,' regarding *māyā* – the illusion of physical reality – and orbs would appear.

'Sincerity is important,' he added.

Souls could take the form of orbs, I'd read. But the technique confused me – did it mean I needed to feel I'd 'had enough' for it to work? I didn't feel I'd had enough. I was the least suicidal I'd ever been as an adult.

We entered his neighborhood. I'd never been here. There was a pleasing variety of plants, many flowers. People walked in pairs.

Once, visiting the north-west coast, my ex and I hitchhiked at dusk to get back to our rental. Months later, we got the car I was driving.

'It's beautiful here,' I said.

The man's house looked small and dilapidated. He seemed to live alone. I saw no evidence of pets. With few attachments, a soul could leave Earth easily when its body died; I often encountered this idea that year.

We stood beside my car. He talked about spices, said he'd been a raw foodist for twenty-three years. I got a banana from my car and ate it as he talked. He asked if I had more questions about pyramids or other things.

'So, I think, "I've had enough",' I said.

He confirmed. He said he'd tried it before – a few times with sincerity – and it hadn't worked. He looked away as he said this.

Looking at my eyes again, he said he'd met the leader of Mars, whose title was 'Dar'. I doubted this because why would the leader of Mars meet a normal guy? In retrospect, this reasoning seems faulty.

He was talking about walking somewhere and being visited by an extraterrestrial – I was feeling a bit overwhelmed, unable to keep track of all the non-human entities. It was starting to get dark out.

I said I was going to go now. He was talking about spirituality. He said he 'mostly followed' *The Essene Gospel of Peace*. He talked at length about the book's translator.

I said something like, 'It's getting dark, I better start heading home,' while backing away, toward my car door.

He asked my name. I said Tao. 'The way?' he said. I said it was a different Tao, related to storing a sword in a sheath, or storing anything, maybe, until the right time – I'd never fully understood my name.

He said he'd read an Eckhart Tolle book and found it just okay but had liked a part about *wi wei*. He said it meant waiting for the universe to act on you, instead of acting on it. He asked if I'd heard of it.

'No.' I suspected he meant *wú wéi* – a central idea in Daoism – but I didn't want to correct him. Except when I said 'Time is money', I'd given no opinion on his thoughts. I'd practiced *wú wéi* that night.

'What's your name?'

'Jota,' he said. It meant something about light or the sun. This seemed to lead him to talk about Hinduism, ancient Vedic texts.

I was interested, but I'd gotten fixated on leaving. The sky was mauve. I said a variation of 'I'm going now' again.

He said something I didn't understand, followed by 'or is it *xiè xiè*?' – 'thank you' in Mandarin.

'Yes, *xiè xiè*,' I said.

'So, not Cantonese,' he said.

I opened my car door and got in. I sat with my arm extended, ready to close the door. I froze in this position, listening to Jota talk. Realizing that a real goodbye was not forthcoming, I moved my hand into my lap.

He mentioned again that he was a working astrologer. He said I could visit him. He was looking for a new rental. He'd be here until August. He said other things that I don't remember.

As I backed into the street, he faced me with his palms pressed together, eyes closed. Then he was pointing at my car, saying, 'You have a Korean car!' followed by something I didn't understand, presumably in Korean.

I smiled and waved, driving away. After a few minutes, I started a voice memo, recording myself talking about the encounter, so that I'd remember it better. It was dark when I finished.

Approaching Pāhoa from the other direction, I realized I'd never seen it at night. The shopping plaza, glowing in the distance, reminded me of childhood. ■

Maggie Millner

First Year Sober

It was like a drug trip
dilated to the length of a life.

Over and over, the mind,
all by itself, ‘coming up’,
then ‘crashing’.

At first the clouds
above the beach were fur:
the fur of white
angora rabbits.

Then they were cake frosting
with candle-holes the sun
came leaking through.

My shoulder burned.
Two kites went inside out.

Attention raked itself through sand
like something crushed
then filed into lines.

A lighter clicked downwind.

Imagine ruining your life,
I thought,
the ecstasy of that.

Sentimentality

The estate sale was over, but the guy,

who introduced himself on Craigslist

as Leonard Melcher, surname included,

was chilling at the condo until nine that night

if I wanted to drop by and see the lamp.

I'd gotten myself into weird situations with men

selling underpriced home-goods before,

like in that dark New Jersey duplex where

the chair I bought was basically embalmed

in scraps of trash I had to peel away myself

while the seller smirked, watching from the door.

But the lamp was cheap and I was driving anyway

and I'd given up a lot of thrills over

the years, compared to which this habit
seemed benign. I pulled up in a pool
of yellow light that stained the snow like piss
and climbed the stairs. Leonard was closing in
on seventy, pretty short, NFL sweatshirt. Smell
of mothballs, folding tables spread
with cups and textiles, some Wedgwood
on the decommissioned stove. Descending
to the cellar, where the lamp had lived,
my eBay Virgil pointed to a photo of two underwater
nudes, all four tits inclining toward the surface
like balloons. 'They lived together forty years,
these two,' he said. 'Very groovy ladies.'

A broadside printed COFFEE MAKES YOU QUEER,
McGovern button, shoebox of Hitachi Magic Wands.
Leonard and I were still testing each other:
'My kind of women,' I said, and he raised me:
'One was Jewish, like myself. The other
was from Cuba, like my wife.' 'I'm kind of Jewish too,'
I volleyed back, plucking an Adrienne Rich chapbook
off a shelf, her signature in Sharpie on the proem.
'Take it,' he said. 'Most of this is headed
to the landfill in the morning. Here's your lamp.'
'I bet you see a lot of shit,' I said, grabbing the green
ceramic object by the throat. 'I really do' – this last
over a spool of salmon bubble wrap, his eyes
like dirty cabochons a pro like him might buff
to list on Facebook or The RealReal for a song.

'One woman died a few years back,' he said; the place
was being sold to pay the other one's assisted living bills.
'Did you know them, Leonard?' 'Nah,' he shrugged,
'I'm just the dude who makes stuff disappear.' I left
with dice, a sugar bowl, a beach rock Leonard said
I should turn over in my palm when I was tense.
I'd do that now, except it's in the car. I told myself
I wouldn't do this anymore, this writing
about people like they're things
to neaten up and sell. Yet here I am,
sitting in the light thrown by that lamp, peddling some lore
about property
changing hands in Connecticut.

HE TRAINS MY HANDS FOR WAR

Zora J Murff

Introduction by Ciarán Finlayson

Zora J Murff belongs to a generation whose political formation was shaped by the social upheavals that began with the killing of Trayvon Martin in 2012 and reached a crescendo with the murder of George Floyd in 2020.

Born in 1987 in Des Moines, Iowa, Murff came to photography while working with children in the state's criminal justice system. At Linn County Juvenile Detention and Diversion Services, he helped young people avoid incarceration by supporting them in meeting the conditions of court orders. In 2013, the year Martin's killer was acquitted, Murff took the first of the photographs that would become *Corrections*, a series of portraits of the teenagers in his care, posed so that their faces are obscured from view.

Over the following decade, Murff produced work that ranged from examinations of redlining and segregation in North Omaha, Nebraska (*At No Point In Between*, 2019), to more personal reflections on heritage and social mobility through family photographs and self-portraiture (*American Mother, American Father*, 2018–2020). In the 2022 monograph *True Colors (or, Affirmations in a Crisis)*, he placed family portraits alongside a newspaper clipping recording the murder of his mother's boyfriend, who was stabbed by neighbors hurling racial abuse during Murff's childhood.

Today, Murff is an assistant professor of Art and Black Studies at the University of Oregon. In his writing, he grapples with racial and class prejudice at institutions of art and higher learning; in photographic self-portraits he flashes gold grills and mugs for the camera in a ski mask, adopting the alter ego Money B. Greene as a way of toying with what he calls 'our collective trade in stereotypes'.

Murff has described his most recent material as 'a visual record of my personal journey towards liberation', a process that has found him, since 2020, engaging in collage – less the Weimar clash of irreconcilable images than the conspiration of related browser windows – bringing together family photos and historical documents, stills from television and radical documentaries, memes and found images from contemporary struggles against racial violence. The photographs gathered here draw from several bodies of work made in the last several years.

For the artwork *I Woke Up Today Wanting To Kill Me A White Man* (2022), Murff assembled four stills taken from local news footage of the 1992 Los Angeles riots, which broke out after the acquittal of four Los Angeles Police Department officers filmed brutally beating Rodney King. One of those stills appears in this selection, at the top of a vertical diptych: it captures the moment just after news of the verdict spread, in which four black men surround white truck driver Reginald Denny. One has his foot on Denny's neck, pinning him to the ground, another throws an oxygenator at his head. The blurry footage was shot by a news helicopter under fire from below; Murff pixelates it further. When Murff first exhibited the full work, its title included the parenthetical '*(N.H.I.)*' – the initials stand for 'No Humans Involved', a designation reportedly used by California judicial officers to refer to incidents involving young, unemployed black men.

Later in the selection here, opposite a distant photograph of a basketball game in a Tulsa housing complex, Murff has placed an image of the shopping center in South Central that was burned down in those same LA riots. In the photobook *True Colors*, he previously paired this image with a photograph of another fire at the affordable housing complex near Minneapolis's Third Precinct, destroyed in the aftermath of George Floyd's murder. The work was titled *The Fire of Revolutions Continuing to Burn (1993–2020).*

Another appropriated television still shows a grainy Obama, as he appeared on *Face the Nation* in 2009, one year into his presidency, flanked by the American flag and rows of leather-bound law books. He lifts his broad, open hands in the universal gesture of statecraft, projecting confidence and control, which nonetheless echoes the raised arms of Denny's attackers in the image above. The rage above is sublimated into restraint below, but the degraded quality of the images suggests an unstable equilibrium. The LA riots belonged to the history Obama was meant to transcend. Instead he presided over a twenty-fold increase in the number of black homeowners with negative equity; as a result of his handling of the 2008 financial crisis, black homeownership rates dipped below where they were before the passage of the Voting Rights Act. Similar contrasts appear throughout this portfolio: enlarged, monochromatic images of pistols face off against black figures and their homes. These scans, taken from police manuals, collapse the distinction between law enforcement and vigilantism.

The found photograph Murff includes here, of a black man in olive drab fatigues posing with an underslung grenade launcher, likely on deployment in Vietnam, poses questions about empire: not simply who wields force, but under what conditions it is judged legitimate. The uncertainty continues into the final photo, a portrait of the artist in training, showing Murff alone at a gun range, his face hidden, bullet case glinting in the weak morning light. This is one way the struggle is overcome. ■

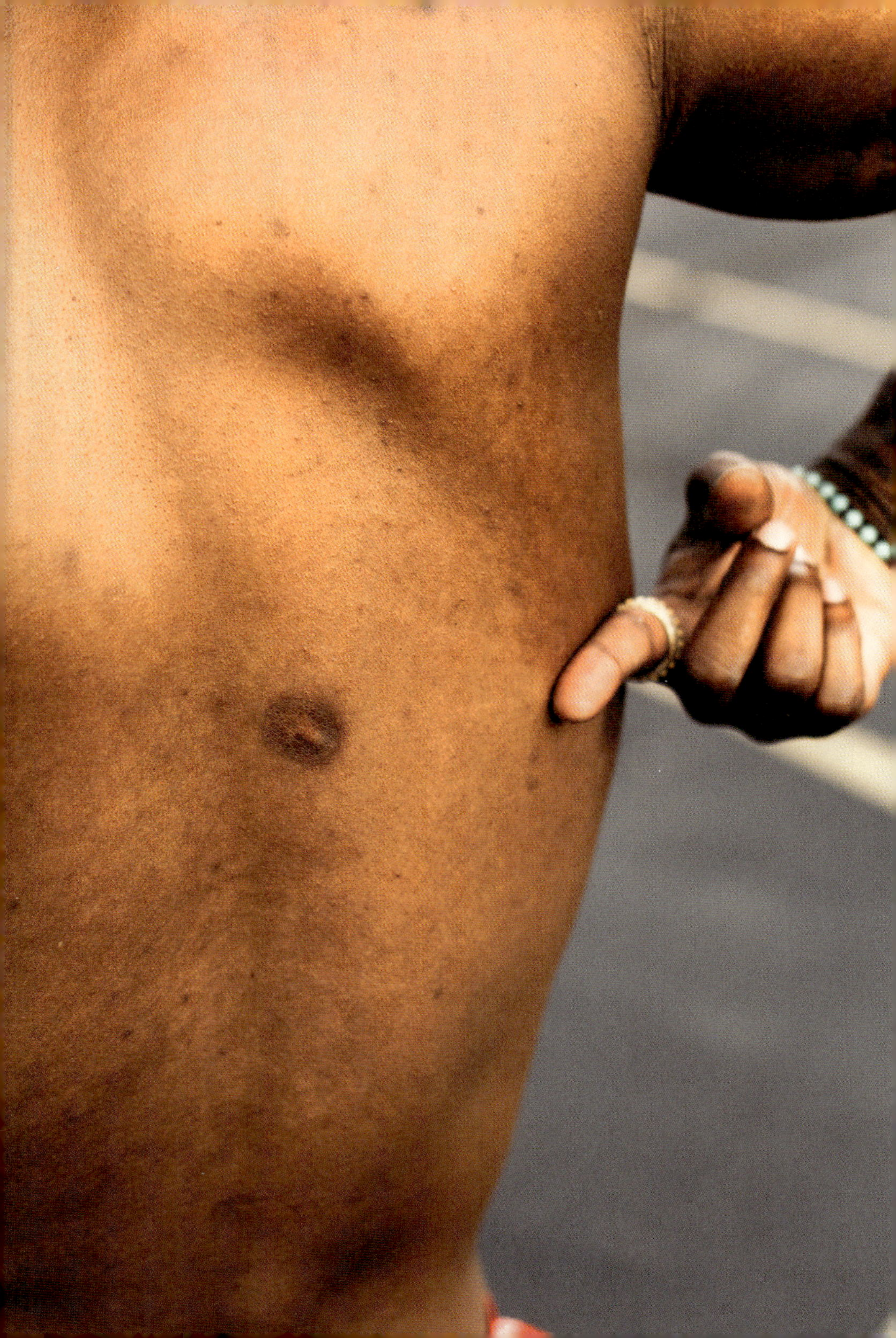

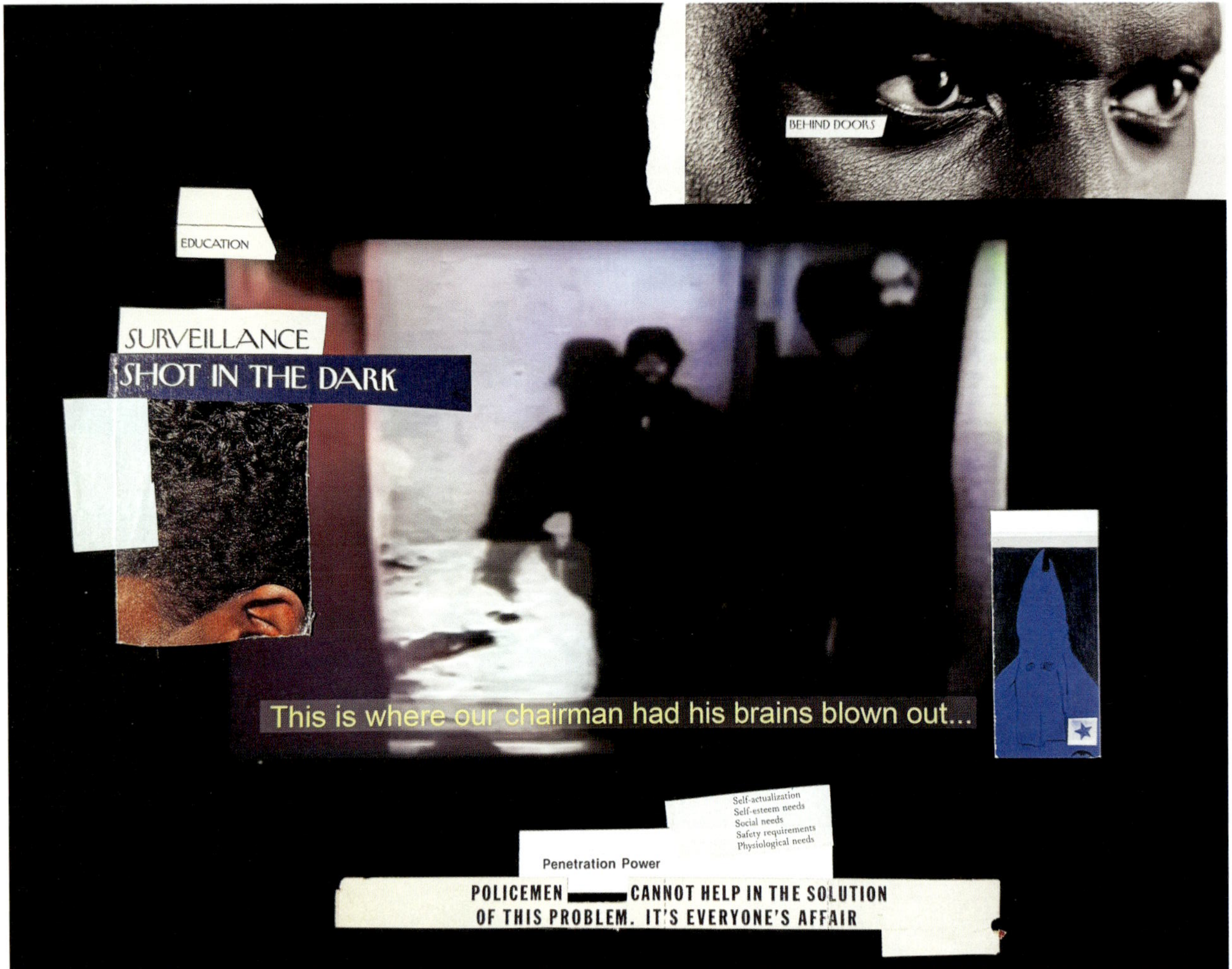
BEHIND DOORS
EDUCATION
SURVEILLANCE
SHOT IN THE DARK
This is where our chairman had his brains blown out...
Self-actualization
Self-esteem needs
Social needs
Safety requirements
Physiological needs
Penetration Power
POLICEMEN CANNOT HELP IN THE SOLUTION
OF THIS PROBLEM. IT'S EVERYONE'S AFFAIR

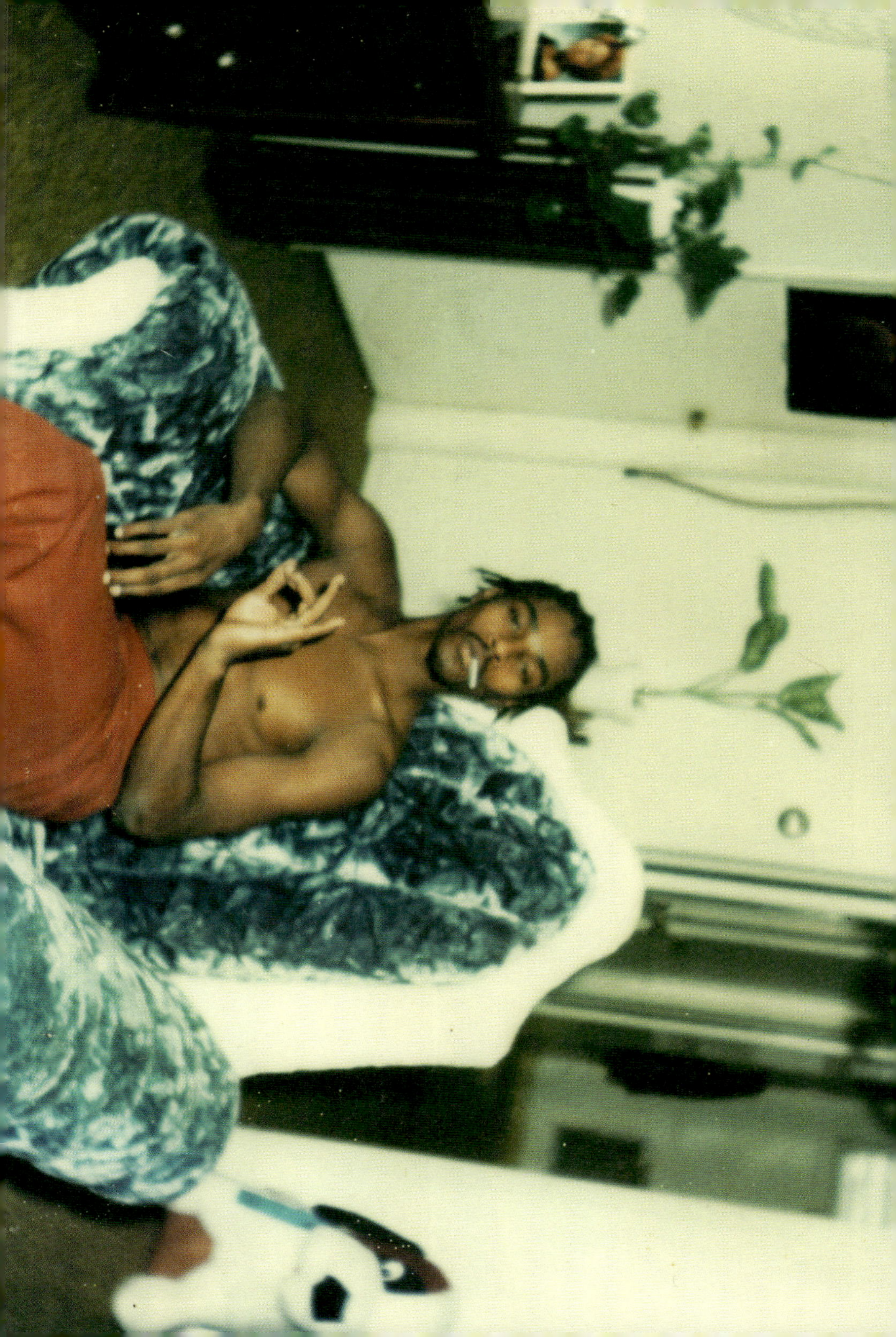

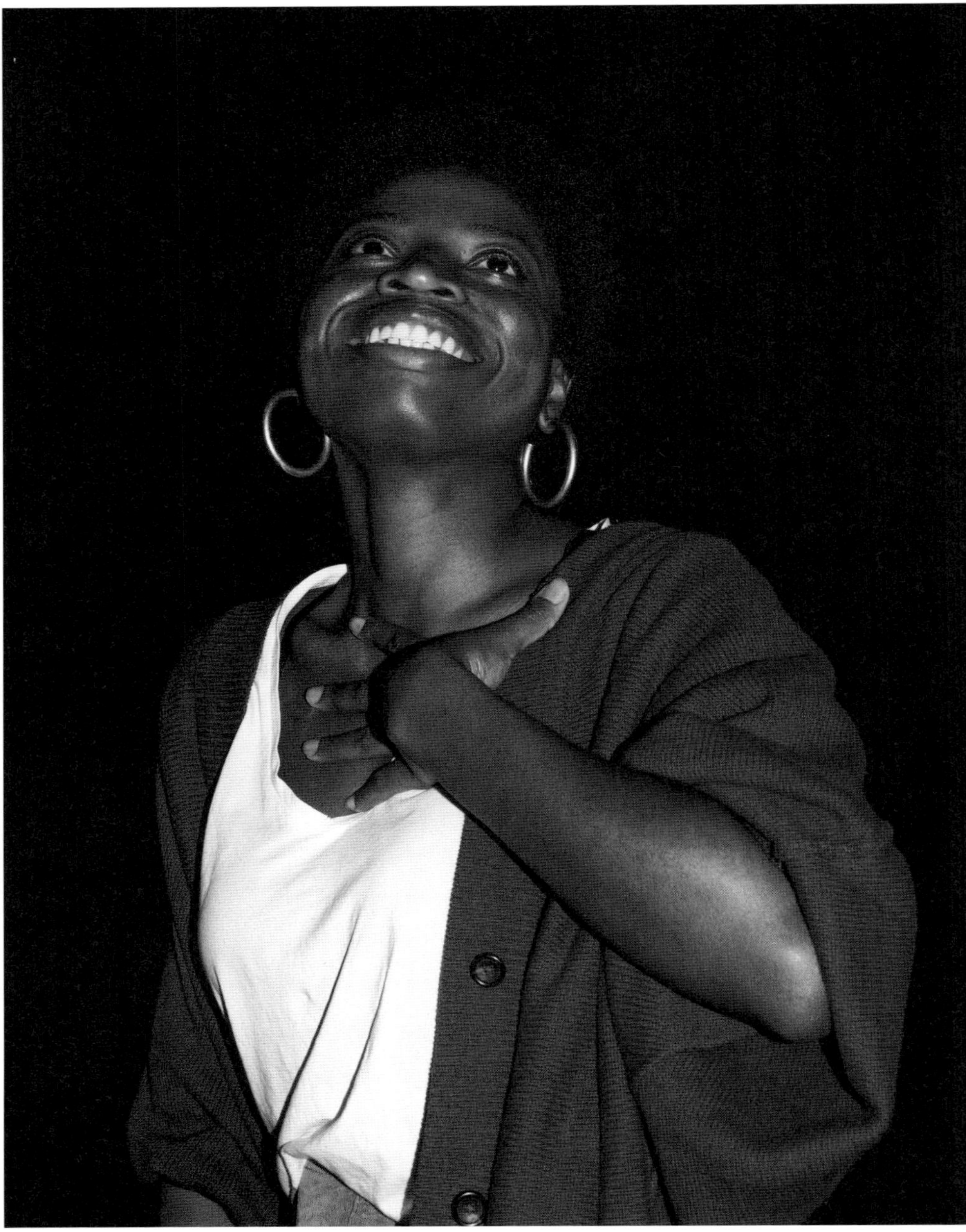

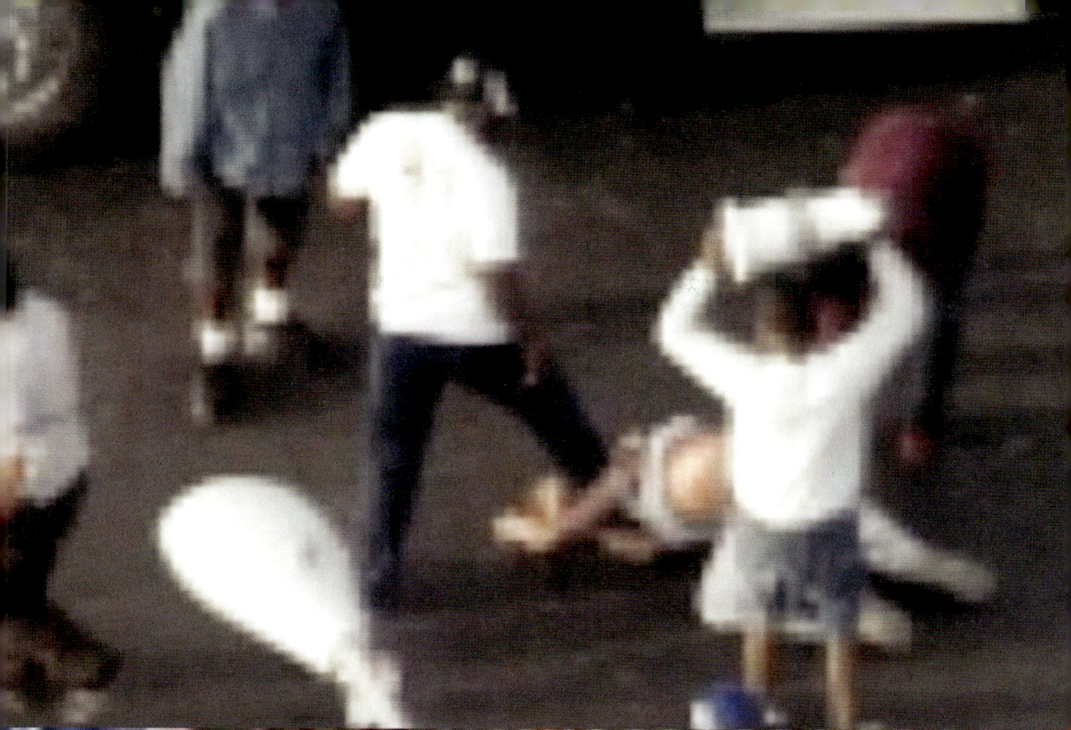

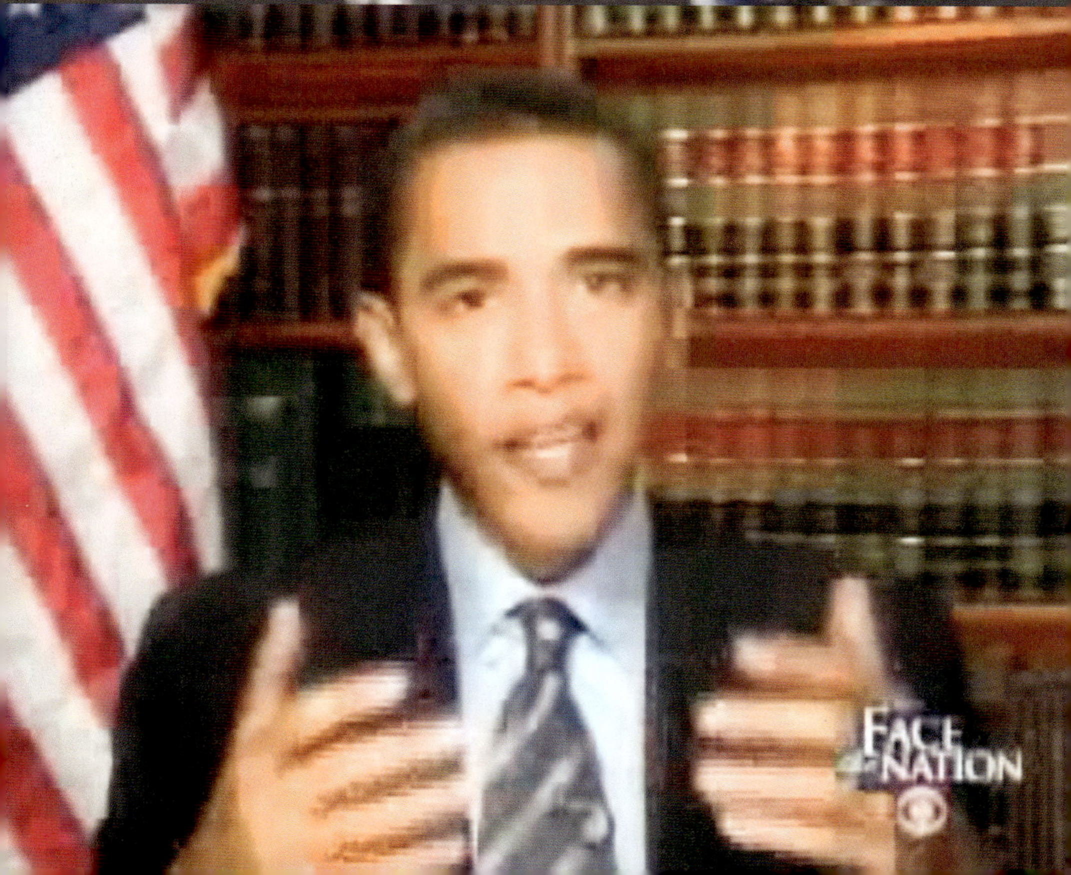
FACE
NATION

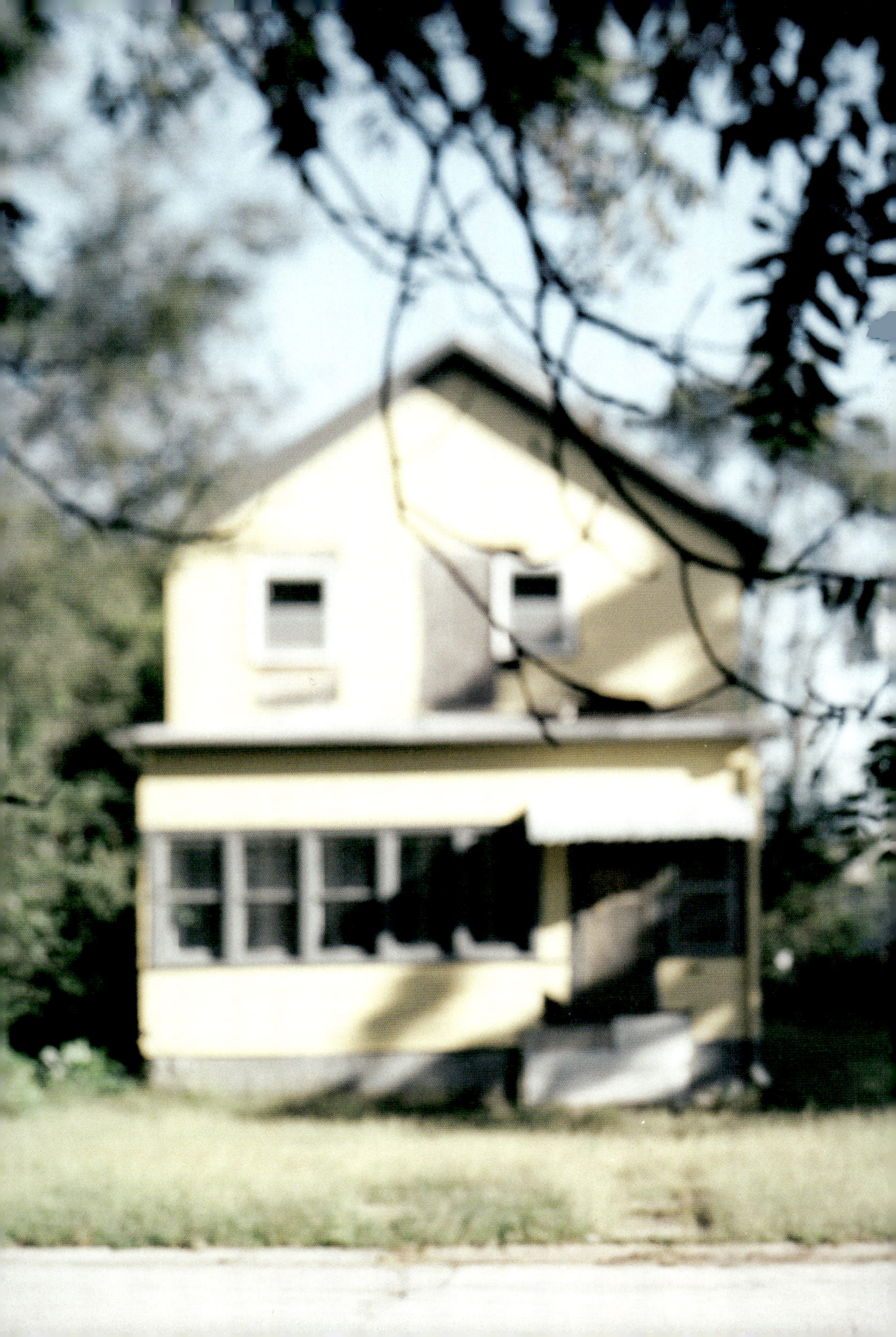

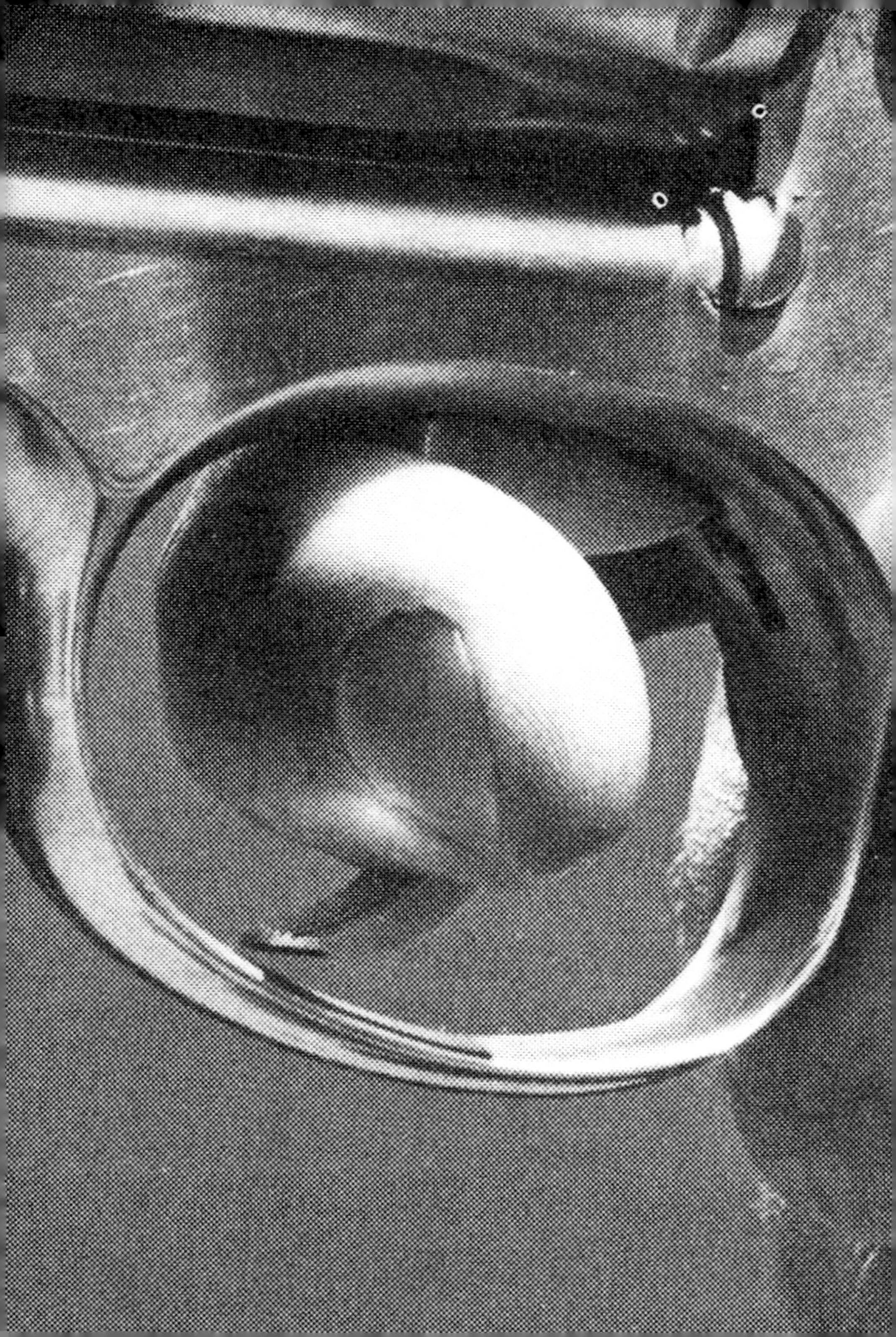

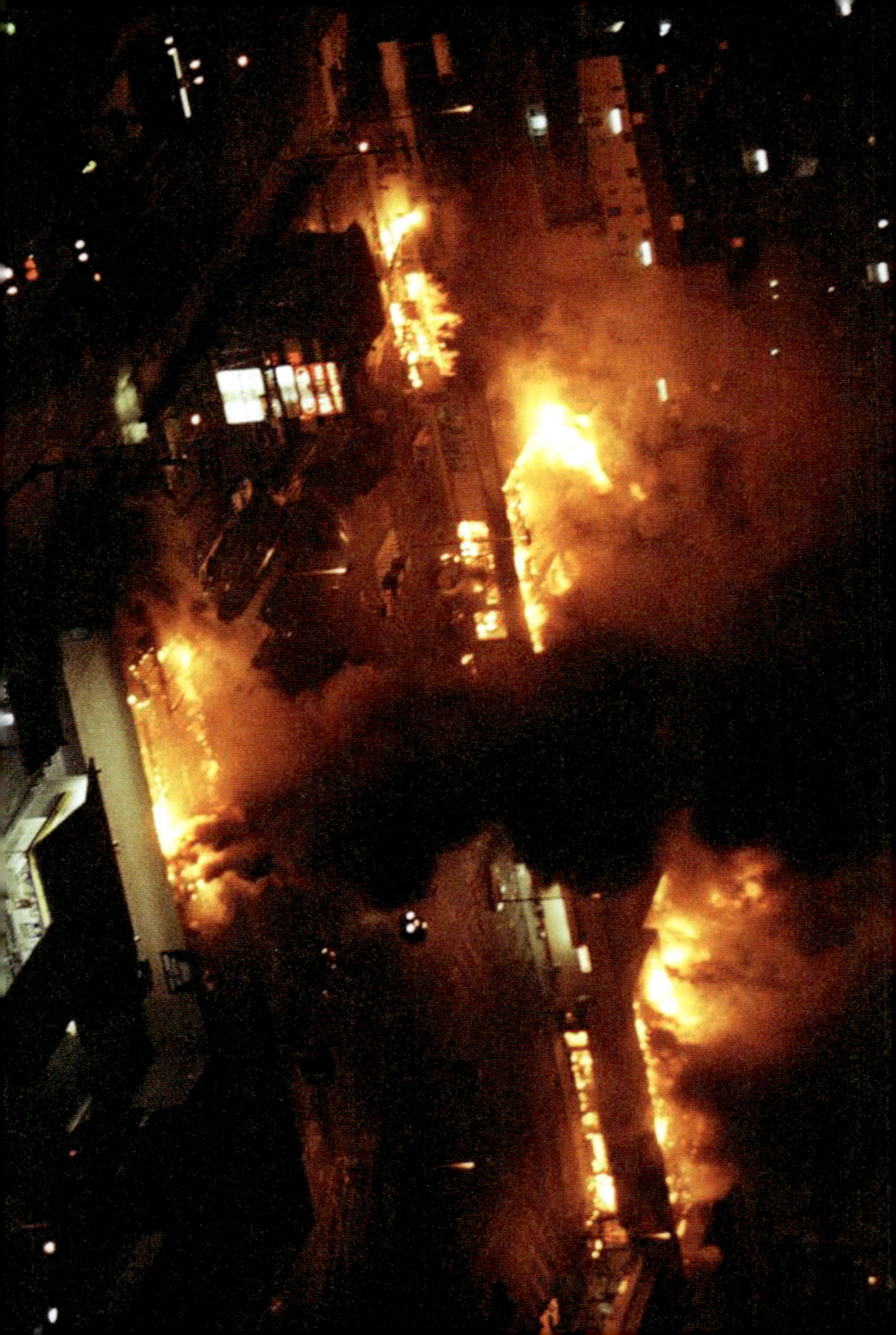

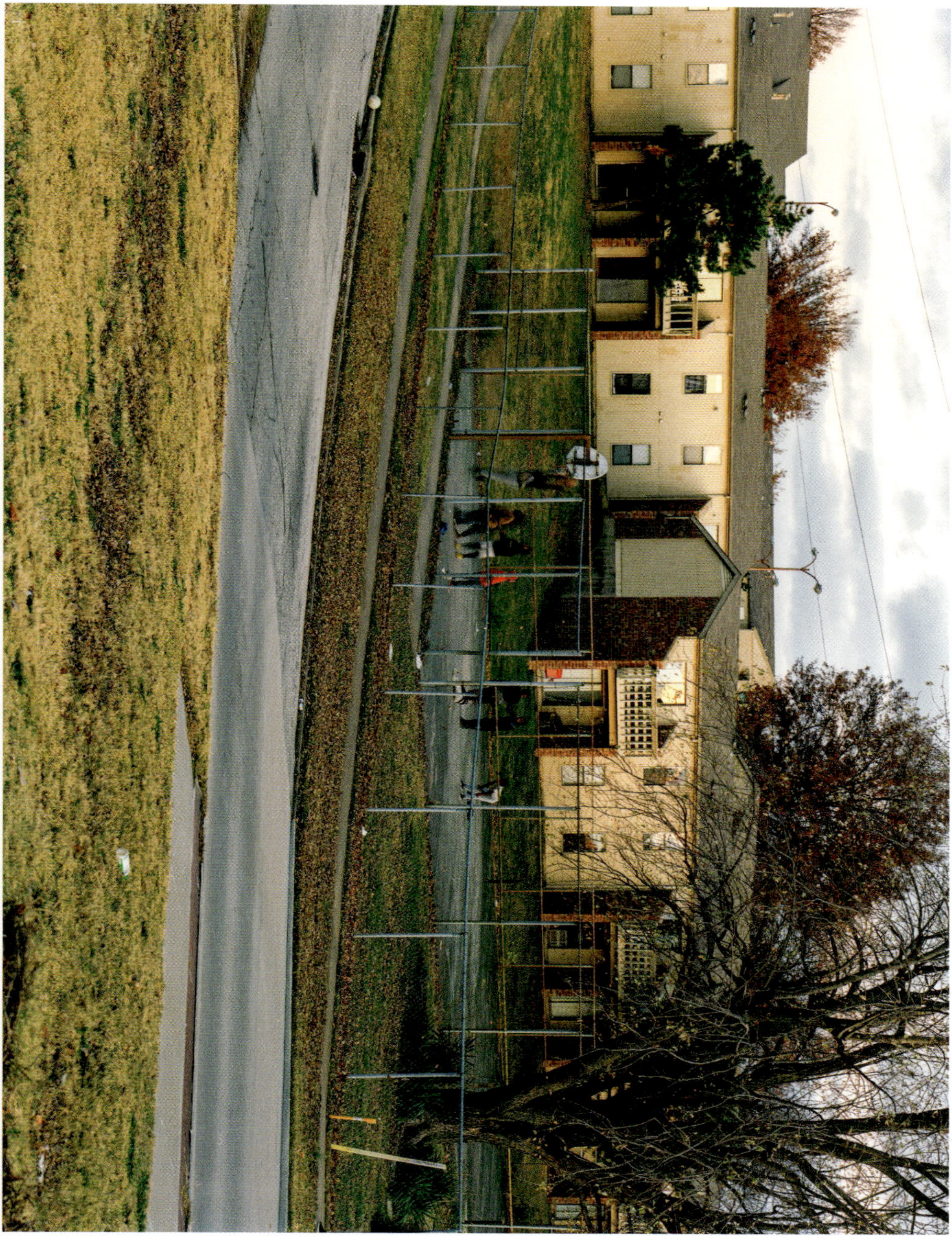

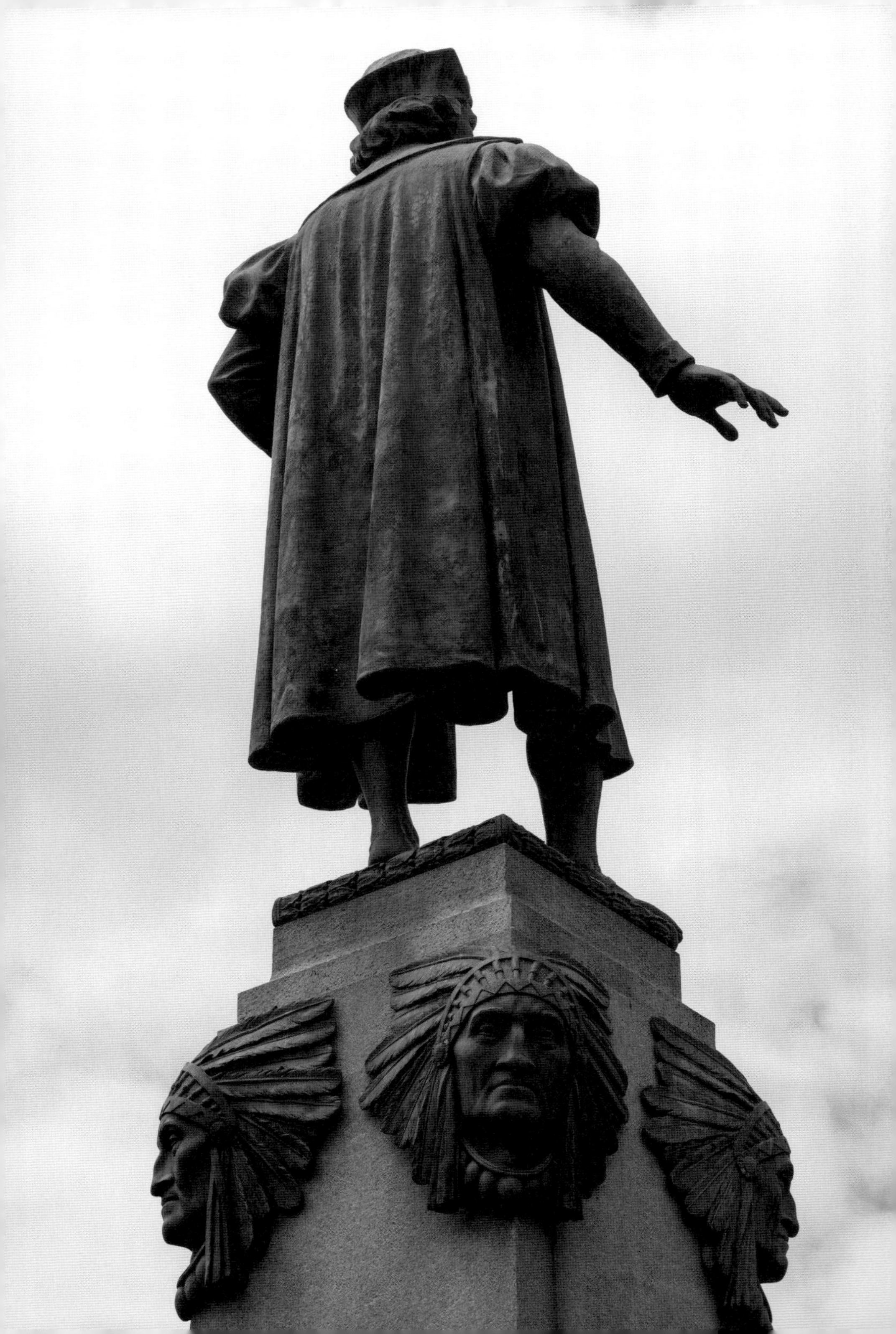

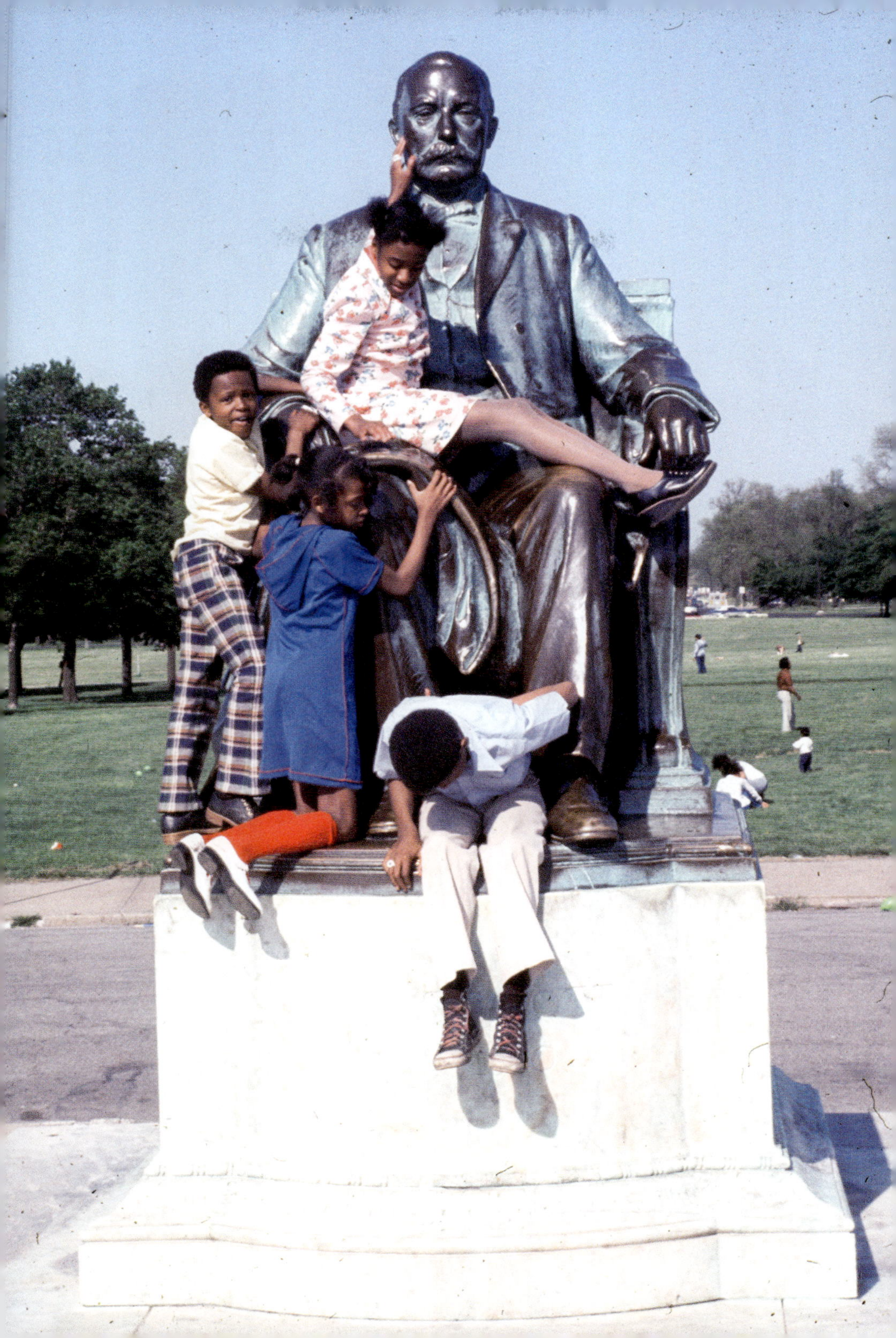

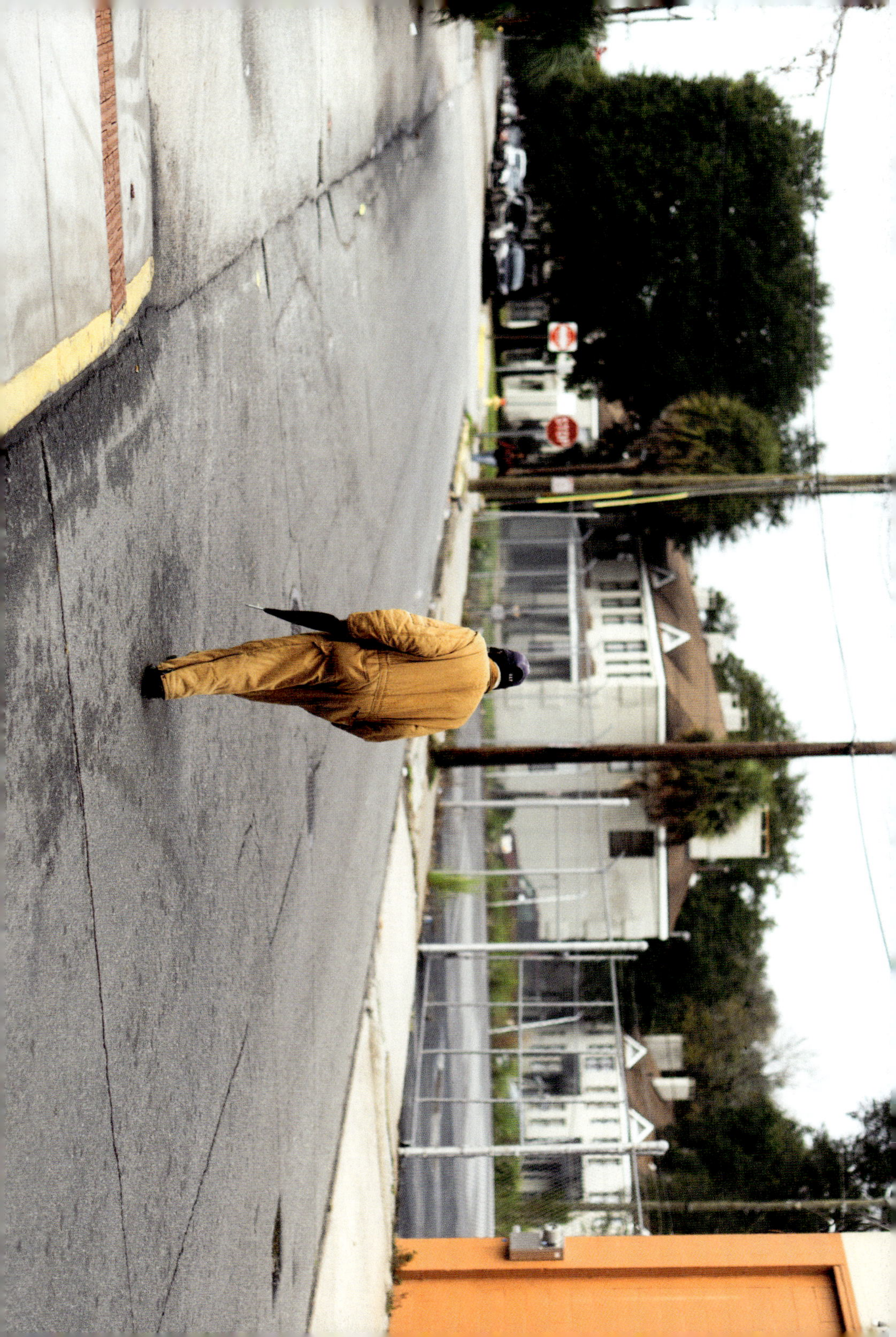

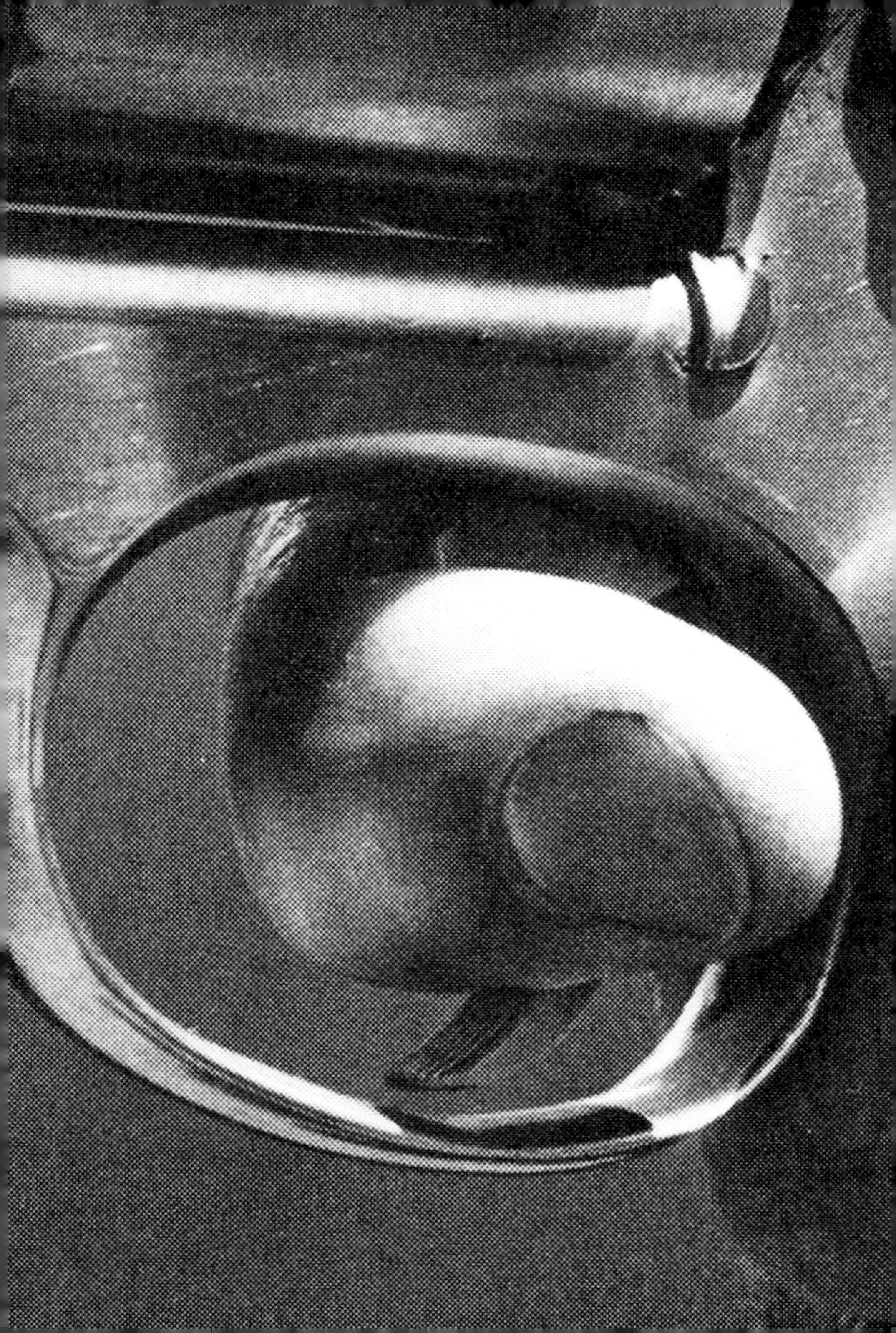

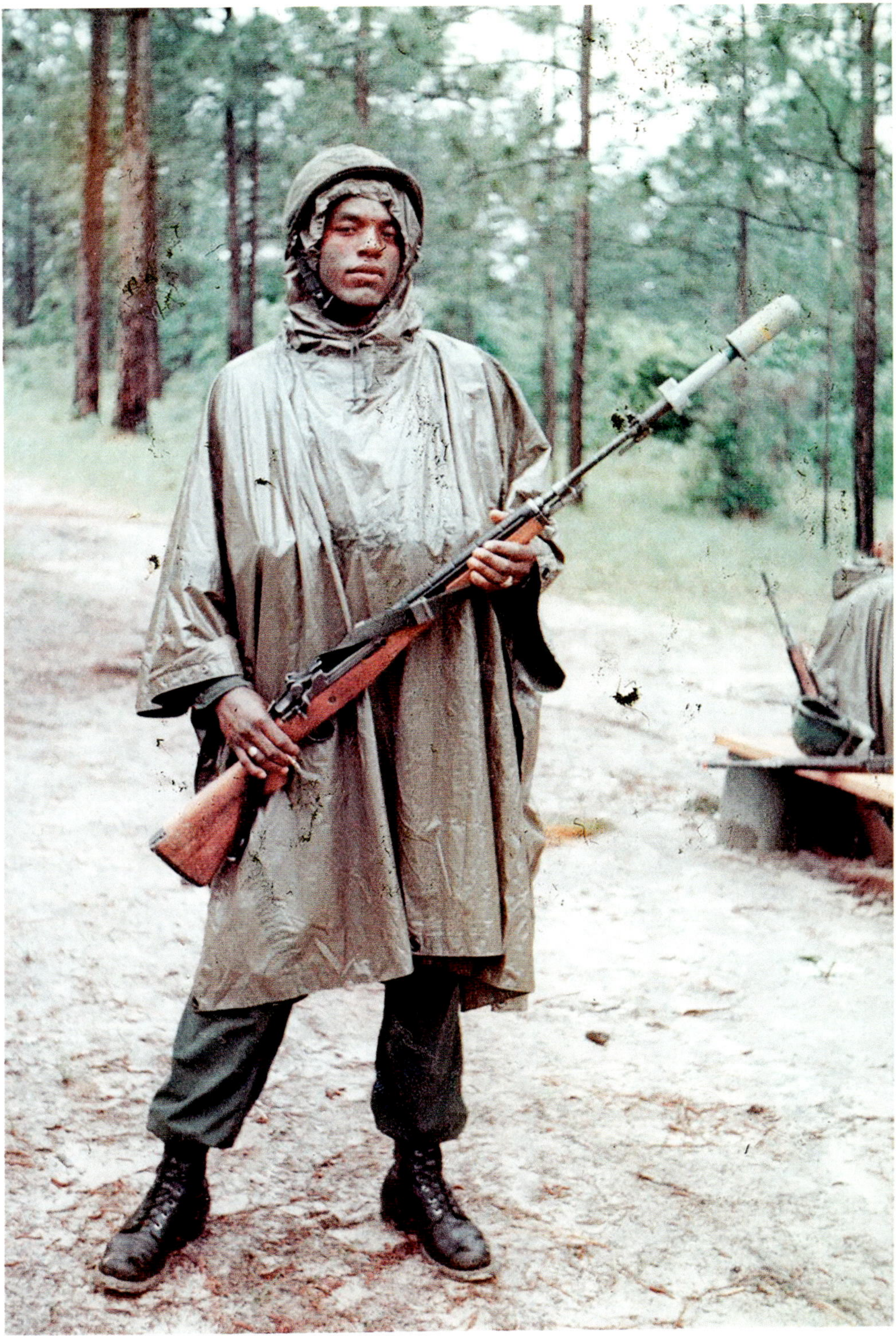

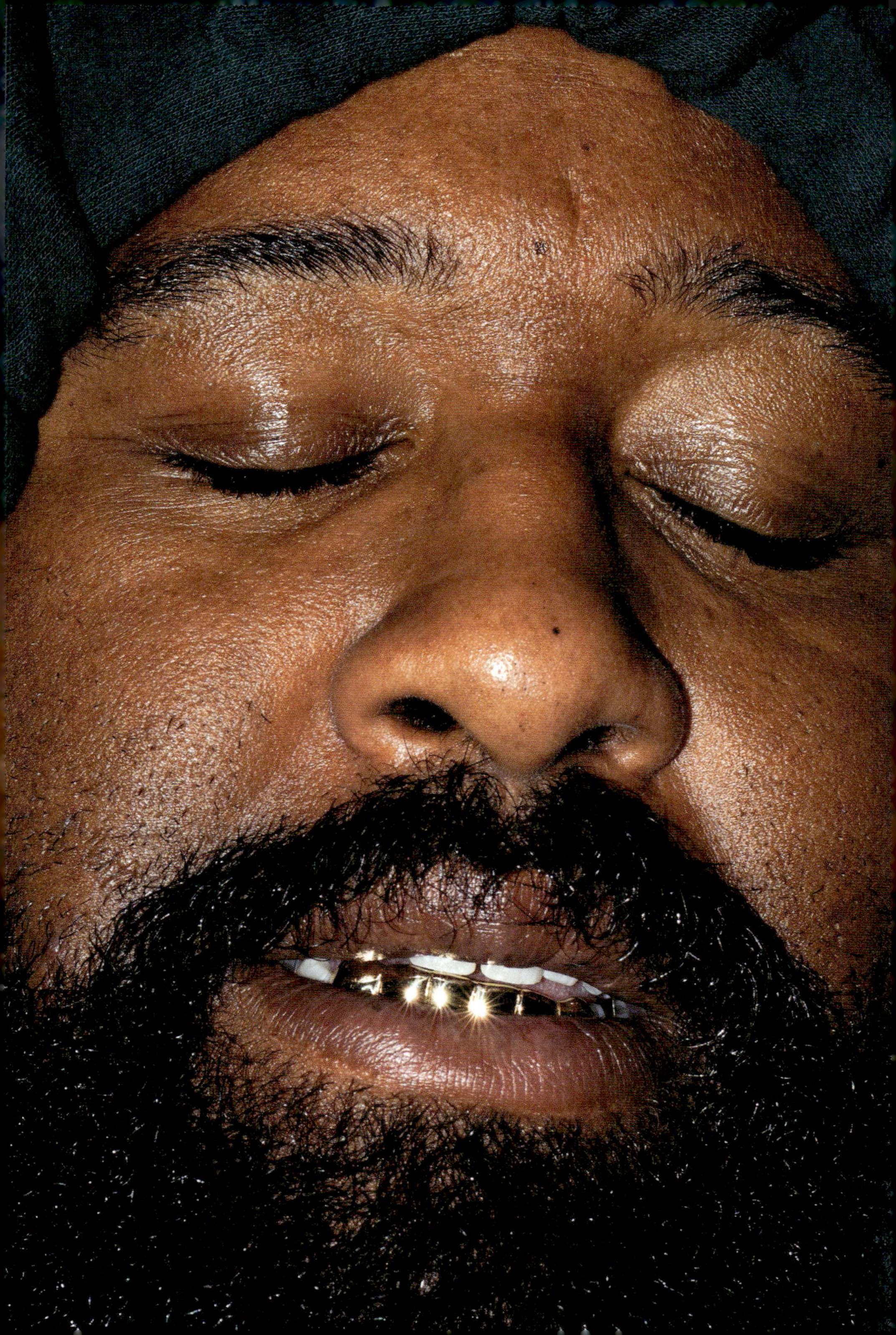

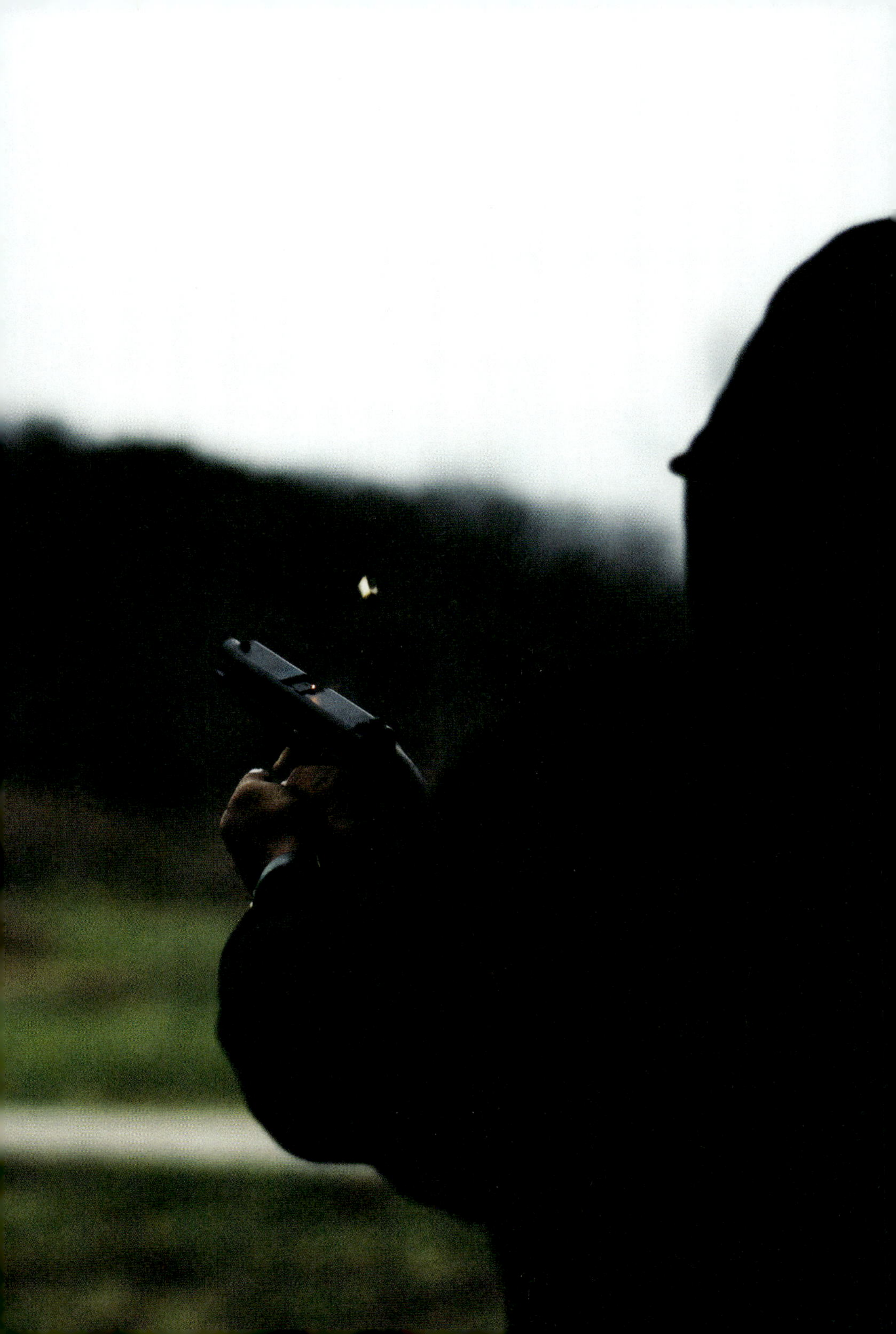

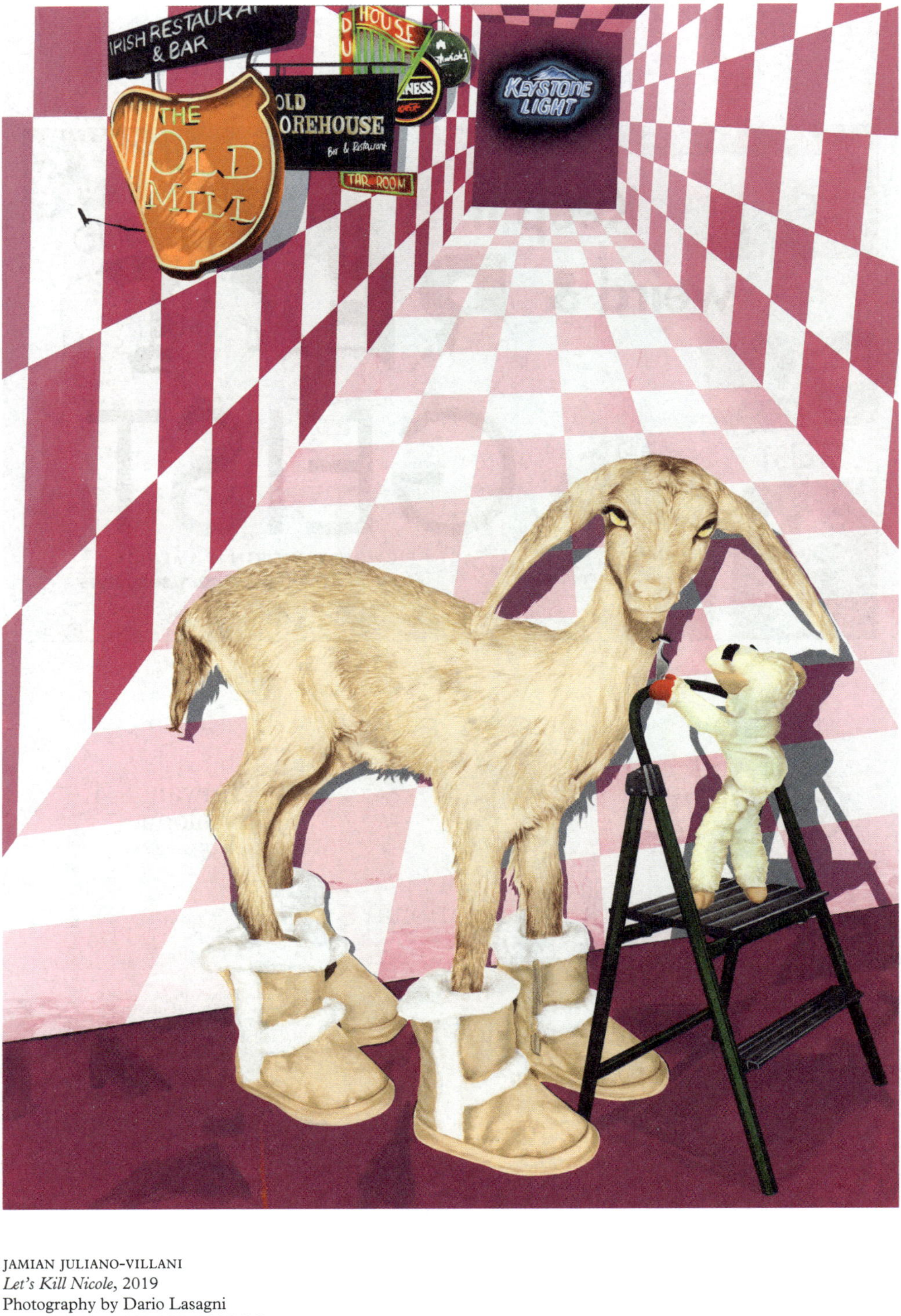

JAMIAN JULIANO-VILLANI
Let's Kill Nicole, 2019
Photography by Dario Lasagni
Courtesy of MASSIMODECARLO

THE YEAR OF THE RAT

Halle Hill

Lee Warwick drove west toward the city. His Chrysler inched through a long, blinding work zone. He worked overnights at the reservation desk of the Ramada Inn off US-129. There was light rain. There was big sky. A deep plum sky. And billboards yelling: REPENT, REPENT.

To the right and left of him, excavation workers toiled under light towers and trails of red tail lights made cherry-colored shadows on his dashboard, face, and his clothes. He slowed, slouching through one-lane traffic. He yawned. He fiddled with the radio.

Major construction had started at the aluminum plant in Alcoa, recently sold to some mega German conglomerate, and all types of scratch-tattooed, red-brick-necked, felony-looking men had come seeking employment. In hard hats and on expansion contracts, they stayed for weeks out in the mountains. Some were staying at the Ramada, ordering soft-core on the en-suite TVs at night.

Lee was a little late when he walked into the motel. Donnie Jenkins was already there, playing around with a Gematria calendar he'd found online. He looked up as Lee took his place beside him at the front desk.

'Lee, listen. It's the Year of the Rat, you know, man.'

'Oh, okay.' Lee logged on to the computer.

'And different words mean different things to the deep state.'

'You told me.' It was going to be a long night.

A recent Facebook IQ test had revealed Lee to be a man at the far right of the bell curve, not just gifted but searingly brilliant, in the upper tenth-percentile of minds, comparable to Benjamin Franklin, Sylvia Plath, Barack Obama, and Ray J.

After the test he had been added to a Mensa-like Facebook group for other geniuses to talk about genius things. Lee found himself relieved to finally be in a place with other thinkers, able to have deeper, esoteric conversations around the meaning of life and hell and protein supplements.

It was the Thursday shift and the motel was mostly empty, apart from the regulars. There were no witnesses when Lee and Donnie felt a major headwind as the front automatic doors opened toward the parking lot. No living creature had passed, and the CCTV confirmed this. The men watched as the doors paused then closed again. Lee spun around in his desk chair. Life felt metaphysically positive toward him tonight, as if he was sophisticated spiritually, as if God-postured to receive secret knowledges, to see and know secret things.

While Lee thought about God's secrets, Donnie tried again with the rat thing.

According to the Reddit QAnon group Donnie was in, Rat represented the number 181, which was the same number as Dr Phil and the same as Big Difference and the same as Asleep and Bismillah. And the End.

'Q says this will be the year of the cipher, Lee. That Rat is the beginning of the astrological calendar, that this will be the end, the turn toward the end, man. You gotta wake up, Lee.'

Then he said all types of slurs and slurry things about Muslims, the End, and Armageddon.

Bismillah, Lee mouthed to himself. An ending didn't feel so bad. And God did feel merciful to him. He saw the generosity of heaven in the majesty of the season. It had been a golden autumn in East

Tennessee, crisp and resplendent, even the rain had seemed dark and comforting. Holy. Lee responded to Donnie's rat excitement and Arab panic with dismissive body language, offering a stale thumbs up. He was getting sleepy. To pass the time, he made himself busy on the Toshiba monitor, moving reservations from canceled to approved back to canceled again.

It was exactly these conversations at the front desk of the Ramada Inn off Alcoa Highway that Lee was beginning to feel were beneath him. He let out a long cleansing breath.

'Loosen up, bro.' Donnie leaned over to rub Lee's bony shoulders.

Lee shrugged Donnie off and adjusted his bowtie in the monitor screen, which had turned black and idle. He worried he looked like a dressed-up infant seal.

Sabrina Cortez, a customer-favorite lot lizard, arrived at the ghost doors and made her way to the elevator, adorned in purple eyeshadow, butterfly clips and Love Spell. Lee stared even closer at his computer as she passed, thinking about the bean pie he'd packed for his dinner.

Donnie flipped his head up toward Sabrina's ass as she waited for the elevator.

'What you need is some Puerto Rican pussy, man.'

But all Lee had was a Charley Pride song stuck in his head:

It's plain to see
That the likes of me
Don't fit with you

Around 2 a.m. the next morning Lee went to the third floor to knock on Sabrina Cortez's door. There had been noise complaints, four calls to the front desk. When she didn't answer, he let himself in and looked around. Cocooned from head to toe in white 100-thread count and Egyptian musk, Sabrina had fallen into a deep hydroxyzine sleep. She glowed like swaddled neon, the duvet around her head, her toes out bare. Poppers were balanced on the nightstands around her altar, as was lubricant, a jelly rabbit, sparkling cock rings and large white pillar candles. He leaned over close enough to smell her eyelids. The bed was shaking from what looked like a plugged-in Hitachi Magic Wand and Lee pulled it out at the wall. Sabrina was red-brown, with hair that shimmy-shimmered like a Lapiz corvid wing. She breathed shallowly. Her fingernails were painted Cajun Shrimp, a bright, orange red, same as his mother's, same as his sister's, the color of wealthy, stay-at-home blondes in West Knoxville. Downstairs Donnie was helping a trucker check in. Lee felt his mouth salivate. The Prophet was testing him. He wanted to enter paradise, just not this way, not through her.

The truth was that Lee felt overdue. Not merely for sex, or money, or hair, but for something. A correction. Some intervention in his favor. Along with the Mensa group he had been added to a covert Herbalife/Nation of Islam FB group where an imam from Detroit took a keen interest in him, writing him messages about discipline, brotherhood and entrepreneurship. He wanted to add Lee to his Herbalife downline, telling him that his energy drink products could offer him financial freedom and flexibility, but Lee felt soul-stirred to something higher.

The following morning, Lee thought of Sabrina as he sauntered through his mildewed apartment, filled with bags of trash he was using as furniture, toward his slim balcony overlooking dumpsters and a gravel parking lot. He took in the bleak 3.30 a.m. morning of his day off. Lee believed, while facing the east before dawn, that praying would ease his fibromyalgia, give him social confidence, and help with his hair situation.

After watching YouTube videos and absorbing the teachings of the Most Honorable Minister Farrakhan, Lee had taken up a sort of pleading to heaven, (change me, change me) leaning on the foundation of the Nation of Islam, channeling prosperity and Black Male Greatness via the Prophet (Peace be upon him) and his teachings. He considered what Donnie had said about how astrologically it was a good time for rat men like him.

Donnie had got him into the Kevin Samuels videos, and soon Lee began ranking his potential through a set of averaged metrics (8.5/10). He was short, yes, but had an above average dick and a solid job. Now he just needed hair. For months he'd followed the instructions from another YouTube video which showed him how to make a homemade toupee out of synthetic braid hair from the Asian-owned beauty supply on Magnolia; hair fibers, super glue and Got2b hairspray. He would pat the fibers down then wrap a washcloth around his pointer finger and sleek back a hairline, carving the black smut into a smudge-less scalp circle. This gave him confidence to face the world and not be devastated by his baldness, which had become a growing problem due to his high cortisol levels and the 'heat-anger' trapped in his stomach, which he had also learned about on YouTube from a Chinese medicine practitioner in South Carolina.

Lee would turn forty soon but knew he didn't look a year past twenty-two. He was considered striking, all symmetrical and lip glossy, with smooth butter pecan skin, an aquiline nose and star-tipped eyelashes. Although, at 5'2, and with his high-pitched voice, dating on the apps was hard, and caused people in real life to double take in awe and in concern or fear as if he were a fresh lamb, a movie star or a pedophile. To maximize his matches, he uploaded photos of himself with Kawaii filters and a black Nike Dri-FIT cap, the first and main profile picture one of him and his baby sister running a 10K. The photo was from seven years ago now, but he didn't want to replace it. He thought he looked handsome. Caring.

Women on the apps were brutal. He received almost no viable matches, only obese whites from Karns, Sweetwater or LaFollette (named Tanya or Kennedy or Connie) or obscenely bold Fashion Nova Black women who he predicted had hood origins and a lack of paternal guidance. Opening lines delivered on the apps frequently began with 'lift UP the cap and let me see'. Or 'Is that your bitch?' Avoiding the hat query, he'd write something like no . . . that's not my bitch . . . that's my baby sister. Then he'd usually be unmatched or called a 'fkn weirdo'. So he deleted the apps. And had taken to supplication instead, speaking directly to God, to channel his sensual energy in a more penetrating way.

Now, standing on the damp concrete of his balcony, face turned east toward the eastern hills, Lee raised his hands before his chest. The parking lot lay mostly silent below him.

Lee found himself distracted by a balayage brunette struggling to get into her rental house across the street. Her keys drunkenly scraped at the front door lock. She stumbled, then fell backward into a large honey-bell bush. Her legs opened, revealing a waxed, salmon-pink furrow in plein air.

Pressing his legs against the balcony railing, he felt the tip of an erection stirring at her misfortune. He considered what it would be like to walk over to her in her unknowing stupor, stroke her pale scalp with his fingernails, then rub the cornsilk tracks of her hair across his face and between his front teeth. God teased him, *the greatest of God's secrets is God himself*, he thought.

Hours passed. Lee thought of Sabrina in the shower and again in bed. He thought of her Cupid's bow, her clavicles, the garlic smell of her armpits. He thought of how long she was. He thought of her people, who she came from, what kind of child she'd been.

That evening, after two more showers and some chicken noodle soup, Lee climbed into bed and opened his laptop. In a private browser he scanned video after video of girls who looked just like Sabrina with bottomless throats and buoyant breasts, searching for JOI clips to take the edge off, women smiling into their webcams and telling him what to do and how to do it. In another blinking tab, viable suitors offering massages from faraway places popped up, opening their glittering pink canyons to their cameras. Juliana looked promising.

He liked her flushed mulatto skin, which looked soft and ripe for bruising. She held her feet to the camera in a sophisticated way, her rib flare prominent and her back softly arched. The balls of her feet were smooth and slightly pink-singed. Reclined on her elbows and with her ankles bound in Shabari rope, she revealed the fat things on herself despite her nymphet body. She wore a rhinestone blue-baby T-shirt and had baby bangs; her palms pressed together in prayer, her nipples slick and thick, protruding through sheer polyester. And she had sad eyes, deep lowlife, sertraline black pools. Above all else, something in the angles of Juliana's features, in her sweet, sweet face, gave Lee a feeling of familiar passage. He missed Sister.

Lee double-clicked. Juliana was live now, taking requests. She was riding a purple dildo, making puddles on the floor. Lee was transfixed. She could smile. She could do a middle split. She was just 632 miles away in Harlem.

Yes, he thought. This is the one.

Lee fell asleep with Sister in his heart and Juliana in his mind, a high-value Discord server crackling in the background. Amorphous male-chatter flowed through his stale apartment, men talking about biohacking, betas, and femme boys. The voices wrapped around his lonely head.

In the early hours of the next day, Lee had slept through six missed calls. His mother, Hortencia Warwick, had been calling, confirming her morning ride. Lee needed to drop her off for her opening shift at the Sunoco in Seymour. He was late but got there at a reasonable time. They didn't speak much about family these days. But on these rides she would say, 'How is she?'

They hadn't heard from Sister in over three years. Sister had sent them no-contact letters. Called them all sick fucks and Cluster B types. But Lee knew she was just playing.

'Sister's good, I spoke with her yesterday,' he would respond almost every time.

All Lee knew was that she'd moved somewhere else, somewhere far away. Started dancing in clubs.

Lee heard from her in his head, though. She was still reaching out. She'd woken him up out of his sleep many times, an archangel visiting him through creamy wet dreams.

When the apparitions became more frequent he'd found a psychic, Veronica, all the way out in Dandridge, and went to see her so he could decode the symbols Sister wanted to send him. 'What is she saying to me, V?' he begged.

Veronica said that Sister was closer to Lee than he realized. She said Sister wanted to see him, needed to, really; she just didn't know how to say it. Needed him to come and get her. That she'd spent some time in New York. Worked as a waitress at some family-owned Italian restaurant.

Sister was the type of sister who was a good daughter, the type who would be a good lover to someone. Lee had always known this. She was smiley and agreeable, always had been. Lee wished that his wishes were mighty horses, that they might carry him somewhere. Sister, a sable-brown-skinned brunette with a sweet face like Juliana. Yes, she was a magnificent woman, and he had always shown tender affection to her.

That evening Lee went to his computer and found the tabs still open on his browser. He closed them one by one, then pulled out his credit card and booked a flight to LaGuardia in three days' time, right then and there. After work on Friday, Lee would get his suitcase from the bedroom, pack his Old Navy athleisure-wear in tight, tidy rows, and get on a red-eye from McGhee Tyson Airport, arriving in New York City around three in the morning. From there he would make his way to Harlem. To find Sister.

The Warwicks had bought that rancher in West Hills and the dirty cousins from Bessemer were visiting. They seemed excited, and poor, running around every room in the house.

'Y'all got TVs in your bathroom?' said Darryl, the light-skinned one with the rash around his lips. 'When did y'all get these TVs? I wont one.'

Lee was silent.

'You hear me talking to you, faggot?' Darryl was also homophobic.

'It's you all.'

'What?'

'It's not y'all, it's you all.'

Darryl rammed into Lee and they fell to the linoleum, wrestled and squirmed. Lee heard his momma yelling for them from their new kitchen, with Cambria Quartz counter tops. Darryl straddled Lee and put his hand over his mouth. The boys struggled there in silence, and Lee looked over to the closet. Sister was hiding like a bush baby, tucked behind his mother's slacks, looking at him and offering comfort. *Be still and know that you are God*, Sister said to the boy through his mind. Darryl leaned over and hovered over Baby Lee's face; his chapped lips were close enough for Lee to see that it was a mix of fungal ringworm and nervous licking. He could smell peanut brittle on Darryl's breath. Darryl's eyes widened. He reached his hands toward Lee's zipper, as if on autopilot.

What a hot day the next morning brought. Mrs Warwick sent Sister out with the boys to play with the water hose. Sister wore a one-piece with a pony over her belly. When Lee couldn't be still, he'd do Baby Sister's hair, make her sit still between his legs while he combed it through and made her wince, creating complicated hairdos like the updo 3000 or the updo 2000 or the updo 4000.

In her swimsuit he could see her growing, the seven-year-old slowly moving toward puberty. Was he imagining that she was already developing hips? She loved the hose. He splashed her and she laughed and asked for more, he splashed her again, hitting her neck, then her chest, then her tiny crotch. The sun was out and the grass was verdant in a way only East Tennessee could be, the white pines above them bowing their heads in shame.

Lee and Darryl and their other cousin Michael all surrounded the baby girl and clasped hands around her, keeping her in a circle. She squealed. Lee held the hose up over the three of them, over the top of Sister's head, letting the cool water soak the crown of her hair. She was soaking and happy, her swimsuit dark with wetness, her tiny fingers pruning.

New York City! Before he made it over to meet Juliana, Lee wanted to breathe in the Greatest. City. In. The. World. He'd gotten some tickets to *The Lion King* for a reasonable price from a blind and deaf man he met on the subway that unfortunately were not real. On the subway, he made eye contact with everyone and tried to smile. In Times Square there was both an Olive Garden and a Sbarro. He decided to treat himself a little bit to both. Everyone around him seemed alive with a certain robust pacing and vitality.

There was a homeless man smoking crack right next to a police officer. And there were all these pigeons flying into electrical lines, honking, and tall buildings, and garbage, and streets slick with motor oil, streets with bright red blood flooding into the drain right by the halal butcher, the kosher one too.

Here he was: this new erotic universe.

Five flights up at a Russian Bath House. Light filtered in through a makeshift window, a kaleidoscope of glass, duct tape and welding plastic.

The room smelled of frankincense and tea tree oil.

Battery powered candles made slender shadows on the glass.

Lee was on his back already erect, lying on top of a heated esthetician table.

Juliana made sure he was comfortable as she took off her top then slowly her tights and then opened her legs to show crotchless panties and a pouting pink outie. Lee's neck tensed. He was nervous and concerned about not getting his money's worth. He hoped she came from a broken home; this thought made him harder.

'Tell me about your day, Lee,' Juliana said, now at his raggedy feet, working her way up from his ankles. He shut his eyes and imagined Mother Mary standing over him. He was silent and stuttered. He wanted a spanking. He felt something moist and warm and oystery slide across his shins then over his knees. He peeked with one eye, his chin tucked down to see Juliana grinding on his thigh, moaning softly and gyrating herself out over him. Juliana had a small stomach pouch, a stomach that would sag with children. Lee then saw Sister at thirty-nine; miserable, married with a husband and a soft apron belly and three children and felt a pang of jealousy in his bowels. New Sister took him in her mouth. He returned to the moment.

Lee began to shake with excitement after the oral part, shuddering, feeling proud of the surprise of his size in her rosy lips. And when she slid on top of him, he almost collapsed from that first entrance into her.

Sister forgot and Sister woke up normal many mornings. Her mouth was so clean, her breath was warm, watery. They were up in the bonus room in their Tuscan suburban home and mother was downstairs making Ritz-crushed chicken breast.

They practiced again: Someday you will make another boy very happy, Sister.

She smiled. Lee told Sister to use her tongue one hundred times to the right then to the left slowly.

Yea, you'll make someone very happy.

Mother was busy making the chicken and Lee got caught up and bit her lip too hard and she bled; he smacked her some. She sat in a corner flustered.

Allah is Forgiving and Merciful.

On a phone call to Sister the last time they spoke before she started doing ketamine-assisted EMDR and got on that Latuda and moved to who knows where with that funny-looking white woman, she would tell him he could tell her anything. But he liked hearing about her whoring. He liked being a corner she could turn into, a final wall.

Lee had requested plain-play aftercare: he wanted to imagine their mundane lives together.

'And after this –'

'Yeah.'

'If you were my man –'

'Yes,' he breathed and moaned.

'You'd take me out for –'

'Yes.'

'Some Peking duck and Szechuan green beans.'

'Yes, and?'

'And we could feed the bones to the rats, and we could get ice cream and walk through the park and by the Met and get back to our apartment on Roosevelt Island via train.'

'Yes.'

'Because we take the train in.'

'Yes.'

'And then we will take a shower and fight about the laundry and throw plates and go to bed angry.'

'Would you like that?'

He finished again.

Her breath smelled of salt water, the saline of his tiny loins.

He nodded and wept, and then pulled mounds of her raven hair, gently, and rubbed it across his eyes and cheeks and chest. Juliana pulled out a baggy of drugs and rubbed a little on her gums then tongue kissed him. The room got brighter. Lee felt like a light bulb. He wanted Baby Sister, but then he felt like he was sweating, like he was hearing vespers, his skin one large sonic tear. The weeping continued. Cathedral bells rang around his ears.

'There, there, Mr Warwick.' He shook, all pitiful. 'You're a nice man Mr Warwick. This is normal. All of this is normal, and you were very gentle.' She cupped his face. She put back on her clothes and asked him for the $850 he owed her in cash.

Lee decided he would become a Roman Catholic to guard against the jumping spirits he felt when leaving the Russian spa. But first, Chinatown!! The smell of oyster sauce and fish sauce and yuzu citrus. Red paper lanterns and candles and red envelopes filled his line of vision. It is the Year of the Rat. Roaches scurried, bowed, at his feet.

'HAHA,' he laughed because he saw an I ♥ CHINA(TOWN) T-shirt. 'Lol!'

He decided to get the one in Mandarin, which he'd been learning on YouTube, too. The shirt roughly translated to I ♥ CHAIRMAN MAO. He also got another new shirt to support his colleague Donnie, one with Jigglypuff on the front saying I'M NOT AUTISTIC, I'M ARTISTIC.

The Peking-roasted ducks smelled gamey and peppery, hanging from curing nooses. It made his stomach sour. The counterfeit markets looked promising. Perhaps some perfume for Sister. Versace Bright Crystal? Yes. He purchased three of the pink bottles, though later a rash on his neck and a DuckDuckGo search would lead him to believe the perfume was filled with gasoline and urine.

I love the city and the city loves me, Lee thought. Yeah, I might move here. He stood on a sewer plate and felt rushing toilet water vibrate underneath him. He had a toothpick in his mouth until a group of Jamaican men robbed him in the middle of 21st street, under a violet violent-crime streetlight. They punched him, pistol whipped him, then kicked him in the bladder and pelvis and kidneys. They took his cash, his credit card, his ID, and his First Bank of Tennessee debit card.

He huddled in a ball and stayed there for what felt like hours imagining being held by a greater divine feminine in the pietà pose; it began to drizzle purple rain and a rat crawled over his back and his head to get to the other side of the sidewalk. Rain soaked the crown of his head. He felt his remaining hair curl in the water. That summer Darryl had run his hands through Sister's hair softly, pulling from root to tip, smiling at the strands of curls that came out in his palms.

He needed to get to the airport. Kept walking and bracing. Walked past St John's Cathedral and coughed in the lingering incense from an earlier mass. He wanted a prayer candle and he wanted his dick sucked again. He passed himself in a mirrored law building, and he was one long torso-warp reflected endlessly in the mirror, one tangled spider of a man. Shaking, he kept saying his prayer, talking about, *You're a nice man Mr Warwick. And this is normal and you were gentle.*

Lee got a taxi to LaGuardia from the church which took his last $200. Surge pricing, the driver said. Halfway there he took a detour, driving Lee through the tunnels of Central Park on a discounted 'locals only' tour, all four windows down and sunroof open.

In the green grass, a man was bowing in sujud on an ivory rug, reverent and dappled beneath the kind of purple violence lights Lee had his ass beat under. Lee's head ached, he wanted to cry. He let out an accidental burp and tried to let it slip through by making his mouth a controlled air-valve, but he smelled the Times Square Olive Garden rising, and stomach-acid garlic filled the black car.

The driver, Abed, waited a few seconds and then pulled out an Oud air freshener, spraying the interior down until clouds of aerosol surrounded both their heads. Lee's face burned, he pulled his shirt over his mouth to stop the smell.

The city was so magnificent, so shining, from the back of the car. He wanted the street to open and swallow him. He asked Abed to turn up the music: 'What a Girl Wants' by Christina Aguilera.

This was the first time Lee left Tennessee ever. He looked in the passenger mirror at himself and saw his damages. His hairline had dissolved in the rain, the black hair filler had turned to tar, it dripped down his forehead and onto his lips. His teeth were all there, but a black eye was now forming. Both eyes had burst blood vessels. He looked, without a doubt, crazy, ugly and broke.

If he could tell anyone he'd say he was very sorry.

Lee made it to the airport three hours late for his flight but hung back. There was a mother holding her newborn, her head a big eggy egg. He waved to the baby and stuck his tongue out, and the mother pulled her head away and walked briskly to another terminal.

When Sister was an infant, he helped turn her over and helped change her diaper and watched her as she yawned and tried to stay alive and grow the rest of her brain at four months premature. Her head alien-like and pricked with a pain port in the vein of her forehead. As the months went on, she developed a type of sugar thrush in her mouth, her lungs fighting, her kidneys still forming. Many times, before he knew how much he loved her, little Lee thought about pinching her nose and mouth until she stopped breathing.

Lee looked up and Boeing 737s were taking off, going every which way. Out past the airport the city was still not sleeping. Juliana was somewhere out there, headed home maybe? Donnie Jenkins was headed home. Sabrina Cortez, too.

Sister was somewhere out there in this big city, headed home to him, *maybe*?

He wanted to pick up the phone and hear her breath. *Tell me about your day, Baby Sister.* Like the old times he wanted to have her pick up and answer him and to tell him things while she spread her legs on her T-shirt quilt.

Everyone was headed somewhere and Lee was not. He lay down next to the baggage-claim conveyor belts and put on his headphones and played a money attraction meditation. His head was hurting again, and he felt a nosebleed coming on. He put some pressure on his eyes. He felt his own warm breath against his hands and on his upper lip. Outside the airport windows, the cars roared on the turnpike. ■

Osdany Morales

What Was Your Hair Color as a Child?

at midnight
they put A BULLET in the leg
of the old woman who demanded to participate
in the celebration of THE REVOLUTION

it was not a bullet
shot from a pistol
around the bonfire lit by rays of matches
the missile sat
heads set ablaze
we had to run
I never knew where the ORDNANCE was coming from

at seven I had escaped
this bullet in the washbasin
of the backyard of a house; during the ritual
they said that when it BURNED it left
the silhouette of a turtle
we spun our heads like an inverted russian roulette
until one of us decided to start the RACE

we poured into the street, running away
without knowing from what

and this, I remember, was
weeks before the host would show us
that by means of an EXTREME CRUNCH
it was possible to blow yourself

What Sports Team Do You Love to See Lose?

under our window
in the house next door, at all hours
we eavesdropped on the CONVERSATIONS

of the other couple
after screaming orgasms they discussed future projects
they named their pet BABY DOG
my lover said that SHE was faking it or that HE
had a big one
we christened them THE MOVIE
shutter after shutter
our youth in splinters

the wall was a sponge
that flooded with rain
it was easy to have sex with my lover
in the humidity and the gloom
she knew the names of IRRELEVANT ACTRESSES
and hip songs of the past
every night she came home from work
with a new theory about her personality

YEARS LATER I would deny those days

only hanging onto a legitimate feeling
an imaginary poster of THE MOVIE
the empty windows
three barks of BABY DOG

On Which Wrist Do You Wear Your Watch?

they tried to steal it from me
two different NIGHTS

the first, I woke from a dream
pulling so hard
on THAT ARM that when he fled
the sleepwalker dragged my bunk bed with him

the second, also asleep
another hand leapt through the window of the bus
his fingers dipping under THE WRISTBAND
I towed him a few meters

I wasn't the one with the invincible qualities
the watch was heir to something that granted
the left hand a survival instinct
stronger than its resistance to water

it has already stopped telling time
at the bottom of THIS SUITCASE

Translated from the Spanish by Harry Bauld

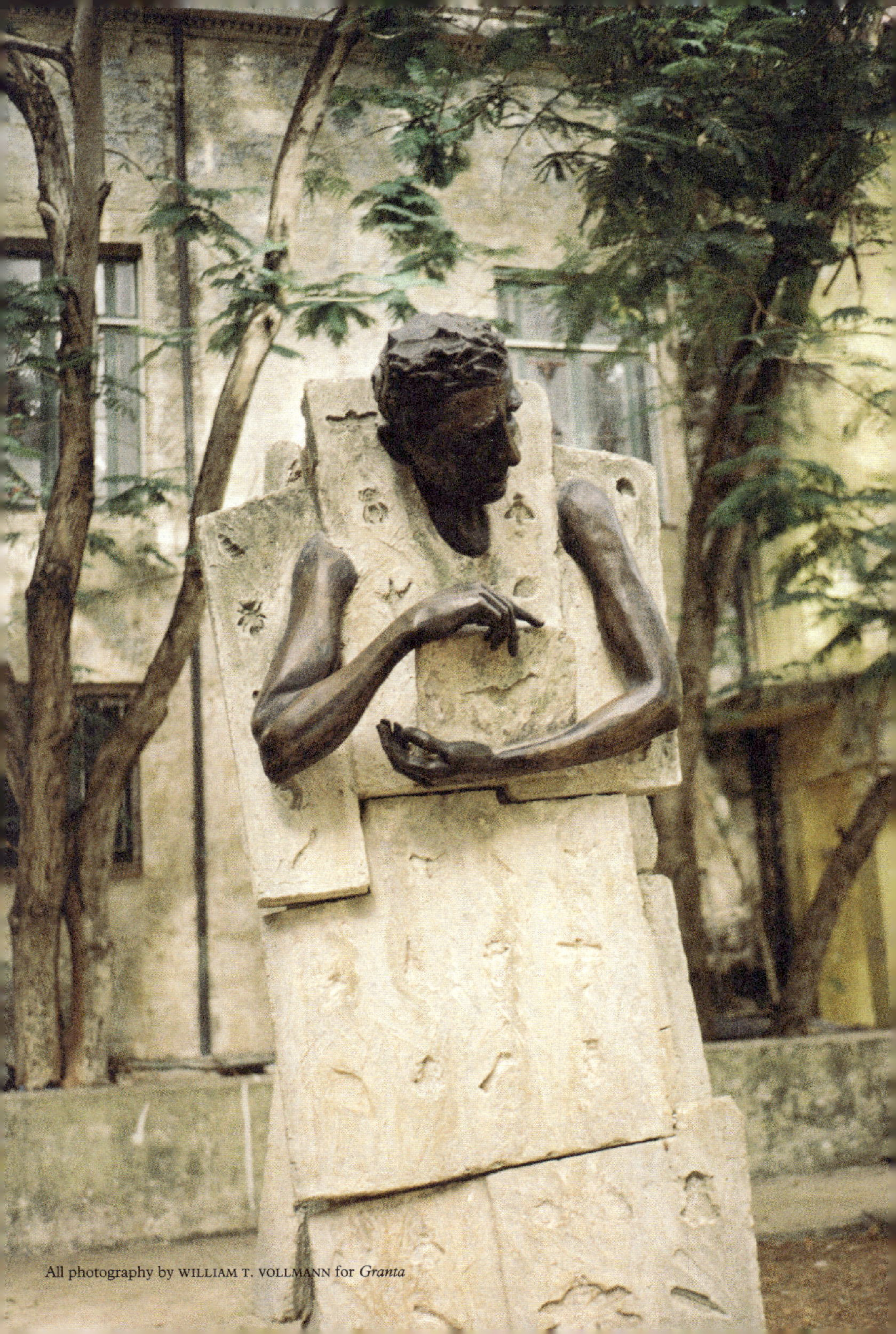

All photography by WILLIAM T. VOLLMANN for *Granta*

MAKING CUBA GREAT AGAIN

William T. Vollmann

Since the King of America's threats to make Cuba great had once again swelled into truly patriotic pustules, *Granta* proposed to send me to that island so that I could report back to you like a good subversive. My brother-in-law remarked: 'We should have taken them out fifty years ago.' A fellow groomsman at my exterminator's wedding said: 'But that place is a hellhole. Oh, well, Bill; that's what you do.' I liked him very much and loved my brother-in-law, so I smiled, poured out more whiskey and kept quiet, because what did I know? You see, I had never been to that *hellhole.* For an interpreter who would not be a secret fink for Havana, I hired my neighbor, a Mexicana called Concepción, and just in case anybody with police powers thought to punish us (she worried that the attention we might draw could lead to detention in the Land of the Free), I asked a prominent social-justice lawyer to accompany us. Both knew Cuba from before. Concepción had volunteered in a labor brigade back when Fidel was still alive, and Mark, a committed Marxist-Leninist, had engaged in various sociopolitical exchanges with the cadres over there. They were brave kindhearts on whom I could count to excavate truth, no matter how ugly it might be, and who would help because they cared for me.

Mark made contact with a woman who catered to left-wing travelers. Despite having had our documents for weeks, two days before we flew out, she announced that my companions could not qualify as journalists. Mark then contacted the Cuban Embassy, which – perhaps out of sheer annoyance at the hasty request, a bureaucratic technicality, or their busyness in the run-up to May Day celebrations – instantly admonished us not to engage in any journalism whatsoever. Thus inspired, we arrived in Havana, where wide uncrowded boulevards and humid glare were flavored by jungle air and smoke from burning leaves and garbage; I could almost have been back in Phnom Penh in the early 1990s, when one could stand in the middle of any intersection and count stars; of course Cambodia had been recovering from Khmer Rouge atrocities committed in the service of quasi-Maoist deindustrialization, while Cuba was proceeding in the opposite direction thanks to our monster in the White House.

Being unaccredited, and therefore discouraged from entering a hospital, photographing a soldier, or decorating my anti-royalism with official Cuban statistics, I began learning from the people around me: 'Concepción, would you please ask him what he thinks about socialism?' That was how I did things. I thought up questions and twiddled the lens-extrusion wheel of my pocket Contax film camera while she did the work, and tireless Mark, almost twenty years older than us, carried our baggage whenever we got faint, stayed cheerful, kept faith in Fidel, outwalked us, and kept his legal powder dry in case of difficulties from one or the other government.

This report now formally commences with the skinny, wild-haired seventy-year-old carpenter who insisted: 'Economically, socialism does not function, as proven in Europe and in ancient times, because there is no motivation. That's what's maybe happening here. But even if we need to strengthen the private sector, no one should impose capitalism from the outside.'

(Now you may return to your dogmatic slumbers. Most interviewees said much the same, and if the King could only redact that last sentence he could pretend to be doing Cuba a favor.)

How had the carpenter assessed the revolution's head in former years? 'I felt good about Fidel when I was young. I consider him a very intelligent man. If he were here now, it would be better. The revolution gave a lot of opportunity for people to learn, but it was always under pressure from the blockade: many restrictions. Life has proved that the system does not work. But democracy itself is a huge problem. Look at Peru. Look at your country. The perfect does not exist.'

He added: 'Young people don't think about socialism. A lot of them, they don't care about working.'

When I wanted to know why he preferred that I obscure his identity, he replied: 'The lack of freedom. Contrary opinions are not well taken. At this time there is so much tension that I would rather you didn't use my name, because somebody may fuck with me.'

CARLOS AND MIGUEL

Two men stood on the street – good enough for me. 'And do you consider yourselves socialist or not?' I inquired.

'Personally, no. In a socialist society everything is equal, and here there are differences. People have nothing to eat.'

'When Fidel was alive was there more equality, or was it bad then too?'

'It was another time. We didn't have internet. It was a blind country that didn't know the reality of the world.'

'You're not the only ones,' I remarked. 'I was in Russia talking to people who said, back in the 60s and 70s they didn't know they were poor, so they were happy.'

'I would like to be able to say the opposite of this, but all my life I only hear *blah, blah, blah* and we are moving backward,' said Carlos.

'Yes, we have gone backward,' agreed Miguel.

'To the point where we are now,' said Carlos. 'There is no water, no gas, no eggs, no milk, no electricity . . . Education is okay. It is free.'

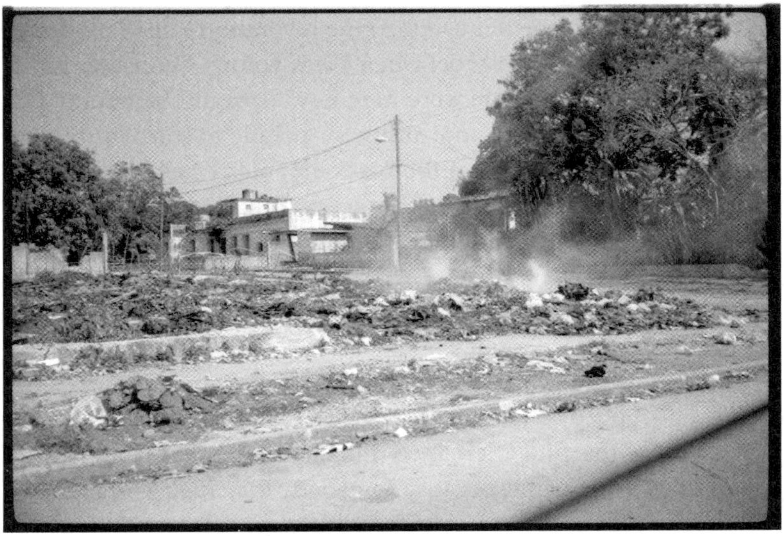

'But in Cuba today,' said Miguel, 'education has declined. Because if the children don't sleep and they don't eat, they cannot attend classes.'

'Señor, is anyone being repressed?' I said. 'We just got here, so we don't know.'

Carlos said: 'I don't know if you heard about 11 July 2021. The whole country went onto the streets to protest about electricity, food, and because there used to be stores that operated using the Cuban convertible peso – which functioned like the dollar. They were removed and replaced with dollar-only stores. And here they don't *pay* in dollars, so people can't go to those stores.'

'Cuban families have people in the United States – some, not all – that help us, and that is why we have not died of hunger,' Miguel explained.

'And when the people took to the streets, what did the government do?'

'The government beat them. They went in dressed as civilians, and said it was the people themselves doing this. Many went to prison . . . Now people are afraid.'

'We do not see the police here,' I said.

'Oh, they are dressed like us. If they see us talking with you like this, it is a big problem, because here we have no freedom of expression, and when you don't agree with the government you are an enemy; you are a criminal.'

'Why did they change to dollars?'

'The Minister of Economy devalued the Cuban peso. He is a crazy man. The devaluation happened right in the middle of Covid – madness!'

'For us to have primary necessities at home, we must acquire the dollar,' added Miguel.

Carlos gazed up at balconies across the street where a couple of people were leaning over, watching us. 'Look. As we were saying, they are paying attention to all conversations, watching everything. We are surrounded. But I don't care; don't worry.'

'I'm sorry,' I said.

'Look, Marco Rubio has experience in what these countries of repressive dictatorships are like. It is like a game of chess: They are looking for the right tactic, the opportunity to say checkmate so that the Cuban people can move forward.'

'And be free,' said Miguel.

'You're supporting what Rubio wants to do?' asked Concepción in amazement.

'No, it's not support. It's a hope for change.'

'Because here we are alone,' Carlos insisted. 'So a quick death is better than sixty-seven years of a system that is slowly killing us. Before, ten-year-old children who went to school were *this* big (gesturing at chest level), and now you go to school and there is a fifteen-year-old child *this* big (gestures lower) due to malnutrition. Children don't know what cheese is, what ham is, what milk is. They don't know.'

TWO SAD SOLDIER-GIRLS AND A FEARFUL MOTHER

Marisol's mother lived in a block of those Communist-era apartments that crumble comparably in Kazakhstan, the former South Yemen and the former East Germany. The flat dated from 'maybe the 1970s'. My 1939 home in Sacramento looks newer. I remember a fan, a flat-screen television over which hung two framed reproductions of flower-prints (bouquets in vases) and a framed daub made stranger through my sweaty glasses. The wary mother prepared chipped little porcelain cups of smooth black Cuban coffee. Marisol's compañera, Ana María, came in uneasily. (All names in this section are pseudonyms.)

'You know,' I began, 'we were a little surprised when the government said no, you cannot talk to anybody without accreditation. We're wondering why, because it would be good for people to understand how the blockade has affected Cuba. What are they thinking?'

Ana María replied: 'It's sad to say this, but this is a country where independent journalists are prohibited. Actually, they are being hunted. I work in a communication faculty involving journalists and I study information sciences – we are one of the most controlled faculties in all of Havana University.

'Whenever they choose a new director for media studies, the military must approve that person!' she said, swinging her right hand upward. 'I had professors who worked as contributors to *El Toque*. They were persecuted because they practiced independent journalism. One of the things we've always demanded is transparency, because there isn't any. The ministries put up information that they want the public to have, but the data on how the budget was distributed and the results of their plans, they don't make available. In the Assembly, ministers are supposed to give an account of their term, how their mandate went. The agriculture ministers have been in office for more than ten years, and none of the agricultural plans were fulfilled.'

'Do they have a Five-Year Plan as the Soviets did?'

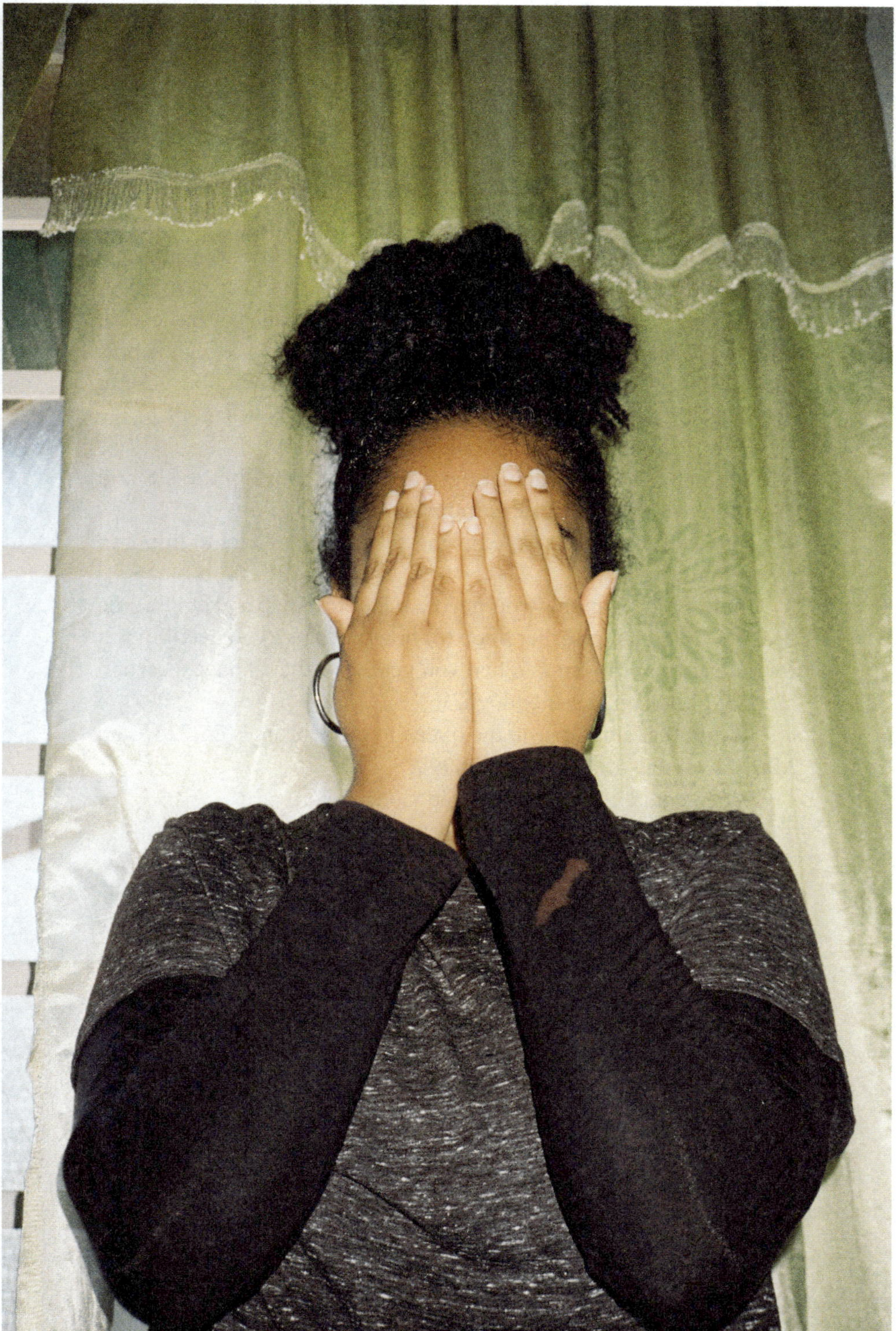

'Yes, they have an annual plan and a national plan for food sovereignty. They want to triple production because right now we have a big problem. Almost all of the food is imported, which makes it very expensive. My grandmother, who passed away two years ago, was retired and received 1,500 pesos a month from her pension. A carton of eggs costs twice that, which gives you an idea of the level of inflation. Whenever that department has to report to the people how they used their budget, they say they weren't successful because of the blockade. It's always the fault of the blockade.'

'How do goods come in despite the blockade?'

'The sanctions are against the state. Companies in the US and elsewhere will sell to private companies.'

'But how do these private businesses get the dollars to import?' asked Mark.

'In the same way that you need a ticket to buy gas,' replied Ana María, leaning forward, her hoop earrings jittering, 'you need a ticket for your turn at the bank. When you get there, they'll have a certain amount of dollars, never enough.'

'My mother's number in the queue to buy dollars is 25,726,' said Marisol. 'Today the queue is at 9,999.'

'When could it be her turn?' said Concepción.

'Maybe at the end of the year, or next year,' said Ana María.

'I come from an extremely revolutionary family,' Ana María told me. 'My grandmother is from Granma; she used to hide ammunition in her clothes and take medicine and messages by bike to the Sierra. My grandfather fought in Angola, fought in the Congo. He worked in aviation, and both worked in associations for combatants. They believed in the dream because they came from poor families. Thanks to the revolution, they were able to study. *The revolution was needed.* The people were suffering under Batista. The problem is that the revolution became twisted.

'They gave their entire lives for a better Cuba. My grandfather and father are still alive, but disillusioned. Everything for which they fought and sacrificed, everything that was promised, never materialized. My grandfather does not understand. He lost many things in the war, children even, and now he has a destroyed country, a retirement that he cannot live on; and he sees us, the new generation, going through the same problems, or worse, than when it all started.'

'We look at Cuba: Free housing, free healthcare, free education!' Mark said, still hoping and believing in the revolution. 'And the costs that you are experiencing for food, transportation, are a result of our government's restricting Cuba's ability to participate internationally.'

All three of the Cuban ladies smiled bitterly. 'The blockade exists and affects us, and always has,' replied Ana María, 'but it is not the fundamental cause. For a very long time things have been deteriorating. My grandmother died of lymphatic cancer. We were taking her to various doctors and medical facilities for six months and got no diagnosis. By the time we found out what she had, it was advanced. I spent two months trying to get her a bed in a hospital, and all the medicines had to be obtained by me separately. The hospital didn't have them.'

'And you think that is the fault of the government and not of the blockade?' I asked.

'The government has the responsibility. For years money was funneled into tourism. Health and education and social security have fallen behind. The hotels are now empty. Everyone questions this prioritization. We are an island and it is incredibly expensive to get fish because they did away with all the fisheries.'

'So, what does Cuba have to export?' said Mark.

'Tobacco, rum, coffee, nickel, cacao. We used to export sugar, but they got rid of the mills.'

'Why?' I said.

'In the 90s, during the recession known as "Vacas Flacas" ('skinny cows'), sugar prices dropped worldwide. Castro, instead of listening to the analysts who said the situation could be temporary, dismantled the mills. And that industry was lost. A few years later sugar went back up, and we didn't have the infrastructure to produce it anymore.'

'When I entered the military at fifteen,' said Ana María, 'my father did not approve. He was a military man and said think twice, because that life is very difficult. I thought as militants our job would be to protect the people and all the revolutionary achievements. But when I joined, I began to see the great difference between those who oversee the system and the vision of Martí's homeland.'

'Why did you resign?'

'The pledge to defend the people was really a pledge to defend the socialist revolution, and there came a point when the socialist revolution appeared to be against the people.'

'How so?'

'We do not have quality education or medicine, people have a hard time getting food, the transportation system doesn't work . . .'

'Repression,' summarized Marisol. I was not surprised.

'New military and penal codes have been passed,' continued her friend. 'If you show up to a demonstration and you carry a DOWN WITH CANEL sign, you can be arrested. If you go against the government on social media, you can be subject to everything from a ridiculously high fine to being incarcerated.'

'When we questioned anything,' Ana María added, 'it was always, no, no, no, it *has* to be this way; the Party and the revolution are all that matter. When I questioned why there was no investment in social and medical programs, I never got a clear answer; my ideology was called into question instead. And then they would just repeat that everything is the fault of the blockade, the sanctions, the Americans, and that we must resist. I would reply that people have only one life, that you can't put politics first and ask for sacrifice and resistance when the people have no food, no medicine, no education, and their houses are falling down! There came a point that I felt ashamed to put on the uniform.'

FINCA VIGÍA

When Martha Gellhorn found Finca Vigía in 1939, the property was about eight miles from downtown Havana. Eighty-seven years later the city has swelled, so that the Finca now lies in 'East Havana'. It was dilapidated, so hard-charging Martha deployed her own funds to fix it up. Her soon-to-be husband Ernest Hemingway fell in love with it, and they moved in. The following year he set off to settle accounts with his second wife Pauline. That accomplished, he married Martha and bought the Finca. Nowadays they call it the Casa Hemingway. It was here that his protagonist-in-progress Thomas Hudson (who would not be published in *Islands in the Stream* until nine years after Hemingway's suicide) enjoyed watching the blackbirds come in and 'the first bats come out in the evening and the very small owls coming out for their night flying when the sun went down into the sea beyond Havana and the lights began to come on over the hills'.

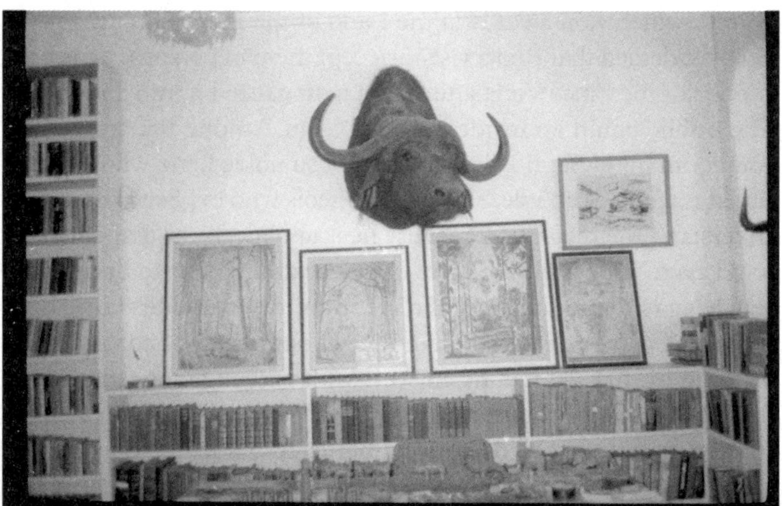

Horned heads stared glassily from the wall. Sometime long ago the authorities had clipped a cord across the doorway to keep out vultures such as yours truly, so for consolation I focused my ancient peepers on an Impressionist-ish bullfight painting. (A Picasso sculpture used to reside in the house, but Concepción overheard the docents gossiping about renovations. 'They're taking a lot of really important pieces out of here,' said one to another. I asked whether somebody might be selling them for hard currency, a possibility that received an admitting smile.) In one of the wooden racks pertaining to Hemingway's generation (for whom printed productions were still worthy of keeping) stood copies of the *New Yorker*, *Look* and other period magazines, many with him on the cover. Everything gets hollowed out sooner or later, but this antique shell was sweet enough, thanks to birds singing and muted light from a cluster of windowpanes. Through interlaced bamboo fronds, I happily mused my way a trifle closer to the man who had been one of my dead father's favorite writers, and whose stoically morbid and brave productions I've loved for fifty years, loyally ignoring their mean parts.

In Tomás Gutiérrez Alea's great film *Memories of Underdevelopment* (1968), which won awards in the Land of the Free (don't worry; in 1970 we denied that Red a visa to accept them in person), we see the interior of the Finca Vigía after Fidel nationalized it into a museum. The public could go inside in those years. Among the crowd let's now zoom in on Sergio, the movie's not so noble hero, who lives the gilded tragedy of an idle, restless bourgeois who explicitly refuses to understand the revolution because he is apolitical – as if apoliticality could even be possible in an era of class warfare ('not to decide is to decide', say the Italians). When a committee examines him about the rents he lives on and the number of bathrooms, bedrooms and toilets in his palatial flat, he answers with pathetic innocence: What could they possibly have against him? His wife has already fled his ennui'd creepiness. With nothing better to do, he seduces pretty, young Elena, who promptly bores him; and now here are those two at some kind of brightly lit night event inside the Finca. Elena finds small use for the dead white hunter's stuffed heads, while Sergio concludes that Hemingway hardly cared about Cuba and must have been 'insufferable' – unlike Sergio, of course.

In some respects Hemingway was more than insufferable. He could be bigoted, vile, abusive even to those who loved him. As for Sergio's charge of indifference to Cuba, that I deny. In *The Old Man and the Sea* (1952), Hemingway draws on the Cuban particularities he knows and loves to create an Everyman whose greatness is magnified by understatement's mysteriously spiritual allusions. We are all dark inside, so why not contain stars? 'I can always come in on the glow from Havana,' Santiago tells himself, sailing ever farther into the true night, which he must make his own. Even if he never comes home he knows where he is in his own night of suffering, necessity and victorious defeat. 'It will be dark soon . . . Then I should see the glow of Havana.'

He knew the glow of Havana, and, as he would have put it, it was what he had and so he'd better love it.

But Hemingway did not love Cuba only as Pygmalion loved the marble woman he had sculpted. Carlos Baker called him 'greatly relieved' when Batista got out of Havana at the beginning of 1959. 'I wish Castro all luck. The Cuban people now have a decent chance for the first time ever.' He denounced the US government's turn against Fidel, and kissed the Cuban flag before a Havana crowd.

All the same, flag-kissing in 1959 did not mean the same as flag-kissing after Kennedy's failed Bay of Pigs invasion of April 1961. Hemingway shot himself in July, while the US went on trying to make Cuba great again, which naturally made the revolution more overtly Communist. By the time of the Cuban missile crisis of October 1962, Fidel was firmly in the Soviet camp.

'I cannot be a communist now because I believe in only one thing: liberty . . .' wrote Hemingway in 1935. As he saw it, any true writer is an 'outlyer [sic]'. 'If he is a good writer he will never like the government he lives under. His hand should be against it . . . He can be class conscious only if his talent is limited.'

I happen to disagree. Platonov, Sholokhov and Lu Xun were great writers and also class conscious. Hemingway had been overtly class conscious in *For Whom the Bell Tolls* (1940). In *To Have and Have Not* (1937), he had been class conscious whether or not he knew it.

Hemingway risked his life for the Spanish loyalists. In Cuba he decided to act against the Hitlerites. No doubt this had something to do with Martha's goading accusations about his staying put while she was covering the war in Europe. So what? He did something: In 1942, when Germany's subaqueous U-boat campaign, Operation Neuland, was causing maximum trouble in the Caribbean, Hemingway established an amateur intelligence network called the 'Crook Factory' to spy on Havana's Fascist set, and began hunting the Nazi U-boats from his boat *Pilar*. Although one US Embassy official in Havana considered the Factory's doings surprisingly professional, Hemingway tired of running it, and after a year, his capricious rages against his associates further damaged that enterprise, which by one account was shut down by the US Embassy and by another simply absorbed into the FBI. As for his submarine patrols, they intercepted German radio transmissions but never stopped a single U-boat. At least he tried, or tried to try.

MARTYR TO LOVE

Our next aesthete, whose writing would have tasted flowery-sickening to Hemingway, was another well-traveled womanizer, readier to spend down to nothing his money, family, liberty and, ultimately, his life. To Cubans he is almost more universally beloved. His name is José Martí.

His prose, as I said, was ultra-purple. When he wrote about the beauties of art, landscapes, bridges and women, he superficially resembled Baudelaire and later French Decadents. His tributes to Whitman and Emerson are beautiful line for line, if sometimes formless. When he wrote about exploitation, colonialism and imperialism, it was with militant sincerity. His ethnic and gender

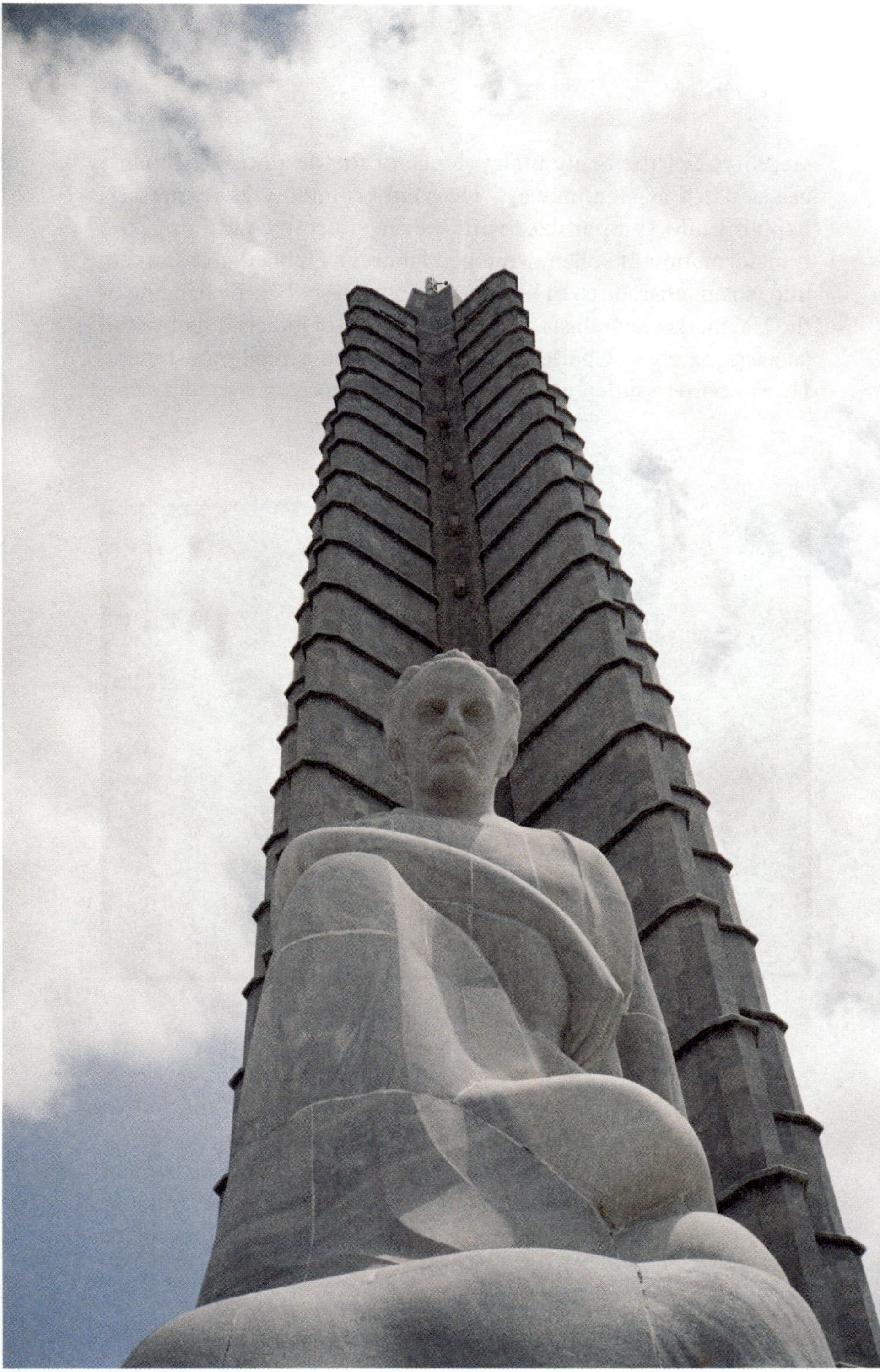

stereotypes ('the brute malevolence of the despotic Irishman') are as dated as Hemingway's He-Man brutalities. He expresses, explains and sympathizes with, never entirely condoning, the transformation of sullen, wretched laborers, clubbed and starved, into violent anarchists. In hideous detail he describes the hanging of the Haymarket anarchists. His denunciations of judicial cruelty read as passionately as Charles Dickens's essay on capital punishment. He was born to suffer, which he did with the grace of a secular saint.

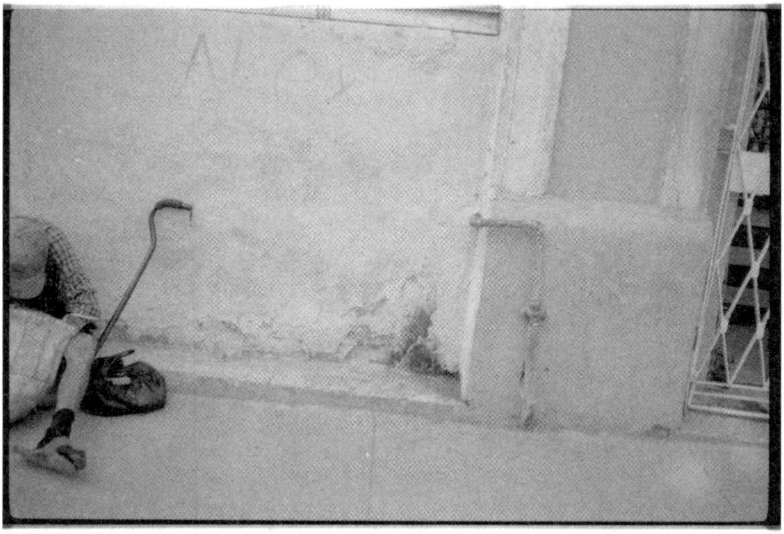

Outside the two-story house Martí was born in, the stench of stale urine greeted me in the hot and glaring streets of central Havana, aka Centro, where, between decaying apartment blocks, boys played ball in scattered garbage between hillocks of the same, while taxi drivers in 1950s Plymouths, Chevrolets,

Buicks and Cadillacs sat dully at the curb, unable to afford the fuel that would allow them to troll for fares – never mind that public transportation often ran up to two hours late, necessitating the hoarding of diesel for special white buses so that doctors and nurses could arrive on time at their filthy hospitals – oh, and let's also celebrate those Trumpian power blackouts, which made for rotting food, stifling flats and dangerous nights. All this brings to ghastly reality and angry righteousness what Martí wrote about Mexico City 151 years ago: A municipality 'asks, imperiously,' whether or not we hear or care, 'for neatness and cleanliness; it asks that its parks be elegant, that its places of transit be easily accessible, and that its impoverished back streets be subject not to a neglect that exacerbates the misfortune of all the needy children, but to tenacious and persistent effort, even though the good thus done will yield no financial profit.' With ever-increasing productive efficiencies, economies of scale, canny distribution systems, *why* should this be so? The answer: Because human decency *will yield no financial profit.* I won't even aspire as high as Martí; if the parks are not elegant I'll never complain; if there be no parks at all I may or may not hold my peace, but *why* must the rest of this be tolerated? Because Kings, Batistas and other stinging parasites would have it so.

In his dramatic poem 'Abdala' (1869), Martí asserts that love for the patria is not affection for her physical attributes but 'eternal hatred' for her oppressors. But two years later, in his manifesto 'Political Prison in Cuba', he addressed the Spaniards in a different tone: 'God does exist, and if you send me from this place before I have torn away your cowardly and calamitous indifference, then give me leave to despise you because I can hate no one; give me leave to pity you in the name of my God.'

Martí flits through Latin America, lives awhile in our States, and to an item in the *New York Evening Post*, which proposes to make Cuba great again, replies: 'It is probable that no self-respecting Cuban would like to see his country annexed to a nation where the leaders of opinion share toward him the prejudices excusable only to vulgar jingoism or rampant ignorance.'

In 1894 he demands: 'Why, O Spanish tyranny, did we fly from you only to find all your horrors in an American republic?' A year later, he sets out to create a patria through insurrection.

On 11 April 1895, Martí landed at the Playitas de Cajobabo in Guantánamo, not the part now held by Americans to sequester terrorists real and imagined, but another subsector just as fertile for crops of misery. His purpose, so he wrote to his friend Manuel Mercado, Mexico's then-Undersecretary of the Interior, was 'to prevent, by the timely independence of Cuba, the United States from extending its hold across the Antilles and falling with all the greater force on the lands of our America'. No worries; my King will save Cuba from dangerous radicals like him! This letter was unfinished when death ambushed him a month later. During the Battle of Dos Ríos, General Gómez commanded him to stay behind, so, much as I might have done, he promptly set out, made a wrong turn and got well peppered.

From his war diary, 25 April 1895, I quote: 'Three heavy bullets come in and hit the tree trunks. "Distant gunfire – what a fine sound!" . . . "It's even better up close," says the old man . . . The gunfire intensifies; Magdaleno, seated against a tree trunk, carves decorations into his new calabash.' 16 May: 'The Cuban people want affection and not despotism . . . what exists in the countryside is a people in search of someone to treat it better than the Spaniard.'

What word has Martí for us now? He sends a message from 1871:

> You, who had not a thought of justice in your minds . . . you, who immolated some on the altar of seductive words even as you were listening with pleasure to others who spoke of the simplest principles of right . . . go on bare knees to collect the broken shards of your reputation that lie shattered across the earth.

GLORIA ROLANDO

'The war started in 1868, the Ten Years' War,' Gloria told me. She and Joaquin were making a film – part fiction, part documentary – to memorialize the Cubans of the Liberation Army, who fought to win Cuba's independence from Spain. 'Later came the Middle War, and Martí re-established the war in 1895. But the presence of the United States began in 1898. This was the so-called Spanish–American War.'

'How important a role did Martí play in this long war?'

'Martí was the founder of the party that was a guide for the leadership, for the army, and especially brought together all the Cubans. This party Martí was creating stretched between Key West and Tampa.'

'And in Tampa now, the people of Cuban extraction, are they on Rubio's side?'

'Yes. They have their own interpretation of the Cuban war. Our project talks about how the United States lies about their intervention in the war. In 1898, they claimed, we are going to help Cuba gain freedom from Spain. We are going to liberate you. You need our support. The speeches they gave at that time are the same ones they give now. The same speech! So, when we are visiting the past, we are talking about the present.'

'Gloria, how is the blockade affecting your work, and you personally at this moment?'

'Personally? With the domestic life, it's the food. It's the struggle with the transportation, because of the oil. Also, for example, the resources to make this film.'

'In your opinion, why did Trump allow Putin to send the oil into Cuba recently?'

'It's part of a strategy to show the people that he's not too bad. But the solution is not to give us one or three drops. They want to destroy our dignity.

'We survive like a big family. This is the only way. If I have some chicken, and I don't have an onion, don't have rice, we share. I am seventy-three years old, and it's the first time that I've seen my country in this condition.'

'It's worse than the special period, when the Soviet Union fell, right?'

'It's worse. Because even then, we had the ration book.'

'Are you still a committed Communist?'

'Oh, yeah. I was a member of the youth organization. But that was a long time ago when I was at the University of Havana.'

'And how many people would you say are Party members now?'

'I don't have any idea. But it's the only party that we have. Of course, the Americans don't agree with that. They want the different parties. And before the revolution, people said there's nothing more equal to a conservative than a liberal. Because everybody promised the same, and nobody delivered. I've heard that ever since I was a child.'

'If you wanted people outside Cuba to have one slogan about what the Cubans are going to do if Trump comes, what would it be?' I asked. 'Like, uh, the one we hear often by Che Guevara: *Until the final victory*.'

Gloria said: 'I am not waiting to fight. I am fighting. One that is popular is *we are continuity*. I see the people fighting for continuity. And you don't have any idea how many weekend parties we have around this neighborhood. You cannot sleep because the people are drinking and dancing!' (While saying this she was smiling.) 'All the places for dancing, they are still open.'

'One thing we know,' said Joaquin, 'is that our society is not perfect; we have many things to change; but I think there is no right for an invasion, to come and tell us what we have to do. With the documentary we show it is a cycle; the same thing is happening: the United States' blockade, invasion; but Cubans continue fighting to have a better society.'

At the end I kissed Gloria's hand, and she whispered, '*Muchísimas gracias*.' She was determined and committed without bitterness.

JANET

'I'm a Fidelista,' Janet said heartily. 'I've lived my life with Fidel. The embargo has always been a problem, but nothing's as bad as this. I'm the daughter of a sailor.' So she was working class; of *course* she held true to Fidel! 'Now the government steals from us. China sent rice and the government is already stealing it.'

Lowering her voice, she repeated her tale, as busy as one of the speeding clouds in the pink and purple sky over the Plaza Vieja where we sat drinking rum, awaiting the next gush of rain and watching boys run around playing at swords while two- and three-story white-arched, yellow colonial facades made backdrops for their performance: 'A bunch of journalists came from Italy, Palestine, Germany, and they announced that China sent us sixty tons of rice, and the people didn't know! There's something happening. They're keeping people pacified . . . I think the world is trying to help but the government is holding them back. Now milk has been talked away! The government wakes up one day and decides there's no cigarettes and no powdered milk . . .'

A kilo of powdered milk now sold for 3,000–3,500 pesos ($6–$7), which she reminded us was 'more than a person's salary'. Retired people received a pension of around 5,000 pesos per month.

When her 77-year-old mother had a fall, Janet had to find $60 before the doctor suddenly 'found' the medicine the old woman needed. (She conceded that at least her mother was allowed to stay in hospital for a week without further payment – a vestige of 'socialism'.)

Leaning forward, gripping the table, she whispered, just as other interviewees had and would: 'They say, "we don't have it", but you ask how much, and it turns out they have it if you pay. I can show you people standing on the corner, selling penicillin donated from churches!' and she laughed bitterly until she coughed. Then she chitter-chattered, eating the dinner she had initially refused before ordering it. 'If Fidel were alive today this would not be happening,' she said suddenly, lowering her voice yet again. 'We've had children die, and he would have moved mountains not to have children die.'

I think it made Mark happy, that she still believed. It pleased me also. I can't say what Concepción thought.

'There are plenty of plain-clothes police around,' she said. 'They're young and they're from the campo. They want to eat, and send clothes back to their families.'

According to her, 11 July had been 'a huge youth movement. It was very close to my home when everything started. People rushed out into the street. A good number got twenty years in prison. The young people have no tolerance. They were yelling *freedom*! When it was over they had nowhere to go. Twenty, thirty, forty thousand of them, all in different provinces . . .'

'How many are in prison?'

'Hundreds. Right here, eight or nine trucks will come, grab the kids hanging out and take them to the police station, arrest them for being in the tourist area and charge them a fee. If it happens two or three times, they put you in prison. That's where they sentence people, in front of the capitol; they do it publicly.'

ZULEICA M. ROMAY GUERRA

'My name is Zuleica. I am a social researcher and the director of the program of studies on Afro-America. I study social inequalities, especially during the revolutionary period, with an emphasis on skin color, social origin, and gender.'

'In Cuba nowadays, is there discrimination on the basis of skin color?'

'For a long time, it seemed like there wasn't. The revolution took very radical measures in its first ten years, and the lives of Black people changed drastically. At that time, it was thought that if people's living conditions changed, then people's mentality would also change. But the society that Cuba managed to create remained class-based, remained unequal, and didn't erase the disadvantages that had accumulated historically. Society functioned horizontally, and those differences weren't very noticeable at first.'

Mark said: 'We understood that it was the common experience that would bring people together, whether they were white or Black. So, in union organizations, for instance, the workers had greater common interests and could unite in opposition to the employers. And this would eliminate some of that feeling of distinction. You don't think that's true?'

'The problem is that the colonizers of today keep doing their job. There are many ways to benefit some workers at the expense of others. Last week I was leaving an academic event at the University of Havana. I was dressed as I normally am, and I went to the sidewalk of the Habana Libre hotel for a taxi. There are two types of transportation there: Cars, which are a little more expensive, and covered electric motorcycles where people sit cramped. When I arrived, there were two cars, and a young Black man managing passengers tells me, hey, ma'am, this costs 300 pesos, you have to wait for the tricycle. I said: why do you assume I can't pay this? It was a Black man reproducing the colonizing gaze, thinking that middle-aged Black women, even if we have university degrees, are poor people.'

'Do you consider yourself a Marxist?' said Mark.

'*Sí, sí.*'

So I asked: 'Do you feel that socialism is working well now, and if it isn't, can it be saved?'

'I think the socialism that's in our heads is not viable because in practice the state is much too important. Socialistic production does not dominate. If a factory that is run by the state says it's representing the workers, but the workers don't have any say in what happens at the factory, that's not socialism, it's state capitalism. And socialism in the twentieth century had that kind of construction. That's why it failed.'

'Trotsky talked about this,' I said. 'He thought that when the revolution in Russia started to go wrong, it was because of this creeping bureaucratization, and we see that in America, too.'

'The bureaucrats never give up power,' she said. 'You must take it away.'

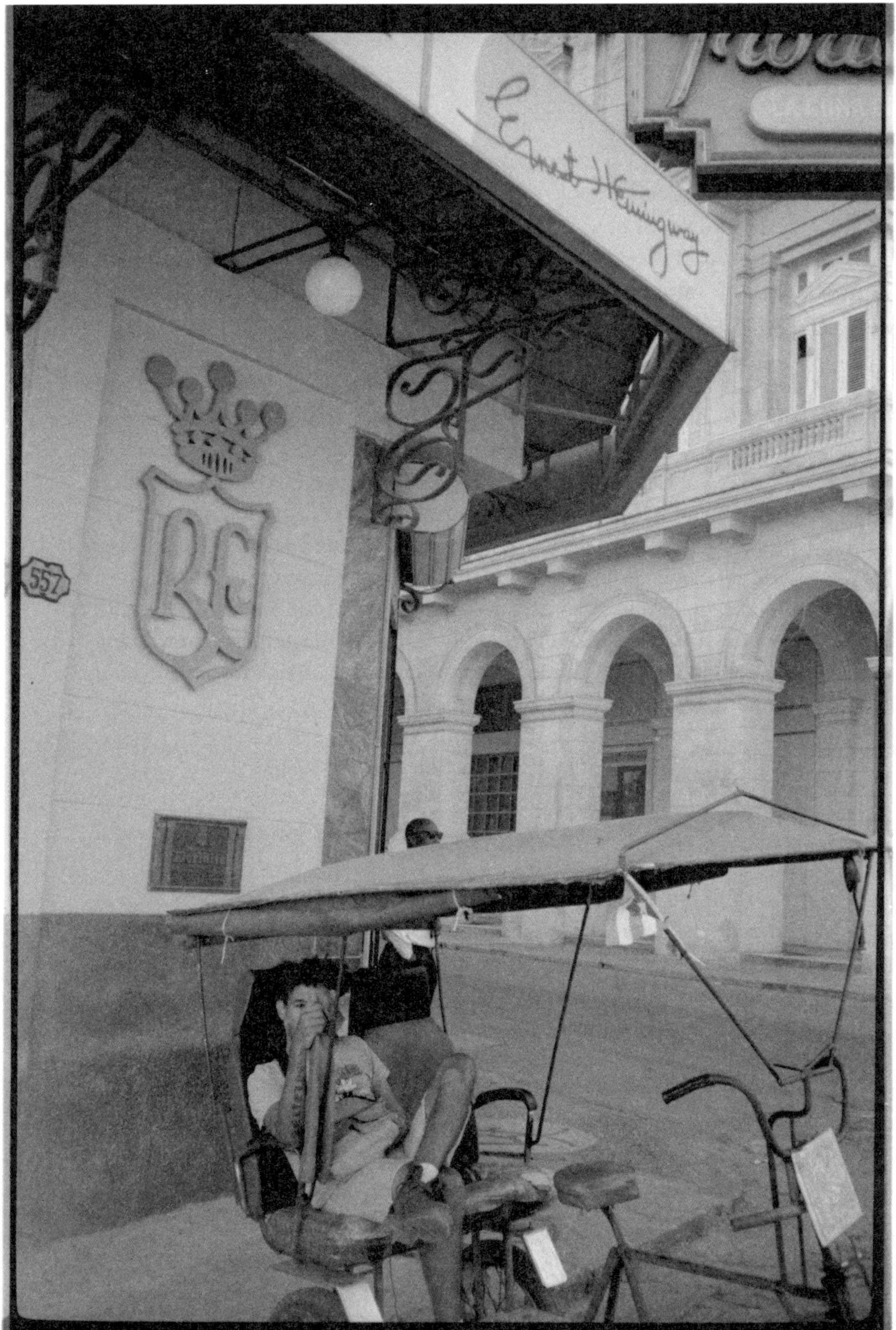
Ernest Hemingway
557

'Yes, they have always been invested in maintaining control,' said Mark. 'That's why Trotsky talked about perpetual revolution.'

'Right,' I put in. 'That's what Jefferson said too.'

Zuleica was expressing in more technical and, of course, more optimistic terms, what other Cubans kept telling me: In the name of representation, the government kept the people down. I could almost have been home in the Land of the Free.

'We live in a very fragile society from a materialistic point of view,' said Zuleica. 'There is a combination of three elements. One, our little natural wealth – the richest products we have are our beaches – two, our mistakes in economic policy, which go back more than half a century, and three, the US blockade, which has been strengthening over the last thirty years. In a society where we lack almost everything, it's very easy for corruption to grow. If you had to get medicine for a family member, you would pay whatever it takes.'

'Do you think Cuba can survive what Trump is doing, and somehow hang together?'

'We Cubans have something in our favor – we are very patriotic. It cost us a lot to come out from under Spanish domination, we were at war with the Spanish for thirty years, and just when we thought we were going to be free, the United States government interfered. Cuban patriotism isn't specifically lined up with ideologies or political affiliations. There may even be people who believe that capitalism is what's best for us, but they don't agree that Cuba should be a protectorate of the United States. Cuban patriots are on a spectrum that goes from the socialists, the Marxists and the radicals, to the bourgeois patriots. And that is always going to be a coalition that will prevent us from losing the ideals upon which the revolution triumphed.'

Mark said: 'In demonstrations in the United States, we say "the people united will never be defeated". It is very important for us. From what I am hearing, it is not so effective.'

'Well, people can lose, but they always lose temporarily. There is no way to definitively defeat a people if they do not surrender.'

By then Zuleica was fond of us. Glowing when she flattered us with the title of socialists, I assured her that she was so beautiful that her touch could turn a glass of water into Havana Club. '*Salud – Salud – Salud – Salud – Salud*!'

'Can I ask you a question?' she said. 'This attempt by Trump to have another term, does it have any prospects? Does it have a chance of going well?'

'No, no. That would be terrible for Cuba and terrible for America.'

'Is it possible that it will happen?'

'Well,' I said, 'all three branches of the government – the executive, the judiciary, the legislature – are corrupted, and the electorate is corrupt. Now the executive has corrupted the Supreme Court and Congress, and the people have become foolish. But Mark doesn't think he will be able to do it. I suspect the opposite.'

'People will rise up,' said Mark.

Concepción added: 'They are trying to manipulate the electoral registers. They are taking away the vote from Latino people, from Mexican people, from Black people. You heard what he said about those Haitians. And we Mexicans are just selling drugs and raping women. In the United States they tell me: "there has always been racism; why are you scared?" Racism has always existed, yes, but people didn't have the right and the power to be so open with it.'

AS THE FUEL RAN OUT

Every few blocks I spied the grafitto YOU NEED TO BE HAPPY. Later on, the taxi driver Ernesto would advise me to take joy in the little things: 'My cousin in the States has the latest model car, a six-pack of beer and a giant TV, but all he does is drive to work and back, and when he gets home he falls asleep before he can watch or drink anything.' A young mother with her baby in her arms begged for money to buy milk, so I gave her five dollars and Mark handed her twenty. Over time more of the street-greetings became importunities, then demands, which, when not fulfilled, improved into spiteful curses, and when gratified, incited other deserving people to place their own orders. I have no regrets; as usual I did what I could and slightly more than I wished to, which presently entailed giving less, so that I might still be able to buy my companions and myself out of trouble. A panhandler named Felipe called us *walking dollars*; we were like Sergio in *Memories of Underdevelopment*, not wanting to understand because understanding would have required us to give up everything and wither away with everyone else.

Just as we left Cuba, Putin's oil ran out – a win-win for our King. Back at home I read in the *New York Times* about the administration's possible indictment of Raúl Castro, evoking their Venezuelan playbook. Meanwhile, the CIA director presented a stark demand: *Shut down Russian and Chinese listening posts and take steps to open the economy.* The indictment would be brought by federal prosecutors in Miami, of course. It could include drug-trafficking charges but focused on an incident in 1996, when Havana shot down two out of three Cessnas flown by Brothers to the Rescue, a Cuban-

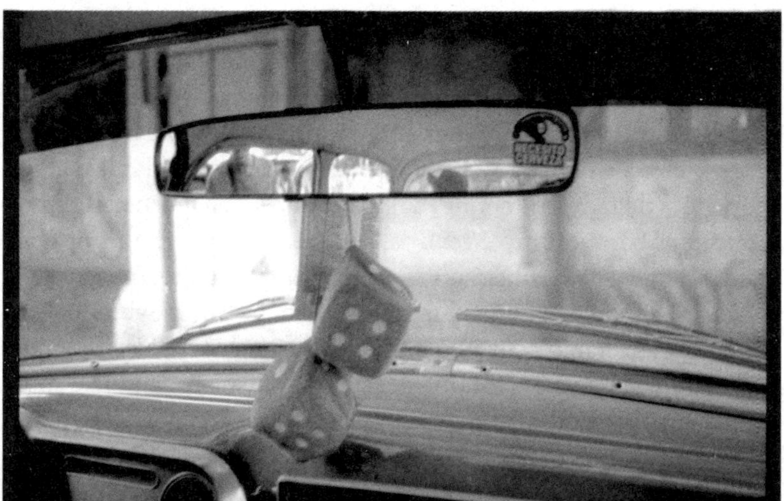

American humanitarian group that helped boatloads and raftloads of Cubans attempting to cross the Straits of Florida – the ninety miles of sea between Havana and Miami. This evoked the playbook indeed, for had my King not blown away Venezuelans in boats? They might have been drug traffickers as he claimed, or even those ultra-terrorists called fishermen. As for the Cuban fighters, on that day in question, they killed four people. Of course the Venezuelan fishing boats were in international waters, and Brothers to the Rescue violated Cuban airspace. This charity, by the way, was founded by José Basulto, a former CIA operative and veteran of the failed Bay of Pigs invasion, who had admitted under oath to firing a cannon from an offshore boat at a Cuban hotel said to be frequented by Fidel Castro. I'm sure he meant no harm. Anyhow, he's still alive and looking forward to the indictment.

This wounded revolution may or may not be moribund. How many of its hurts are self-inflicted I can hardly estimate, given that I spoke only with the people for whom the revolution was made, not with the policymakers and apparatchiks who might have plausibly directed more blame at the United States. The closest I came to hearing an official line was when I asked the old sunburned cadre at the Centro Fidel Castro Ruz what Fidel would have done about my King's threats. 'He would get right in Trump's face and say, we impressed you with Bay of Pigs and we will do the same to you now.'

As a mere American citizen I doubtless understand far less about geopolitics than my blathering, bullying King. Each morning I thumb the rubber band off my *New York Times* and search the front page to see whether he has begun stomping Cuba into greatness. As his subject, I offer up my due hatred and despair. But maybe I can do better, for as Hemingway wrote in *To Have and Have Not*: 'You just go dead inside and everything is easy. You just get dead like most people are most of the time . . . I guess that's just about what happens to you.' ■

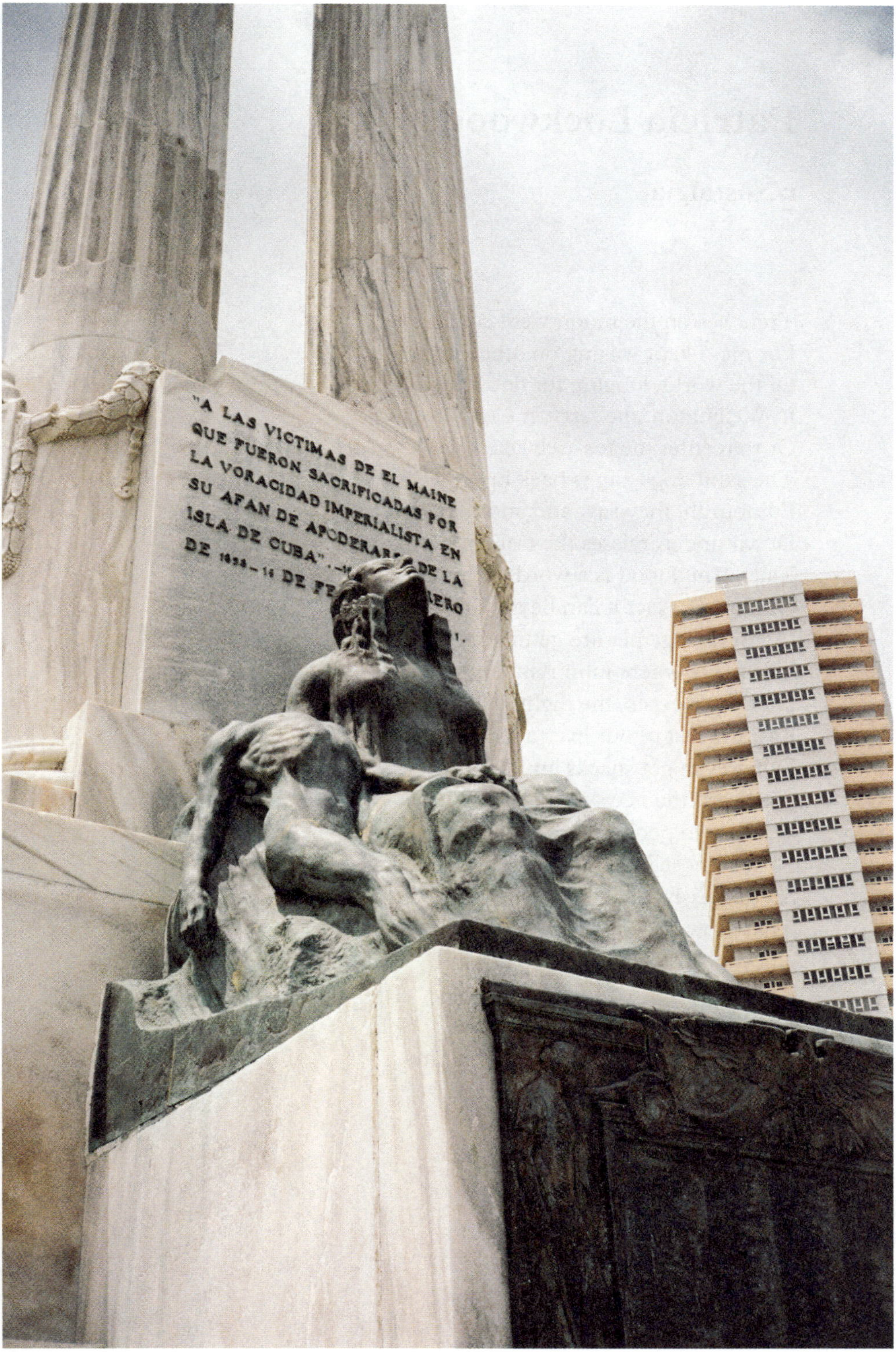
"A LAS VICTIMAS DE EL MAINE
QUE FUERON SACRIFICADAS POR
LA VORACIDAD IMPERIALISTA EN
ISLA DE CUBA".

Patricia Lockwood

r/Nostalgia

Trenches on the moon were coming
For me. I kept waking on other sides
Of the world, longing for flat whites
In Wellington, the ferry in Cong,
Or to reenter the tea-tree lake.
The sand dogs guy is back in
Edinburgh, they say, and another,
Down under, misses the taste of roo
Tails. Childhood is a word like poem
Or clue – in fact it can be anything.
'All of us together are getting on
The plane where John Ashbery
No longer exists, the flight will
Last the rest of our lives and we
Don't even get snacks anymore.'
We heard the news in the airport
Where two people were standing
Nose to nose and kissing almost
Motionlessly, 'like the tree fern
That grows one inch per year,
They look related but who doesn't,
They may not read poetry at all'.
John had the transmissions,
The words were going on all the time
And once in a while he just reeled
Off a length. So see, Jason said,
They must come from somewhere.

He was reading out the names
Of old literary magazines –
'Your youth!' he said, but no,
It was his. '*Zyzzyva* still comes
At the end,' he said, happy,
The house of letters always wins.
'I am taking off from Australia myself,
Being in another country is like
Being dead, you see how people
Go on without you, how someone
Is winked up – and up! –
Into the wide woolgathering head.'
I couldn't finish an ode for anything.
Even Joseph was still breathing,
Twelve fingers and three kidneys,
And the doctors saying it was
The moon, he could not live there
Long. 'So I thought to you here
Is the alphabet, big clear embrace
Of the bathwater, your city's idea
Of pizza, which you'll miss
When you move away.' Phrases
Like *the wild lung of the day* –
I didn't know about dead back then.

I thought you went up but you go
Down. You keep your torso and
Your heart and your eyes,
But the place where you walk
Turns to water. Someone posts
A blue jellyfish, frilled like a portal,
And all of us enter it from above.
A mermaid who has the whole ripple
For her bottom half, networks of light
Thrown casually as a fishing net.
Nothing caught? No, nothing today!
Pull them in, then, the tides.
As you ride out what you long for
Will be particular. More than anything
I want to sit somewhere on earth
With a plate of clams and angel hair.

Goodnight Moon

I wondered if I would write a poem about Nelson.
He was nearly the last in line, young, clean-cut,
Moon-faced (the moon was full, behind us)
And not obviously mad. David probed him
About Venezuela: Everyone must be asking.
Nelson began normally, and then halfway
Through a sentence, lapsed into a happy
Unhad childhood, safe, secure, protected.
I *love* Trump, he said, with his shoulders
Releasing, and in the sound of our speech-
Lessness he went on, When you were a baby,
Do you remember anyone besides your parents
Changing your diaper? Maybe my grandmother,
David said, taken aback. My parents let other
People change my diaper, Nelson told him,
And now, I think, they should not have done
That. Next to David was the One-Day-Old Pro-Life
Jelly Baby, which he pretended I had miscarried
In the green room toilet. 'I sponged it off,
Still warm, still breathing, and now it eats me
Out of house and home.' Neither had ever
Touched a diaper, I realized, or seen one
Be pinned after death. There is a picture
From that night of me kneeling on the marble,
Teaching a grown man to *homologous rock.*

It's a developmental movement, I told him,
You go back, let go of your postures of pain –
Do you trust me to hold you? May I lift
Up your head? Beyond was David, signing,
Salt Lake, and the moon. And there –
Was that Nelson, in a blue sweater, patient,
Waiting? To be fed, bathed, tucked in,
Read to? Suddenly I felt we were
His mother and father, in pearls and Comme
Des Garçons. When would we, out for a night
Like this, return? Years past his bedtime,
To find him climbing through the bars,
Demanding different voices, chanting
Change me, change me, change me.

The Subject Had Become Poetic Logic

Itself. Exhibit: You know what I love?
Establishing shots, more than the actual
Show. How it felt to type EXT. NIGHT.
SOLITAIRE PAWNSHOP. WE BUY
GOLD. And just a fragrance of the light
Of the people inside. The bars are to say
Let me in – into the three-act structure,
And wanting a glass of water. Like
If you mention the Eastern Shore, for
A moment I live there, and my whole life.
Possibly in the witness protection program,
Or because my parents are in the weather
Underground. A trailer, beaded curtain,
The blanket we called The Birds,
And nine-month-old me, in the photograph,
Making intense eye contact with a conch.
Before books I read clear cursive objects.
One must have been this. The other,
Two petrified bookends so far from
Each other they held the complete A-Z.
See what your special baby is doing?
I asked on Mother's Day. Follow her gaze.
Where is she looking. She answered,
Laughing: at food! At me. I must be
Standing out of frame, in the doorway.
Speaking in her child voice again:
I was there, wasn't I? Yes, always there.

What's the wave that puts waves in hair?
The thing that just keeps coming.
The shell flares at the rim, is finger-
Nail ridged, blares its message
In perpetuity. Holorhymes, word
Avalanches, our fall down stairs
In spiral mansions, the rushing
Roaring not-there sea – brief
Home, blue lease, long vacancy.

GRANTA TRUST

Granta would be unable to fulfil its mission without the generosity of its donors. We gratefully acknowledge the following individuals and foundations:

Ford Foundation
British Council
Jerwood Foundation
Pulitzer Center
Amazon Literary Partnership
Sigrid Rausing
The Hans and Marit Rausing Charitable Trust
Anonymous
Bloomsbury Publishing Plc
SALT
Open Society
The Common Humanity Arts Trust
Jonathan and Ronnie Newhouse Fund
Hawthornden Foundation

We also thank the following readers, including those who wish to remain anonymous, for their kind support:

Anonymous
Alex Fardon
Jared Hameloth
Michael Isard
Bee Wanono-Samuel

CONTRIBUTORS

Amie Barrodale is the author of the novel *Trip* and the story collection *You Are Having a Good Time*. Her second novel, *Homestead*, is forthcoming from FSG.

Harry Bauld's poetry collections are *The Uncorrected Eye* and *How to Paint a Dead Man*. His translation of Osdany Morales's *Security Questions* is forthcoming in 2027.

Rebecca Curtis is the author of *Twenty Grand and Other Tales of Love and Money*.

Ciarán Finlayson is the author of *Perpetual Slavery*, a book of art criticism, and an editor at the New York City Policy Forum.

Mary Gaitskill's most recent works are *Stauf: A Tragedy*, a retelling of the Faust story, and the novella *. . . And This is Pain*, forthcoming in spring 2027.

Seth Harp is an investigative reporter, Iraq War veteran, and the author of *The Fort Bragg Cartel: Drug Trafficking and Murder in the Special Forces*.

Halle Hill is the author of *Good Women: Stories*. Her short fiction and essays have been published in *Joyland*, *New Limestone Review*, *Southwest Review*, *Atlanta Magazine* and the *Oxford American*.

Antonia Hitchens is a staff writer at the *New Yorker*. Her work has been supported by the Pulitzer Center.

Tao Lin is the author of ten books, including *Leave Society* and *Taipei*.

Patricia Lockwood is the author of six books, including the forthcoming poetry collection *Agate Head / Stone Soup*, published in October 2026.

Maggie Millner is the author of *Couplets* and the forthcoming book-length poem *My Funeral*. Her work has appeared in the *Best American Poetry* series, the *New Yorker*, the *Paris Review* and the *Nation*.

Osdany Morales was born in Nueva Paz, Cuba. *Security Questions*, translated by Harry

Bauld, will be published by Fitzcarraldo, Giramondo and New Directions in early 2027.

Zora J Murff is an artist and educator. His work has been exhibited internationally and is held in public collections. Murff's forthcoming book with KGP MONOLITH will be published in 2027.

Michael Robbins is the author, most recently, of the poetry collection *Walkman*. 'People Keep Finding Bodies in Joshua Tree' is from his new manuscript, *Safe Word*.

Kathryn Scanlan is the author of *The Dominant Animal*, *Kick the Latch* and *Aug 9—Fog*. A new novel is forthcoming in 2027.

Frederick Seidel's books include *The Cosmos Trilogy*, *Ooga-Booga*, *Poems 1959–2009*, *Nice Weather*, *Widening Income Inequality*, *Peaches Goes It Alone* and *Selected Poems*. His latest collection is *So What*.

Hansen Shi's first novel, *The Expat*, was published in 2024.

John Jeremiah Sullivan is the author of the essay collection *Pulphead*. He is at work on a new book, *The Prime Minister of Paradise*, about a forgotten eighteenth-century utopian experiment.

Nikita Teryoshin is a photographer whose genres include street, documentary and 'everyday horror'. His project *Nothing Personal* was published as a monograph in 2024 with GOST books.

William T. Vollmann's books include *Europe Central*, *Imperial* and the *Seven Dreams: A Book of North American Landscapes* series. His latest novel, *A Table for Fortune*, was published in 2026.